All the King's Ladies

Other Books by Janice Law

Fiction
The Big Payoff
Gemini Trip
Under Orion
Shadow of the Palms
Death Under Par
Nonfiction
Preachers, Rebels and Traders
Women on the Move

All the King's Ladies

Janice Law

A
Joan
Kahn
BOOK

ST. MARTIN'S PRESS · NEW YORK

Design by Paolo Pepe
Copyeditor: Robert Hemenway

Library of Congress Cataloging in Publication Data
Law, Janice.
All the king's ladies.

"A Joan Kahn book."
1. Louis XIV, King of France, 1638–1715—Fiction.
I. Title.
PS3562.A86A78   1986   813′.54   86-12672
ISBN 0-312-01966-1

10 9 8 7 6 5 4 3 2

To my father

All the King's Ladies

VERSAILLES—1680

The King woke up, his heart pounding. The night breeze stirred the heavy silk curtains of his bed, and in sudden anguish he wanted to fling them aside and run to the windows overlooking the moonlit gardens. But that would wake Bontemps, asleep at the foot of his bed, and doubtless the Swiss Guards, who would shuffle in, sleepy and unshaven, to see what was wrong. In the morning, his physicians would record that His Majesty had passed "a bad night" and a dose of medicine would follow.

The King wiped his face on his fine lawn sleeve and found that he was dripping wet. The same dream! Although not excessively superstitious, he knew it was an omen and felt a flutter in his chest. Perhaps, he told himself, it was only the salad, the pies or the second platter of partridges, yet no sooner had he closed his eyes than he opened them again on the gray darkness of his curtained bed. He had dreamed he was standing on the great terrace overlooking the canal, the parterres and gardens. The building behind had been quiet, eerily so, and he had had the suspicion of a dream combined with a deep uneasiness. He had called for music, but the violins seemed slightly out of tune, and, restless, he had walked along the terrace, past the orange trees in their silver tubs. But here, too, was cause for annoyance: dead leaves on the trees, faded blossoms in the borders, tarnish on the silver tubs and a crack in the marble basin that had been seamless only the day before.

What was more troubling still was that, while at first glance all looked the usual perfection, at every turn a closer examination revealed some foulness, and the King had found himself anxious to escape from the gardens, yet fearful of what he might discover if he should return to the palace. His heart raced, and with a horrified embarrassment, he felt himself, who never showed his emotions by more than the faintest flicker in his lips or eyes, trembling.

"Will we not return, Sire?" a voice had asked.

His Majesty was conscious that he must have kept his court standing about a very long time. He nodded and, as he turned, saw the palace stretching across the top of the terrace, white and gorgeous, its windows and the immense gallery reflecting the sun, bringing him an instant of relief before his heart again knocked in his ears: it was all wrong! Those mean, pinched windows, that heavy, clumsy cornice! The proportions were not like a palace at all, but like some giant tenement, erected by a malicious fairy in the midst of the gardens. And sure enough, now the palace began to shrink and dwindle until it was no more than a collection of pale hovels, then still more until terrace and all vanished, leaving only a wagon such as traveling players use, a creaking, battered vehicle with flimsy sets hung on one side, and, leering at him through the windows, a set of faces, pale, thin and depraved. In a fury, the King had raced forward, shouting for the guard, for the troops of his household, but this effort awakened him, and he lay sweating and tossing until, just as the cocks began crowing and the first wagons bearing provisions for the palace began rumbling through the village, he fell asleep.

"Sire, it is time," Bontemps said.

The King opened his eyes: the rose curtains glowed like a sunrise.

"Thank you, Bontemps." He took a deep breath and said his prayers with more than usual fervor before ordering the bed curtains opened. His confessor, Père de la Chaise, his doctor, Daquin, the Gentlemen of the Bedchamber, and the Princes of the Blood were already assembled, murmuring greetings. Then his son, the Dauphin, held out his shirt; Bontemps brought the wig for the morning; the First Gentleman of the Bedchamber, his coat.

"I had a disturbing dream," the King confided to Daquin, who listened gravely to the narrative.

"It is plain, Your Majesty, that your care is still on your kingdom after the recent war. You are naturally anxious about any threat to France."

"Yes," agreed the King, but his relief did not go deep. The doctor knew little or nothing of the secret Chamber at the Arsenal, of the recent police reports, of the internal threats. Of witchcraft, of poison, of treason.

"Your Majesty, I am certain, but to be safe, a purge tomorrow. I have a new medicine for you."

The King nodded in resignation and went to sit on his commode. In the outer room, he could hear those waiting for admittance to the Grand Levee, gossiping, arguing, pushing for position. One of his Gentlemen whispered a petition as he handed him the toilet paper.

"I will see," said the King.

Another added a bit of gossip. The Dauphin announced his favorite bitch had whelped. "I will take a pup," said the King.

Presently the outer doors opened and the mob for the Grand Levee poured in. This was one of the times when courtiers could catch their master's ear, and they cooed like a flock of doves.

They wanted a commission for a son, a monopoly for themselves; they wished to dedicate a poem, launch a privateer, curry favor for some scheme. They wanted to ruin a rival, to advance a friend. The King listened impassively, as grand as a galleon among fishing smacks. To their requests he replied, "I will see," and went on with his breakfast.

Finally, after hubbub, ceremony and gossip, the levee was finished. The hungry courtiers rushed to grab a bite and rest their feet before they accompanied the King to Mass in late morning, and His Majesty summoned his two great ministers, Colbert and Louvois, and retired to his council chamber. The business of the day included financial projections for the coming months, the completion of the new fountains, a plan for the northern fortifications and citizens' complaints from the Auvergne, but throughout, the King was tired and preoccupied. He was waiting for the reports from the Chief of the Parisian police.

"Well?" he demanded at last. "Is there nothing new from Lieutenant de La Reynie?"

Louvois, his plump, swarthy face serious, passed over the latest dispatch. "Madame de Montespan has been mentioned."

The King's violet glove stopped in midair, and his expression, still controlled and grave, shadowed as if the sun had gone in. Then he took the packet, opened it and read through the report quickly. "This is not proof," he said, though his heart pained him. He had loved Athénaïs de Montespan for twelve years. That he loved her no longer did not make his pain less.

"No, Your Majesty," said Louvois. "But the seriousness of the charges was such, and the persons so close to the throne, that we believed—"

The King waved this aside. "Without question, de La Reynie has done the right thing, but we must have proof. These—accusations—come near to high treason. It is essential that we know."

"Nothing will be left undone, Sire. Nothing."

"See it is not. These witches must be questioned again. And the priest, this Lesage. I want a thorough report."

"Of course, Your Majesty."

"At once," said the King, "for this is unendurable." He rose so abruptly that old Colbert nearly fell over his little stool trying to follow, but His Majesty was not quick enough to escape the mood of the dream. Wherever he looked it seemed there was corruption, sacrilege, poison, treachery; even in the court, even in the inner circle dearest to him. How had this happened, he demanded of himself, of his ministers, of the saints. When he reached the outer door, the courtiers once again crushed forward, trampling the attendants and each other, whispering, whining, bellowing, showing the worst manners imaginable. The King's face hardened into his dignity; his self-command was his armor. But it was a bad day for the petitioners, for anger twitched across his brow and lips, and his heart was too disturbed to grant any of their requests.

SPRING 1663—BELLEGARDE

I

"Oh, look, Madame. It's a players wagon." Marie pushed the window further open and leaned precariously out on the thick stone sill. "Yes, it is. Actors! They're coming here."

"Why else would they drive this road?" asked her mistress drily.

Marie made a little face but nothing could spoil her pleasure in any novelty. "There are five or six of them. Do look, Madame, and one has a bagpipe. Here they come!"

There was a rumble of wheels below, a creaking of harness and brakes, and the high, leathery squeal of a small pipe. All the dogs in the courtyard exploded at once. Madame's little lap dogs danced and yapped, the ancient mastiff that slept at the threshold raised its heavy head and bayed, and the master's hunting dogs, lean gray and buff hounds bred for stags and wolves, hurled themselves at the ends of their chains and howled to tear the intruders to pieces. The two old horses pulling the wagon stamped their feet and shook their bridles nervously; the pigs, disturbed from rooting through the dooryard rubbish, trotted off with their snouts in the air, and the fowls, whirled into motion by the arrival, began to flutter back to their accustomed perches.

"Ah," said Madame, looking down with amusement, "the Théâtre de Paris. They are far from home."

"Truly, Madame?" Marie squinted at the faded lettering on the wagon as if concentration would give her literacy, but before her mistress could elaborate, the bagpipe player jumped onto the driver's seat on the wagon and bellowed greetings to the mob of maids and footmen, cooks, scullery boys, grooms, vagabonds and children who came running from every corner of the sprawling, tumbledown chateau. The piper produced a handful of balls from his coat and juggled, found a pear behind a footman's ear and a mouse in a maid's pocket, told an impolite story and then, with a flourish, introduced the rest of the troop: a sallow young man with a vacant expression, the short, fat driver, a plump middle-aged woman who sang well, and a thin child who danced to castanets.

Upstairs, Marie itched to be away and hopped from one foot to the other in excitement. "It's just the thing for the master, isn't it, Madame? Will take his mind off his troubles. Shall I run and tell him?"

"The master's troubles are nothing to you," Madame de Montespan said sharply, but, of course, the girl was right. Monsieur the Marquis was whimsical and eccentric, his moods more variable than the weather in the mountains. When he was sunk in gloom and unwilling to stir from his room the only cure was such a distraction.

"See that one of the footmen informs Monsieur," the Marquise said with dignity, and Marie bobbed the slightest of curtsies and raced out of the room. Now it was Madame's turn to lean her elbows on the window sill. Théâtre de Paris! Her smile was scornful. The wagon was high and solid but much battered, the red-brown paint on the body chipped, the blue-and-gilt sign faded, and the theatrical elegance of the whole compromised by the kettles and washtubs hanging down the back, the jumble of props and baskets stacked on top. Yet the name was enchantment, and even the crude caperings of the players awakened memories of the Comédiens, of Corneille's noble lines, of the troupe of Molière. Paris! The Marquise took a breath of the dry mountain air and counted the months, pressing her fingers one after the other on the cool stonework. Six months until the child; another two, then Paris! She sighed like an exile, although she had been born in the province, within sight of the Pyrenees.

The Marquise Athénaïs de Montespan was twenty-three and had been married for just over a year to her husband, Henri-Louis, an intelligent, impoverished and unstable Gascon of twenty-one. Although this young man had a certain charm, living intimately with him required both resilience and ingenuity. One morning, he would rise early and clatter out of the court with all his hounds baying like demons, as hearty and happy a man as could be found. The next, he was so depressed he could scarcely lift his head, and old Jacques, the majordomo, would send out frantically for an acrobat, a wandering musician, players, a fortune-teller, even a peasant with a trained beast. This mood over, the Marquis breathed fire and rejoined his regiment; tired of soldiering, he would return to pester the household with some fantastic scheme: a telescope in a turret, a new ram to improve the breed of sheep, a different well in the court, an experiment with gunpowder.

Emotionally faithful and sensually promiscuous, the Marquis had fantastic lapses and extravagant repentances, a combination which his lady was gradually turning to her own advantage. At the moment, although he still loved his beautiful wife, the whole chateau knew he was sleeping with her pretty servant, Marie. In compensation, he was wonderfully solicitous, preparing costly and beautiful rooms for his lady, creating the only comfortable accommodation in the whole leaky, neglected and dirty chateau. He loved her, spoiled her and neglected her by turns and believed that he could keep her contented with a lovely cage of fine paneling, imported silks and Persian carpets.

The performance, admittedly rather silly and crude, was held in the long hall of the chateau after dinner. The players had less skill than energy, but the Marquis's appetite for diversion and his lady's nostalgia for the theater excused many faults. The Marquise returned to her rooms in a good mood, and when Marie whispered that one of the visitors was waiting to see her, she consented.

It was the players' child, a tall, skinny girl with a tight, smooth face, an ugly mouth and a long, straight nose. Her eyes were very light, a yellowish gray, her hair was black. She entered the room without a sound or greeting and took in the white stucco work, the gilding, the mirrors, the flowers and painted birds.

"Well," said the Marquise in her soft, slightly drawling voice, "my servant was incorrect. She said you were one of the players but you stare as if to take my likeness."

The girl gave a start and then curtsied very low with a queer, elaborate gesture learned for the stage. "Please, my lady, I would serve you."

This was so preposterous that the Marquise laughed. "In what way?" she asked, more to tease than to learn.

"I am skilled in dressing hair, my lady, in all forms of makeup, in the sewing and refitting of costumes."

"I plan no career on the stage," the Marquise said, highly amused.

"A great lady has her own stage, Madame."

It was a line from a play, of course, but now the child's solemnity struck the Marquise. Hope and ambition urged this pale and dirty brat as an omen. "Where are you from, girl?" she asked sharply.

"I am Parisian born, Madame, though I was raised in the provinces."

"Ah, Parisian. That explains your boldness. Without excusing it." She fiddled with one of the ribbons that caught up her light brown hair. "Though I love Paris, I don't always like Parisians. They are apt to forget their station."

The child curtsied again, another large and artificial gesture.

"And your parents?" the Marquise inquired. "The man below is not your father." There was no doubt in her voice.

"Both dead, my lady. They were actors. My father was on the stage with Molière before he left Paris."

"Indeed. He would have enjoyed success had he remained with Molière." She looked at the girl thoughtfully and uncurled a strand of hair. "Have you no desire for a theatrical career?"

"I lack the talent, Madame."

"I agree I've seen better," the Marquise said coolly. "But I don't need a provincial dancer as my lady's maid. Come here instead and tell me what my child will be."

The girl knelt obediently at the Marquise's feet and touched her belly like a gypsy midwife. In the glow of the candles, the Marquise noticed the bruises, blue and yellow, on the girl's thin arms and the swelling below one eye, half hidden by paint. She wondered idly why the child was beaten and noticed that her eyes were wild and secret and without hope. "It will be a boy, my lady."

The Marquise smiled. "That will please my husband." She gave the girl a close look and decided she was not pretty and never would be. For some reason the Marquise found this agreeable.

"Well," she said impatiently, "Fix my hair."

The girl sprang up and went to the dressing table. For a minute she hesitated, looking at the expensive silver-and-ivory combs and brushes, the little Chinese dish of pins, then, fingers trembling, took up the implements. "A style for evening, Madame?"

"A style to please my husband," the Marquise said, shaking her head coquettishly.

"Then not so many pins, Madame." The girl began work with quick, clever fingers, catching up the curls at the side with ribbons. "I can curl hair, too, my lady, and lighten it, if required. I have heard one cannot be too fair for Paris."

"We are far from Paris," said the Marquise tartly, "and mind you do not pull my hair or I will box your ears."

The girl bit her lip and worked in silence. When she was finished, the Marquise had a cascade of curling hair on each side of her head and an elaborate decoration of ribbons.

"Not bad," was her reaction.

"It requires pearls, though, my lady." The girl traced a line to show her, and the Marquise gave a smile that was too quick and clever to be altogether sweet.

"You have tastes above your station."

Before the girl could reply, the door at the opposite side of the room opened and the lanky figure of the Marquis appeared. His mobile face turned down into a frown. "Who is this ragamuffin?"

"The players' child. Surely you have not forgotten our evening's entertainment."

The girl flushed a little, but the Marquise kept her eyes on her husband.

"And what of Marie?" He looked around the room as if she had been hidden somewhere.

The Marquise gave her cat smile. "I've a mind to try something different. This child assures me she knows a hundred styles in all the latest fashions."

Her husband sniffed and gave a sour look. "She is too tall for a child and too thin for a woman."

The Marquise ignored this and touched her coiffure. "What do you think?"

"You are as lovely as always."

"There," she said. "I am as lovely as ever and you need not miss Marie. I need a hairdresser more than you need a playmate."

"We are overrun with these creeping beggers and mountebanks," the Marquis said crossly, raising his hand toward the child, who prudently fled to the hall, her wooden shoes clattering.

The Marquise took no notice. "It is time Marie was married," she continued serenely. "The second groom would be a good choice."

"Do not concern yourself with my servants, Madame."

"As *femme de chambre,* Marie is my responsibility," the Marquise replied, taking up a book. "I fear she may be pregnant. I would not have scandal."

"The baggage!" her husband exclaimed, indignant. "It was not me, you know. You need not look at me in that manner." He stormed around the room, stamping and swearing, but his wife did not lift her nose from her reading, and gradually the Marquis's anger ran down like a top and he dropped onto the floor beside her and laid his head in her lap. She closed her book and began to stroke his dark, tangled hair.

"I should like a hairdresser," she began now in a sweet and wheedling tone. The Marquis looked stern, crossed his arms and twitched his thin black moustaches, but she had not misjudged him: he was ready to be generous, to be indulgent, to adore her, so his lady secured a new servant and, because the others, born and bred in the peculiar air of Bellegarde, did not realize their exile, a confidante.

Right from the start, the girl could not hear too much of Paris. The balls, the belles, the court fetes, the gallant gentlemen, the players, the palaces—talk of these was as good as meat and drink to her. She was always teasing for news of the courtiers, of the wonders of Paris, of the distinction of her mistress's relatives, and out of her loneliness the Marquise responded. When her hair was being dressed, she would remark that the style was fit for Paris; when her gowns were laid out for repair or inspection, she would decide that such a one would suit a morning at court. Madame would look out the window and remark that the weather was fine, the King might hunt, or note the day and predict a fete, or observe it was the morning of a ball or the evening of a wedding. She had her plans and hopes. She would count the months on her fingers and sigh.

"What is it, my lady?"

"Three months until the child. Another two, then Paris."

"Will you take me, Madame?" This question was the only thing that produced a show of emotion in Claude des Oeillets.

"If I go, I will take you. My hair will need to be blonder."

"Yes, Madame, so it is said for Paris."

"And for the court. I think for the court, too." She touched her hair and looked thoughtfully into the mirror. "Ladies at the court must be very beautiful." Then, restless despite the weight of the child, the Marquise would examine her jewels and have out all the now useless dresses, for she pined for the capital and the court as vagabonds for the road. The morning after her delivery, she sat up in her bed and cried for her hair to be dressed and her best clothes brought.

The old nurse and the midwife were beside themselves, frightened she might try to get up, alternately scolding and cajoling. But, as was the way at the chateau, the wilful Marquise got what she wanted.

"Claude! my ribbons and my mirror," she called. "I have done my duty, I'll have my reward. I want my perfume and my pink gown. It will fit me now, surely. Haven't I a lovely boy?" she demanded. "And healthy! Is he not healthy, nurse?" she cried, looking herself as strong and healthy as a brood mare.

"He is, indeed, my lady."

"I think his wet nurse will do."

"Surely, my lady, if only you will rest."

But the Marquise had her mind set on preparing for Paris, and she sent her servants running between her bed and her cabinets, laying out dresses, fixing her hair and trying this jewel with that gown until, finally exhausted, she was content to lie, arrayed like a princess, on her satin bed. Then, through her half-closed eyes, the Marquise contemplated the room and her future. Her son lay in his basket near the fire; his nurse, a plump, cheerful looking girl, lay asleep on the rug beside him. The blue autumn afternoon hung cold outside the window, but inside it was warm from the fire that cast a dancing gold light over her pink gown, the baby's lace-ruffled basket, the nurse's gray stockings. The fantastic birds and flowers that ran up and down the walls were reflected again and again in the facets of the mirrors, and the Marquise felt her hopes, her excitement permeate the room. The servants quietly working, the child asleep, the rose of the fire and of the low autumn sun might have been but phantoms in her dreaming eyes.

"In two months we will be in Paris," she said softly, and the beauty of the room at that moment was like the first faint glimmer of the glories she expected.

PARIS

II

The roads were frozen and rutted, and the heavy carriage rocked and bounced, jolting the two sisters into each other, crushing their fine dresses and bending the feathers on their large plumed hats. "We shall look like ragamuffins before we reach the court," Athénaïs de Montespan said, but she reached out to knock her sister's hat down over her eyes and burst out laughing.

"Stop it! It is easy to see you have been away from polite society." Gabrielle smacked her playfully, then tickled her with feathers pulled from her coiffure until they were both breathless.

"I am so glad to be back," Athénaïs exclaimed. "I have missed you so." She gave her sister a hug. "There was no one to talk to—nothing but soldiers, peasants and pigs, and which smells worse, I don't know."

"Then there's your husband. Quite handsome," remarked her sister. Her own was rather older, rich but depressing.

"Henri's mad."

Gabrielle gave her a look.

"In a nice way," Athénaïs said, "in an entertaining way, but quite mad."

Her sister poked her ribs. "Mad about you, I'd say. You can't complain, dear child. He has given you a son immediately. That way you needn't be bothered with any more, you know. You can be spared." Her sister raised her eyebrows and nodded sagely. Gabrielle de Thianges was a bit darker than her sister, a little more angular, but vivid and attractive like all the Mortemarts. "How do you think I keep my looks?"

"Not to mention your lovers," Athénaïs teased, and her sister tried to box her ears.

"I can see you are not interested in serious conversation," Gabrielle said, a little miffed that her sophistication was not appreciated.

"No, I am not. I want only gossip and scandal and news about the court. I am starved, Gabrielle," Athénaïs said, taking her arm affectionately, "and I would rather have half-a-dozen children than spend another year in the provinces."

"Poor darling! Well, all has been so amusing. The King is still sleeping with Louise, and she is still a lady to Madame, and Madame has still not forgiven her for this royal triumph!"

"Not yet?" Athénaïs asked, surprised and yet delighted. This was the extravagance of the court.

"Never. She barely speaks to her. If Louise offers a tray or a skein of thread or picks up a napkin, Madame will not accept it. Though the English princes are not an old family, she was royally bred. Her severity is unrelenting. Oh, you will enjoy her, Athénaïs."

"Yet Louise is still her lady, her *fille d'honneur?*"

"But of course! How could that change? His Majesty is besotted with her. And now she's had a second child—"

"Another?"

"See you don't mention the little bastard. A big secret. Louise was at Christmas Mass just five days after it was born."

"Poor creature! Preserve us from the love of kings."

"He will have her with him, but he will keep the affair from the Queen—as if two pregnancies could be hidden. It's worthy of Molière. You will be diverted. And her brother! The scandal! His greed is not to be believed. I am doing my best to interest His Majesty in one of the older families before the wealth of the kingdom falls entirely into the hands of nobodies."

Athénaïs laughed at this, knowing her sister's immense pride in their family. "Dear Gabrielle, you are a tonic. Now, there are others. The Comtesse de Soissons, for example."

"Oh," said her sister, drawing her head closer, "there are the most extraordinary stories about her."

In this way, shaken and jounced, the two sisters entertained themselves on the way to Saint-Germain, running over all the gossip of the court. "How I have missed you!" Athénaïs exclaimed again and again, and she kissed her sister with every piece of news. She'd felt torpid and lazy at Bellegarde and lonely, so lonely. Now here with Gabrielle and their brother, Vivonne, and her two sisters, the Maries, their own circle was restored and with it almost the happiness of childhood again, with their own pet names and private jokes and turns of phrase. She hadn't dreamed how she'd miss that—or the court. When at last she saw the castle, she cried aloud and leaned out the window, pushing aside the felt-and-leather curtains.

"You fool," said Gabrielle, but she laughed to see her sister's enthusiasm and high spirits.

"Now I am home!" Athénaïs's eyes were alight with the sight of Saint-Germain. The sound of the courtiers' carriages, the clattering hooves and metallic rattle of the household cavalry, the bustle of the court at high tide, these were like music to her, and she was in a frenzy of impatience to reach the tall, ugly buff palace. But the road was jammed with carriages and riders, the bridge over the empty moat full of courtiers and soldiers, great lords and ladies, petitioners, pages, priests, cardinals and clerks, all pushing and quarreling over precedence. The crush was so great, the ladies had to leave their carriage and work their way on foot to the entrance. There, Madame de Thianges disappeared on business to the ministerial offices, while Athénaïs went up-stairs to resume her duties with Madame, the King's sister-in-law.

Saint-Germain was private home, public gathering place, mili-tary barracks, government office and ceremonial center; from morning to night, its halls were crowded with officials, soldiers and servants, and Athénaïs had to push through the knots of petitioners and hangers-on to reach the small antechamber jammed with ladies in the most elaborate morning gowns. Madame's attendants were straightening their hair, putting on their paint and jewels, trying to get their billowing dresses smoothed after bumping out from Paris in hackney carriages and coaches, a process they tried to hasten by screaming at their dressers and swearing about their hair. Joining the crush, Athé-naïs began a frantic fuss with her coiffure which ended when the main doors opened. Instantly, paint and mirrors were abandoned, the ladies' voices sank to genteel murmurs, and they trooped off to attend their mistress, whom they found sitting in her fine rose-and-gold chamber, drinking chocolate. Curtsying in turn, the ladies scattered about the room to sew or gossip, but kept alert for a chance to entertain Madame, to fetch her gloves, to under-take some errand.

Henriette, Duchesse d'Orléans, called Madame, was young, vi-vacious and clever, and her chambers were the center of a con-siderable little court. As sister of the King of England, Henriette was a personage in her own right, and an important conduit between the French King and the English court. Every day, she worked on an enormous correspondence, keeping her brother apprised of affairs in France, passing on various messages too vague or delicate to go through conventional channels, and re-ceiving visits from messengers, diplomats and officials. A good deal of serious business was transacted around Madame's tea table, in spite of the laughter of her ladies-in-waiting, the flirtations of the courtiers, the interruptions of messages and servants. There was always a scent of intrigue, diplomatic as well as erotic, in the air.

"Dear Athénaïs, you have returned! And your son?"

"Very well, thank you, Madame. He is in good health."

"And you, my dear? Maternity seems to have suited you." Madame smiled gently. Her own confinements had been difficult so far, and Monsieur's sexual tastes had not prevented him from keeping her almost constantly pregnant.

"My sister says it is not ladylike."

Now Henriette laughed. "Indeed, it is not! But we have missed you." Athénaïs curtsied deeply. Outside in the hall there was a flourish and heralds thrust open the doors. "Especially Monsieur," added Henriette. "He will be delighted." Athénaïs curtsied again, and then to Monsieur, who wafted in for his ceremonial visit. There were formal greetings; the assembled ladies bobbed up and down with a rustle of silk and taffeta, and Monsieur swept his hat to the ground and bowed to his wife. Then the royal couple exchanged a few words, but coolly, for if they lived together amicably enough, there was no love between them. Monsieur, though charming, generous and brave, much preferred the company of handsome men, while only the King's sudden and, to all intelligent courtiers, unthinking, infatuation with Louise de la Baume le Blanc had prevented a liaison with Madame. Still, all the salon was aflutter, and Athénaïs was pleased when, after her long absence, Monsieur suggested a hand of cards.

"With pleasure, Monsieur. If I still remember how to play."

He sat down and ruffled the pack, diamonds flashing on his elegant hands, on the buttons of his coat, on the brooches of his large feathered hat. He really was very pretty with all his jewels and curls, his small dark features, his flowery scent and his little touches of paint.

"I feel I've returned to the living," said Athénaïs.

"You've been lost in the wilderness, my dear."

"Nothing but soldiers and peasants."

"Nothing wrong with soldiers," said Monsieur, and cut the deck.

"You have not seen my husband's regiment. Very rough and dirty."

"Dirty, I don't like," agreed Monsieur wickedly, and laid out a coin.

Athénaïs saw the stake was going to be high and hoped she would play well, but the cards ran against her and in no time her purse was empty.

"That is too bad," said Monsieur, who loved to gamble and who hated to cut short his game. He looked around as if to summon another lady, but Athénaïs was inspired.

"I'll play for your buttons."

"Buttons? What an extraordinary idea." He leaned over the table and examined her dress. "Yours are mostly pearls. Mine are diamonds."

"Two for one," said Athénaïs.

Monsieur laughed. The idea put him in good humor; if the Marquise should lose her whole bodice it would be a splendid joke. "Agreed," he said and called for a pair of scissors.

Then, to the amusement of the court, the two of them went at it in earnest, aces, jacks, queens, spades and clubs. They cheated shamelessly, pulling cards from their ruffles and arguing each point before triumphantly snipping off yet another button. They played so long that when the clock struck the quarter before the King's Mass, Monsieur's coat was hanging askew and Athénaïs's sleeves were drooping from her elbows. They had to jump up and call for help, and there was a flurry of stitching and patching before the whole group rushed out to the chapel, ladies and gentlemen shoving and arguing, gorgeous, noisy and careless.

On the way downstairs, Louise de la Baume le Blanc slipped up behind Athénaïs and touched her arm. "How clever you are! We have not laughed so much since you went away. You must come one day and visit with the King."

"Dear Louise." Athénaïs stopped and kissed her. She was one of the few ladies who did not snub the favorite. "I am told you have had good fortune."

Louise blushed and held her little dog more tightly. She was the palest, prettiest, meekest lady, a blonde and delicate *jeune fille* who, on stage, is safely married off in the third act. "Do not mention," she said quickly, "but it is a little girl. So pretty."

"That is lovely. Can you see her often?"

Louise shook her head and her eyes grew shiny. "Not often. She is at Madame Colbert's. I try, but it does not please the King."

"She will be well, I'm sure," Athénaïs said to comfort her, for Louise's first baby had died soon after birth.

"I pray so."

"And His Majesty?" Athénaïs asked as they crossed the court toward the chapel.

Louise allowed herself a shy smile that lightened her transparent skin and darkened her blue eyes.

"That is good. You must ask him for your child."

"He gives me other things." Louise touched the magnificent diamonds at her throat. "My rooms, furnishings, all are splendid."

Athénaïs thought fleetingly of her own drafty town house just on the edge of the Marais. "I congratulate you."

Louise stopped and pointed to the attic of the chateau. "See that window? I was happier in that little room under the tiles. I was nobody and nobody knew and His Majesty and I were the happiest lovers on earth. I wonder who has that room now—just some servant, probably, or an aide-de-camp. I wish he'd let me keep it."

"My dear," said Athénaïs, surprised and a little shocked, "the favorites of kings deserve an honorable station."

Louise smiled sadly, but the bell for mass rang before she could answer and the two women hurried in with the last of the court.

"Well, there you are," the Comtesse said briskly. "Of course, she's not happy. How could she be? She's quite unsuited." Olympe de Soissons wiped her upper lip delicately with a fine lace handkerchief and fixed her brilliant eyes on her friend. "There's a place to be filled. Do not deny it, dear Athénaïs. There is a place at court for a brilliant woman. It is truly a necessity."

Athénaïs laughed. Olympe was clever and worldly and more than a little wicked. An afternoon with her was always stimulating. "His Majesty would be touched at your concern for his dignity."

Olympe took another sip of her chocolate, then set down the cup and opened her pretty ivory fan. "It is too bad for him that we are not as close as we once were." She seemed to pity the King for her fall from grace, and Athénaïs could not help adding, "And bad for you, too, Olympe."

The Comtesse's black eyes narrowed. They were dark like the King's and she had thick honey-colored hair and a strong Mediterranean face with a bold red mouth and a long, straight nose. A niece of the King's mentor, the great Mazarin, she was one of the entertainments of the gods. Her intellect, energy and appetites had marked her for power, destined her to be a worldly cleric, perhaps, or a politic soldier. Then, prankishly, nature had made her a woman. Her consolation was intrigue.

"I think nothing of myself," she said melodramatically. "Nothing. *Nulla*. My heart has had its moment, as you know." She raised her eyes dolefully. In fact, the King had loved her younger sister, Marie. When high policy forced him to marry the Infanta of Spain, Marie had declined to become his mistress. Though Olympe had been less scrupulous, the affair had not lasted. In comparison to that great opportunity lost, her present Count was of little value.

"Dear Olympe, no comtesse has ever suffered so becomingly."

"Nor lady been as heartless as you." But still the Comtesse laughed. She liked Athénaïs, who was not taken in by her cant and scheming, and hoped to shape her career. "But listen, there is a place. That is sure. A place beside His Majesty. No, no . . ." She waved away objections. "You realize the Queen Mother is sick."

"I had not heard."

"Nor will you for a while, but I pay a certain lady in her entourage. They say it is a lump in the breast. Saints preserve her, but still she is old. When she is gone, the court must have a lady. The Queen is incompetent; she is the queen of priests, dwarfs and little dogs. That she should ever influence the King is impossible."

"The King is his own First Minister," Athénaïs said carefully. "Perhaps no lady will have influence, just as no gentleman has."

"Don't you believe that." The Comtesse tapped her knee for emphasis. "Don't you believe that for a moment. Look at that simpering Louise. Though she is too timid to seize her chances, every petitioner worms his way into her presence." As she thought of the great opportunities being wasted, opportunities which she could have turned into the most significant and unassailable position at the court, the Comtesse allowed herself a few words of impolite Italian.

"Perhaps her humility is her recommendation."

"It is not fitting! It is an affront to every woman of quality at court. The family is completely unknown; the brother, an upstart. She has asked, you know, for the rights to salt fish in Rouen— that is for him."

Athénaïs betrayed some interest. "That will come to a tidy sum if well managed."

"It would keep us in jewels and horses," the Comtesse agreed, "and that won't be the end of their wishes, either. Don't deceive yourself with her meekness. Her little hand is always out. Did you hear her the other day when the Sisters from the Ursuline convent visited? 'I must ask the man who takes care of my affairs,' she said. It was all I could do to sit still. I will not rest until she has been removed. It is a patriotic duty."

"It is not often that duty is so agreeable," Athénaïs teased.

"The only thing disagreeable is the choice of agents," the Comtesse said, warming to her work. "He smiles on the Princess of Monaco, but I do not like her."

"That will rule her out then, for His Majesty will not be impolite."

"You are malicious, Athénaïs, but the agreement of the chief people of the court counts for something. Louise cannot maintain herself forever in the face of the present opposition. That even you must admit."

Athénaïs looked thoughtful but said nothing.

"Then there is little Mademoiselle de la Mothe-Houdancourt."

"Her nature is agreeable."

"Too agreeable. She has slept with half a dozen already. His Majesty will enjoy her but not trust her. He has his illusions," she added cynically.

"There is nothing for it, then, Olympe, the new lady must be a mature woman of good sense."

"I'm glad you see that, Athénaïs! You have saved me a great deal of argument. Our clique must put you forward at every opportunity. The great admiration you have already aroused must touch the King as well, and then, my dear——"

"Do not talk nonsense, Olympe," Athénaïs said sharply. "I have a husband and am not seeking a lover." Whether or not she was genuinely surprised, Athénaïs was disturbed. The Comtesse noticed and drew her own conclusions.

"The King is the king and not just a lover. I am surprised you are so lacking in duty. Think of your family, of your brother, Vivonne, of your younger sisters, as yet unprovided for. And your husband——though it is probably just malice and gossip, it is said his affairs are in difficulties."

"What gentleman's affairs are not in difficulties? It is practically the brevet of nobility."

Olympe smiled and moved her fan languidly. "Consider it before you argue. You have an opportunity if you are patient—— particularly now that Louise insists on your company." Her eyes narrowed. "Your strategy has our admiration, my dear. You can't deny it; that is a strategem of genius."

Athénaïs did deny it quite angrily, and, when the Comtesse was gone, she went straight to her prie-dieu and said her prayers, then sat for another hour with a long treatise by St. Augustine on grace. But these devotions failed to settle her spirit, for when Claude foolishly remarked that the Comtesse de Soissons seemed a sensible woman, her mistress was angry.

"You needn't praise the Comtesse to me. Her disappointments have made her bitter and allow her to suggest a dishonorable course."

"Certainly, my lady," the girl agreed, but she was thinking of her mistress's gowns which were beginning to show some wear, of her jewels which had more than once been pawned. Perhaps the Marquise had thoughts of her own along those lines, for she was very subdued and when, as was more and more frequently the case, the Marquis came home late, they had words in her chamber.

The young couple were not so happy in Paris as they had been in Bellegarde, and Olympe de Soissons had inadvertently, or more likely, deliberately, put her dainty finger on the sore point: they were desperate for money. Both were sensitive about this. The Marquise needed only to raise one elegant eyebrow and to remark the hour for her husband to feel that he was being criticized. A word about her gowns brought one about his drink and whores, and very soon their voices were raised.

"Had your father paid your dowry, we would not be in this predicament," the Marquis shouted. "Yet when I ask you to apply again to him—"

"What will it matter what I ask—or get—if you will loan it out again to your father? And without interest? Dear God, the interest alone on that third of my dowry would be our rescue."

"What do women know of money? Nothing!" the Marquis thundered, and he slammed around the room trying to make this point unassailable.

His lady was unperturbed. Athénaïs no longer wept when he was angry nor moped when he was absent. "Tell me not of your management when our chateau is falling to bits, our rent ruinous, our debts unpaid and my jewels pawned."

"It is for you now, my dear, to make our fortune," the Marquis shouted. "You are the one who attends Madame; see if you cannot turn that post to favor. Let me remind you what we spend to keep you at court! I could live with my regiment and let Bellegarde fall to ruin. I could return, Madame, I could return home. A man can hunt in the mountains and find all he needs in the country."

"Indeed, as you do in the gutter here."

The Marquis smashed his hand across her dressing table, sending a vase to the floor with a great shatter of glass. His lady jumped up, flushed and angry, the book she had been reading still in her hand. Behind her, Claude pushed open the door without being summoned, took in the little tableau and came forward. "Has there been an accident, my lady?"

Without a word Athénaïs pointed to the shards of glass.

"Leave them," said the Marquis, who knew perfectly well that the girl had been listening outside the door. Claude bent to pick up the pieces anyway; she was quite fearless where her mistress's welfare was concerned.

"Tell your servant to leave, Madame." Henri was angry, angry enough to kick them both.

"Claude will never leave," Athénaïs said with a cruel laugh, "for she fears some brutality."

"So you have turned the servants against me! You make out that I am cruel to you!" He was tempted to stamp out, to get on his horse and ride straight to a convenient house he knew and get gloriously drunk, but with her thick hair down, his lady looked remarkably pretty. The Marquis felt his emotions begin to shift, and to cover his uncertainty he seized Claude by the arm and jerked her to her feet. "She has turned you all against me, isn't that true?"

"My lady speaks nothing but good of you," the girl said; she was trembling, but her flat, cold little face gave nothing away.

"That is a lie," he said, wrenching her arm. "That is a lie!" But it was really a question.

"It is the truth, sir. You could not have a more loving lady."

"She does not look very loving at the moment," he said, but now there was a slight smile at the corners of his lips, and he released the girl's arm. Athénaïs gave a coquettish shake of her head, dropped her book onto the chair and walked to her dressing table. "Throw away the glass and come brush my hair," she commanded.

Claude obeyed without mentioning that Madame's hair had been finished just minutes before the master returned home, and while she worked Athénaïs examined her face in the mirror, added a touch of paint to her lips and ordered more ribbons for her coiffure. Still sulky, but not unappreciative of these efforts, the Marquis dropped down on the end of her bed, his muddy boots staining the ruffles. His wife opened her perfume bottles, sniffed them speculatively one by one, and glanced at him in the mirror as she did so. His lazy, sensual expression pleased her, for she began to come into a better humor. "Was she pretty?" she asked after a time.

Her husband shrugged. "Not so pretty as you."

"That goes without saying." She criticized the placement of a ribbon and requested a different arrangement of some curls. "I was told today that my looks might make my fortune."

The Marquis looked up, half hopeful, half angry.

"I, of course, said my husband was an honorable man." She looked at him teasingly in the glass.

"That was wise, Madame. I'd have killed the rogue."

"Indeed. I expected no less."

The Marquis came to stand beside her, with one of his large hands on the dresser. "We are not so poor as to be dishonorable."

"Nor so abandoned as to be devoted?"

"It is mere follies!" he exclaimed. "You cannot think otherwise, when I have half ruined myself to keep you at court. Stop fussing with your lady," he added sharply, pushing the brush aside. Claude curtsied, and at a nod from her mistress, vanished. Henri ran his fingers through the Marquise's thick, curly hair. "Were you to love me, I would be more faithful," he muttered.

"Were you more faithful," she began softly, but he did not let her finish, preferring not to know too much about her emotions. "I would not lose you," he said, wrapping his arms around her and kissing her. "I would not lose you."

That night produced a daughter for the Montespans, but not happiness. In a week, the Marquis was up to his old tricks, Athénaïs's dresses were still shabby and their fortunes no nearer mending.

III

Real spring came at last. The roads were a mire and the ladies' dresses were banded black in mud. Laundresses labored from morning till night on sodden petticoats and on spattered socks and breeches, while grooms struggled to turn out their horses with gleaming coats. No one complained. The air was warm; the chill in stone rooms lifted. The King's gardens came into exuberant bloom and the court, like a dainty orchard, blossomed forth in pastel colors. True, the old Queen was sick with the cancer that would bring her death; the young Queen, ill with her latest pregnancy. There were courtiers in debt and ladies without hope. Servants were whipped, hearts broken, horses ruined. The poor went hungry and convicts died at their oars, yet there was enchantment. Never did violins play so sweetly, never were woods so fresh; comedies, so amusing; wits, so sharp. For the young people of the court, all was intoxication, and they sought dizzily for pleasure from afternoon hunts and picnics in the forest, from evening musicales in the gardens, from boating parties on the river, from late suppers in open rooms ablaze with candles. Everyone was in love; no one more so than the King with his shy mistress. Delighted with their little daughter, he doted on Louise, showered her with jewels, enriched her grasping family. His heart was lost; he was wild with desire and with the dream of romance.

But as there are those unlucky in love, so are there those whose love is not destined to bring happiness. His Majesty loved Louise after his own fashion and sought to please her in his own way without considering her feelings or her nature. While he had been trained from birth for a public position and cultivated the ceremony and attention of his court, she was shy in crowds, aware of her modest abilities, and sensitive to the resentments caused by his favor. She had been happiest when the King, still shy and uncertain with women, had wished a secret affair, when their love had been simple, when she had been allowed to be herself. She had not foreseen how her love would give him confidence and how that confidence would impel him to flaunt his happiness before the world. From birth he had been urged to glory, and it was impossible for him to be content forever with a secretive, childish affair. His vanity demanded a splendid show, the envy of his courtiers, the lavishness which was the only outlet he allowed his rigidly controlled emotions. Since an official position for his mistress would have wounded his wife and his dying mother, His Majesty overwhelmed Louise instead with gifts and attentions. That spring, giddy with the season, with love, with the completion of the beautiful gardens at the tiny hunting palace at Versailles, he planned a great fete.

It was the talk of the court for weeks: there were to be plays by Molière, music by Lully; there would be masques, ballets, pageants, fireworks. Seamstresses worked until they nearly lost their eyes sewing gowns, and fine coach horses went on the block to pay for a lady's new jewels, for a gentleman's diamond-buttoned court attire. The most miserable room in Versailles village was suddenly worth a fortune, as the court bid up the prices in order to enjoy a few days of spectacle and glamour in what turned out to be a perfect theatrical setting. Acre after acre of the scrubby plain above the Seine had been transformed with fountains, lakes, groves and parterres. Orange trees bloomed, casting their scent over the graceful arabesques of hedges and borders. At night, candles glowed in the trees like fairy lights, and servers laid out lavish buffets by torchlight. In the elegant little temporary theater, Molière's troupe played and laughter floated on the night air to hurry on the dancers readying their ingenious machines so that gods, goddesses and monsters would appear to fly. There were animals, costumes, wonderful sights and surprises at every turn, and though the courtiers might sleep on straw or ride home in the dead of night with their servants armed around them, they would have died if excluded. They were enchanted, every one, except the lady who had provoked this incredible display.

"Athénaïs."

There was a light step on the gravel and the Marquise de Montespan and her servant stopped. The last of the evening light was fading over the woods, leaving the ponds awash in lavender that illuminated a lady standing in the shadow of the beeches.

"Louise! What are you doing? Shall we not be late for the dancing?"

"Oh, I hope not. I was waiting in hopes of catching you." She fussed nervously with her hair.

"Let Claude help you. There is a ribbon loose."

"She is a treasure," said Louise graciously.

"There, you look very nice," Athénaïs said when the repairs were finished. "Perfectly lovely and lacking but a smile."

Her friend took her arm in agitation. "There are so many, are there not? And another play tonight. I can never think what to say about them and His Majesty is sure to ask my opinion."

"Say Molière is the very soul of wit and our chief social anatomist. You will not go wrong with that."

"Yes, that is good. You are very kind, Athénaïs." She wiped her eyes, nearly weeping with anxiety. "And the actresses—one can always say they are delightful. But what of the dancers!"

Athénaïs could not help laughing. "You make work out of pleasure, Louise. The King wants only your compliments. Tell him you are in paradise and he will be content." She patted her friend's arm and they started down the path.

"This is not the paradise I would have chosen."

"Kings choose."

"Yes, but the Queen will be unkind. It is hard, Athénaïs, to have to enjoy everything when you are miserable."

"How true. His Majesty is tyrannical only in his pleasures—which ought to keep you safe from rivals, Louise."

"Were that the case, it would be worth the misery."

"You are in a wretched mood! See you deceive the King with smiles or he will think his gifts wasted. Come, leaving aside your sorrows, is this not magnificent?" Athénaïs smiled as she spoke and stretched her arms to the night, the candles, the whisper of Lully's violins in the groves. It was magic, a dream, and Athénaïs could feel her vitality and imagination expanding in the softness of the night. She felt for a moment that she could do anything.

A temporary pavilion had been erected for the buffet, and under the gilt and silks the whole court was assembling. The light of the torches and candles revealed the splendor of the Queen's table—already full—with Her Majesty bedecked in a cloth of gold as pale as her fine hair, a little blonde dog on her lap and two dwarfs capering beside her. Next to her, Madame wore a pretty blue silk overlaid with silver. Louise stopped.

"I cannot go on, Athénaïs."

"You must! What excuse could you possibly give? He has done all this for you."

Louise bit her lip and fiddled with her jewels, overwhelmed by the brilliance of the company, the malice of her enemies, the nervous paralysis of her wits. "He adores you, nothing else matters."

Louise clutched her hand. "Do not leave me! I cannot appear alone!"

"Dear Louise, of course not. But I am not invited to your table."

"You shall be! I will insist," she replied with a show of spirit. "He cannot refuse me that. Oh, Athénaïs, it would be such a comfort. You will be able to make him laugh and you can whisper whether the dances are done well or not." She clapped her hands in relief. When she was happy, her skin seemed transparent and through it her personality glowed, innocent and shy. She was the youngest and prettiest ingénue ever and needed only a young man as silly as herself to be perfectly happy.

Athénaïs gave a little bow. "You are too kind, Louise."

"I insist. I insist. You said it was all for me. Now I shall be happy." And quickly, before she could lose courage at this boldness, she drew her friend after her to a front table and commanded the servants to lay an extra place. Athénaïs smiled as calmly as possible, sat down and noticed with a little start that the King had taken his place between the Queen and his sister-in-law and was watching. His black eyes roamed over his guests and though his firm mouth and strong chin were as still as a mask, yet they were eloquent enough: they spoke of his self-control, his gravity, extraordinary in so young a man, his punctilious observance of the minutiae of court etiquette. He will be cross, Athénaïs thought. Beside her, Louise flushed under his gaze, but Athénaïs lifted her head, returned his glance and smiled boldly. There was an instant, too slight for even the watchful court to notice, but for that second, Athénaïs felt his interest, felt the sudden leap of his personality, as if the King were, after all, more man than monarch, as if behind his handsome person, his politeness, his severity, there was someone else, lively, eager and vital. Then his eyes slid away and the banquet began.

"Perhaps he will not be angry after all."

"Oh, no," Louise agreed. "It is too perfect to spoil."

That night Athénaïs was witty, charming and beautiful. The ambassadors took note and the courtiers admired. Susceptible young men thought the Marquise de Montespan ravishing, the most brilliant woman of all, and the King, who noticed every-thing, now and again glanced at her slyly and decided to ignore that little breach of protocol. For how pretty Louise looked! Her friend helped her to relax, to shine, and they looked quite charm-ing together. As for the Marquise, she was interesting, but too fearless and sharp-tongued to inspire the more delicate emotions. Still she was handsome, an ornament of his court; he appreciated the interest she aroused. Yes, he could forgive Louise for putting her forward; he would not complain if she were present some-times when he visited. He smiled slightly and raised his glass, so that Louise flushed scarlet and hung her head gracefully, making His Majesty's heart beat faster with her beauty and submission.

The demands of such court fetes made Athénaïs indispensable to Louise, and she was soon the repository of the favorite's little secrets, of her sorrows, her joys, her overwhelming religious scruples. More and more, Louise begged her to visit her rooms to help entertain His easily bored Majesty, and when he was not expected, she still wanted her friend beside her, to appraise her wardrobe, to listen to her troubles, to bring along the clever Claude to fix her hair. Many a day the two women sat with chocolate if it were early and brandy if it were late, talking of clothes and courtiers, of fetes and finances, and, especially, of Louise's two favorite topics, her horses and her sins.

"I sinned out of love," she would say. "He was the only one to care about me. Ever. No one else noticed me at all. It was always my brother."

"It was ever thus," said Athénaïs complacently. "That is why we women must keep our wits about us."

"And then he was the King—the most handsome man on earth. That was when he was coming to see Madame more than was fitting."

"He was too wise to continue such folly."

"Indeed. He is wise and sees everything—even me. I am punished properly with my unhappiness at court, Athénaïs, for I have had my season in paradise."

"You are too hard on yourself. Too unrealistic. A flirtation may be hidden, but the amours of a king, never. You have more reason, Louise, to be discontented with the smallness than the greatness of your position. Why isn't your child recognized at the court? Why have you not the honors and titles which the close companions of Kings merit? There is where your griefs should lie."

At such common sense, Louise would weep a little and worry that her child would be neglected at Madame Colbert's now or left unprovided for in the future.

"The more reason for you to speak frankly with His Majesty," Athénaïs would urge. "Ask now when he denies you nothing. You are too generous with your relatives and too miserly with yourself."

But this was impossible for the unhappy favorite, who meekly suffered indignities and wept behind her fan. When the King belatedly decided to present her to the royal ladies, it was obvious she would need some friend within the family circle. Louise requested Athénaïs, and the King, for once realistic about his beloved's temperament, made the Marquise *dame d'honneur* to his wife. At a stroke, Athénaïs moved into the Queen's household, where to everyone's surprise and the King's relief, she became a particular favorite.

She managed this by being pious as well as witty. The Queen cared nothing for clever conversation and generally distrusted high spirits, but she was religious to a fault. Next to her dwarfs and dogs, her pet clergymen held pride of place, and she even had a pretty religious habit which she sometimes wore. As her health was ruined by successive pregnancies, and her hopes by the deaths of her children, the Queen turned to the consolations of religion, sustaining herself with the regimen of feast days and fast days. Ignorant of theology or scripture, she was content with simple prayers, lavish Masses and little austerities. Athénaïs, who weighed her bread in Lent and would not have missed Mass for a coach, suited the poor Queen very well.

She had another recommendation, too, though the Queen would rather have died than admitted it: she was able to entertain the King. It was humiliating for Her Majesty to see her husband tapping his feet with boredom or rising from a visit when he had just sat down, and she was wounded when the courtiers said that the King went to Madame's salon to be amused. Although unwilling to relinquish the dear, dull Spanish ladies who attended her, the Queen was pleased to acquire a companion who could talk to the King and make him laugh.

As a result, Athénaïs was soon spending her mornings with the Queen and her afternoons with the favorite. When the ladies of the court accompanied the King to hunt, she rode in the Queen's carriage with Louise. When there was a fete or party, she enjoyed a place near the royal family. People noticed; the ladies with envy, the gentlemen with flirtation, and Athénaïs could have felt content with her success had she not been so poor. Although a social success, her attendance at court was still a financial failure, for Louise, so generous to her family and to the swarms of religious who cultivated her favor, never thought to spread bounty to a friend already richly endowed with all the talents she herself lacked.

But despite this oversight, and the hints and poisons her sister, Madame de Thianges, and their friend the Comtesse de Soissons were ever ready to pour into her ears, Athénaïs still had not seized on the way to make her fortune. She kept hoping the Queen would do something for her or that Louise would plead her poverty to the King. It was well over a year before a certain incident unsettled all her admirable resolutions.

Old Madame de Mortemart, her mother, died in the late winter of 1666. The death was sudden, and because they had been estranged since the difficulties over her dowry, Athénaïs felt remorse as well as grief. She dreaded going back to the court where all must be smiles and chatter, but no sooner had she returned than the old Queen was released from the torture of her illness. The King wept and ordered a splendid funeral; the courtiers sank into the dullness of official sorrow.

At this sad time, Athénaïs felt her own unhappiness redoubled, and occasionally, worn out by Louise's complaints, the Queen's inanities and the anxieties of both over what changes might ensue for the court, the Marquise walked in the wintry gardens. One afternoon when there was still frost on the ground and dwindling piles of snow lay heaped around the roses, she and Claude went out with one of her little dogs. The Marquise glided in her heavy winter skirts, sunk in thought, her hands deep in furs, leaving Claude to lead the animal about on a string. Delighted to be outside, the little creature lunged here and there, yapped at the blowing leaves and sniffled among the roots for mice. The women wandered idly after it until they reached one of the sculptured groves where lovers or thinkers could sit in chilly privacy. The Marquise stopped and sat down on a marble bench. The little dog put its feet up beside her and studied her face with bulgy brown eyes.

"How cheerful Hector is," she remarked, "yet Monsieur Descartes assures us he is merely a machine."

"Machine or not, Monsieur Descartes should have been as happy," Claude said tartly, "and why not, seeing he is always well fed and generally spoiled?"

"All things need not be useful," the Marquise replied, chafing her hands and returning them to the fold of her muff. "Have you any money with you, Claude?"

The girl shook her head and Athénaïs shrugged. Although she made it a point to pay her servants promptly, she was always borrowing little sums.

"Not even a sou? I thought we might get some chocolate."

"I'm sorry." The girl sighed, thinking longingly of a cup of steaming chocolate, but the palace servants would expect a coin and she had none.

"We are genuinely poor, I'm afraid." The Marquise looked across the brown gardens and wiped a tear from her cheek. "Be wise and never marry, Claude. Had I not married, there would have been no quarrel over my dowry, and we wouldn't be sitting here shivering." She wiped her eyes again.

"Don't upset yourself, Madame." Claude put a friendly hand on the Marquise's shoulder but could not think of any more positive encouragement.

Athénaïs sighed heavily and seemed about to speak, when her little dog jumped down, barking frantically. There was His Majesty, quite alone and as long of face as they were. The women jumped up and curtsied, then Claude lifted the dog and retreated several paces.

The King raised his hat, and for a moment it appeared that he would merely nod and pass on. Then he noticed her distress.

"Why Madame, I have disturbed you."

She denied it very prettily.

"Yet you are not often alone."

"I am not always so sad, Your Majesty. To a loss of my own has now been added your loss, the court's loss and the country's loss. These gardens, so beautiful in design and so logical in all their parts, are soothing."

"That is my feeling!" he exclaimed, a sudden sympathy lightening his face without noticably shifting his features. "When I walk in my gardens and see what Le Nôtre has so beautifully said with plants and trees, I am always consoled." He sat down on the little bench and gestured for her to join him. "I had thought none but he and I understood."

"It takes, perhaps, a sorrow," she whispered.

"Yes." His voice, usually so firm and resonant, trembled. "She saved my crown, tended my youth, protected my interests, and when I became a man, delivered the throne and turned away without the slightest thought of interference. She was a princess most worthy of love." He wiped his eyes with his velvet gloves, and Athénaïs offered him one of her lace-trimmed handkerchiefs. The King held it to his face and smelled the faint perfume of crushed roses.

"The Queen Mother was the greatest of ladies, Sire."

"Yes, yes," said the King. He was deeply affected and the tears ran down his face. "You understand."

"Yes," she said and found herself trembling. She was touched by his agitation, and more, by a wave of sympathy for him, a sense almost of camaraderie. He had always been the King— remote and splendid, a capricious force of nature whom the courtiers propitiated in hopes of making their fortunes. Then he had been Louise's lover, masterful, lustful, easily bored—to be entertained, managed, coaxed. But now here he was a man alone, human as herself, in need of comfort. "And how fortunate you were, Your Majesty, never to have any but the warmest relations with your mother. There were differences in our family. Oh, you are fortunate that your conduct can cause you no regret."

"Do you think that truly?" he asked, catching her hand. He knew that his romance with Louise and his bastard children had grieved his mother greatly.

"Did you not see her daily? Were you not beside her always so that any difference, any misunderstanding could be made up? And did she not live to see you great and happy, the greatest of kings?"

"By the grace of God!"

"By the grace of God, she must have left you with all her prayers answered."

The tears flowed down His Majesty's face—he was quick to weep and tenderhearted where his own feelings were involved. Athénaïs, a little pale, put her hand on his shoulder.

"Poor lady," he said at last, "if you have not my consolations." Athénaïs turned from him and covered her mouth, but the tears which had refused to come before for her severe, infuriating, beloved mother now broke through and, in a confusion of feeling, she let him draw her sobbing into his arms. For a few minutes they sat weeping together, then Athénaïs wiped her eyes and nose, bit her lips and smiled faintly at the King. His black eyes were warm, his curly black hair soft and feral like the pelt of some beautiful wild animal. She was aware of his strong well-shaped features, of the personality normally hidden by the barriers of court and etiquette. For a moment they were both nervous and awkward, then he touched her hand. "How cold you are! We will have a chocolate." He looked around automatically for a servant, an aide, then laughed. "And there is no one to go! I have not a valet, not a footman in sight!" His eyes sparkled with the novelty, with the sudden freedom from service.

"My woman can go."

"We will all go in. We will not freeze to death and deprive the court of our company." His face was red from the wind, and despite the black and deep purple clothes he wore he now seemed almost merry. And so handsome. Athénaïs bowed her head and took his arm. On the way back she spoke with difficulty, but the King was still charmed. He insisted they see Louise, and when they reached the favorite's splendid apartments the three of them sat and talked, tears in their eyes, and clasped hands like old friends.

"Take care of your friend," the King told Louise as he was leaving. "She's had a great loss." He raised his hat to them both and when the door closed, Athénaïs fell into Louise's arms and cried—for the loss of her mother, for the loss of her innocence, for the end of her tranquility at court.

IV

"**M**y head aches," Athénaïs said.

Claude took out some perfume to wipe her forehead. "You are wearied of books, surely, Madame." Her mistress had spent most of the afternoon reading a tedious religious work aloud to the Queen.

The Marquise shrugged and didn't answer.

"Perhaps it would do you good to take a rest from the court. You haven't been off your feet for months."

"How should I afford a rest? You might as well suggest that to the laundress," Athénaïs replied crossly. "Put away that perfume."

"Mademoiselle de la Baume le Blanc should be less demanding," Claude said, not daring to criticize the Queen. "She never thinks about your health."

"It is not Louise who tires me," Athénaïs said as she looked out the palace window at the road boiling with dust. Things were going from bad to worse. All summer Henri had spoken of permanently rejoining his regiment, and then, as the autumn days shortened, of returning to Bellegarde. If only he would do one or the other and leave her alone. But he always had a thousand schemes for recouping their fortunes, for clever investments and new devices, none of which progressed beyond his first enthusi-

astic pronouncements for want of hard cash. His real employ-
ments were what they had always been: the seduction of pretty
servant girls and drinking parties with his military cronies.

Athénaïs's face tightened; it pained her that she was coming to
despise her husband, whose mercurial intelligence had once been
so charming, so amusing. Yet she could feel her store of affection
eroded by his compulsive infidelities and violent outbursts. Since
the birth of their daughter, she had begun to lock her door at
night and to eat alone like the great ladies. Conversations with
her husband were now devoted almost entirely to money and to
her failure to secure more through her position at court. "A *dame
d'honneur* to the Queen!" Monsieur would shout, "and worthless
in spite of that. What about that little trollop Louise de la Baume
le Blanc? Surely she might open her white hand and give you
some bounty. They say she has asked for the rights to a bastard's
estate in two provinces! When the rent of one abbey would save
us!"

Against his passion, it was vain to plead that such favors were
not gained overnight, that one did not demand of the Queen nor
pressure the favorite. These conferences usually ended with her
as angry as he, and it was better when Henri stayed out late or
quietly drank himself into a stupor by the fire so that the
footmen had to carry him off to bed in his boots. Yet she had
loved him once.

For these domestic troubles, her position at court offered small
consolation. It wounded her pride to be dressed in made-over
silks and dunned by the dressmakers for her last petticoat. She
might smile for the Queen and commiserate with Louise, but she
was frustrated and humiliated by the neglect of her abundant
gifts and frightened that, at twenty-five, her time might soon be
past.

Even worse was her proximity to the King. Since the fatal

afternoon in the gardens, she had been all too aware of him. Her eyes followed him through the patterns of the dance; she saw only his horse at the hunt. He had so impressed himself upon her that she could feel her blood rise when he was near and feared her face must give her away. Then, too, she had the suspicion, long suppressed, that it would take very little exertion to make him hers. Scruples, piety, duty to the Queen and friendship with Louise could not make her forget this. She knew him now: behind the facade he showed the court he was a man of strong appetites and emotions. There were days when she felt she had the key, then she would be angry with herself, fast for a day, say the rosary until her voice gave out, and spend hours on her knees with the missal. But no matter what she did, she knew there was change in the air. The old Queen was dead. Louise, though still in favor, was not as pretty since her last child. Every baby cost her teeth and drained her vitality, and Athénaïs wondered how many more confinements would find her still in favor. Yet the Marquise could not bring herself to give the look, the smile, the hint, which she guessed the King required. He would be all-conquering; he would not try his luck unless he was sure. She could make him sure and yet, tormented, she could not do it.

It was this struggle, not Louise or the Queen, that tired Athénaïs and rubbed the luster from the court. When, shortly after the New Year, the Comtesse de Soissons sent an invitation to her chateau, Athénaïs was eager to be away and accepted with delight.

"I feel better already," she said as her sister's carriage rolled out of the city gates. She threw back the hood of her fur cloak and leaned recklessly from the window. "We are like school girls out of the convent for a few weeks. I mean to be wicked and gossip scandalously."

"Dear Athénaïs, you must," her sister drawled. "Your goodness has been much remarked at court. Patience, virtue, fidelity, we will go to Olympe's for the cure." Gabrielle giggled as she spoke, but remembered to add, "Though I don't like her much. They show their origins, all the Mazarinis do. What they were in Italy, I can just about guess."

"See you don't. Olympe is a comtesse now."

"A comtesse is cheap today. His Majesty creates nobles as a cow does manure. Remember, we Mortemarts were noble before the Bourbons."

"Yes, yes," said Athénaïs, "but money is necessary too."

"We have discussed that already," her sister said coldly. "You won't take advice."

This was treacherous ground, and by mutual consent, the sisters moved on to family gossip, to their brother Vivonne's chances with the army, to his wife's infidelities, to how much the Carmelites would expect if Marie-Madeleine should decide to join the order. They were deep in this latter topic, when they rumbled onto the gravel drive of the chateau and were met with a great hallooing and hollering, and by the barks and growls of a multitude of lean, stiff-hackled hunting dogs.

The footman jumped down as the coachman swung his whip to clear the dogs. Then servants bustled in and out of the chateau; the boxes, baskets and trunks of the ladies' finery were bumped down from the top of the carriage and the majordomo appeared, to bid them welcome with bows and flourishes. Leaving Claude and the footmen to deal with the luggage, the sisters started up the icy flights of steps to the main entrance.

Olympe's chateau was old—a mixture of brick and blue stone like the hunting box at Versailles—with steep slate roofs. Although Gabrielle sniffed that such unfashionable trappings wouldn't add age to Olympe's title, Athénaïs thought it imposing. A row of paired pavilions formed a substantial court to the front, and on the sides were long terraces, ornamented with statues in the Italian manner. Later in the year, when the gardens came into bloom, it would doubtless be charming, but now with the sky low and gray, the fields brown, the statues rimmed with ice, the effect was grand but chilly, and Athénaïs wondered momentarily if she had been right to come.

"I hope we'll have lots of company," Gabrielle said. "All this and Olympe, too, could be wearisome."

"My thought," admitted Athénaïs, laughing. Well, she'd come to be wicked, to gossip and flirt. Perhaps the young Comte de Saint-Pol would ride out from Paris; perhaps she would let him make love to her.

"Come along then." Gabrielle seized her arm. "We will insist on parties. We'll make Olympe entertain us royally. She's had a royal share after all."

Athénaïs scolded her and felt her spirits rise. For the next few days, she was delighted to be away from court, glad to fill her time with letters and gossip in the morning, rides in the carriage before lunch and afternoon visits from the troops of Parisian gallants who rode out daily to console the Comtesse in her husband's absence. In the evenings there were more visits, cards, music, more or less serious flirtations—the usual things—until about a week into their stay when unaccountably the women found themselves alone for an evening. Perhaps unwilling to amuse their hostess, Gabrielle declared herself indisposed and retired to bed. Athénaïs and the Comtesse were left sitting together in the pretty smaller salon, a beautiful room hung with patterned cerise silk and decorated everywhere with real Chinese porcelain, which glowed softly in the candlelight and in the red-and-yellow flicker of the fire. Olympe was working a dragon in gold thread on a dark ground, her large, strong hands not so much embroidering as tattooing, her swoops at the fabric interrupted with

bursts of imperious conversation. Now she raised her long face
with its thin straight nose and said, "I'd had hopes of your sister." Her voice was severe, as if Madame de Thianges had of-
fended her.

Athénaïs looked up from her book. "In what way, dear
Olympe?"

"Do not be deliberately obtuse, Athénaïs. It does not suit you.
You were not cut to play the sphinx. You should be all vivacity
and anticipate your interrogator. I speak, of course, of our great
task: securing a new favorite for the King."

Athénaïs yawned, but did not break off the conversation.

"Your sister flirts with His Majesty shamelessly, but she is not
the one."

"You seem sure."

"She bores him with the greatness of the Mortemart family. It
is her monomania, and it makes him shy. Any mortal man would
wonder if he is worthy of the favors of such a house."

"It is incorrect, then, to say that pride goes before a fall. Hers
has secured her virtue."

"So it seems," agreed the Comtesse. She finished off a stitch,
snapped a thread with her white teeth, and held out her hand to
Claude for another spool. "But seems only. The future is not
such a closed book, Athénaïs."

The Marquise waited without speaking and listened to the
wind smacking against the shutters. She was beginning to tire of
the Comtesse's cryptic remarks, of her absorption in intrigue.

Olympe gave a throaty laugh that was neither seductive nor
pleasant. "Dear Athénaïs, do I not know that you are bored?
After your arduous sessions reading the *Lives of the Saints* to the
Queen and listening to Louise whine? I've planned a little divertissement for you, and knowing your intellectual tastes, I've arranged it should be educational as well." She stretched her hand

and rang a little silver bell. When a footman opened the door and bowed, she commanded, "Bring in Madame Voisin."

A moment later he returned with a plump bourgeoise of perhaps forty, who wore a very neat, plain dress of good gray silk, lots of expensive lace and a white cap over dark hair just touched with gray. She had a round jolly face like a motherly nursemaid, a long nose, and shrewd dark eyes. Noticeable too, was a certain forcefulness of personality, and despite as compliant, even as servile, a manner as might be required, a great sense of self-possession. She curtsied deeply to the Comtesse.

"We are obliged to you, Madame Voisin, to have ventured so far on such a cold night."

"No trouble is too much for you, Comtesse."

"Indeed, we are engaged on great affairs." Olympe turned to her friend. "Madame Voisin is most incredibly skilled. She roams the future as you and I travel the Ile de France."

"A not always enviable skill, I should imagine."

"You speak truly, Madame." She gave a profound sigh and turned up her eyes. "I have heard the sorrows of the world," she added, and without being asked, or even introduced, hitched up her skirts and knelt at Athénaïs's feet. "However, there are good hands. Happy futures, customers one can help." Her sharp eyes probed here and there restlessly, taking in every detail of face and dress.

"Indeed! And what solace can you offer one who draws an evil fortune?" Athénaïs wished to know.

Madame Voisin gave a little smirk. "It depends, my lady, on what is needed. There are many arts." She addressed the Comtesse. "Another candle, if you please."

"Quickly, quickly," Olympe said sharply to Claude; she was always imperious and cold to servants.

Claude put down the embroidery stuffs and lifted a candelabra from the table. Madame Voisin beckoned her closer. "Ah, it's a pity she's not younger. We might read the crystal."

"I should think my servant young enough," said Athénaïs. "She's a mere girl yet—in her teens."

But Madame Voisin shook her head. "For the crystal, one needs a young virgin—the younger the better. Much more than ten or eleven is too old."

"How extraordinary."

"Well," said Madame Voisin, taking her hand, "the mind is soft at those ages and easily catches the impression of future events. I, myself, have seen the conclusion of a horse race or the cards of a hand of *Hoca*—even the contents of a will. But then, I had the gift, lady, as perhaps you will see."

She ran her plump fingers up and down the Marquise's palm and peered at the lines.

Athénaïs was between interest and amusement. "Really, Olympe, you think of the most unusual entertainments."

"Let Madame Voisin concentrate," the Comtesse said. "Many times she has read my lines."

"And with what result, Olympe?"

The Comtesse's face grew stiff. "With such results that I have set my hopes elsewhere."

Athénaïs lifted one eyebrow, but having no desire to quarrel, said no more.

"Ah," Madame Voisin exclaimed, "that is good."

The ladies forgot their little differences and leaned forward with anticipation.

"See this?" One of her disagreeably sharp pointed nails traced a line. "That's a long life, Lady. That's a principal thing."

"Without doubt. But am I to have happiness? To linger in misery is not my desire."

Madame Voisin returned to her examination and the ladies

held their breath. Claude was quite white in the face. Even in fun, she knew it was a frightening thing to disturb the future. Once told, events take on a kind of shape, a shadowing of reality.

"I see a great love. You will be fortunate there, Lady."

"A Count, perhaps?" Athénaïs asked a shade too casually. She had begun to think Saint-Pol would enable her to forget other temptations.

Madame Voisin shook her head, and Athénaïs was faintly disappointed.

"Well, you are wrong in any case, as I have a husband already."

"That goes without saying, Madame," replied the witch saucily. "It is only with the price of a husband that our sex has any freedom."

They all laughed at this.

"I see more children for you."

"How many?"

Madame Voisin shrugged. "Half a dozen, maybe."

"Alas, poor darling!" exclaimed the Comtesse.

"I see a great future for them. And for you, Madame, I see wealth. A carriage, a great chateau."

"I might have those already."

Madame Voisin looked her in the eye and studied her face without speaking. She was no longer the jolly nursemaid or the amusing witch, but the Sibyl herself, remote, indifferent, perhaps unkind. Her head swayed and her sharp eyes glazed. "You have a chateau," she said in a voice that was deeper than her usual one, with a hollow resonance. "Set high in the mountains, gray and lonely. The roofs leak when it rains, there are pigs in the court and beggars in the galleries. Your rooms may be stucco and gilt, but the house is in ruins and your jewels are gone."

Claude was frightened: no one there had seen Bellegarde but

she and the Marquise. Not even Madame de Thianges had set foot in the chateau. Athénaïs was angry; she flushed and glared at the Comtesse.

"I know what you're thinking," continued the witch in a more normal tone, "but she hadn't told me anything. I don't know your name, nor do I wish to. Your present interests me not at all; it is your future, Madame, that holds promise. I have seen greatness for you. I read fame, honor and fortune in your hand."

Athénaïs snatched her fingers away, but already she was seized with the idea that it was not too late, that the years at court had not been wasted, that her moment would come. She felt the future like a physical thing, like an animal in the room beside her.

Madame Voisin got heavily to her feet, her face blank as though all were a matter of indifference, and wiped her forehead with a handkerchief.

"Something to drink, Madame Voisin?" asked the Comtesse.

"If you please." Her voice was weary.

"Seat Madame and fetch her a drink," the Comtesse ordered. "A brandy, perhaps?"

The witch moaned her assent and dropped down into a chair.

"My fortune must indeed be great to have wearied you so in the telling," Athénaïs remarked. She felt a need to be light, to be frivolous, for she was on edge.

Madame Voisin took a thirsty gulp of her drink before answering. "Is not your chateau far, my lady?"

"It is."

"Think you it is easy to go so many leagues, to peer into so many rooms, to avoid your husband's spotted hunting dogs and the cannon in the turret?"

Athénaïs felt the blood drain from her cheeks and Madame Voisin chuckled. "Do not distress yourself. The future is based on the present and we who would read its lines must not be afraid of a little fatigue." She took another long swallow of brandy, wiped her lips with satisfaction and held out her glass for another.

"You have impressed my friend," said the Comtesse, "but she is a lady of the utmost virtue, the most sensitive scruples. I'm afraid she questions your art."

"Why there is no harm in futures, Madame," the witch exclaimed. "Even men of the cloth consult me, and I consult them in turn, for little favors for my clients."

"What sort of little favors?"

"Does not God give all things for a reason?" the witch asked in return.

"Surely."

"Even knowledge of the future?"

"That might seem the Devil's gift."

"Even the Devil exists but by the sufferance of God," Madame Voisin said confidently, "but as for my gift, I doubt not it came from God, for I had it in my cradle." She nodded and half closed her eyes dreamily.

"This does not account for your clerical friends," Athénaïs said.

"Only this: forces are tending toward the future I described. Yet, consider, my lady, how many are the spirits of the earth, how many are the influences both good and evil. Your fortune is like a candle set on the wastes, needing but a breath to blow it out or to coax it into flame. Prayers, Lady, are the good breath, prayers that harness powerful forces may make all the difference! My friends are truly special men, well fit to serve the interests of a lady who would be great." She smiled, gave Athénaïs another shrewd glance, then returned to her drink.

"And they can guarantee—" Athénaïs whispered, only half intending to speak.

"Yes, Madame. Though all things are uncertain under the moon, yet in your case, I feel so strongly I would not hesitate to guarantee."

In the long silence that followed, the candles whispered softly, the wind rattled along the panes, the Comtesse's needle punched stiffly through the canvas. Then even this stopped, and the women were as still as if they had fallen under a spell. The night flowed out like a river around them, and all the spirits the witch had spoken of seemed to be passing in the wind, in the billow of the drapes, in the sudden smoky cracklings of the fire. A dog howled in the court, and Athénaïs clasped her hands nervously and said, "Tomorrow. It may be I will summon you tomorrow."

Instantly, Madame Voisin roused herself, her dreamy air replaced by a businesslike bustle. "Of course, Madame. You consider it well. I am at your service, Madame, always. And at yours, too, Comtesse." She rose and curtsied to them both. The little silver bell rang, and a moment later a footman appeared to escort her away.

Gabrielle de Thianges clapped her hands and began to bounce up and down on the bed like a naughty child. "How delightful, Athénaïs! How amusing Olympe is! There is something to be said for these new families."

"How you go on. It is nonsense, a trifle for our amusement, although when she spoke of Bellegarde as if she were standing on the drive, my heart jumped."

"And to think I was up here alone and missed everything! It was too bad of you, Athénaïs; you ought to have sent for me."

"You claimed to be ill."

"Ill, ill. You know how a lady's illnesses are. I am vexed with you both."

"The Voisin woman is for hire. You can invite her to your next soiree."

"Indeed I shall, if she is always so interesting. But come, Athénaïs, surely there is more."

"She offers me certain priests."

"Ah," said Gabrielle and her face grew more sober. Her sister looked at her quizzically. "Nothing." She waved her diamond-sprinkled hand. "Just that I have heard of such."

"As though I needed anyone except my own confessor," said Athénaïs, but there was no certainty in her voice.

"You must take all this more seriously," her sister scolded. "If there is any chance—even the smallest—that you might come into favor with His Majesty, it must be taken. Must. I speak not now of myself, for as you know, my affairs are sound, but do consider your own. Montespan's debts are shocking. Then you must think of our sisters. One or both may have a true vocation, and any good convent, unlike your compliant husband, will demand the dowry in hand."

Athénaïs flushed at this and to cover her indecision, picked up a heavy silver-backed brush and hurled it at her sister's head. Gabrielle ducked and laughed, then snatched up a pillow as a shield. In a moment, the bedroom was a field of combat with combs following brushes and pillows, until Athénaïs began on her stack of books and her sister threw up her hands in mock surrender. "Stop, for God's sake! I shall be destroyed by your library."

They collapsed in giggles on the bed and wound up lying side by side, talking companionably, while Claude tidied up the results of their tomfoolery.

"There is Vivonne, you know," Athénaïs said after a time. "His prospects are good."

"Men look after themselves; it is we women who must consider our families, and really Marie-Christine and Marie-Madeleine will be in serious difficulties if something is not done. Not to mention Father. His affairs are grave."

Athénaïs sat up, brushing back a loose strand of hair. "I don't like it, Gabrielle. We are warned of superstition and sorcery."

Her sister put aside this fear with a laugh. "You are too wise to take such things entirely seriously. It will be an amusement, entertainment to help pass the time on a tedious visit. What harm can anything done in the spirit of fun do? And by priests at that! Their prayers may do good. Besides if this woman has the knowledge she claims, all is decided already. It is fated."

"Perhaps I should leave the matter to fate."

Gabrielle laid a hand on her shoulder. "We must accept our fate, we must take it up. That is where the magic lies. You must will what you would have. And if it is to be the King——"

Athénaïs jumped up. "Do not speak to me of that. I serve the Queen and Louise has confided in me."

"Very well," drawled her sister, "yet they cannot expect you to be ruined with debt for their friendship." She leaned her handsome dark head on the pillow and watched as Athénaïs paced up and down, fiddled with a curtain and stared out at the fields cracked and whitened with frost. It was a long time before the Marquise spoke.

"Of course, as you say, it would be a game—this business with the priests."

"Dear Athénaïs, merely a game."

But still she hesitated, ordered her hair done, began a book and laid it aside, took up another and read out a poem. She was restless and nervous and nothing suited her, not her hair, not her ribbons, not her lace or her paint. At last she called for brandy and sweet cakes and by the time the sisters descended the stairs for supper they were in a silly humor, their voices a shade too loud when they spoke to the Comtesse.

"I am jealous, dear Olympe," Gabrielle pouted. "Do let us have this marvelous fortune-teller back again."

"It can be done! I will send a servant immediately."

"And let her bring her priest."

Athénaïs looked away. Only Claude saw the smile of triumph on the Comtesse's face and the look that passed between her and Gabrielle de Thianges.

There was a great deal of merriment that night at the Comtesse's table. Every course featured some new delight and no glass went dry for an instant. Athénaïs was reckless with gaiety, with hope, with the wine her sister and Olympe urged on her. As for those two great and playful ladies, their emotions were a mixture of power and envy, and when the witch and her companions arrived, their hard eyes grew large with anticipation. But the Comtesse was well able to conceal her interests, and after she had ordered the visitors seated and given refreshment, she did not mention them again until the ladies had finished their cups of café au lait.

"I have no idea what Madame Voisin may have brought us," she said. "She has the most extraordinary tastes in men."

"Really," drawled Gabrielle. "What of Monsieur Voisin?"

"A tailor of no account. But her lovers are quite interesting. There is a certain gentleman of the court—"

There was a murmur at this.

"And, it is said, the headsman of Paris."

"A combination to give one pause," exclaimed Athénaïs.

"A woman ought to be interested in both politics and the law," the Comtesse replied smoothly. She rang and gave commands. A few moments later, Madame Voisin was ushered in, followed by her two priests, Father Mariette, a smug, lazy-looking fellow with a round, oily face and a well-padded frame, and Father Dubuisson, lean, sallow and alert, with a long stringy neck that rose from his cassock like a turtle's from its shell. Both were a good deal younger than Madame and both paid flattering attentions to her, transacting their business with many winks, bows and sidelong glances. Athénaïs felt a twinge of disgust even under the wine and spirits, but her sister and Olympe were in high good humor, and soon there was much laughter and joking. If the ladies were resolved to take the evening as a lark, the accommodating Madame Voisin was content to humor them. As for the two priests, they were ready for anything. Their tongues hung out like famished hounds and every other word was "of course" and "at your service, my lady."

At last Madame Voisin interrupted the banter and compliments by lifting a candelabra and asking if the "little service" might proceed.

"Very well," said Olympe, still laughing. "We are at your command."

"It would be better with some preparation and in some special place."

The Comtesse nodded that she might proceed.

"The chapel, perhaps?"

Athénaïs disliked this idea and Father Dubuisson and Father Mariette had to go all out to persuade her. They bowed and scraped, commended her piety and spoke of spiritual forces. "Madame can move the spirits," Dubuisson whispered. "Her talents are amazing. But for piety's sake, they must be under the guidance of the church."

"Of the holy Mother Church," intoned Mariette solemnly. "We are specialists in this sort of thing—many times we are called. It is dangerous to approach the spirits without a proper spiritual director. That is what we do for Madame Voisin. We see that her talents are kept within suitable boundaries." He crossed himself ostentatiously, and his partner waggled his lean head and rolled his eyes and whispered "the powers of prayer" in his Norman dialect.

Athénaïs agreed at last.

"A few moments then, ladies. A few moments, only, we will beg your indulgence," said Madame Voisin. She has the voice of a mountebank, Athénaïs thought with contempt, but she could not forget that the woman had seen even Henri's spotted hunting dogs. It was true; there were people with gifts, with powers.

A footman led the guests away to the chapel and the ladies had another brandy, exchanged quips and congratulated the Comtesse on the novelty of her entertainments.

"It is all in having connections," Olympe said. "Too many think only of the court. A wise lady has connections everywhere and neglects no source of information, though, of course, Madame Voisin is quite special." She had begun a discussion of Parisian fortune-tellers and was explaining how her own superior intelligence had winnowed out impostors, when, quiet as a shadow, the footman returned and, with the barest of nods, indicated all was ready. The Comtesse dismissed him, then picked up a candelabra herself and led the way.

Without the usual escort, the corridors were even darker and colder than usual. The candlelight ran along the gilt frames of such ancestors as the Comtesse had managed to collect, over swords, hung unscabbarded, over old helmets and new bronzes, over fine marbles, ormolu clocks and polished brasses, all glimpsed for an instant, then sinking as quickly as they appeared into darkness. The door of the chapel was ajar, and as they approached, the women saw the faint flickering of the large altar candles and heard the soft murmur of the priests' chanting. Madame Voisin, attired in a vast black velvet cloak embroidered in gold, met them at the door. "The lady will approach the altar," she told the Comtesse. "The rest of us will be witnesses."

Gabrielle looked around. "A very Italianate entertainment," she said drily. Athénaïs giggled nervously but did not release Claude's hand.

"And what is to be done?" asked the Comtesse in her imperious voice.

"They will read the Evangels over her head," said Madame Voisin. "That is a sovereign charm. Very potent."

"Such private services are forbidden," Athénaïs protested.

"Well now, they are and they are not," said Madame Voisin in a soothing way. "If the King or Queen or any of the great ones desire a prayer in their own chambers, who would say no? Those who wish to be great must act greatly. And these are very holy gentlemen," she added. The two young priests smiled wolfishly, their eyes glittering in the candlelight.

Athénaïs hesitated, tempted, yet annoyed, but her sister and Olympe mocked her scruples until she knelt before the altar. The priests opened an immense and ornate Bible, and one began to read rapidly in Latin while the other swung a censer full of incense. Madame Voisin, doubtless the better to affect the spirits, began to chant with a monotonous hum. Their voices spun out a soporific Latin line and with that drone and the heavy scent of the incense, Athénaïs began to nod. She felt as if everything was happening elsewhere, as if it was all a spell, a dream, a story merely, like one of her brother's much-embroidered escapades, to which she need not pay attention. The candles flickered, the service stretched out interminably, the cold of the chapel crept into her bones, then with a shock, she realized that one priest had begun to pray loudly and resonantly in French.

"You must repeat, Madame," he prompted.

"I ask the favor of the King," she said obediently.

"And for all bounties."

"And for all bounties."

Madame Voisin prompted them in a hiss.

"That the King may leave and neglect Mademoiselle Louise de la Baume le Blanc who now shares his bed."

With a mixture of dread and ambition, Athénaïs froze. They had seen into her heart. "I cannot," she said and realized with a kind of horror that she could.

"You must," Olympe said imperiously. "If she has him, you cannot."

"Athénaïs, dear," said her sister.

"That the King may leave and neglect Mademoiselle Louise . . ." Athénaïs whispered, twisting her hands in remorse.

"That the Queen shall be neglected and her children die," continued the priest pitilessly.

"I am her lady," Athénaïs exclaimed. It was not a dream but a nightmare and she wished to awaken.

"Would you be great?" demanded the Comtesse.

"Her children die anyway," Madame Voisin said carelessly. "They are of a sickly nature."

"I cannot pray for that!" Athénaïs said, her voice rising dangerously. "For the deaths of her children, I cannot pray."

"I ask that the Queen conceive no more," intoned the priest in a moment of inspiration.

"That were a blessing to her, surely," Olympe whispered.

"A safe prayer, indeed, even for a *dame d'honneur*."

There was a long pause. The chains of the censer rattled and the candles fluttered, casting the faces of the priests and the witch into black-and-gold masks. Athénaïs felt the greatness of her will—on which all depended—and the nearness of the spirits that would bend events to her desire. This was the point at which everything was balanced, and she tasted it for a moment before she leapt to her fate: "I ask that the Queen not conceive again," she whispered, then covered her face with her hands and slumped until her head almost touched the marble floor. "But demand of me no more!" she cried. "No more!"

"We ask these things in the names of our Lord, Jesus Christ, the Holy Ghost, the Virgin and all the saints," said the priest. His plump colleague began to sing in Latin. Their words vibrated in the freezing air and Athénaïs started to weep. Claude picked up her shawl and draped it around her shoulders, and before the last whisper of the priests had died away, the Marquise stood up.

"We must leave," she said. "We must leave this place." She walked out of the chapel without another word, leaving her servant to snatch up a candle to light her way, and didn't regain her composure until Madame Voisin and the priests had been dismissed. When they were gone, she was as arch as ever. "A most eccentric evening, Olympe. You know such interesting people. From your early life, most likely, from before the late Cardinal brought you here."

Although the Comtesse was angry at this reference to her former poverty, she managed a smile. "You will be great, Athénaïs, and then you will be grateful."

"They will waft me to favor with their garlic breaths," Athénaïs said lightly, but even the candlelight showed she was pale.

The Comtesse called a footman and ordered some brandy. "The chapel is cold," she said. "I see you are shivering."

"It is the bare floor. It needs a Turkey carpet."

"It is that woman Voisin. She is a dragon. I was quite frightened; no wonder Athénaïs is shivering," Gabrielle said, but her eyes were bright. The evening had excited her and opened possibilities.

"Would you have a meek witch?" Olympe asked. "A timid, shrinking witch, afraid of her shadow?"

The others laughed.

"Afraid of potions, afraid of spells?"

"Afraid of wickedness," said Athénaïs, but she found solace in brandy.

The Comtesse refilled the glasses herself. "To our success," she said, raising her glass. "To Athénaïs." The fine crystal clinked, the golden liquid wavered.

Athénaïs lifted her glass boldly. "To his Majesty," she corrected. "To the future."

When Claude opened the curtains, the pale winter sun was long up, the fire was burnt out and there was ice on the window panes. She crossed to ring for a footman, but her mistress raised her hand weakly from the bed and said, "Don't."

"But the fire is dead, Madame."

"Don't." Athénaïs touched her forehead delicately. "He will clump in with his heavy boots and drop the logs and my head will split."

"Very good, Madame."

"Well, bring me my fur if you don't want me to freeze to death!"

Claude brought the robe, perfume to wipe her face, and brushes and ribbons. Her mistress sat motionless, her eyes still closed as if it hurt them to be open. "I have been foolish."

"The brandy was foolish. The rest, Madame, was but prudent."

"You are a pagan, though you attempt to deceive me and carry your beads."

"My mother carried her beads—and her missal, too—but the Church would not put her in the ground," Claude said bitterly.

"Players have always been outside the church," her mistress answered indifferently.

"She was a good woman, player or not," Claude said stubbornly, and she gave her lady's hair a tug as she fixed the curls.

"Ouch! I'll dismiss you and take on a proper hairdresser."

Claude put some perfume on Athénaïs's temples and resumed work more carefully. A lady can indulge little angers, but her maid cannot. When she was finished, she fetched a mirror.

"There, Madame."

Athénaïs was pale, but her image in the glass was as lovely as ever. In surprise, she touched the surface of the glass and then her cheek. "Nothing shows. I had thought"—she gave a little unconvincing laugh—"but it was just a game. A divertissement, a novelty of Olympe's."

"To be sure, my lady. Nothing more."

"Then why am I so uneasy? Why does my heart beat so?"

"That is the brandy and sweet cakes and late coffee."

Athénaïs reached out and hugged the girl. That was her way—sudden sweetness after anger. "Yet I do not wish to stay here. Gabrielle must lend me her carriage."

"It would be better perhaps, my lady, to postpone a day."

Claude had been well trained in exits and entrances, and Athénaïs saw her point.

"Tomorrow, then," she said with a shrug. "The Comtesse must be content if we stay until tomorrow."

V

Athénaïs left the Comtesse's chateau determined to have no more to do with Madame Voisin's unseemly services, sly priests and cryptic prophecies, but the witch's offers and promises had stolen into her heart. Before the month was out, Athénaïs had dispatched Claude to Madame's remote house on the Saint Denis road. From then on there was a constant traffic: Madame had charms that never failed; she said the most efficacious prayers. She could look into the crystal and pluck from its misty swirls jewels and matched coach horses, noble titles, pensions and offices. She could shape the future; she could make it so real that Athénaïs found herself interpreting all the minutiae of court as an augury and searching the still lineaments of the King's face to discern her fortune.

This concentration on the financial and romantic future—very necessary since Henri's debts were monstrous and her last good jewels were pawned—had another effect. Unforeseen by her, but perhaps anticipated by the Comtesse, dealings with Madame Voisin hardened the heart. Athénaïs found herself impatient with Louise and bored with Her Majesty. Certainly it was cruel that Louise, in possession of all that would have made Athénaïs's life comfortable, happy and glorious, should spend her time bewailing her sins and fretting over the King's little flirtations. When

Louise became pregnant again, she was more weepy and insecure than ever; her pretty eyes filled with tears as she smoothed the folds of some ravishing brocade or accepted her commission on a request passed to the King. Neither wealth nor grandeur cheered her, and it was hard for a woman of Athénaïs's quick, and slightly malicious, humor to keep from thinking that it would be a positive favor to take the King from her.

As for Her Majesty, Madame Voisin's crystal seemed to have cleared Athénaïs's sight. There the Queen sat, with her dwarfs around her, dumpy and misshapen, singing sad Spanish songs. The Queen patted their heads, called them nicknames, straightened their lace. Or else she played with her little dogs, tittering when they messed the chamber for want of being let out, and cooed to them like babies. Despite the ambassadors, courtiers and dignitaries of all sorts that passed through the chambers, there were days when Athénaïs felt paralyzed by boredom.

Her chief happiness that spring was to get away from court on the trips to see the army which His Majesty had collected for the invasion of the Spanish Netherlands. It was a force such as the Continent had not seen since the days of the Caesars, and often the whole court rode out to see the soldiers maneuver.

Their encampment stirred Athénaïs to the heart. Tens of thousands of foot soldiers, scores of cavalry detachments, musketeers and artillerymen, all led by the flower of the nobility, gorgeously dressed, splendidly equipped. The horses were magnificent; the drills, impressive; the uniforms, as covered by lace and ribbons as any ball gown at Saint-Germain. Colbert might complain of the expense, of the useless ornamentation and opulent fittings, but the King loved splendor, and the trips to the camps were like fetes. Arriving with the Queen and Louise, the Princess of Monaco and the other chosen ladies in Her Majesty's coach, Athénaïs would be almost intoxicated with the pageantry, the music, the rows of glorious men and horses. She adored it; her pleasure, and her intelligent interest, pleased the King.

For he, too, was bored with routine and was feeling the exhilaration of spring and the coming campaign. Sitting on the back of his beautiful war-horse, his power arrayed before him, he thought that he could do as he pleased and that it might please him to change his mistress. In this frame of mind, he made Louise the Duchesse de La Vallière, legitimized her daughter and gave them the duchy of Vaujours. But though he conferred this with all the required flourishes, Athénaïs found her friend on the brink of tears when she went with congratulations.

"Madame la Duchesse," Athénaïs said, crushing her envy by curtsying almost to the floor.

"Do not mock me." Louise bit her lip.

"My dear, what do you mean? Your child is recognized, you are elevated, and you have Vaujours. Though the duchy is not rich, I think these tears foolish."

"You may think so, but you don't know the King. I'm in the greatest danger and he is buying me off," she said and burst into sobs.

"Dear Louise, it does not do to put such dark colors on everything!"

"Don't you understand? It is all for our daughter! Do you think any of this is for me? I am made a duchesse so her rank is respectable."

"But haven't you wanted your child legitimized?" Athénaïs asked with a touch of exasperation. "If you must be a duchesse for that, so much the better. How rarely our children bring us glory."

"Oh, do not tease," Louise said so unhappily that Athénaïs regretted her sly tongue, put her arms around her friend and turned the conversation to Vaujours. "But he has provided for Marie-Anne! That is important."

"He is not providing very well," Louise said sniffling. Although in many ways a silly woman, she had a sound head for figures. "Marie-Anne will not be independent with its rents. We will be asking for charity at every turn."

"She is legitimate and the daughter of the King. You will marry her off easily enough."

"If I am still at court! But what will happen to her if the King is tired of me? No, no, I fear it is true! His attention wanders." She rose from her chair and cried out in anguish. "Who will it be? The Princess of Monaco? That wretched little Mademoiselle de la Mothe-Houdancourt? Your sister? Who does he smile at, Athénaïs? I feel in my heart that he will abandon me."

Louise refused to be comforted or distracted, and that same day there was a scene with the King. She wept and told him no one would ever love him as she had. He comforted her and became solicitous, concluding the conversation by telling her that she must not risk her health and the child by following the armies. Surprised, Louise protested that she was not five months gone yet, but the King overwhelmed her with fears and cautions, saying he would not for the world have her miscarry.

All her pleas to be included were in vain. In early May, the King left Fontainebleau at the head of his troops. The dust from his escort had barely settled before the Queen ordered Louise to her new estates in Vaujours. A few weeks later, minus Louise, the court ladies set out with an immense and wonderful equipage to see the towns captured in the Spanish Netherlands. Since these were taken for Her Majesty, heiress of Spain, it was proper that the peasants whose stock was seized and the burghers whose towns had faced French artillery should see the lady for whom they had suffered. For them, the Queen came in her gilded coach, wearing her court dress ablaze with jewels despite the heat and the powdery white dust that blew into the windows. Around her came her escort, thousands strong, and the wagons with the servants and tents, food and forage, hairdressers, cooks, priests and little dogs essential to her ladies. Almost 30,000 horses and mules ate their way across the northern countryside so that stunned farm laborers and provincial merchants could see their new queen—and so that rumor could run to the ends of the Continent that the King was on the move like Darius the Persian, with such wealth, splendor and confidence that no mortal power could stand against him.

Day after day, like a great gilded serpent, the Queen's entourage made its slow progress north, the carriages bouncing and swaying over the roads ruined by the earlier passage of the armies. The ladies planned to join the King at Avesnes, and they pushed on until they were a day short of their goal. They were at La Fère, resting from the unseasonable heat, when a page arrived, whispered a word to the guards and was led into one of the luxurious silk-walled tents.

"The Duchesse de La Vallière has arrived, Your Majesty."

The Queen stood up in an absolute fury, dropping her little dog, her beads and her embroidery. She hated Louise more than any other creature on earth. "That whore has disobeyed me! I will not have it! Here, you say? She dares not. I will send her back." With this the Queen's face puckered, and she began to cry with anger and with fear, too, that on this triumphal promenade she might be forced to accept her husband's mistress. It was unbearable, the more so when her own little daughter was dead, gone to the saints, while Louise's brat was given Vaujours! And another yet to come! "May she die of it," the Queen shouted. "Send her back!" and she wept again, while the page rubbed his foot on the carpet and picked at his lace ruffles. The Queen's ladies tried to calm her.

"You need not see her, Your Majesty," Athénaïs said. "You need not receive her."

"And I will not!" exclaimed the Queen, fastening on this. "She may sleep in her carriage. I'll not receive her. Tell her that and see she understands it."

The page bowed and left.

The Queen sat down, spiteful and delighted. But though she clapped her hands at the murmurs of her ladies-in-waiting, her triumph lasted only a few hours, for Louise had a better grasp of strategy than of court etiquette. When the ladies arrived at the little country chapel to attend Mass, her carriage was waiting in front. Before the Queen's foot touched the ground, the Duchesse rushed up and curtsied. There was nothing poor Marie-Thérèse could do but turn red and white, twitch up her skirts and, when the party returned to camp, order the Duchesse de La Vallière served nothing for lunch.

At table, Athénaïs could scarcely keep a straight face. Poor Louise, she was so weary and worried. But it was funny to see the servers dodging around her chair, leaving her hungry, while the Queen ate greedily and almost fainted with spleen.

"God keep me from being mistress to the King," Athénaïs remarked to the Princess of Monaco, who sniffed as if she did not quite believe her.

Piqued, Athénaïs added, "But if I were so unfortunate, I'd be ashamed before the Queen." To which all the other ladies quickly assented, although they were half laughing. It was a comedy for everyone but the Queen and Louise. They were in deadly earnest, and early the next morning, Louise rose, determined to stake everything on one last gamble. Had she not been so heavy, she would have ridden, for she was a superb and fearless rider, but she was now far too pregnant. Instead, she ordered her carriage readied, and, without considering the risks, sent her driver off the road and in a direct line over the fields toward Avesnes. By the time the other ladies of the court were ready, she was long gone. The Queen seethed, then fretted that such a dash might win her husband's sympathy. Her ladies took little bets one way or the other. Only Athénaïs had no opinion. She was too nervous to think, but as soon as they arrived at Avesnes and found the chateau which had been commandeered for the court, she sent Claude to find out what had happened. Her servant returned in minutes.

"Oh, Madame! Madame! It is your opportunity!"

"Do not speak nonsense but give me the news!" she cried, catching Claude's shoulders and shaking her in anxiety.

"Madame, you might have heard it from your window: Madame de La Vallière is in disgrace."

"No!"

"Yes, a thousand times. The King said, 'What, before the Queen!' He was angry, Madame, that she had left Vaujours, and angrier that she had preceded the Queen. You will see, Madame, she will be hanged as a sheep and not as a lamb."

"Do not give me your opinions," Athénaïs said in exasperation. "Was there no more? She must have pleaded. Certainly, she cried."

"To no avail. He told her, Madame, that he did not like to have his hand forced."

"No, no, that is true. He will be the master and have his way no matter what," Athénaïs said and began to pace around the room. Unlike her servant, who was delighted, she found herself in a great confusion of emotions. She was so near, her goal was in sight, yet the cost was there, too. She had seen the Queen's fury, Louise's tears. Worse yet, there was no guarantee. She might risk so much and still watch another take the prize. "And is the Duchesse sent home?" she asked.

"Some say yes and some say no, Madame. She has cried a great deal."

"Then doubtless she will stay."

"It does not matter," Claude said confidently. "She has come on without her cue and spoiled her entrance. The spells have worked. You see it has all been worthwhile, Madame."

But Athénaïs would not let her speak of such things; she preferred not to know what her left hand did. Instead, she dressed with the greatest care and made Claude slave over her hair until it was coiffed in a mass of curls with dozens of ribbons. She could have wept then at the loss of her diamond earrings, but Claude assured her they were unnecessary, and, appraising their work, Athénaïs saw that was almost true: the face in the glass had beauty and needed only luck to triumph.

That night at supper, the Marquise charmed the officers, consoled the Queen and avoided Louise. It was only luck she needed. When she thought of that, her breath grew short and she touched her beads, but without comfort. The church was deficient in worldly council; the Virgin knew nothing of passion. But there was one who did. Twice, Athénaïs almost left the salon, crowded with young volunteers, their opulent battle dress now worn and stained. Twice she promised herself she would not. But His Majesty's black eyes were secret, his face still. He is trapped, she thought. He is under a spell; I alone can free him; I alone can smash that suffocating and useless reserve. She thought she would scream or cry, her nerves were so tight, and when, after hearing of Vivonne's valor before Tournai, she found herself near the main doors of the salon, she slipped past the guards and up the staircase.

Her silk slippers whispered on the steps and on the polished stone of the corridor. Her room was at the back, and, seeing that Claude was out—having dinner with the other servants or flirting with some guardsman—Athénaïs gave a sigh of relief. She felt she could speak to no one. She went straight to the casket where she kept the bits and pieces of jewelry she still possessed and took out a packet wrapped in silk. Her heart began pounding. Madame Voisin had promised this was the sovereign charm, requiring a single hair from the King's head. Athénaïs had managed that just before he left Fontainebleau, and now, trembling and on her knees, she wound the black strand that she had worn in her locket around the little bundle.

"My own ingredients," the witch had said. "I gather the herbs myself. All things are given in plants. And there are other very secret and costly ingredients, my lady. If your heart is bold, this cannot fail."

Athénaïs held the packet to her breast. Yes, she would have him. The thought of his eyes, his shoulders, his strong legs in their red stockings took her breath. Yes, she would. She got up, smoothed her dress and slipped the charm into the pocket of her overskirt. Then she stood in the middle of the room in a patch of clear, golden late-evening sun and waited until she had shut out every impression, every thought, every awareness but the King. The sky had turned lavender and was already darkening when she finally stepped out into the shadowed corridor. Athénaïs moved slowly along the hall, chose a turning at random, then another. She climbed a stair, crossed a gallery, took a passage. Below, she could hear the guards in the courtyard, hear the rattle of their swords and muskets as they paced back and forth. Horses, restless on the lines, shook their heads and whinnied to their fellows, and further off yet, the voices of the infantry detachments mingled with the wood and fat smell of their cook fires. When she passed windows opening to the yard below, she smelled the earthy, ammonia-laced odor of horses and men, the perfumes of the officers, the dust from the wagons. At certain turnings, she caught the voices of the ladies, the faint sound of lute or violins. She touched the charm in her pocket, and continued like a sleep-walker, all alone in the labyrinth of passages and stairs. Above the ground floor, the chateau was tenantless, as empty as a desert, with not a servant, not a page. That was unnatural, and Athénaïs felt her heart pounding in her ears as she climbed higher, up to the medieval tower that buttressed one wing. Below she could see a group of sutlers joking with the guards, selling them drink, and an officer, his particolored coat open in the heat, teasing a lady. The square of the sky visible over the courtyard was grow-ing dark, and Athénaïs had to feel her way back down the nar-row stair to the main corridor. She had just reached the far side of the chateau again and a shallow balcony that fronted over the fields to the north, when she saw him. She touched the charm and was sure: the King was walking slowly toward her, his face still but intense, the crimson feathers of his hat stirring delicately in the breeze. He did not speak.

Athénaïs waited a long time to curtsy, then, when he had almost reached her, inclined her head and dipped to the floor. He extended his hand, and she grasped it to rise. The sky was deep blue now, and against it his face was dark as a phantom's, his hat, with its crown of feathers, shading his eyes. I have raised a devil, Athénaïs thought, with a stab of fear, then the King slipped his hand around her waist and she felt his warm mouth, the stiff embroidery of his coat, the ribbons on his sleeves. She reached up to his face, to the thick tangled hair, and drew him into her arms, and he began kissing her with ecstatic hunger and running his hands over her bodice, feeling for the laces.

"We are at the windows," she whispered. Though the chateau was empty, the courtiers gone, enchanted, vanished forever, he

drew her back from the balcony. In the hall, he began to fondle
her again, loosening her skirts and tearing her lace. She pushed
back his hat, slid her hands under his waistcoat and kissed his
eager fingers, so that their erratic progress down the hall left a
litter of clothing, ribbons and feathers. At every other step, he
stopped and pressed her against him, gasping and laughing. Athénaïs felt drunk with power, with the scent of his thick hair, with
the touch of his strong body. At last they reached the steps to his
rooms and stumbled down, still in each other's arms, the King's
shirt open, her breasts naked in the night air. He still did not
speak, but pushed open the door and led her into the darkness
under the silk-draped canopy of his bed. The King sank to the
mattress and, lifting her skirts, pulled her onto his body so that
she gave a cry and plunged with him into delirium.

It was weeks, months, before they woke. Louise went to Vaujours for her confinement; the court returned to Saint-Germain
during the siege of Lille and then, in July, migrated again to
Flanders, meeting the King at Compeigne. Their separation had
been like a break in a fever—Athénaïs had visited Louise, seen
her own children, managed business for Henri, and secured, with
a new, careless confidence, extensions of several big debts. When
they reached Compeigne, passion seized her again.

"Are you not wearied after your journey?" the King asked her.

"A little, Your Majesty."

"You ought to rest," he said and gave a look to old Madame
Montausier, who had apartments with Athénaïs and knew what
was what.

The two women curtsied and went upstairs.

"Be a darling and call me when he leaves," said the old lady.
"I'm the one who needs a rest."

Athénaïs kissed her with pure joy.

The King arrived before she had time to finish straightening her hair, in tears to see her. For him, the Marquise was by no means the least of his summer conquests. He could not do without her, could not resist her, had to have her with him. Her slightest gesture aroused him, and her passion, her carnal appetites and enthusiasms, so like his own, so different from Louise's, were a source of delight. Now, by way of greeting, he picked her up, flung her onto her bed and made love to her until they were both exhausted. Then she began to tease him and torment him until he was almost cross. He spoke to her sharply and she threw his hat across the room, burst into tears, swore, stamped and returned to his arms so sweetly that his head reeled. She was a maddening, enchanting woman, and when, one day after he had drawn up his dignity over some trifle, she asked if she was to love him as King or as man, he picked the latter unhesitatingly. With her he could be free.

On that trip, Athénaïs was indisposed nearly every afternoon and every evening. The King teased her that her eyes were too bright, she must rest, or her color too high, she ought to avoid the sun. If she smiled at him, he immediately insisted she had a headache; if she danced particularly enchantingly, he was sure her ankle was turned. Then Athénaïs would wipe her forehead in a pantomine of languor, give a signal to old Madame Montausier that she was to stay downstairs, and take herself off to her rooms. In a few minutes, she would hear him on the stair, taking the steps two at a time before he ran in, throwing his hat, his gloves, his coat to the floor and tearing the buttons off his waistcoat in his eagerness.

"You come to besiege a city," she teased, the day after Alost had fallen. "You still have your boots on." She dodged his rush and hid behind the posts of her bed.

He cut off her escape with his scabbarded sword, so that Athénaïs ducked this way and that, shaking her curls coquettishly, her thin petticoats clinging to her slim legs.

"Madame, I'd sooner have you than Lille!" he shouted. He cornered her against the wall and made love to her fully dressed, his sword still dangling from his belt.

"You are, indeed, ill and you've given me the fever," he said when he was finished and trying to untangle himself from his ruffles and laces.

Athénaïs laughed. "I could try to recover."

"Never," said the King, pushing her back against the pillows. "You are to be in bed early tonight." He kissed her greedily, teased her, smiled at her jokes, made her imitate again the officers and ladies who annoyed him until his still, controlled face was broken into laughter. When he was with her, his heart pounded and his body caught fire. When he was away from her, he was lighthearted and full of energy. When he saw her across the room, when he saw his officers' heads turn as she passed and noticed the desire in their eyes, he felt triumphant, glorious. She was worth her weight in diamonds.

As for Athénaïs, she had never been so happy. She sent Claude with orders for dresses, and, as the King was always generous, installments on her debts. She drooped in the Queen's presence and made her excuses to the company, then ran laughing to her lover. She was so giddy that even the discomforts of following the armies—the heat, the dust, the cold, the rain, the moans of the wounded, the appeals of the abandoned, the gore and misery of battles, even a panic by the sutlers' wagons on the way home that stampeded the carriages—were as nothing. She was in a dream until one day just after they reached Paris, when she and the King's cousin, La Grande Mademoiselle, and Madame de Montausier were sitting alone with the Queen in her chambers at the Louvre. The old lady was sewing, the Queen was drinking chocolate, and Athénaïs and La Grande Mademoiselle were discussing a fine hunting hack that Prince Condé had just acquired.

"You know," said the Queen, "I received a letter yesterday." The ladies looked up, smiled and waited to hear the rest. Marie-Thérèse's pale eyes scanned their faces. "It contained information which I refuse to credit."

"Yes, Your Majesty?" said Mademoiselle.

"I am advised," said the Queen, "that the King is in love with Madame de Montespan . . ."

"Oh, Your Majesty," said Athénaïs, going quite white. "There isn't the slightest—"

". . . that he cares for La Vallière no longer; that it is Madame de Montausier who is conducting this intrigue . . ."

Now it was the old lady's turn to blench and protest. None dared look at the others. They had smiled behind their fans all summer when the Queen complained that His Majesty was kept up to the small hours by "dispatches."

". . . that the King was with Madame de Montespan in her apartments nearly all the whole time we were at Compeigne. There are a great many details." She looked around the circle again, then shook her head like a child and announced, "I do not believe a word of it."

The ladies vented their relief, their indignation, their devotion, but when Athénaïs left the chamber she was wide awake, and when the King read the letter, he, too, woke with a start. "There is only one solution," he said. "Louise must return as soon as she has the child."

VI

Louise was delivered of a son in October and urgent orders for her return to Saint-Germain accompanied the King's congratulations. In the interim, the malice of the court was exercised with innuendo and speculation. Like other scavengers, the courtiers knew when one of their number was mortally wounded, and though still uncertain of her successor's identity, they occupied themselves with blackening Louise's name and casting doubt on her child's paternity.

Mercifully, the Duchesse heard none of these rumors at Vaujours, but she was still anxious about her return to court. She feared disgrace, and though reluctant to confirm it, she was incapable of long enduring the suspense of ignorance. As soon as she could travel, she left for Saint-Germain, and, on her arrival, demanded to be taken to her rooms at once. She trembled on every step of the way upstairs, but when the page stopped in front of the usual door, she gave a sigh of relief: she still possessed the suite directly below His Majesty's rooms. With a prayer to the Virgin, Louise followed the page over the threshold and stopped. What had been her reception room was now fitted out as a bed chamber, and, beyond, from the rooms that had been her private quarters, came voices, the clink of cups, the sound of lapdogs, a lady's laugh.

I am lost, thought Louise, something has happened. She dropped her fan, her gloves. The door in front of her was half open and she was standing there, stunned, in full view of the occupants beyond, when she heard someone say, "The Duchesse has returned."

She thought she would faint. She was still weak from the birth and the trip had tired her terribly, but there was no question that she had to go in. If she could not face the court, she could never recapture the King's esteem, could never hope for his love. Louise took off her shawl, smoothed her hair, then pushed open the door.

Athénaïs de Montespan was sitting at a little table pouring chocolate for her sister, Gabrielle de Thianges, and Olympe de Soissons. This was so unexpected and surprising that, for an instant, Louise thought her friend had arrived to greet her. Then she saw the look of triumph on the faces of the Comtesse and Madame de Thianges and comprehension flooded in.

Seeing her confusion, Athénaïs flushed, rose, stretched out her hand. "Dear Louise."

The room grew dark, then wavered into focus. "So it was you, Athénaïs," she said at last.

"Delicious," exclaimed the Comtesse with a delighted titter, but the Marquise's bright eyes grew pained and she came around the table and took Louise's hand, willing her not to faint.

"You've had a son. His Majesty will be so pleased."

Louise felt dazed. She jerked her hand away, then in desperation, clutched Athénaïs's arm. "He will be christened Louis," she stammered.

"Other names have been suggested," the Comtesse said archly, but Athénaïs glared at her. She had not expected Louise so soon, had expected to see her alone, had, perhaps, expected her charm to cover even this fault.

"You must be tired. Come and sit down."

Louise wanted to flee to the ends of the earth, but she knew it was impossible. She had to sit down. Had to smile at the two—was it three?—ladies who hated her. Had to take the dainty chocolate cup—much nicer than Athénaïs's former service—and sit on the heavily carved blue settee that had once been hers. She took a sip of the chocolate and found she could barely swallow; she was choking on strangled tears.

"So many interesting changes," Gabrielle de Thianges said. "You will have to catch up." She smiled unpleasantly and waved her hand to encompass her sister's apartment.

"Yes, it's been a splendid fall. A fall to remember," the Comtesse added, placing the accent on "fall" and looking at Louise.

Athénaïs broke in. "Such parties, and of course the celebrations since Flanders. They are still catching up on the Te Deums the King ordered. And hunts! The foxes have been very good, Louise. You will have to get your horses back into shape."

Louise felt as if she were drowning and struggled to speak. "The grooms never exercise them enough," she said, her voice unsteady. "I will find them winded and lathered before the hounds have raised the first scent."

"I had forgotten what a rider you are," drawled the Comtesse. Her eyes danced. She will say something awful, Louise thought; she will tell me I am displaced and I will weep before her. Her hand trembled on the cup.

"Vivonne's got a new horse," Athénaïs said, rescuing her. "An English horse, very thin, very fast. He has won fifteen thousand livres with it."

"I prefer the cards myself," said the Comtesse, "and other bets. Lately, I've been lucky. I've wagered on changes, on affections."

"All affections alter." Athénaïs's voice was sharp.

The Comtesse shrugged and took another biscuit. She stayed for an hour, tormenting Louise with insinuations but not quite daring to cause an open quarrel with Athénaïs. Finally, tiring of this tepid sport, she and Gabrielle made their adieus and allowed Louise to escape to her room.

A little while later, Athénaïs knocked on the door.

The first thing Louise said was "Don't lie to me."

"What would be the point?" Athénaïs drew one of the blue brocade chairs near the bed, where, her hair down and her face tear-stained, Louise was lying in dishabille. "Though I can't regret my good fortune, I'm sorry it is at your expense."

"Go away," said Louise, turning her face to the wall.

"I can scarcely go very far."

"As far as you can. To the devil," said Louise.

There was a pause, though, of course, it had been only a manner of speaking and Louise knew nothing. Athénaïs looked out the window at the leafless trees of the park and turned her rings round and round. "We must talk," she said finally. "Delicacy, anger, regrets aside, we must talk." When Louise didn't answer, she added in a low, intense voice, "I have prayed for the right words."

"What are the 'right words'?" Louise demanded. "What will justify your betrayal of my trust?"

"Nothing will justify me," Athénaïs replied calmly, Louise's weakness, her easy tears and fragile temper giving her confidence. "But if we are foolish, you will be exposed to much unpleasantness and I"—here she hesitated, for there was a certain danger—"I will risk ruin, Louise. I am putting my life in your hands."

The Duchesse swallowed and wiped her tears. "What do you mean?"

"To speak of your affairs, first. You need to seem under the protection of the King."

"Seem," exclaimed Louise. "Seem! You are no woman at heart if you can counsel this way. I had his love once and now—"

"And now," Athénaïs said coldly, "you have his child. Young Louis is not yet recognized. Nor will he be for a while. Resign yourself to that."

"What do you mean?"

"Your enemies whisper that you have had another lover. That the child is not the King's."

"It is not true! How can they be so heartless! You can't believe it!"

"Of course not. But it is the weakness of your position that prompts such malice. You will need a stalwart friend."

"You offer yourself," Louise said bitterly, slumping back against the pillows, "when you have taken the King from my bed."

"Would you rather it had been my sister? The Comtesse? The Princess of Monaco? I am your friend still, would protect you, would see your child settled and legitimized." Louise turned to face the wall again, her eyes streaming, overcome with the misery of the moment, the misery of the future, the misery of what might have been.

"I am sorry, you are right to hate me," Athénaïs whispered, then added subtly, "but I still trust you."

Louise moved so that her profile was visible. The fine contours were sharper, more abrupt. The child, her fifth, had stripped the flesh from her face, leaving it beautiful but mortal.

"My position is vulnerable," Athénaïs went on, wondering at her own daring and yet exhilarated: such an offering must surely erase her guilt. "My husband is a man of strange humors and tempers. If the affair becomes public knowledge too soon, he might cause trouble for the King."

"His Majesty would not like," Louise whispered, wondering if there was yet a chance. Surely she owed Athénaïs nothing. Nothing!

"I would be lost." She waited a moment, then added, "Of course, the woman who betrayed me would be destroyed forever in His Majesty's favor. Her daughter would be left with a meager estate; her son, a bastard. Do you see how it is, Louise?"

"It is too cruel!" she cried, covering her mouth to stop the sobs. "He will pass through my rooms. He will pass through my rooms to your bed."

"He can do as he likes," said Athénaïs with a touch of bitterness.

"But why did you do it? Why, Athénaïs?" Louise gripped her hand so hard it hurt and Athénaïs thought of the service, the doubtless sacrilegious prayers, the charms, and shivered.

"I could not resist him," she said. "I fell in love with him. Surely you know what that is like."

Then Louise gave a sob and opened her arms. Athénaïs knelt beside her bed, weeping and begging her forgiveness, promising to defend her. Louise declared it was all fate, that it was too cruel, that it was no one's fault. "It was my sin," she cried at last, "that has left me defenseless." And Athénaïs shivered again, stroked her hair and told her not to talk nonsense, though later, in her own rooms, she threw Madame Voisin's charm into the fire and promised the saints on her knees never to touch magic again.

When Athénaïs rose from her prie-dieu she felt clean and peaceful, but this mood did not last long. She and Louise were now inextricably bound together, and each one's safety lay in the other's deceit. They had to be together at every function, ride together in the Queen's coach, sit together at table, pray together at Mass, and live together in the same apartments. It was hard for Louise to receive the hatred of the court without the compensation of the King's love, and it was galling to Athénaïs to be denied the little marks of preference given an acknowledged favorite. Necessarily, too, the joy and triumph of the one and the sorrow and jealousy of the other made for awkward scenes and hard words.

Under the strain of this unnatural companionship, Louise gradually devoted herself to prayers, priests and penances. Soon she was fasting in and out of season, wearing a hair shirt under her court dress and speaking, often and with evident sincerity, of taking holy orders. Helping Athénaïs dress for a ball, she would mention some new austerity she intended to undertake; waiting for Claude to do her coiffure, she would remark that she was lightheaded from fasting or that she was wearied of the profane entertainments of the court. Athénaïs could not help feeling that this show of virtue and repentance was a reproach aimed at her and, practical as always, she wondered if it might not touch the King as well, pricking his piety or whatever guilt he might feel over this new, double adultery. She was still uncertain enough of her position to fear that the weepy repentance of the old mistress might dampen the King's enthusiasm for erotic adventures with the new, and she found herself growing impatient with Louise and indifferent to her tears. Though for appearance's sake the women remained courteous, inevitably their emotions grew separate, their amity a matter of form.

At this point, Athénaïs, like Louise before her, found that life with a man as demanding, imperious and all powerful as the King necessitated some woman friend. True, he was ardent, generous and devoted, visited her often and delighted in her company. He gave a fete for her nearly as lavish as the one for Louise and showered her with gifts and bounties. Still, he demanded a lot in return. The King's favorites could never be weary, out of sorts or indisposed. She had to be able to ride for hours on end in his carriage—and never mention a need to stop—devour enormous amounts of food at his parties—hungry or not—and be lively and gay whatever her private feelings. She was to come when he called, be absent when he wished, fit her moods and humors to his entirely. Though Athénaïs was far bolder and more spontaneous than her predecessor, she still had to deal carefully with His Majesty's desires and caprices. This put a strain on a temper unimproved by dealing with the suspicious Queen, Louise, and Monsieur Lauzan, Captain of His Majesty's Guards, with whom, they had given out, she was in love.

These pressures and intrigues made it important to have someone to confide in, someone to talk to of books and plays and court gossip, someone entertaining during long trips and dreary ceremonies. But though Athénaïs wished a confidante, she was determined to avoid Louise's mistakes. Just as she did not plan to weary His Majesty with countless small petitions or shame him with timidity, she was determined never to introduce any witty and attractive woman with ambition. No. Her choice, she often thought, was genius: Françoise Scarron, widow of the poet and satirist, a very proper, reserved and intelligent woman, three years older than the King. Françoise was attractive, certainly— dark, shapely, fine-featured, much admired, but quite unflirtatious and modest. Although the family was anciently noble, she had been born in debtors' prison, the beginning of a hand-to-mouth existence in France and the Caribbean which had left her with a fervent respect for both religion and rectitude. Athénaïs, who took delight in her cheerful, high-spirited company, saw this fervor for propriety as a guarantee of her own safety. That the King disapproved of the Widow Scarron and thought her a prudish bluestocking was the seal of approval. Athénaïs was soon inviting her protégé everywhere, commiserating with her poverty, giving her such little commissions as she could. They were often

together in Athénaïs's rooms, and, since Françoise was wonderfully discreet, the Marquise seldom thought to ask her to leave
when business was being discussed, not even when the War Minister, Monsieur Louvois, visited. He was a man without vivacity
or small talk, who tended to fall silent after the ritual greetings.
On that particular day, he made even less effort than usual and
sat glowering at them both until Françoise, sensing what was
wrong, rose to make her farewells.

"It is too bad of you to leave," Athénaïs pouted. "His Majesty
will be busy with the treaty. I shall be alone all day."

"I have promised Madame de La Fayette to attend her.
Madame de Sévigné will be there. I will bring you all her news
tomorrow."

"Pray leave out everything about her daughter. The boy is
much more amusing. Very wicked."

"Madame is a darling, though, and so clever. When she de-
scribes something you think of it that way forever."

"Well, I'm to be denied such delights," Athénaïs said. She had
some idea of why the War Minister was using up his afternoon to
visit her and she would just as soon have put him off. "Good-bye,
Françoise." She kissed her friend.

"Farewell, Madame. Monsieur Louvois."

Athénaïs resumed her seat, stretched a little like a cat getting
ready to hunt and turned her brilliant smile on Louvois. They did
not care much for each other. Louvois had a brutality of manner
that put her off, and she had a careless wit that the War Minister
feared might do him harm. Nonetheless, they needed each other.
Her husband was a fool whom Louvois was buying off. In return,
he expected to remain in the King's good graces and to earn the
new favorite's gratitude. Personalities hardly entered into it.

"Well, Monsieur. You must have something of importance to

tell me, else you would not have stayed through so much chatter."

"Madame." He stopped and sighed. Louvois did not care for dealing with women. His passions were power and the army; on these topics, women were invariably frivolous, sentimental—or subversive.

"Yes?" said Athénaïs when the silence had grown noticeable.

"It is the Marquis."

"Ah," said Athénaïs with a little gesture of indifference. These great men were not used to dealing with madmen. She had had a fairly long experience. "What has he done now?"

"He is demanding more than I can give him, Madame. A post with one of the household regiments is out of the question. His Majesty would never—"

"Certainly not. Nor is that my wish, either, Monsieur."

Louvois nodded. She was no fool, which made it both better and worse. The Duchesse, now, had been content with money. This one, he suspected, was both greedier and more subtle. "His pension has been arranged. The equipment and supplies for his regiment have all been forwarded. I have paid for their billeting. Given him a better commission."

"I have been pleased with your generosity."

"Thank you, Madame. I have even ignored reports which I would otherwise have had to investigate—he put one of his peasant girls in uniform, Madame, to conceal her abduction!"

The Marquise laughed. Of all the madmen, hers was the maddest, which gave her a certain pride. "You don't realize that this marks an improvement for Monsieur the Marquis. Concealment is something new."

"The local bailiff did not take your attitude. He seized the girl and your husband led some of his regiment to reclaim her. The bailiff was beaten. Had he not recovered—"

"Yes," said Athénaïs. "But that is not why you have come to see me."

"I present the facts, Madame, so that you can see you have nothing to reproach me for. Your husband has been generously treated."

"Monsieur Louvois, I have no complaints."

"He does. I have now had three peremptory letters asking for a household post, or, failing that, for one of the elite regiments. Madame, this I cannot do. The new reorganization of the army is taking place along different lines altogether and, as for the Marquis's obtaining a post in the capital, it is not His Majesty's wish."

"Nor mine, as I have said. My husband must remain in Gascony."

Louvois looked down, sighed, then raised his heavy, fleshy face and pursed his lips. "Monsieur the Marquis informed me that he was returning to Paris. Not knowing whether or not this was mere talk, I have had some of my agents on the lookout. He is at this moment in your house in the city."

Athénaïs gave an exclamation of irritation. "Does His Majesty know?"

"He will have to be told."

"At once! Henri will come to court. That is sure. You don't know him."

Louvois shook his head, the fat rolls of his face rippling with distaste, as though he were turning the idea in a mangle. "What is to be done, Madame?"

"Hope he will go away, Monsieur. And hope he stays in good humor." Athénaïs spoke lightly, but when the war minister had gone, she was in a fury. She would send Henri home, have him arrested, tell the King to lock him up, but while she stamped around, complained to Claude and threw her books to the floor, she knew quite well she could do none of those things. She would have to coax him, keep him in good humor, remind him of their paid-off debts. Why hadn't he taken after his father, who had thanked heaven for the good fortune of her "fall." It was infuriating, but she had no choice except to borrow Louise's carriage and rush to Paris, where she found Henri in the main salon of their house. He had his boots up on a pretty inlaid table—one of her new acquisitions—and his filthy riding jacket and breeches were soiling the green satin pillows of a new armchair. He was tanned and wild-looking, and his hair, left undressed and uncurled, fell limply to his shoulders like some poor foot soldier's. When he saw her, he blew out a cloud of smoke and set down his pipe. "My darling Athénaïs, I am a fool."

Athénaïs stood still and looked at him with an irritation not unmixed with amusement. Beyond his handsome face he had little to recommend him, but after the rigidity of the court his indifference to form was a novelty. "Many would agree," she said tartly.

"I have been in the wilds laying peasants when I might have been sleeping with you. You're as lovely as the dawn."

"Like the dawn, I have not always been here. The court has followed the armies. It's as well you stayed home, Henri. When I'd have seen you, I can't imagine."

But this mention of the military was a mistake, one Athénaïs realized instantly.

"The armies! You know, darling, how I long for glory."

"It has not been evident so far, Monsieur."

"You are unkind." He stood up, seized her hand and kissed her. Athénaïs annoyed him by turning her head.

"Is that how things stand?"

She shrugged.

"I would have glory, Madame, and failing that, I'll have you."

"Stop playing, Henri. What is it you want?"

"A new mannerism. I like it." He caught her round the waist and flopping down in a chair pulled her onto his lap. "I like a lady of spirit."

"You would find more spirit if you kept better company."

"Agreed, agreed! I am wasted with my regiment. I need more scope, my darling. I would be in action before the King, I would receive honors, I would be dressed like one of the gods of war."

"You will not get a household regiment, Henri, that is sure. His Majesty does not wish it."

"I bet he does not. Yet I deserve it, for he has enjoyed my wife!" Henri shouted suddenly and threw her off his lap, so that she barely saved herself from hitting the floor. "He has taken the one thing I possessed—like the rich man in the Bible. Like David, he has set his eyes on Bathsheba, and I, poor fool, must grow horns like Uriah the Hittite."

"These Biblical similes are tedious, Henri," Athénaïs said as coolly as she could. "Our debts have been discharged, Monsieur Louvois has been most generous with your regiment. If you are too greedy, you will find yourself back where you were."

"That would suit me, Lady. Then I had my wife." He seized her arm violently, his dark eyes brilliant with anger. "And I will have her back!" He twisted her arm for emphasis, before stalking upstairs to begin a series of letters and petitions to the King. All couched in ornate Biblical language, they described his sufferings and wrongs and demanded leave to remove Athénaïs from court.

His Majesty avoided these documents with difficulty, and he was furious, first that the Marquis could irritate him in his own court, and second that the aggrieved husband was set on removing his wife. But Henri was indifferent to his wife's pleas and his sovereign's displeasure. This was the antic phase of his campaign, and when Henri was in the grip of such a manic and exalted mood, there was no talking to him. In vain did Vivonne beg him as a brother-in-law to consider the family. In vain did Athénaïs hold out hopes for further bounties—she was angling for the dues from the Parisian meat trade. Nothing moved him. He fitted a pair of straw-stuffed horns onto his carriage, talked loudly of adultery at court and behaved like a perfect fool. Nothing could be done; they must wait for his mood to shift.

During this time, Athénaïs avoided her husband, afraid he might remove her south by force. But one afternoon when she had been visiting Françoise, she impulsively had the hackney driver stop at the house. The King's painter and decorator, Le Brun, had suggested two different drapery silks for the main salon and having the samples in hand, she thought she would see which looked better. Henri was unlikely to be home in daylight, and, in any case, her conflicting emotions had narrowed into anger: she would not be kept from her own house by her fool of a husband. She ordered Claude to ring the bell. When the footman reported that Monsieur had been out all afternoon, the women made themselves at home in the salon.

The windows to be curtained looked out onto the garden, recently cleaned up and replanted by the King's gardener. The sun poured in, golden and beautiful, and dark against the light, Claude balanced on a high stool, holding one length of drapes then the other. Athénaïs couldn't decide.

"I think the blue-green, Madame." Claude had excellent taste, and Athénaïs was tempted to accept her suggestion.

"It's different in the light, though. Of course they'll be lined."

She crossed the room, turned the fabric this way, then that, and risked Claude's neck by having her hold both lengths up at once. "They're not quite straight," she complained. "It's so hard to tell. Perhaps I should wait until the new paper is up."

Claude, her arms ready to drop off, agreed and scrambled down. She was folding up the material when they heard footsteps in the corridor—defiant, angry, imperious footsteps. The door banged open: Monsieur was home and his antic mood had evaporated.

Claude looked at her mistress and crumpled the paper around the fabric. "We must leave, Madame."

"Good afternoon, Monsieur," Athénaïs said.

Henri's face was dark, and she knew, before he came close enough for her to smell the wine, that he had been drinking. "More rubbish from the court, I see." He snatched the package from Claude's grasp and shook the wrapping so that the silk brocade fell in a swirl to the floor, a rich, satiny expanse of blue and turquoise.

Henri kicked at it irritably. "They pay you like the whores of the savages—in trinkets."

"And you, Monsieur, who left me undefended and allowed His Majesty to settle our debts? What's the word for you?"

Henri slapped her but she struck him back, her nails leaving a streak of red against his cheek. He gave a short laugh and jerked her into his arms. "I could forget, Madame. I could erase the slate."

Athénaïs stiffened. "But I could not," she said and pulled away. "You demanded money; I have gotten it for you." When he let his arms drop, she walked to the window. "I did as you wished," she said, addressing the well-pruned trees, the elegant parterres, the young hedges. "Now I have another life that suits me." Below, the bulbs and begonias and primroses burned red and yellow and pink against the green. They were the badges of her new life, visible signs of her favor, as the mess and rubble of Bellegarde had spoken of her poverty.

"You loved me once."

"I loved you—once."

"I was in error," Henri said. There was a new note in his

voice—affection, longing, remorse, or just cunning? After so long, she found it hard to tell. "Things change. We could go back to Bellegarde."

Athénaïs looked at him over her shoulder. He was a thousand men in one—each different, a few desirable, all feckless. She knew too many of what he was, and she was angry that he dared reproach her. He had been unfaithful with any servant girl he could catch; she had slept with the King and made his fortune. "And when you are broke, Sir, will you plan to sell me again?"

"Do not speak to me like that! I am a man of honor; I cannot bear this shame," Henri cried and crossed to where she stood. "I would see you dead first."

"Man of honor!" Her scorn burned her mouth. "Fool! You bore it well, until Louvois denied you a household regiment. While the purse was open, you were content."

"I did not know how I was earning it," Henri said, but Athénaïs laughed. She tasted the madness of anger and her voice rose. "You lie! You knew."

Henri struck her so hard that she was knocked back against a chair, and then again. She felt the blood in her mouth and the pain through her ribs and thought he might kill her. But when she stumbled onto the floor, he dropped beside her, caught her shoulders, seized her throat. He kissed her, then slapped her again, his mind between desire and hate. But one was as frightful to Athénaïs as the other, and she thrust him away with all her strength. Claude, having no doubt now of her mistress's revulsion, flew at the Marquis and tried to pull him away. Then, taking a sharp blow, she jumped up and ran into the hall, screaming for help.

"The King's bounty to any man who helps my mistress!" she cried and the confusion, the running feet and Claude's screams distracted Henri, so that Athénaïs was able to scramble free. The

Marquis leaped up after her, his hand on the hilt of his sword. Mad with fear and anger, Athénaïs lifted one of the light tables and swung it at his head. Henri dodged the blow, but stumbled over the table's spidery legs. Athénaïs grabbed up her trailing skirts and ran for the hall, where two burly footmen were standing uncertainly while Claude shouted abuse at them. Now, seeing their mistress bruised and bleeding, one slammed the salon door and the other, leaping down the steps to the foyer, opened the front. The two women ran out, their hems catching and tearing in their court shoes, and flung themselves at the hackney carriage. "Quickly, quickly," Athénaïs screamed as the man opened the door. The driver began to argue, not wishing to be in the middle of a family quarrel, but when Monsieur appeared on the step, his sword naked in his hand, his face scratched, his eyes black with rage, the man slashed his whip across the backs of his thin hacks. They bolted forward as Henri leaped into the street, his blade scratching the side of the carriage. He grabbed for the door, but the heavy vehicle pulled away in a spatter of mud and garbage, leaving him wiping the filth from his face and shouting curses, oblivious to the laughing servant girls, to the tradesmen with their barrows, to the passing carriages: a mad, sorry, hopeless man.

"Oh, Madame, you're all over in blood!" Claude exclaimed.

Unable to speak, Athénaïs seized her hand. Claude took a handkerchief and wiped her bleeding mouth.

"It's not a tooth," gasped Athénaïs, clutching her side and trying to get her breath. "It's not a tooth, is it? It can't be."

"It's your lip. It will be awfully swollen."

"So long as it's not a tooth. Louise lost teeth before she lost the King." Athénaïs began to feel her teeth gingerly with her tongue, while Claude tried to straighten her hair.

"I will not hide what he has done to me," Athénaïs said

furiously, jerking her head away. "Let the King see what he has done. Henri has gone too far; he is in our hands! Let it alone; let them see!"

"Let His Majesty see you beautiful," Claude said slyly. "The blood on your dress will be sufficient."

"Yes, yes, you are right. But my mouth is a mess. And we have no paint! Nothing to wash it off with."

Claude got out the perfume—which stung like fire and set the Marquise to cursing—wiped her face and tied up her hair. When they got to Saint-Germain, the blood was dry on her lace and on her silk bodice and crusting on her lip. Shivering with nerves and anger, the Marquise sent Claude with a message to His Majesty, then cried and carried on until he arrived. He stormed into the room, very tense and upset, took one look at her, called for Captain D'Artagnan, and ordered the Marquis de Montespan confined to Fort Eveque until he was willing to return to his lands.

Then he took Athénaïs in his arms, gently because of her injured ribs, stroked her hair and examined her torn lip. She was precious to him; her vulnerability added a new dimension to his passion. And though he showed merriment or lust easier than his other emotions, his fears for her disturbed him greatly. Even after Monsieur the Marquis had been returned to Bellegarde—where, a frolicsome mood returning, he held a funeral for his "dead" wife and dressed his poor children and staff in mourning—the King continued to feel uneasy. When Athénaïs told him she was pregnant, his first thought was the difficulty the Marquis could cause. He sat up out of her arms and ran one finger nervously over his thin moustache.

"You are displeased?"

"My darling, I am delighted. I should love a child from you." He kissed her ardently, then drew back and looked at her seriously. "But there are certain dangers. Legally, the child will belong to your husband. He could take it away from us. You understand."

She took his hand. "We must get a deed of separation."

"I have asked; I have had all the documents submitted again and again. But the Parliament of Paris will take its own time." His face was rigid with annoyance. "They can defy me in few ways, but in this matter they hold the upper hand. It will please them to delay. And your husband has his supporters, as you know."

She did. She could not take communion while the court was at Fontainebleau because the priest refused her absolution, and the archbishop, Montespan's uncle, backed him up. It was maddening. "We will have to conceal the child."

"Yes." Though he didn't like it. Though he was wearying of concealment. Athénaïs was as conspicuous a woman as there was at court, outshining the Queen, but their connection was still, officially at least, a secret.

"We must find someone," Athénaïs said. "Someone to take the child as Madame Colbert did for Louise."

The complications of a disorderly sexual life made the King sigh, but he had to consent. When it grew near her time, Athénaïs suggested the Widow Scarron. It took some persuasion to get the King to agree, and then, when she spoke to her friend, she was taken aback to discover that Françoise had reservations. Propriety being her god, she must speak to her confessor.

A few days later, they spoke again: Madame Scarron would accept the child but only at the King's request. Athénaïs's irritation at this punctiliousness did not change the fact that Françoise would be an ideal governess and negotiations continued until, touched, perhaps, by the widow's piety, His Majesty said the word. At once there was a flurry of preparations, a house was rented, a nursemaid and a wet nurse hired. Françoise was kept running with purchases and arrangements for fitting out the house and the two women were together, going over the final details, the night Athénaïs's pains began in earnest.

"You must not stay here," Athénaïs said when they had gotten her to bed. "This will not be long."

Her friend was flustered. Françoise knew little about sex, nothing about birth. She had been nurse to her crippled husband, and had never had to fear a confinement. "Will you be all right?"

Athénaïs gripped her hand strongly for a moment before she relaxed. Her hair was down, her face flushed. "I never have much trouble." Then she gritted her teeth and threw her head back in a spasm. When it was over she said, "Leave, Françoise. Lauzan will bring you your baby by dawn."

Her friend kissed her and Athénaïs lay back on the pillows. Claude wiped her forehead and the midwife drew down the covers to place cold red hands on her belly. Athénaïs wished she could have had her sister, Gabrielle, with her, or better yet, her old midwife from Bellegarde. As the pain surged and ebbed, Athénaïs thought of the old lady with affection. She had given her good advice, had taught her how to endure, had whispered the secret. "You must go with the pain, My Lady, submit to it. It is like a man in the night. You must give yourself up to the pain, go where it takes you." Her other deliveries had been easy, even she had to admit that. And quick. She took a deep breath, felt the terrible tightening of her body, felt her strength, felt the fear going. "I would sit up," she said in a loud commanding voice.

Claude and the midwife brought the chair. The King had wanted her to have his doctor, but she preferred women, so Monsieur d'Orme waited at home. The only man around was Lauzan, who sat drinking brandy in the next room, ready to take the baby to Françoise.

The pain came violently as they were lifting her, and, for a moment Athénaïs forgot wisdom, forgot courage. When the scream died away, they eased her into the chair. "Very soon, Lady," said the midwife, "very soon." She brought clean cloths, put them over the basin which she laid between the Marquise's feet, and lifted her patient's petticoats. Athénaïs pressed back against the chair, put her feet on the rail and arched her back, breathing in rhythm with the pain, which now came low, steady and terrible, stirring her warrior soul so that she cried out loud like a swordsman in battle.

"Yes, Madame, now," commanded the midwife.

Athénaïs contracted her body with all her strength, gasped, struggling in Claude's arms, then bore down again. Pain sang in her ears, raced the length of her flesh, hooked her vitals and dragged her body inside out. She felt a tear, the blood, the midwife's hands, the emerging child.

"All right, Madame," Claude said, holding her back against the chair.

"Ahh," said the midwife, "here we are."

Athénaïs gasped. There was another agonizing pain, then the midwife called for water, fresh cloths. Athénaïs leaned back exhausted, her damp hair in her eyes.

"A girl child, Madame."

The infant, small, red and naked, squirmed and whimpered in the nurse's grasp.

"A girl," Athénaïs repeated, still stupid with pain.

"But alive and well."

"Yes," she said. His Majesty, like all men, would have been better pleased with a boy. Yet he loved Louise's girl. She reached out and took the child for a moment, seeking the mark of royalty in its scrunched face, still webbed with her blood. Then she nodded. She could feel the pain again for the afterbirth. "Give her to Captain Lauzan with my compliments."

Claude lifted the child from her arms and she felt another thick ooze of blood. "I would be done with this," said the Marquise and signaled the midwife to attend her.

Claude wiped the child's face, wrapped it in a thick blanket, and put the little bundle in a basket. The captain was waiting behind the doors.

"The Marquise?" he asked.

"She gives you this with her compliments," Claude said.

"Well, she is a cool one." He crinkled his nose at the infant. "Not too promising."

"Go away, it's a fine baby! Lovely and fat."

The Captain opened the blankets curiously. Although well acquainted with women, he was quite ignorant of babies. "It will last till I reach the Widow?"

"Of course, but see you don't crush it, leave it air." He tucked the basket under his arm, and Claude arranged his cloak to conceal the container. "All right. That's fine."

"A fine thing to be carting off from my supposed lady love," Lauzan teased her.

"Quickly," said Claude. "It will not do to let her catch cold."

Lauzan clapped his big feathered hat down on his head so that it shaded his wide Tartar cheekbones, tightened the cloak around him and strode out, his sword and spurs clicking, his boots rattling on the stair. Claude ran to the window and leaned out into the moist spring night. The street was empty; Lauzan and his bundle ducked into the waiting carriage, and with a shout from the driver the heavy horses broke into a trot.

A few miles away, Françoise Scarron sat in the foyer of the small house rented to receive the infant. The wet nurse had long since fallen asleep on the floor of the nursery, and the other nurse, a fine, sober-looking girl with long fair hair, dozed by the fire in the salon. Françoise could not share their rest. She kept running over her arrangements and thinking of Athénaïs, of the smell of sweat and perfume in her bedroom, of the flush of strain on her round cheeks. Though it was her third, it might still go badly; children might grow harder, rather than easier, to bear, and even under the best circumstances, it was a terrible thing. She had been fortunate to have a husband too crippled to rise from his chair.

She heard horses and jumped up, then sat down again, disappointed. Her eagerness and anxiety were not all for her friend. Athénaïs's request had unexpectedly created a desire. She, who had had no wish for a husband, had discovered in herself a passion for a child. In the last months she had felt such longing, had spoken so often of the coming infant, that Athénaïs had teased she should have been the mother. Yet though the idea made her blush in secret, she could think of nothing else. She waited with feverish impatience until she heard the sound of horses, this time accompanied by the rumble of carriage wheels and the squeak of the harness, and ran to fling open the door. Lauzan emerged from the carriage, took the steps at a bound and entered the hall. With a flourish, he slid the basket from under his cape into her arms, then bowed and left as silently as he had come. Françoise heard his feet on the stone, the voice of the driver, the diminishing clatter of the hooves, and stood, still trembling. Then she found her legs, set the basket on the table and lifted the baby. The small body twitched sleepily, the fingers, tiny as the toes of a frog, found the quivering mouth. Françoise felt her heart. The child stirred and she held it more tightly, touching its fragile red body, feeling the wonder of its possession. Had she known she held her fortune that night, Françoise Scarron could not have been happier. With careless largesse, Athénaïs had given her her heart's desire. And with that gesture, all unknowing, the King had secured yet another lady: Madame Scarron, who wished only to be a mother.

VII

"Le Nôtre left this wood for a background," Athénaïs remarked to her sister, the Abbess, as the carriage approached Clagny. "I had wanted it down, but I'm glad he resisted."

"It is delightful."

"He is a genius! And when you see how he has laid out the orange trees and the palisade of flowers he has devised to hide the tubs! The effect is lovely."

"The gardens must be almost finished."

"They are. You see there he has laid out new planting right to the road. When the chateau is complete we will need the balance of the landscaping."

"You couldn't have balanced all this land with your first house."

"It was only fit for an opera singer—as I told His Majesty."

"You were wicked and ungrateful," her sister teased. "It was as nice a house of twelve chambers as I've seen."

"Now there you're wrong, dear Mother Marie, the Abbess. His Majesty wants a woman who is grand. I intend to give him grandeur." She smiled and nodded toward the strong white bones of the chateau emerging from the trees. The main section of the building was completed, except for the dome, and men were swarming over the two massive side wings slating the roof. The forecourt was crowded with horses, wagons and supplies, and the shouts of the workmen, the crack of whips, the creak and rumble of heavy carts forced the sisters to shout to be heard.

"Grand, indeed," said the Abbess, "it is almost as busy as the palace."

"We've had twelve hundred men working every day—give or take a few injured. It is to be complete by fall, for I want the winter season in my own house."

"And the children? Will you have them here?"

"Only sometimes. Officially, Maine and Vexin are at the palace with Madame Scarron. As soon as they were acknowledged, His Majesty insisted on having them. Louise-Françoise, the baby, I don't know."

"He will do right by her."

"I have no doubt," said Athénaïs with a triumphant smile. "He has treated our family well."

"Indeed," said her sister. She had been too poor to enter a respectable convent; now she was Abbess of the nuns and monks of rich, ancient Fontevrault. Their brother was Captain-General of the Galleys, their father Governor of Paris. Dozens of other relatives had obtained lesser posts and bounties; Athénaïs had been careful but thorough. It was only right that for herself she should have this splendid chateau, the coach and six, the garden by Le Nôtre. "It will all be marvelous," her sister said, patting Athénaïs's hand.

"You will see."

The coachman drew up to the main door and Athénaïs stepped out eagerly. She hardly ever missed an opportunity to check on the progress of her chateau, for she loved the bustle and energy of construction: the huge cranes, the powerful horses, the smell of dust, sweat and sawdust, the sound of tiles and slates and blocks. Just as the fury of construction around Versailles was tangible proof of His Majesty's power and the expansion of his domain, so Clagny was evidence of her success, her power, her visibility. The deed of separation had come through; the children were recognized; she was acknowledged before the court. Today—one reason for the Abbess's visit—Louise de La Vallière entered the convent of the Carmelites. As of this moment, Athénaïs was supreme. "Careful of these cloths," she said to her sister, taking her arm. "The floor is laid, so they are trying to keep the marble clean." She pushed aside the canvas with her foot, revealing the polished blocks at the entryway.

Overhead, painters called back and forth from their scaffolds as their assistants ran up and down the ladders bearing newly ground colors and clean brushes. Some were adding trompe l'oeil marbles to the gallery's stucco work, others, panels for a series showing the myths of Apollo.

"I think you might have left out the Daphne," the Abbess teased. "No lady has turned into a tree around our Sun King."

"Merely symbollic," Athénaïs said lightly. "His ladies run to Le Nôtre and blossom into gardens."

"So I see." The Abbess had stopped by one of the windows. "You have made your fortune in orange trees! What a lovely view!"

"Did I not tell you?" Athénaïs asked delightedly. "We will go out so you can smell the hyacinths. And for later, we will plant tuberoses and summer lilies. You must come then, when the dust from the work has settled."

A raw stretch of dirt separated the chateau from the neat gravel paths of the gardens, but once in Le Nôtre's preserve, all was perfection. The sisters inspected the orange trees and the orangerie being prepared for them, admired the ponds and fountains, the massed bulbs and the arabesques of hedging, then returned to the artistic wonders of the house: here was a painting by Mignard waiting to be hung, there one by Le Brun or Poussin, and everywhere, fine Savonnerie carpets and Gobelin tapestries lying rolled in corners waiting for the walls to dry. Athénaïs had the workmen unwrap these costly fabrics so that her sister could imagine the final effect.

"The furniture," the Abbess said, warming to the task of decoration.

"Oh, yes, I have been prodigal. There are orders in to Boulle and Gobelin and to half the workshops in Paris. His Majesty denies me nothing," Athénaïs said complacently, then stopped. Church bells were dying away in the soft air. "Is it eleven?"

The Abbess looked out a window and checked the sky. "I think it must be, by the sun."

"We must go; we cannot be late." Athénaïs gave some final orders, then they hurried downstairs. "I have promised Louise a final meal at court," she explained.

"The Carmelites," said the Abbess as they entered the carriage. "Will she endure such severity? I had expected some fashionable convent, some lenient place where she could retire elegantly."

Athénaïs's face grew serious. "You have misjudged her. She has petitioned the Carmelites again and again. She told me that she would rather stay at court than enter an uncloistered order."

The Abbess crossed herself. "God has touched her heart. May He give her strength." She straightened the wimple of her habit severely and gazed out at her sister's rich landscape. She herself had no vocation and, though her abilities as Abbess had surprised everyone, a completely sequestered life repelled her.

"And you, Madame?" Athénaïs asked cautiously.

"I am as I was. Our Lord gives me wisdom to do my job; he has not added His grace. If Louise truly has a vocation, she is much blessed."

Athénaïs touched her hand gently. "Perhaps our souls are too worldly. Living as you do at Fontevrault, you, at least, have hopes."

"Indeed. But I am content, Athénaïs. You may assure His Majesty that I am content. We may be useful to God without the highest spiritual gifts. A life of poverty and contemplation, devouring the riches of my soul, would not delight me."

"What a horror," Athénaïs exclaimed sincerely. "I have begged Louise to reconsider. It was not, believe me, all expediency. I would be happy now if she would stay—wherever."

"If God has given her a true gift, she must use it," said the Abbess. Both women crossed themselves and fell silent as the coach rolled over the flat valley toward Versailles. The roads were hard, dry and fast; the horses' hooves rang like clean, hollow bells—like the bells of a convent, Athénaïs thought, like the sound of her own triumph. Surely this marked a point in her career. She had not wished Louise to leave, had disapproved of her immurement with the Carmelites, and yet, this day made her supreme. Or rather, it made her officially supreme; for the last few years, her triumph had been unmistakable. His Majesty kept her with him at every turn. She rode in his carriage; he worked in her rooms. She was beside him when the ambassadors visited, she greeted him early and said farewell to him late. Now that her two boys were in the palace, her surviving daughter would soon follow. There was nothing more to wish; once Clagny was completed, she would live like a second queen. She could say farewell to Louise with a light heart.

The carriage raced into the Marble Court with a great deal of shouting and trumpeting by the footmen, arrogantly leaving behind the vehicles of lesser mortals who were forbidden such proximity to the King. When they emerged by the caged birds and decorative fountains of the inner court, Athénaïs was immediately besieged by petitioners, hangers-on, courtiers—full of needs, of requests or, like Monsieur Racine, of gratitude.

"Dear Lady," he said, "the history will be such a success. Each year when we leave with the armies, I must thank you again for suggesting it to His Majesty."

"His Majesty's pleasure in the results is thanks enough for both of us," Athénaïs said. "He has been very pleased—and rightly so."

The poet bowed and bowed again and embroidered compliments until even the stolid Abbess shifted her feet and Athénaïs was sure they would be late. "The bell for Mass," she said firmly, and with many flourishes the poet took his leave.

"I fear now we shall have no more plays from him," Athénaïs remarked. "As King's Historiographer, he does not need the stage."

"You cannot blame the man for wishing to be a gentleman and be buried in Church," the Abbess said as they made their way through the crush. Athénaïs now sat with the royal family in the little circle facing the King. Louise was there, too, wearing a very severe dress of black silk, her only jewel a crucifix set with pearls, a dark veil on her pale hair. Her little girl, also in black, sat beside her, looking like an angel and wiping tears from her eyes. How can she leave such a child, Athénaïs wondered, but Louise was perfectly composed, her features and her transparent skin which had always betrayed her emotions revealed nothing but tranquility. She will never see the light beyond the walls of the Carmelites, Athénaïs thought, and her soul shivered. What had Louise done that she must bury herself in black and spend her days weeping on her knees? Nothing but love the King, and Athénaïs refused to believe that evil. Even she, who had been led into temptation and follies, even she—but Athénaïs found herself unwilling to follow this thought, and knelt instead and whispered the prayers with passionate fervor, her emotions in turmoil, triumphs and misgivings following each other in a bewildering sequence. In the homily, the priest spoke of the sacrifices of the religious as the incense of the earth, and the congregation wept silent tears of pity, of regret, of envy. After the last words of the benediction, the whisper of the strings and woodwinds followed like the echoes of another, more spiritual language. In this uplifted mood, Louise went to make her farewell to the King and, very privately, to the Queen, who at the sight of her rival sanctified yet prostrate before her and asking forgiveness, forgave her everything, begged to be remembered in her prayers. "Would I were going with you," she cried in all sincerity, for she had herself taken third orders.

Louise said Her Majesty had been her inspiration, and the poor Queen wept again. When her ladies returned, they wept, too, very daintily, wiping their streaming eyes with fine handkerchiefs. The whole court was in floods of tears as if to float Louise to her convent, and many who had hated her most and envied her most bitterly hid their red eyes behind their fans and felt a thrill of religious fervor.

By the time Louise reached Athénaïs's chambers, she was pale and half exhausted. She curtsied to Madame de Fontevrault, the Abbess, who embraced her and advised her kindly not to overtax herself with austerities.

"In that holy atmosphere, I think I will be sensible," Louise replied calmly, and the Abbess smiled, embraced her again and then withdrew, leaving the King's two pretty ladies alone. Athénaïs rang for the servants, but when the food arrived, waved them away and poured the wine herself.

"I wish for your happiness," she said, raising her glass.

"I seek only contentment," Louise replied.

Athénaïs tasted the wine then asked, "And do you think you will find it in the Rue Saint-Jacques?"

"I have not found it in the world."

Athénaïs looked at her carefully. Over the last few years, Louise had lost the fussy uncertainty of manner, the whining self-pity which had aroused both sympathy and irritation. "You have no doubts?"

Louise shook her head. "None."

"My sister is right then: God had given you grace."

"Not grace, not yet, but He has touched my heart. It knows its sin."

"You are hard on yourself," Athénaïs said uneasily.

"We are born into sin; we are all in need." Louise looked across the table then and smiled. "You know I have waited for this for three years. Yet you are sad."

"There is no expediency in my sorrow, Louise. Loving the court, I cannot imagine being happy away from it."

"I looked for happiness at court," she said thoughtfully. "It eluded me. Perhaps you have found it for a time."

"I have found it," Athénaïs said defiantly.

"And I contentment." She raised her glass and touched Athénaïs's goblet. "Whatever brings one to God is to be praised," Louise said, then she laughed softly. Their farewell dinner was merry, and Louise, who was preparing to live on bread and vegetables and water, said farewell to all the rich foods and wines, the confections, the stews, the dainty partridges, the wonderful creams. "I am ready," she said when at last she wiped her fingers on her napkin.

Athénaïs stood up, her face serious. "Have you forgiven me, Louise?"

There was a moment, a hesitation. "Yes, you will be in my prayers always."

Athénaïs felt the tears in her eyes. "Good-bye, dear Louise," she said.

Cynics, of course, pretended that such tears for Louise were fake, hypocritical, self-serving, that the hearts of the worldly are never touched. But excesses of ambition and desire bring their own reactions. Courtiers could be devout and pray and fast in silence. Sensation being the chief drug of the idle, rich and anxious, the frisson of religious dread sometimes survived the dulling of the other senses, and ill luck could blaze formal piety into fervor. On the first anniversary of Louise's retirement, the King had just such an experience. The reasons remained enigmatic to his court, although they whispered their opinions. There was, of course, the example of Louise, now fresh again as she approached the veil. There was the war with the Dutch, which despite the Te Deums for captured cities every summer, had not reached a victorious conclusion. By opening their dikes, the Hollanders had flooded their lands and preserved their freedom. The resulting stalemate encouraged hostile coalitions, and each year, sending his armies far afield, His Majesty felt anxious and uncertain: God who gives victories might turn His face from France. His father had placed the kingdom under the Virgin's care in hopes of a son. In the spring of 1675, when the King and Madame de Montespan were again denied absolution, His Majesty felt the need of some grand gesture of faith. He was determined to take communion at Easter Mass and this required his absolution. When he consulted with Bossuet, already writing a triumphant sermon to mark the end of Louise's novitiate, the Bishop risked a very high card: the King blenched, but did not argue.

"Your Majesty seems weary," Athénaïs said when she saw him that afternoon. He was late, delayed by consultations with Louvois, his generals—and the Bishop.

"The grass will be long enough to feed our horses in another few weeks. If I'm to take the army north, everything must soon be ready." He sat down heavily. Usually he enjoyed military planning and preparations, but today he was depressed, and the Marquise, sensitive to his moods, sat beside him and took his hand.

"I am sure it will be a great success. Having taken Maastricht last year—"

"We will strengthen the fortress there and give ourselves a rational line. This campaign must bring the Dutch to the table." For a moment, a ruthless anger passed over his face: republican, mercantile and Protestant, the Dutch were everything his soul detested. Surely God would give His annointed King victory. "If God wills," he added and sighed.

"There can be no doubt," she said.

"I would make it surer."

Athénaïs knew that something was coming, but even her delicate antennae did not detect what it was.

"I would be absolved this Easter."

Athénaïs sat up straight. "Father Lecuyer is making difficulties for me again. I do not see why he could not be sent elsewhere."

"I have been consulting with the Bishop and with Father de la Chaise. I have given them my word"—he rose abruptly and took a few paces about the room before facing her—"that we will part, Lady."

Athénaïs jumped to her feet. "I don't believe you, Sire. Now? When our children are in the palace, when I am recognized, when the separation order has at last come through?" Her voice rose. Of all the court there were only two people unafraid of the King: Athénaïs and her son, the little Duc du Maine.

"These very things have become a scandal, Madame. What was concealed was not so offensive to the Church."

"Yet God saw," Athénaïs said sharply. "We have loved each other in His sight these many years. It is these bloodless, cruel-minded churchmen! They are proud to have beaten Louise into a convent and would do the same with me. I tell you that Bossuet suffers from the sin of pride."

"There is no question of a convent," the King said mildly. "But you must withdraw to your house in Paris. For a time."

Athénaïs was wounded to the heart. "But Clagny is barely finished! This will be the first spring in the house you have given me. Not to let me see my new gardens is too unkind!"

"It must be," the King said miserably. "It must be."

And though Athénaïs unleashed her sharp, scornful tongue, then her tears, then every coquetry in her extensive repertory, all was in vain. The King might weep, but he was resolved.

Later, when the Bishop came to cement his conquest, Athénaïs worked on him. She tried flattery and offered preferment; this failing, she accused him of spiritual arrogance so tartly that he had to mount all his ecclesiastical dignity to escape unwounded. But the results were no better. Bossuet was as immovable as the King, who had embraced piety as passionately as he had taken her into his arms at Avesnes.

Nothing had prepared Athénaïs for such a calamity. She had been clever. Had ignored his little infidelities—even a romp with Claude in the foyer of Clagny that produced a girl with the King's black eyes. Had outmaneuvered ambitious ladies. Had pruned from the Queen's *dames d'honneur* any likely to attract his eye. Had cultivated and kept on good terms with virtually the entire court. Had not hesitated, though she hesitated to remember now, to consult the ubiquitous and obliging Madame Voisin for certain charms and powders—and now! She slashed her arm across her dressing table, clearing brushes, combs, perfumes, bibelots, a fine silver mirror, books and flowers onto the floor in a clatter that left water, paint, glass and china in a spreading pool and brought Claude running.

"What is it, Madame?"

"We are ruined."

Calmly, Claude began to tidy up the mess. Exposure to wealth and power had not had an altogether happy effect on her character. She had developed a certain hardness to go with her vastly improved manners. All that remained of the ragged player's daughter was a love of the stage, a detestation for the Church, and a devotion to the Marquise. "Is there another woman?" she asked.

Her lady raged at this, threw another brush, cursed her stupidity. "No, but there will be. He cannot go a day without a woman."

"He has taken the army into Flanders without the court."

Athénaïs did not answer this, for she was engaged in a very careful examination of her physical assets. "There is not yet one at court to match me."

"That is the truth, Madame." Unbidden, Claude began to fix her lady's hair; she knew how to soothe the Marquise.

"It is that officious Bishop."

"His Majesty will return at the end of the summer."

"That will do me no good if I am locked up in the rue Vaugirard! And the children. And Vivonne—I had intended to make him a marshal of France!" She wiped away tears of anger.

"When he returns, His Majesty will be in an ardent mood," Claude suggested.

"Yes, yes, that is obvious and don't pull my hair! But I must see him. Nothing works at a distance."

Claude looked at her mistress in the mirror. "We might—," she began and stopped. Madame was sometimes sensitive about dealing with La Voisin. Every time they consulted her, Madame promised the saints it was the last time.

"What?"

"Madame Voisin has many arts. Her powders have done wonders in the past. And her charms. You yourself said—"

"What good will that witch do me if I am sent from court!" Athénaïs was furious, and yet she saw before her, clear as though she stood on its stones, the corridor at Avesnes where she had wandered in a dream.

Claude stroked her hair and set the ribbons into place. "There are other things. La Voisin has prodigious resources. It would do no harm to inquire."

Athénaïs did not say yes, but she did not say no, either. Instead, she had Claude change her hair, her usual gambit when she was thinking things over, and put on a dark sober dress, chastely trimmed with white lace. Then she sat down at a ravishing Boulle desk—all fine inlay and gilt-bronze acanthus leaves—and wrote a letter.

Early that evening, Bishop Bossuet arrived, piety, gratitude and triumph moving over his large ugly features and enlivening his fine, dark eyes.

"My daughter," he exclaimed as the Marquise fell to her knees in tears. He knelt beside her on the carpet and raised his hands in prayer. The Bishop and the sinner were together a long time, talking and praying. In those moments, in the Marquise's beautiful blue-and-gold reception rooms, the Bishop had hopes of a religious court and tasted the triumph of the devout group. It was in a mood of exultation and thanksgiving that he went home and wrote the good news to the King, commending military glory to wean His Majesty's mind from sin and reporting at length on Madame de Montespan's repentance.

As for the Marquise, she wrote a long, tender letter to the King, badly spelled like all her others, but literate and full of clever allusions. She praised piety, begged the favor of a pure friendship, described her new life of seclusion. When this was finished, she called Claude.

"Have this given to Monsieur Colbert. Any of the footmen can take it. He will put it in the regular mail pouch to His Majesty." Claude took the letter with a curtsy.

"And, Claude . . ."

"Madame?"

"You will go and see that witch La Voisin at once."

VIII

M adame Voisin's house was along the road between Paris and Saint-Denis in a suburban neighborhood of small villas set beside orchards and gardens. Although not in a fashionable district, the house was conveniently secluded. Approaching along the Paris road, all travelers saw was a large stone wall and some dark cedars, but behind the tall iron gates were elegant formal gardens and a well-proportioned house of pale stone. On pleasant evenings, the passerby might hear Madame's violinists playing from their alcove in the main salon or out in a pretty arbor in the rear garden, making music by the light of large bronze candelabra. On these nights, there would be laughter in the house and a coming and going of Madame's eclectic clientele. There might be a duchess or even a princess and surely several marquises along with bourgeois ladies of advanced morals and bottomless purses, dukes with gambling debts, valets with ambitions, and always, because Madame was known for her piety and for her devotion to all matters of religion, a variety of priests of no certain order or parish with confidential voices and speculative eyes.

Yet for all this—the flowers, the violins, the candles, the wine, the witty, colorful company—one could not say that the Voisin residence was either cheerful or festive. The gloom of the wall and the cedars was not dispelled by a few chords and even over Madame's parties there hung an air of nervous tension and expectation, as if everyone were assembled for a lottery drawing of enormous value, or as if the whole room were a table at which one played for the highest stakes. Certainly, it is true that no one went to La Voisin's for pleasure. One went for knowledge—often painful in the getting—for advancement, for little favors, more or less expensive, for gossip, likewise. Certain pretty and indiscreet ladies came for assistance in matters both painful and compromising, arriving cloaked and masked in hired carriages and departing later in the day, pale and trembling in anonymous hackneys. In all these operations, except for the parties where everybody pretended surprise, innocence and a general air of doing "for once" something outré and daring, the clients of Madame Voisin came singly, secretly and silently, and it was this constant surreptitious traffic which had finally impressed its mark upon the establishment, leaving it cold and mysterious, with a slightly sordid and transient air, like an infinitely better class of traveler's inn.

Indeed, as the sun set behind the black cedars, and the wall and garden cast a jagged and unbroken shadow across the road, the house created a troubling impression, strengthened by a spectral figure muffled in a long hooded cloak and a black silk mask. Tired from picking her way through the sog and puddle of the roadway, the woman stopped at the gate to shake her damp skirts and raised her mask to catch her breath. Claude des Oeillets had left Madame de Montespan's carriage well out of sight of La Voisin's residence, and she was not used to walking so far: tonight's commission would have to be substantial.

"Is Madame home?" Claude asked the girl in the severe black dress and gray apron who met her at the front door.

"If you will please come in, Mademoiselle," the child said quickly, curtseying as if to a duchesse.

Loosening her cloak, Mademoiselle entered a small reception room, elegant in white stucco work with a black-and-white marble floor. There were bouquets of white flowers at the windows, but stronger than the narcissus was a scent of incense which caused her to sniff the air and raise her eyebrows expectantly. Then the door opened at the side of the salon and Madame, fashionable in fine gray silk petticoats and a low-cut bodice, bustled forward.

"Mademoiselle! Such a pleasure! We did not keep you waiting too long, I hope. Oh, how close it is." She carried a little ivory-and-silk fan, very pretty and elegant, with which she stirred the damp air.

"Good evening, Madame Voisin. I hope you are well."

"As well as can be expected. My heart is delicate, and this damp weather——" She fanned herself vigorously, all of a flutter it seemed, unless one noticed her shrewd, sharp eyes and her mouth, which, despite its smiles and chatter, fell most naturally into a thin, hard line. "This way, Mademoiselle," she said, leading her guest into the fine, large salon. "Is it business of your own this time or something for your lady?"

"I came to inquire if you had any of Galet's powders."

"Indeed I do. I went just recently. I had to go myself by carriage," she said as she went to unlock an upright chest of inlaid ebony. "You may assure your mistress these are the very best."

Madame Voisin took out a sheaf of small packets, opening one to show Claude the whitish powder inside. "We must check them," said Madame. "I always check twice. Once when I have them of Galet, once with the client. That is the safest way."

"And these, Madame," Claude asked, pointing to another stack of envelopes.

"Do not touch those, Mademoiselle. Those are not for your mistress." She looked coolly at her visitor then moved them to the back of the cabinet. "Those are not for love but for money." She smiled cynically and rubbed the tips of her fingers together. "Powders for inheritance."

"Pray God, you do not confuse such deadly things!"

"That is why the cabinet is kept locked, Mademoiselle," La Voisin said, turning the key. "Yes, this is a business of infinite pains and care." She smiled again, thinking of her fee, and laid the envelopes of white powder out on the table.

Claude produced her purse, laid ten coins on the table and stopped.

La Voisin shook her head. "The carriage alone, Mademoiselle. Think of the horses—and Galet, of course. His prices go up all the time."

"He has no idea of the purchasers." Claude's voice was sharp.

"No, no, Mademoiselle, I can assure you. Still, he has his reputation."

Claude laid out more coins. "It would be dangerous for anyone to know but you and I, Madame." Her hand paused at thirteen, but La Voisin took no notice of the interruption.

"You need not remind me how much I have risked for your mistress."

Claude continued dropping coins onto the table. When she reached twenty, Madame stopped her, pushing five of the silver pieces back. Claude slipped these into a small bag suspended around her neck, then put away her mistress's purse.

Madame Voisin smiled expansively, rang for her servant and ordered cordials. Their business completed, she and Mademoiselle always sealed the bargain with a drink. "There is no truth in the rumors, then," she said when they were alone. "I had heard your lady was set aside."

"His Majesty has turned devout—temporarily."

"Oh, you are too cynical!" Madame said with a rich laugh. "A pious King—if there is such a thing—would be a mighty treasure."

"But not for such as you and I, Madame."

La Voisin's face grew serious. "You are right, Mademoiselle. We must not let piety get in the way of business."

"Nor of my lady's ambitions."

"Ah," said Madame. "Those powders will help your lady's situation."

"The art of preparing powders is certainly admirable," Claude said cautiously, "but nothing under the moon is certain."

"It were blasphemy to suggest otherwise, Mademoiselle." She gave her visitor a look. "Still, we are saved by our own exertions, are we not?"

"Most certainly. And the more one does—"

Madame nodded sagely. "The greater the chances of success. Would your mistress consider—other remedies—do you think?"

"She hesitates, Madame, but she has asked for your advice."

Madame leaned forward. "If your mistress is resolved, a great deal may be done. There are certain priests who are ready to do particular services. With special prayers. Your lady can have no doubt of their efficacy."

"Yet my lady is pious; she disliked the procedure."

Madame's face took on a scornful and rather bitter expression. "She would have the prize without the stain—such is the way of the gentry."

"She is, of course, willing to pay."

Madame was thoughtful, but cautious. "There is another rite, but I don't recommend it too often. The magic is so powerful that it may be done with a surrogate. Your lady would not need to be present, although, of course, the forces would be immeasurably greater if you could persuade her."

"My lady would have it done and not know too much about it."

Madame Voisin's eyes took on the dreamy look with which they contemplated especially large profits. "I could manage everything—for a fee, of course."

"That goes without saying, Madame."

"Well, then, we will need a priest for the Mass—that is no trouble, I know a specialist—and for his acolyte, our own Abbé Lesage will do nicely. Then, there are certain—necessities."

"Such as?"

"It requires, as you must know, a blood sacrifice. The more valuable the creature, the more efficacious. Then for the chalice—the Abbé is particular about his ingredients. All must be rare, fresh, magical. Oh, it is an undertaking, Mademoiselle, an undertaking of some moment! I don't think it could be managed for much less than two hundred livres."

Claude hesitated. From the household and petty cash she might be able to steal so much, yet no, it was of too much moment. "I must ask my lady."

"See you do it delicately, Mademoiselle. Tell her the Abbé who would officiate is a great man in such things. Tell her that as for the necessary lady I can make all the arrangements. She need not even think of providing a substitute! I have many times served ladies of such disposition," Madame said with a perverse and unsettling smile. "And then there is my daughter. Marguerite is very fit for such things, too."

"I will tell her that for two hundred livres you can perform wonders," Mademoiselle said as she pulled on her fine Spanish gloves. "But can you give her back the King? That is the question."

"You know nothing can be guaranteed without impiety, but I

feel the chances are good. If we persist, Mademoiselle, we can hardly fail."

Claude rose, very serious. "You will get word."

"Very well, I will see you out, Mademoiselle." They had just reached the door when they heard two voices talking in the hall. Madame Voisin stopped Claude with a gesture.

"Tomorrow?" one asked.

"Yes, yes, I assure you, dear Sir. So many consult me, you understand."

"It is a matter of the greatest urgency," the first voice said. It belonged to a gentleman and was very low, strained and anxious.

"Of course, of course," the other replied impatiently. "Yet these matters cannot be hurried. It were impolite to attempt to hurry the great spirits. Most impolite and most dangerous. Not that I am unwilling to take risks for your benefit, Sir, but it would not do to have our enterprise miscarry."

"I'd better take you out through the garden," Madame said as Claude hastily replaced her black silk mask." Some client of the Abbé's. So many come to him for advice."

She gave a little smirk and went to open one of the long windows.

"No, no," said the gentleman in the hall. "But tomorrow. You can't imagine my anxiety, Abbé. I do not think I could stand an extra day."

The reply was lost as Claude stepped onto the grass.

"Remember, I am ready at any time to serve your lady," Madame Voisin said.

Claude nodded and headed toward the gate. A groom and two horses were waiting on the road, but she pulled the cloak over her hair and walked on swiftly. From the open door, only the flash of her black skirts was visible as the Abbé Lesage bid his client farewell.

"Ahhh, Abbé," Madame said cheerfully as he opened the door of her salon. Without his wig, the Abbé looked more like the ex-galley slave he was and less like the priest he had been. His strong, aquiline features were marked by hardship and ill-usage, and a thin white scar ran like lightning from just above his small cold eyes to the top of his long, close-cropped skull. "That was the second gentleman this evening. I am astonished."

"While you have social calls, I labor, Madame."

"Social!" La Voisin exclaimed. "Not with that lady, Abbé! She is the emissary of a woman of standing."

"She came on foot and unattended."

"Fool, she leaves the carriage down the road. It is her habit, though she would be safe enough with me, surely."

"Surely," Lesage echoed, though he thought it would be interesting to watch next time and see whose arms were on the carriage. "And was she satisfied?"

"Oh, she will be back. We have possibilities there—and for you, too, Abbé," Madame said, resting her hand coquettishly on his knee. "And your gentlemen, Abbé?"

"One horoscope—very favorable and profitable for the Marquis de Ternes—and this." With a laugh, Lesage produced a small wax bottle from the folds of his cassock. He held it up for her, then slit the soft side with one of his long thumb nails, revealing a closely folded slip of paper. "Our latest request from the Chevalier," he said.

Madame held out her hand. "He doesn't want much, does he?" she asked when she'd read the note.

Lesage shrugged. "The death of one old man," he intoned in a hollow voice, "What is that in the great scheme of things?"

"A hundred thousand louis d'or, I'd reckon," Madame said. "To his wife, of course, but he'd have control. With his debts"—

she flapped the fan back and forth as she calculated—"yes, yes, even so, a nice profit."

"And for you and I, Madame? For you and I who know these things and how to bring them about?"

Madame smiled. "We must answer him, or rather, Satan himself must speak through your furnace. Really, I congratulate myself, Abbé." She touched his hand. "Whatever trouble I had in securing your release from the galleys has been repaid. These clever hands have brought in more custom than I had anticipated."

"You old tart, remember I'm a man of the cloth," Lesage said, but he bent and nibbled her fingers, making La Voisin laugh. "We have decisions to make, Madame. Decisions. Do we play this fish longer or do we squeeze him now? A letter to his father-in-law, perhaps. Oh, we could squeeze him dry."

"He's in debt to his eyes. You are too impatient."

"Any man will find money to avoid losing a fortune."

Madame paused. In the silence her fan began tracing a lacy course through the incense-laden air. "He will find the money to secure it, too," she said.

"And more afterwards to keep the secret, eh?" Lesage leaned forward eagerly, his avarice checked only by this hint of greater things.

"Of course. If you do not frighten him off."

"Frighten him off! Madame, I have landed many such fish. Why, even when I was third on the oar of the good ship *Calix,* may her timbers rot in Hell, I beached such quarry. The tricks I've pulled, Madame."

"And very likely you'd still be pulling that oar, Abbé, but for my timely intercession." Madame leaned back in her chair, her back stiff, her mouth in a firm, straight line. Occasionally, the Abbé, for all his talent, needed a reminder of his position in the household.

"Madame!" The Abbé protested, his hollow voice hiked up into a whine. "How can you imagine my ingratitude?"

Madame shrugged and flicked her fan rapidly back and forth, while Lesage turned the wax bottle, the tool of his trade, in his supple fingers, making it appear and disappear into the folds of his sleeve. What had upset the old cow now? Her moods annoyed him and even more her habit of command. Almost since he had arrived, he and Madame Voisin had been engaged in a contest of wills. He had expected to establish an easy dominance over her and had been surprised to find that the fringes of Parisian society had produced a character as ruthless as any the galleys had molded. For her part, Madame was surprised at very little. By mutual consent, they had settled down to a long struggle.

"It will be best for you to answer him cautiously," she said at last. "The answer must promise great things if he acts boldly."

"Kill the old bastard and be rich," Lesage said with a hoarse, barking laugh.

"He will be interested," Madame continued smoothly. "We will see how interested he becomes. Once he is committed, we will decide whether to furnish the means for his inheritance or to contact the old man."

"Very well, but let us not waste too much time with this. You have the powders already, don't you?"

"We will use someone else for this job. Your friend Marie Bosse. It's her specialty," Madame replied, beginning to fan herself again.

"I'm not sure I want to be involved with her," Lesage said. "She has a loose tongue. We will use your supply."

The fan stopped, and Madame leaned onto her little, plump, lace-covered arms. "I choose to have no such contacts between your clients and my house, Abbé. They must go to Marie Bosse or"—she straightened up and touched the fan to her lip thoughtfully—"you must move yourself to Madame Bosse's. Of course, you might find her class of clientele less to your liking."

The Abbé clenched his teeth and gripped the edge of the table. He should cut the old tart's throat. He would draw his knife. He was not her servant.

Madame did not move except to raise one of her eyebrows very slowly. The fan, too, hung motionless in the air with not so much as a tremor.

The Abbé leaned back in his chair, controlling his anger. It was not the time. But he would pay her back for these humiliations. He would.

"Very well, Madame," he said. "How wise of you to avoid any occasion for scandal."

"I do believe so, Abbé. And you should be grateful—as a man of the cloth." With this, Madame rose, nodded and left the room.

IX

It took Claude some time to convince her mistress to let Madame Voisin try her skills. At first the Marquise was irritable and undecided and would set the whole matter aside. Then, just when Claude thought there was no hope, Madame Scarron arrived in great good humor.

"I've signed the papers," she announced with unfeigned joy. "The deed is mine and Maintenon, too." She opened her satchel and drew out an official document, heavy with seals.

"My dear, how lovely." Athénaïs glanced at the deed and saw that His Majesty had made the estate a marquisate. In addition to enabling Françoise to buy the estate, he had raised her rank. "So now you are Madame de Maintenon," she said and wondered if she had reason for jealousy.

"It is a dream come true," said Françoise, too happy to pick up the subtle currents visible on Athénaïs's features. "You cannot imagine what it means to have a piece of land of my own after all these years." She kissed Athénaïs. "I owe you a great deal. A very great deal."

"And will you retire there?" Athénaïs asked, perhaps too quickly.

"When the children are grown. And periodically, when I need a rest from court."

Athénaïs managed a smile.

"Have you heard from His Majesty?"

Although it galled her, Athénaïs shook her head. She and the King had agreed that their correspondence would remain a secret.

Françoise produced a letter, the red royal seal broken. "He is pleased with the progress of the Duc du Maine."

Athénaïs ran her eyes over the familiar handwriting. "And my son's leg? How is it?"

"The doctors have been tormenting him again trying to lengthen it. Poor child, he bears everything very well, but I am not sure they are doing him good."

"He will need plenty of courage."

"What about a trip to Bagnères for him? The waters are said to work wonderful cures, and since they now think there is infection in the leg . . ."

"Most likely from the apparatus the doctors have put on it," Athénaïs said. She was sceptical of the medical faculty and of all their works.

"The waters would be a more humane treatment in any case."

"It is a good idea. I will mention it to His Majesty when he returns. The Bishop can scarcely object to a conversation about our son."

"I hinted in my last letter," Françoise said carefully.

"But I will suggest, it being my child," Athénaïs said firmly. Just as she had anticipated, Françoise had proved a marvel with the children, especially with the crippled Maine, but she took a lot on herself. And she was in high favor.

"As you like. So long as it is done."

"I have never neglected my children's interests."

"Madame, I suggest nothing of the sort," Françoise protested. "I merely mentioned the efficacy of the waters." At the thought of Maine's illness, her face grew strained. "A child is a fragile thing to fix one's heart upon."

Athénaïs laid her hand on the governess's arm. Despite the tensions over the children—and increasingly, the King—a certain sympathy remained between them. "There are few sure foundations for our affections," she said. "Children's lives are fragile; man's love is fickle."

"Our faith must be our refuge." There was a touch of regret in the governess's piety.

"Do not forget that so long as we live in the world, we depend on the favor of one man."

"Yet if his mind is on earthly things, nothing but caprice can be expected," Françoise said.

Athénaïs could not help raising her eyebrows. "I am not so sure about the evils of earthly things."

"No, Madame?" Françoise asked, taking up her ironic tone. "Have you taken to doubt?"

"I must, Françoise, for your prayers have sent me into disgrace, while my follies have made you a marquise."

Françoise flushed but she spoke earnestly. "Is a pious life, then, a disgrace? Whatever your pride, this separation must be good for your soul. All the court is moved, Madame, by your example. I have written to tell His Majesty that there is no word but of your renunciation."

Athénaïs looked at her with her eyes narrowed and wondered how far this was sincere, how far it was the subtlest of torments, how far Françoise, herself, knew the difference. Her naïveté was shocking; she knew nothing of love except her affection for the children, which Athénaïs was sure was quite pure. The erotic passions she did not know; she was not, perhaps, capable of knowing.

"It has made such a difference to the Queen, to the court,"

Françoise continued. "Whatever the delights of worldly glory, we must think of our souls."

"You have Maintenon and now would save souls," Athénaïs said drily but when Françoise protested her entire sincerity, Athénaïs did not take up the quarrel. Though she would have liked to relieve her feelings, she could not risk it. Not now, when, she suddenly decided, she was going to commission Madame Voisin to . . . "Yet I am wrong to tease you," she said. "I have seen the Bishop almost daily. He has been a great comfort."

"I knew it!" Françoise said; her happiness was genuine, an overflowing of estates, bounties, titles. Athénaïs remembered the feeling well. "It is all a miracle, a wonder. I know the Bishop is happy: he sees the great example for the children, for the Dauphin."

"Then perhaps he will not beat the poor boy so often."

"The Bishop is firm," Françoise admitted uncomfortably, "yet as you must surely see, his heart is good."

"Well, I trust I shall have his goodness in milder doses than the Dauphin," Athénaïs said. It was a relief when the conversation left her reformation and turned to the unrepentant still at court and better still when she saw Françoise sweep down the steps toward the carriage. It is my own fault, thought Athénaïs, I have repeated Louise's mistake and now Françoise's prayers for the King's piety have cost me my place. This conviction was suddenly so overwhelming that Athénaïs was almost choked with anger before Claude answered the bell.

"If you must go to that witch, go," she burst out. "But see you take her the money, no more. I never want it said that I've been near that woman." She threw a book to the floor to punctuate this order.

Quickly, before she could change her mind, Claude curtsied. "You will not be sorry, Madame. The King will change his mind."

"He will or I will die of grief," said the Marquise and put her face in her hands.

"Whew, what a walk!" Madame Voisin patted her heaving chest protectively as they rested under the porch of Saint-Julien's. The unpaved side streets of the poorer quarters were little better than sewers and it was heavy work slogging through the spring muck and garbage. "This business will be the death of me. I tell you, my dear, learn from my example and don't be taken advantage of by these grand folk. They never think of the effort involved, they don't, and they're always disinclined to pay for yours. Remember that."

The sallow girl beside her was watching the antics of a beggar. With only one arm and leg, he was performing a variety of contortions for the passersby.

"Do you hear me, Marguerite?" La Voisin gave an exasperated sigh. "Do stop sulking! You'll do nothing in business with that hangdog attitude. There's nothing for it, we must walk. Though why the Abbé Guibourg cannot keep regular hours and regular lodgings is beyond me."

"The Abbé Guibourg belongs to the church."

"Yes, yes, I know quite well that if he did not neglect the church's business, he would be no good for ours, but still it is a nuisance. And to up and change his lodgings again! It is quite, quite inconvenient," La Voisin said irritably as they set off again over a patch of filthy cobblestones which were soon swamped in mire, dirt, and manure, old cabbage leaves and turnips too filthy for the beggars to glean and not soft enough yet for the scavenging pigs to devour. Around them surged the tradesmen with their goods, the washerwomen returning from the river with their baskets, the beggars, hungry and importunate, the children, dirty and larcenous, and the bravos of the neighborhood, as dirty as the beggars, as larcenous as the children and more dangerous than either, their long cloaks pulled over forbidden swords. The streetwomen, tough and foul-mouthed, shouted to them over the cries of the vendors.

"Would this be it?" Marguerite asked when they reached a narrow, unpaved track that was very nearly roofed over by large wooden signs. The first of these, a crude design of a cat carrying a fish in its mouth, was placed above a little cramped *biberon*.

"Yes, it must be. The Abbé never lodges too far from drink. Come along then, and look lively. I trust you soon will be able to do these errands for your mother. You cannot rely on my support forever, not when I am so killed with work." Madame began to pant and puff, so aggravated by the distance they had had to walk, the unreliability of the priest, and the incompetence of her daughter that she did not find her breath again until they reached a hovel with a small cobbler's workshop on the lower floor. "Pah! What a stink. A disgrace for a man of the cloth."

"You might take him in," her daughter said with dry malice," and keep him as you do the Abbé Lesage."

"Mind your tongue," Madame Voisin said. "Abbé Guibourg has other arrangements that no doubt suit him well enough. But"—and she looked disgustedly at the stairwell they were ascending which was not quite dark enough to conceal a great mess of excrement and rubbish—"cleanliness is suitable for all habitations. No matter how peculiar." Pausing a moment to catch her breath, Madame surveyed the doors on the landing, chose one and knocked.

There was a long wait. Undeterred, Madame hammered again.

"He is not home."

"Nonsense. He was not at Saint-Marcel's, was he?"

A third summons brought the sound of small footsteps, and, with a creak and a rattle, the door opened perhaps an inch.

"Is Abbé Guibourg here? An old friend, Madame Voisin, has come to call."

The door closed again and there was another wait while the child disappeared into the recesses of the apartment. Finally, after most callers would have given up hope, the door opened, and a child of indeterminate age and sex, barefoot and clad only in a short frock and a piece of old blanket, stood aside to let them pass.

"And where is the good Abbé?" Madame asked in the high, effusive tones she affected on social occasions.

The child's solemn face resisted even the slightest emotion. It shrugged in reply and pointed through the anteroom, close-shuttered and dark as a cave, to a chamber barred yellow in the warm afternoon sun.

"Very good," said Madame Voisin, although she found it difficult to sustain her society tone when faced with the child's blank indifference and the piles of bedding, both empty and occupied, which all but blocked their path. "Come, come, don't loiter," she snapped to her daughter and stepped around the shapeless, ragged bundles. In the room beyond, someone began singing an old nursery song in a very low, hoarse and disagreeable manner.

"I hear visitors," a thin, excited voice cried.

"Hang them."

But there was the sound of bare feet, and a small boy—or at least this one seemed to Madame clearly masculine—appeared in the doorway. Like his companion, he was scarcely dressed at all, being more nearly draped than clothed in a length of old and dirty velvet which had been wrapped around his waist and drawn up over one shoulder like a Scotsman's kilt. He was fair, with fine gold hair hanging to his shoulders, and he possessed a smooth, round, sharp-chinned face with unnaturally cold, sophisticated eyes. "Visitors," he repeated and turned to put out his tongue at the massive old man, whose answering blow he evaded by squeezing past Madame Voisin.

"Wretched brat! Ah, Madame." Surprised and disconcerted,

the Abbé drew himself up to his full height and wiped his lips. "Madame and Mademoiselle." His one good eye swiveled to follow the boy who disappeared somewhere amongst the rubbish of the anteroom; his other, blind and covered with a thin blue film, remained focused on some remote point to his left. "An unexpected pleasure." He straightened his wig and smoothed his cassock. "Do come in. Madame, take a chair." There was only one, but the Abbé produced a stool for himself from a corner of the chamber, and, fastening one massive paw about Mademoiselle Voisin's waist, summoned her to share it with him. When she jerked free, Guibourg laughed, pursing his thick lips and shaking his red, hideous head. "There's little blood in your daughter, Madame! Little, indeed."

"She is not needed for our conversation," Madame said complacently.

"Well, go speak to La Chamfrain. She's in the kitchen. Through there, through there," he said gesturing abruptly. "Any of the children will tell you. There's enough of the brats around. Though I do fancy children," he added with a certain sinister smoothness of tone. "There's no denying it."

"Children keep you young," Madame remarked, "when they do not send you to your grave."

"How true, Madame! How true!" He gave a low, unpleasant laugh. "My love of children has recently sent me to this address. And might well, as you have observed, have sent me to my grave." He laughed again, then, as if reminded, stamped his foot on the floor. "Didi, Didi!"

The blonde child appeared in the doorway. He had, Madame Voisin noticed, a clever face. "That is a likely boy," she said.

Guibourg laid his finger against his nose. "One La Chamfrain had of a guardsman. That's dainty stock. A little rose." The old man smirked, then turning stern, thundered, "Get the lady some wine."

The boy put out his tongue and ran off into the other room. "He has had no discipline," the Abbé said. "None whatsoever. I try, of course." A smile disturbed the raddled contours of his face. "A beating a day would set him in order. But he's a treasure." The Abbé ran one of his large purple fingers across his lips. "A treasure."

"And Madame?" asked La Voisin, who knew all about the Abbé's little weaknesses and preferred current gossip to old scandal.

"Well as ever. She's a bit——" The Abbé tapped his temple. "I have to watch her, of course. You see how I must live," he added, brushing the dirty front of his cassock as though he had been used to better things.

"Better days may be coming." La Voisin shifted her feet and made herself comfortable with an expensive rustle of stiffened silk.

"Little have I been remembered." The Abbé's head dropped down toward his chest, and he remained thus like a figure of Vice sunk in Apathy until the boy reappeared with a tarnished silver tray, two goblets and a bottle of red wine.

"Here, bring it here," the Abbé said, pulling the child onto his knee. He poured one glass of wine and passed it to Madame Voisin, then prepared another for himself. "You may have a sip," he told the child, who managed half the glass in a gulp. The Abbé watched him with an interest that mimicked benevolence and stroked his thin neck.

They finished that glass and the better part of another before La Voisin turned to business. "You have not been entirely forgotten," she remarked. "Some have but recently inquired most urgently for you."

The Abbé straightened up and his hand stopped exploring the smooth contours of the child's back. "Who might they be?"

Madame smiled and raised her glass. "It is a matter of the utmost discretion."

"Leave us," Guibourg commanded, tipping the child unceremoniously off his knee, "and close the door."

The boy skittered off without a word.

"Well?"

"This lady is no ordinary client, Abbé. She occupies the very greatest of positions. It is impossible for any lady to aspire further."

"Ahh," said the Abbé, his evil face showing his pleasure. "We move into higher circles again, do we Madame?"

"We do, indeed, Abbé. If you are interested in serving this lady."

"Well, what fee, Madame? A man of my position cannot work for a pittance."

"Fifty. How does that sound, Abbé?" Madame drew out her purse and placed the first installment in his hand.

"I like this, Madame. I like this very much." He leaned forward eagerly. "But what is to be done? How are we needed?"

Madame sighed, as if some personal problem of her own were at issue. All her clients agreed that this way of entering entirely into one's troubles, ambitions and interests was Madame's most endearing trait. "A crisis, Abbé," she said. "A crisis." She tapped his knee for emphasis. "His Majesty has turned devout! He would repent, Abbé, of his sins."

The Abbé crossed himself. "A habit to be praised, Madame."

"Indeed, indeed, in other times, it would. Yet in this case it brings grief to a lady. Whom you have assisted before."

Guibourg looked up curiously.

"Have you not arranged powders for me?"

"Have I not! Do I not set the altar, have charge of all vessels and vestments? Yes, many a time I've blessed your powders. And for this lady, too?"

"Yes," said Madame, encouraging him.

"The church is a great engine, Madame." He nodded his head. "A mighty engine. It were a shame to leave its direction only to the narrow-minded."

Madame Voisin laughed. "You are a man after my own heart, Abbé. Now, listen, we have much larger game in mind this time than powders."

"Ah," said the Abbé.

"The lady is resolved to do everything in her power. There will have to be a Mass. In my chapel," she added with emphasis.

"Who is to be involved? The lady?"

"Oh, do not dream of it! She is occupied from morning till night at the court. And this is a lady of nice temperament. She would have it done and not know it is done. No, nor any of her retinue, either."

"That makes it more difficult," said the Abbé. "It is less effective, less sure." He seemed genuinely distressed.

"We may have to repeat the service in that case. Several times."

"At the same fee each time? I see your game, Madame. And I approve! But who will stand in for this great and squeamish lady?"

"I myself have often—"

"Perhaps your daughter," Guibourg suggested smoothly. "She is young. It would be better."

Madame Voisin was glad she had only offered him fifty. He was a repellent man. "We will see. And do be realistic, Abbé, about your needs for this service." Her expression turned severe.

"I thought we spoke of an affair of the greatest importance."

"Cats, puppies, pigeons—I will get whatever."

The Abbé's bloated face took on a dreamy expression. "Of the very greatest importance. Madame, we can alter the course of events. It can be done," he added, his voice tense.

"I should have thought, Abbé, that recent events would have—"

"The ignorant mob, Madame, jumps to conclusions. Accidents happen. Children are so—such sickly, delicate creatures." He rubbed his hands together, over and over, as though washing them clean of some invisible stain. "And some operations are delicate, Madame."

"Pigeons, Abbé, will be sufficient. There are risks I will not take."

Guibourg straightened up and looked at her thoughtfully. After a moment, he said, "Your friend, the abortionist, that Lepère woman. See her."

Madame Voisin smoothed her skirt and spoke with affected niceness. "It is a disagreeable, immoral business, Abbé. I have warned Madame Lepère she will come to no good. And she is always looking to my garden, she is."

The Abbé reached out and seized her hand. "When she is finished, they are dead anyway. A little blood more or less makes no difference to an 'angel.' See it is done if you want my help." His breath sounded hoarse in the afternoon silence and his fingers were damp against hers.

"Very well, Abbé, you know your work. But see there is no trouble in the meantime. None. You know I have friends. And our lady—you can imagine her power, Abbé, and her anger should any of her servants disgrace themselves."

"Madame, Madame," Guibourg said in a genial tone, but with a high pitch that betrayed his extreme interest and excitement, "you are the same as ever. So conscientious, so alert to all the niceties of society. Do they appreciate that, your ladies, I wonder?"

"My clientele is large and honorable," Madame said smugly.

The Abbé laughed hoarsely. "When, Madame, when?"

"In three days. In the early evening."

He nodded, content.

"This is a considerable business, Abbé."

"And Madame, our influence will have a long reach. But get me what I require," he added in a threatening tone, "or I will provide myself."

"Of course, Abbé."

"I will fix everything. I will arrive in the afternoon."

"That will be agreeable."

The old man stood up with a laugh. "Yes," he said. "Yes. Didi! Didi!"

The fair child appeared in the doorway. "Find Mademoiselle and show her and Madame out." He gave another coarse laugh. "Then bring me some more wine. He is a treasure, Madame, as you can see. A little rose."

All through the early summer, messages went between the Marquise's house to the rue Vaugirard and Madame Voisin's establishment on the road to Saint-Denis. Once set on this dark course, the Marquise was determined to make her future certain, although she still preserved a certain innocence by indirection. Claude would be given a purse without comment. The purse would be passed to La Voisin, and Guibourg and Lesage would be assembled. Their sinister and sordid business accomplished, assurances were relayed through Claude to her mistress. It was a nice little racket for the sorcerers, and had they not fallen out over the profits, their future might have been assured. As it was, Lesage took it into his head that he was being cheated, and, bitter and angry, expanded his interests to include the political ambitions of the Marquis de Ternes, a strange and mysterious gentleman, distantly related to Madame de Montespan. The Marquis had come to Lesage for a horoscope and, it being good, had returned to feed the Abbé's unstable mind with hints of glory. Lesage and the Marquis were to be as bad a combination as could be imagined, but that summer the sorcerers enjoyed a burst of prosperity and their predictions and encouragements kept up the Marquise's spirits.

Soon, she had other little consolations as well. The longer he was away, the more solicitious His Majesty's letters became. Not a day passed without assurances of his high regard, some gift for her or for the mansion at Clagny, or some service performed by Colbert. In return, Athénaïs wrote about her pious conversations, about her new life—and, because she knew all this was very dull, about card games with Monsieur at Saint-Cloud, about amusing court gossip, about a charming visit or a naughty joke. When, a month or so after the break, the King's letters began to grow more intimate and ardent, she was pleased, but not completely surprised. She was, after all, paying very well to rekindle his passion.

And whether it was because of those peculiar and sacrilegious rites conducted in Madame Voisin's very private chapel, or because of the memories of his happiness with Athénaïs, or simply because of the exhilaration produced by a grandly executed and highly successful military campaign, His Majesty's feelings did undergo a change. Standing alone outside his ornate silk tents in the mild twilights, or riding with Vauban to see the new fortification of Maastricht, now blooming into mighty stars of wall and trench, or watching the detachments of his guards and musketeers run through their drills, it grew harder to remember why he had set the Marquise aside. Away from her and without the distraction of the easy and voracious ladies of the court, the King was lonely. Who could make him laugh as she could? Who could raise his spirits and entertain him, who could arouse his deepest passions? He would sniff the dry white dust of the Low Countries, listen to the dull clatter of the cavalry detachments passing and think there had not been so much harm in it. He had never admitted the Marquise to any influence; his duties as King had always remained sacred to him. Then he would speak to his officers, go over the arrangements of the camp, the passwords for the next day, the order of march if they were to advance, but always there was a hunger at the center of everything which even his delight in military business could not fill. By the middle of July, he was restless. He was not needed; the campaign had been a splendid success; he could leave his officers to carry out the occupation. One night in his beautiful tent with its silver fittings and gold fringes, he wrote a letter to Versailles. When he finished, he prayed for strength without any real hope of obtaining fortitude: His Majesty was going home.

When the Bishop heard of the arrangements, he went about the court asking if it were true, but of course it was. Madame de Montespan's carriage with her splendid bays was already standing in the Marble Court, and her servants were running in and out, transferring all the dresses, jewels, pets, trinkets and books that a great lady needs to her old rooms at the palace. The lady herself looked ravishing, curtsied deeply to him when they met in the halls, then put her nose in the air and sailed into her chambers. The Bishop ordered his coach brought round and drove out until he saw dust on the horizon. Out of the cloud came the jangle of bridles and harnesses, then a line of horsemen, the *Gardes françaises* and the *Gardes écossaises,* the two divisions of musketeers mounted on their grays and blacks, and in the middle, riding glorious in his red-and-gold battle dress, his dark hair falling to his shoulders like a lion's mane, his face burned dark, his carriage easy and robust, the King.

Spurring his horse, a guardsman raced up to see who was waiting at the roadside. But though the King dismounted and did reverence, the Bishop was to be disappointed. He had spoken only the first syllable of her name when the King stopped him. "Say nothing to me, Monsieur. Say nothing at all. It has been decided."

Then His Majesty swung up onto his horse, touched his hat and waved his troops forward at a trot, their polished bridles and fittings gleaming, the plumes on their hats rippling in the wind, their silks and velvets and gold-and-silver braid resplendent under the sun. They crossed the flat, featureless woodland and the peasants' fields, they swung around to the front of the great chateau and clattered up the wide cobbled courts to the cheers of the townspeople, the workers on the new construction, the gardeners and servants and courtiers. His Majesty was like a man in a dream. As soon as the ceremony of their arrival was over, he left the shouting officers, the cheering crowd and the forest of silk pennants and went upstairs to his own chambers and through the connecting passage to see Athénaïs. At the door, by his orders, were two old dames, the most venerable and proper of the court. Standing by the window, in cloth of gold and diamonds, was the Marquise.

"Madame," said the King. He could say no more.

"Now the court lives again," said Athénaïs, rising.

He took her hand and drew her away from their duennas. "You have been well?"

"Yes. Well but lonely."

"As have I." A quick glance over his shoulder. The two old ladies were watching them without expression.

"Your armies took Limburg and Dinant and Tongres and Saint-Trond! A most wonderful summer."

He thought no woman on earth could smile like Athénaïs. "God be praised," he said. He drew her closer to him. "I have come back for you. I could not—though I tried, God knows—I could not be without you."

Athénaïs clasped his hand in both of hers, her tears spotting the deep velvet of his glove. "I thought I would die of grief."

He glanced behind him again—the old ladies' watery eyes were unblinking and unbending—then he put his arm around Athénaïs's waist to comfort her and stepped further into the corner of the windows. "I thought it was necessary; a king has many duties." His throat ached with tears, and in his desire the room seemed to have darkened and shrunk until it contained only the two of them.

"And the man?" Athénaïs whispered.

"The man cannot endure to be without you."

She looked up, trembling. The King clasped her for an instant, then stepped back and tucked her hand formally under his arm. He bowed to the two old ladies, still sitting motionless in their somber dresses, and the Marquise curtsied deeply. Then he opened the door to the bed chamber, and, with another nod to the ladies, drew her inside. Within the hour, the entire court knew that Athénaïs de Montespan was supreme again.

X

It was a triumph beyond reason. Passion had sprung up from the embers and the blaze burned the hopes of the Bishop and his devout circle to nothing on its hot breath. Athénaïs knew this was magic and soon she knew its price: the love which had been feckless as a dream was now marked with their guilt. Athénaïs concealed her uneasy spirit—and any hint of sordidness—with a new style, more magnificent than ever. She began to gamble recklessly, losing enormous sums. She began to drink more and stopped watching her appetite, so that with each new baby she put on weight. She was as bewitching as ever, but also wildly temperamental, jealous, capricious, quarrelsome. When she wasn't fighting with Françoise, she snapped at the King, and when she was in a fury, it seemed that all the demons La Voisin raised had settled in her heart. She was not such a nice person, nor such good company, nor such an amusing guest as she had been, but for these failings she had only one answer: another charm, another spell, another powder.

As for the King, who had broken a holy vow, he tried to pretend it was simple desire and not the Marquise that ruled him. Periodically, he became wildly promiscuous, visiting two or three women in a day and arriving to enjoy Athénaïs after an hour in bed with her sister or the Princesse de Soubise or Madame de

Ludres or some yet briefer and shabbier liaison. There was a fever in his blood which could outrun his control and his dignity, so that the courtiers chuckled and every young woman with a decent figure and a good head of hair began to angle for his favor.

These indulgences did not keep the King from being restless and unhappy. Longing for the old, easy companionship with the Marquise, he took to having long talks with the governess Françoise de Maintenon, a habit which scarcely eased Athénaïs's temper and insecurity. And in the back of his mind, old fears lingered. When the report of the great Marshal Turenne's death came shortly after his return, the pious murmured it was punishment for his sin. His Majesty could ignore such superstition, yet at the setbacks of that fall—the capture of another general, the invasion of Alsace—he felt a twinge.

Still, for these doubts Athénaïs had answers. She was beautiful yet. She went to the spa at Bagnères with an entourage befitting an empress and returned slim—thus purchasing another few months of glory. She erased the dull Princesse de Soubise with her wit, and defeated Madame de Ludres when her effortless fertility produced another daughter at a crucial moment. When all else failed, she fed the King powders from La Voisin. He complained of headaches and blamed her perfume, but he remained.

So the moment of joy when he returned to her at Versailles was stretched and extended, diluted and perverted but never quite forgotten. One year went by, two, three. In spite of other pretty ladies, Athénaïs de Montespan held on until just after the birth of her last child, the Comte de Toulouse. At this point, when she still felt heavy and dull, a new personality arrived at court, Mademoiselle Marie-Angélique de Fontanges, lady to the second Madame.

Unlike Athénaïs, this provincial beauty loved the hunt. Her

heart rose with the sight of the fierce, long-legged hounds, the spirited horses, the grooms and courtiers all straining against their beasts and eager to begin. When the chief huntsman sounded his horn and the dogs were released and the court plunged forward, ribbons and feathers flying, Mademoiselle de Fontanges was always in the vanguard, racing up beside her mistress, the Princess Palatine, the Dauphin, and Monsieur, who was wildly brave, however effeminate. She was carefree and out for blood, hurdling recklessly over fallen trees and brush and risking her horse's legs and her own neck at every obstacle. Too dull to shine in the salon, La Fontanges was astonishing on the hunting field, where precedence and formal etiquette could be set aside, and where courage and energy counted for more than tact and wit.

"She rides well," admitted a lady-in-waiting.

"A very pretty carriage indeed," replied the old Prince de Soubise, who, like her, was disinclined to risk his neck for a fox. He sighed profoundly.

"The spectacle does not please you? Shame on you! She is as lovely as an angel, however stupid."

"In that lies my hope," said the Prince. And the lady-in-waiting laughed, knowing like all the court that the King's afternoons with the Princesse de Soubise were making the family rich.

"Yes, His Majesty will be bored," agreed the lady, although she added maliciously (for all the ladies out of the amorous sweepstakes were malicious) "but when? That is the question."

"Yes," said the Prince gloomily, "it is harder to perceive intelligence in a plain woman than stupidity in a pretty one." He dug his heels into his mount's side and with the lady following, caught up with the hunt. The dogs had lost the scent, and the mass of riders were milling around a clearing, laughing and flirting. The more passionate riders like the Dauphin and the Princess

Palatine berated the huntsmen and cursed the dogs, but the rest of the party, including the King, called for the carriers to bring up the wine, fruit drinks and light refreshments. They were enjoying the sun on the forest leaves, their own fine clothes, clever remarks and sleek horses.

"She rides beside the King," observed the lady-in-waiting.

"Athénaïs has made a mistake."

"She dressed La Fontanges for the last ball herself. She said the girl amused her."

"Well, she is deep," said the Prince who was not. He wondered if there was a more serious rival whom the subtle Marquise might think to forestall with the simple young Mademoiselle de Fontanges.

"What is this child but a country girl?" asked the lady. "She has the manners of a peasant. Listen to her laugh."

The Prince wheeled his horse. The King had stopped under a large beech tree where the undergrowth was thin, and Mademoiselle de Fontanges was beside him on a gray mare. She wore a hunting costume of pale blue that brought out her astonishing eyes, and she was laughing with her head back in a way that would have been considered coarse if she had not been so beautiful. Her hair had become entangled in a branch and the golden curls of her coiffure were coming loose and spilling over her shoulders and over the King's gloved hand which was trying to extricate her. The horses pawed the ground and shifted restlessly, and the blonde coil of Mademoiselle de Fontanges's hair unfurled like a banner. The King guided his mount this way and that as he loosened the leaves and twigs, while Mademoiselle shook her head impatiently and became caught again and laughed her coarse golden laugh so that her long white throat arched from the lace of her bodice and her fine, slim body curved back against the horse's flanks.

"Ah, you are free," said the King, holding up a long twig. Mademoiselle de Fontanges thanked him and tried to repair her coiffure, but after a moment and much laughter she simply took a ribbon from her sleeve and bound up the curls on the top of her head. Then, resuming her mare's reins, she bowed to His Majesty—and smiled at the hand that rested for a moment against her knee. He is lost, thought the Prince. Soubise spurred his horse irritably and left the clearing, thinking as he went of the interest on his loans and of the capricious amours of kings.

The Prince was not alone in his observations. No sooner had the hunt returned than gossip rustled through the corridors at Versailles and made its way to Clagny, where, bored with the card table, Athénaïs had gone into her cabinet to dress for evening at the palace. Although nothing constructive could be accomplished until Claude returned from Versailles, she occupied herself by rouging her cheeks and sprinkling perfume about and scolding the little undermaid whom she sent back and forth to the armoires for dresses and fans.

"So pretty, Madame," said the child, holding up a magnificent gold lace gown.

Athénaïs's deep violet eyes flashed. "Put it away," she said. "Go and find Mademoiselle des Oeillets. She should be back."

"The carriage has not come, Madame."

"Then go and look for it, stupid girl." And quite forgetting herself, Athénaïs hurled a brush at her head. The servant slid behind the screen and was gone in a flash, and Madame relieved her feelings still further by sending several perfume bottles and a pot of rouge against the door. Then she planted her small white hands on the dressing table and glared into the glass. Before her sat a magnificent woman. Yes, still. Her hands touched the thick, blonde curls that showed not a trace of gray despite nine children, a dozen years of power, a mad husband and the demands of

His Majesty. The eyes, of course, were superb—not a line, not a wrinkle, the little bit of weight did that—but at this thought, Athénaïs's inspection was irresistibly drawn to her now frankly plump wrists. More lace, perhaps, at the sleeves tonight. She turned her head, surveying her neck and chin, which a less charitable observer would have characterized as double, then lingered on her perfect shoulders and décolletage: no nymph, surely, but Juno herself, regal and bountiful. And, Athénaïs added candidly, fat, particularly about the waist. For years she had eaten extravangantly, matching the King's platters of partridges and quail, whole joints and roasts, basins of salad and soups, pyramids of pastries and cakes, and dishes of creams and fruit compotes. And wines, of course, and spirits, for she was very fond of brandy, and chocolate to drink and sugared oranges. Then, all of a sudden, the slim girl was no more. She was tempted to clear her dressing table again in a gratifying explosion of glass but remembered that she was running a trifle low on some of her favorite perfumes and refrained. She must not keep losing her temper, especially when the King had come to admire gravity and control. Here, Athénaïs felt a stab of rage: he was the one becoming old, not she; he was already fat. He was, perhaps, tired of his infidelities, his baseness. Could a man fall into piety as he fell into debauchery? Yes, by the grace of God, but then to fall into hypocrisy, into tepid passion, pure calculation and prudish religious discussion? No! She would block that, and Athénaïs looked again defiantly in the mirror. She would wear the gold tonight; it was a dress fit for a queen. In days past, when the courtiers fawned at her feet, one had given her that marvel of workmanship. Well, they were at her feet still, but now they were weighing up the other candidates, backing one or another, while the women, having lived hopeless for a dozen years, each now began to feel she had a chance. He would tire of them, surely, but the sillier his choice—

With a brisk knock, Claude entered, her sharp, slightly protruding eyes bright with malice and excitement, her thin, clever hands already assembling brushes, powder, lace, ribbons, pins. Athénaïs noticed with distaste that the cords were visible in her neck—Claude was too thin.

"The gold dress? I think not tonight, Madame. I would advise the green—more severe, more elegant for a great lady."

The Marquise was nettled. Her inventory of her personal assets had not cheered her as much as usual, and she was in no mood to be contradicted. "More severe," she said, mimicking her servant, "plainer, duller—more like that governess prude, Françoise, the poet's widow!" She banged a fan down on the edge of the table so sharply that its lacquer cracked.

Claude was unperturbed. She was at ease with the great and accustomed to her mistress's rages and insecurities. "More like a woman of intelligence and character," she replied, "and less like a provincial beauty newly arrived at court."

"I see you have news," Athénaïs said after a few moments of silence. "You were late enough to have gathered plenty."

Claude smiled, showing long, yellowed teeth, and began undoing the ribbons which had secured the Marquise's afternoon coiffure. "Everyone is talking of the hunt today, Madame."

"And what are they saying?" she asked coolly.

"They say, Madame, that Mademoiselle de Fontanges has made a great impression on His Majesty."

Athénaïs laughed, a low, rich sound. "A donkey's mind in an angel's skin. You will not frighten me with tales of her."

"She rode beside His Majesty throughout the hunt. They were seen talking and laughing."

"She's safe enough as long as she stays on the horse," Athénaïs

said, but she could not help remembering that Louise de la Vallière had ridden like an Amazon.

"Her hair became caught in a branch."

"And her neck broken? I shall weep at her funeral!"

"The King himself untangled the curls."

"He will sleep with her and give her a necklace. She can barely
open her mouth without some stupidity."

"Her hair was quite disarranged, so she tied it up with a ribbon."

"A cleverness I had not suspected! You will tell me next she
quotes the Greek and sings in Italian."

Claude paused a moment in her ministrations. Her dark eyes
met her mistress's in the glass. "Half the ladies of the court have
ordered their hair done up so. Tonight you will see many
coiffures à la Fontanges. It is a bad sign, Madame."

Athénaïs did not answer immediately. Her life, like those of all
the other courtiers and people of quality, hung by threads and
depended on trifles. Would not a gentleman offer a hundred
thousand livres for the privilege of offering the King paper at his
night commode and were not dukes in ecstasies at the chance to
hold his bedtime candle? One might be undone by a jewel or
made by a ribbon.

"What else will she wear?"

"La Fontanges, Madame? More blue, I should think, and as
overdressed as her means will allow. No diamonds."

"Then I must be splendid. The blue diamonds and—"

"The deep violet, Madame. It is a royal color."

"Yes, and pale blue ribbons for my hair."

"A direct challenge? Of course."

Athénaïs laughed. Then stopped abruptly. "Call the seamstress
in. The waist may have to be let out." Damnable fat. She tapped
on the dresser with one of her perfume bottles, examined her

nails and straightened a ruffle. "Have we any more of the powders?" she asked, ostentatiously casual.

Claude stopped, put down the brush and exchanged a look in the mirror with her mistress. Then she took a small key from the bunch she wore at her waist and opened a small chest. "Only one, Madame."

Athénaïs wet a finger, straightened her eyebrows and cocked her head to examine the result.

"Madame?" Claude inquired.

Her mistress gave a little wave of her hand. "Do not bother me with it now," she said as if she had not just raised the subject herself. "And leave me for a moment. I must say my prayers."

"Of course, Madame." Claude made a little face behind her mistress's back and went through to the outer chamber. Athénaïs rose from her dressing table, smoothed her skirts, then hesitated and stood gazing thoughtfully into the dim silvered circle of the mirror. There she read glamour and confidence, and yet— No, she would not! Biting her lips, she crossed the room to the table which held her folded altar. She opened the wings, revealing the tiny carved-ivory Passion, crossed herself, and, dropping to her knees, began a Paternoster. But no sooner had she finished the familiar lines than other words came, a rapid and intense whisper: for favor, for success, for the King. Her fine round face grew as white as the ivory crucifix she addressed; her hands twisted and turned as though she shared the grief of the Magdalen, and her large, violet eyes turned dark with sorrow. One would have said she mortified her soul, but it was her pride which suffered. Ahead of love, ahead of extravagance, ahead of sensuality came pride: in her family, her blood, herself. The Mortemarts were as ancient as the Bourbons; it was only fitting their place should be nearly as high. For position, for family, all their lives had been sacrificed, and for her, love, passion and power had been so long conjoined that the loss of one seemed to presage the diminution of all the rest. She must keep him! She must! The saints must help her, the Virgin must come to her aid! Athénaïs extended her hand toward the cross and breathed her petition. It must be given! It must come true! Then she crossed herself and rose, her face still pale, her eyes still restless and intense. She rang the bell.

"My clothes," she said when Claude appeared. "I am expected soon at the palace."

Claude brought the tight-fitting bodice of purple silk embroidered with gold-and-silver thread and set with sapphires and diamonds, and the fine, thin satin overskirt, and helped her mistress dress. Madame de Montespan, usually so fussy and impatient, stood motionless and silent.

"A perfect fit, Madame, a splendid effect."

"Is splendor enough?" the Marquise asked seriously.

"Madame—"

In the silence, the two women looked at each other. Then Athénaïs's face grew tighter and she raised her chin and held out her hand. Claude turned without a word, took out her keys and, opening the chest, produced a small paper packet which Athénaïs slipped into her bosom. Claude brought her gloves and her fan, and smoothed the ruffles on her dress. The packet did not show through the silk and she gave a slight nod. "Set your mind at ease, Madame," she said in a soft, insinuating voice.

The Marquise tossed her head and opened her fan with a snap.

"It will work, Madame," Claude said. "You will have a great success." Then she opened the door of the chamber and stood aside to let her mistress pass.

It was evening when Athénaïs's carriage rumbled up the crowded way to the palace, but though the workmen were gone, dust from the construction still filtered through the windows and settled on her satin overskirts. Cranes rose black against the purple sky and the side of the white palace was spidery with scaffolding and ladders, while everywhere lay timbers and blocks and big pipes for the new fountains in the gardens. Many of the court complained: the heat, the dust, the stagnant water, the unhealthy air, the constant noise and confusion of the construction, the unending alterations to the gardens, the frantic din of the new building in town. But Athénaïs smiled as she did each time she approached the palace. Tumult suited her; she liked the restless building and alteration as she liked the court: the intrigue under ritual, the danger beneath monotony. This was a special taste, as irresistible to those susceptible to power as high stakes to confirmed gamblers. Athénaïs was both, and, even now, when the skillful balancing act, the graceful intrigues, the provocations of love seemed at last in danger of failing, she felt her heart beat and her body tense as the carriage passed the blue-and-gilded gates to the courtyards. There a mob of carriages and horsemen were arriving, and the cobblestones reverberated with the sound of the horses' hooves and the tramp of the troops of guards. Sedan chairs, too, crowded the outer court, and the bearers shouted back and forth and cursed the carriage drivers, who, in turn, lashed their horses and bullied everyone. About them, the crowd, resplendent in their silks and feathers and jewels, pushed this way and that, quarreled over chairs and precedence and jostled in lines about the public privy concessions. Where their arguments left off, they were taken up by the swarm of valets, lackeys and grooms that accompanied them, until the Provost of the Household's men would come out with clubs and threaten the most fractious. In this way, with greetings and warnings and shouts, the crowd moved toward the brilliantly lit salons, but the Marquise's carriage swept past them all to stop at the Marble Court before the King's own apartments. Her footmen jumped down and lackeys ran up with torches to light her way.

Inside the palace, the rooms were hot, although the doors and windows stood open on the soft, black night. Burning candles were reflected in the silver candlesticks and reflected again on the silver tables that held them and in the mirrors. From there the light glittered on the gilt frames of the paintings and on the ormolu chests and cabinets and twinkled on the ladies' necklaces and the gentlemen's rings, touching their gold lace and silver buckles before at last expiring, a soft glimmer, on the marbles of the floors and stairs. Athénaïs surveyed the first salon, stirring the heavy air with her fan. The palace had its own scent, a heady compound of smoke and musk, of perfume and incense and flowers: orange blossom, tuberose, jasmine, hyacinth—all sweet and cloying and able to override even the pungent and earthy odors that rose from the outer courts and the inner corridors. And the palace had its own sound, just as rare. In a distant room, she could hear Lully's violins singing in complex harmony and the gentle click of the billiard balls from the Salon de Diane and everywhere the murmur of voices in a tone peculiar to the place and to none other, a soft and intricate composition of compliment and criticism, of wit and malice, of hope and flattery.

"My most beauteous niece! Good evening, Madame."

Madame de Montespan did not trouble to turn her head, but her fan flickering like an angry cat's tail told her annoyance. "Good evening, Uncle."

The Marquis de Ternes laughed. "I see you have not regretted my absence."

"I have rejoiced, Uncle, in your good fortune."

"My good fortune?" His long reddish, sour face twisted into a puzzled frown.

"Of course, Uncle. When I see you not, I know your fortunes are good, for whenever you arrive at court, I can be assured you are in need of money." Her violet eyes flashed over the top of her fan as she took him in: a man well past middle age, thin but paunchy, with a long jaw, small eyes and a high, narrow forehead. His wig was jet black tonight, quite unsuitable for his age and complexion.

Now he laughed. "Your wit is still as biting as ever, my dear. Whatever the years have robbed from you in other departments, Time has kindly spared that."

"I must have some defense against importunate suitors, Uncle."

"My dear, the saints alone should be our refuge."

"You might take your own advice, Uncle."

"Charity starts at home—or, at least, with family. A proposition, dear niece, of the most modest sort." He took her arm and began to whisper confidentially, but after a minute or so, Madame de Montespan stopped.

"It is not to be dreamed of! The grain supplies for the army are already arranged. As for the shipments into the capital, every office imaginable has been created to live off them. It is politically impossible."

"Once all things were possible for you," the Marquis said nastily.

"And you have gotten your share, Uncle. Need I remind you that you have had the rents of two abbeys. It is enough. You must live on your means or find another patron. Now, I beg you, release my arm." She drew herself up, very tall and proud, and her uncle, who knew her temper as well as any other courtier, stepped away, although angrily.

"I have great needs, Madame," he said earnestly.

"For the last time, it is not my affair." Without giving her uncle an opening to renew his pleas, she walked into the Salon de Diane where the King was playing billiards.

"A brilliant shot, Your Majesty," exclaimed a courtier.

The King nodded, raised his eyes and saw Athénaïs.

"You are triumphant," she said with a smile.

"Tonight I am in luck," replied the King.

"A day of good fortune." Her eyes were challenging and the courtiers shifted their feet and smoothed their ribbons, their delicate social antennae sensitive to the slightest change in the royal mood. Each thought: what news, what hopes?

"We killed a stag," said the King, taking refuge as he so often did in hunting. By speaking of hounds and horses, he avoided those topics upon which the courtiers' hearts were set: favors, bounties, commissions and monopolies.

"A splendid stag, Madame de Montespan," said a Duke. "His Majesty's hounds were in superb form."

"They lost the scent a dozen times," the King corrected.

"But found it again," the Duke persisted.

"A lesson for us," His Majesty replied sententiously and took up his cue.

Athénaïs felt her back stiffen. Once he would have joined her instantly, abandoning any number of billiard games; now he preferred a silly pastime and the stale compliments of the courtiers. With a curtsy, she moved on to the tables in the adjoining salon, resolved to play recklessly. Monsieur, all diamonds and paint, waved to her. "A hand, Madame de Montespan? Our usual stakes?"

"Of course, Monsieur. With the Marquis?" The Marquis de Dagneau rose and bowed. Although ordinarily Athénaïs avoided cards with the professional gamblers, tonight she did not care. She sat down and took up the deck. "Lansquenet?"

"Hombre," said Monsieur. "We are three."

Athénaïs nodded and, as she began to deal, one of the Swiss guards assigned to watch the tables stopped beside her. He had a flat, impassive face, a broken nose and clear, pale eyes. After a moment he shifted toward Dagneau's chair, but Madame de

Montespan, superstitious, stopped him. "I won one hundred thousand ecus last time you stood at my table."

She passed him a coin and the Swiss remained.

"A most unusual mascot, Madame de Montespan," said the King's brother.

"More suitable for you, Monsieur?"

He laughed easily. "Perhaps. But I have the cards." A large handful of gold joined his stake, and Athénaïs was forced to open her purse.

"You would make someone jealous," she teased.

Monsieur ran his jeweled hand over his immense wig and winked. "Some say that is your condition," he replied.

"I am content, Monsieur. The newcomers to court do not impress me."

"They are most satisfactory at the tables," said Dagneau, arranging his hand and smiling at the thought of his recent winnings.

But Monsieur, who loved gossip and adored scandal, was not willing to let the topic drop. "Novelty, Madame, novelty is a great blessing."

"But Monsieur, is not the craving for it a failing? It may lead us into vice."

"Yet it is a princely vice. It is not a low and common vice. Do you not agree, Dagneau?"

The Marquis chose this time to reveal his hand.

"That is too bad, Dagneau!" exclaimed Monsieur. "Send away your Swiss, Madame de Montespan! He is bringing the Marquis luck."

"Everybody brings Dagneau luck for he never lets his attention wander from the cards. But I will keep my mascot and double the stakes."

"Reckless, reckless." Monsieur chuckled with delight as he

shuffled the cards with practised skill. Behind him, Athénaïs saw the slim figure of Mademoiselle de Fontanges enter the salon. Her blonde hair, elaborately dressed and bejeweled, was drawn up at the back in a cascade of curls and ribbons.

"Like a mare at a carrousel," Athénaïs remarked.

Monsieur turned, saw La Fontanges and winked. "The very latest fashion. The hairdressers are in ecstasies."

"They should be in the stables," Athénaïs murmured. Another thousand ecus disappeared, and she began to feel a certain excitement in the cards. She would have liked to stake all she possessed on a single hand: to constrict her life to the green leather square and reduce the haunting uncertainties to one terrifying question. Then, like a diviner, the pack would unfold her fate and in a moment display the future. "Shall we raise again?" she asked negligently. "I'm not in the mood for long play tonight."

"You will cut short our evening," protested Dagneau. At the other end of the salon, Mademoiselle de Fontanges laughed with one of the courtiers in a loud careless manner and began recounting the highlights of the hunt. Athénaïs yawned and fanned herself. "There were no such stags in the Auvergne, I imagine," she said, loudly enough for Mademoiselle to hear.

"Oh, yes, Madame de Montespan," the girl replied brightly. "But we never hunted with the King." Her face was flushed with pleasure and excitement.

"No, His Majesty does not care for the provinces, nor for provincial manners," Athénaïs replied coldly. She turned back to Dagneau. "Your loss, Marquis."

"Fortunately, I am to be rescued from your good fortune, Madame," said Dagneau, rising and bowing. "His Majesty has come to join us."

Victory lighted Athénaïs's face and when the King sat down, she laid her hand on his shoulder and whispered to him, so that his grave expression was disturbed by a faint, fleeting smile. That evening, he belonged to her alone and she rested her head against his shoulder and smiled on everyone. But occasionally her vivid eyes strayed over the crowd to find Mademoiselle de Fontanges, who was taking a cup of chocolate or giggling with another of Madame's ladies-in-waiting or boring a courtier with her chitchat. Yes, La Fontanges's conversation was an embarrassment, her manners a scandal: the King did well to ignore her. Yet however satisfying Athénaïs found the situation, a doubt remained. As the evening progressed and the cards grew worn, and Dagneau strove to win back from her and Monsieur what he gallantly lost to the King, Athénaïs began to think her lover ignored Mademoiselle de Fontanges too pointedly. He was a man full of secrets always, yet it seemed to her well-developed sense of intrigue that this abstracted air held something new and potentially dangerous.

"Lully wrote that air for my lute," His Majesty remarked.

"Indeed, Sire, it is very pretty," said Monsieur.

"But now I think it needs the lute," said Athénaïs who saw her chance.

"Why is that?"

"Why, Sire, the violin is a treble instrument, high and shrill like a woman's voice. However lovely in a choir, it is not so suitable for this air, which should be whispered in a low voice by one who knows his instrument well."

"Yet," said the King, "a lute would be lost in this company, and if Lully's new songs are to be heard, it must be with his violins."

"Most certainly, but I should prefer to hear it as it was intended."

Pleased, the King nodded, and Athénaïs, understanding, smiled her brilliant smile, smoothed the lace at her neckline and touched the twist of paper that held the powder. No one, after all, had managed him as she had. He had always returned and she resolved to keep her temper, to forget the slights, to remain serene. But even in the instant of this wise resolution, her nature rebelled, and when the King arrived in her apartments after supper, it was all she could do to keep from breaking into passionate scorn for Mademoiselle de Fontanges and his other conquests.

"Are you thirsty, Sire?"

"A little . . . Mostly water," he added as she reached for the decanter.

She nodded, reassured. The precious powder had been dissolved in the water. Now its murky tinge was hidden by the deep red of the wine.

"I will follow your example." Although she usually took her wine uncut, she tasted the mixture. The wine was the perfumed sort he liked, and she could detect no foreign taste. "We must drink to your triumphs," she said. "To the success of the hunt."

The King sipped the wine. "This is no setting for blood sports, Madame."

Athénaïs smiled over her goblet. "A King has many triumphs," she replied, "and many kinds of victories."

"To the victories of the heart, then, Madame," he replied and drank again.

Athénaïs followed suit, gulping the watered wine so that it warmed the back of her throat. Her eyes grew more brilliant. She seemed to feel the years and the weight sliding away, the powers of her days of glory returning. She moved slowly toward the King, her eyes fixed on his, her smile soft and sensual, and sat down on the stool beside his chair. "You had promised me the air by Lully."

His Majesty touched the thick curls at the side of her face. "Madame, I am uncertain whether you compliment me or not."

Beneath his practised and habitual solemnity, Athénaïs saw a glimpse of the man she had loved, the reckless, playful young man who had made her, in all but title, queen.

"Why, Sire, your playing is beautiful." Her smile was wide and full of mischief and promise.

"Madame, you do make me believe you, but the lute is merely the voice of love and more suitable for bridging separations than for intimate meetings."

Athénaïs raised her glass. "To love, Sire."

He lifted his goblet, crystal, gold-trimmed, and the pinkish wine within stirred with a curl of sediment, a magic plume. Athénaïs willed him to drink and not notice; he raised the glass to his lips and drained it. Then she drank, too, and with the last drops of wine, felt its magic, the soft onset of passionate sensual oblivion. She wiped her lips with her lace handkerchief and saw the desire in the King's dark eyes.

"Take off my gloves," he commanded.

Athénaïs knelt beside him and took first the rings from his fingers—the diamond large as a pigeon's egg, the emerald flanked with rubies, and the magnificent signet ring. The King sat perfectly still, his eyes never leaving her face. She drew off the violet gloves, the very color of her gown, and kissed the tips of his fingers, which, released from their velvet prison, ran down her cheek and throat, across her shoulders and over the exposed tops of her breasts. Athénaïs closed her eyes and threw her head back, drawing the ribbons out of her hair and letting the jewels and curls fall over her shoulders.

"Madame," whispered the King, "we will forget the lute. We have no need of music."

Athénaïs laughed, a soft, broken, sensual laugh, and drew his mouth against her throat, her long violet skirts melting into his stiff brocade, their goblets tipping onto the rug to stain its blue-and-gold design with a few red, cloudy lees.

XI

S uch were Athénaïs's victories in the years of her decline. Nights could still be passionate and passion was still sweet on the tongue, but by day matters were difficult. There were quarrels with Françoise over the children—which were, in reality, over the King. Whenever he returned to Athénaïs, the two women fell out in a fury of jealousy, ingratitude and piety, each bringing out the worst in the other yet unable, by any exertion, to separate. Then, as the summer died in the hunts and revels of fall, His Majesty began to pay more attention to the silly, blonde Fontanges. On nights when the King flirted with young Mademoiselle, Françoise de Maintenon would retire early to prayers which were very serious, prolonged and patriotic, while Athénaïs, less devout, drank more wine than was good for her and lost extravagantly at the tables. One night she was down two hundred thousand livres and only recouped half her loss by keeping the party at play until after three in the morning. In her rooms, undressing in the pale morning light, she burst into tears.

"Madame!"

She threw down some handfuls of gold coins, then her diamond earrings, and began wrenching at the clasp of her large and splendid necklace.

"Madame, it will be broken. Calm yourself. What can be the

reason for this? Has His Majesty said a thing about your losses? No, of course not. He will cover them all."

"Fool!" exclaimed Athénaïs. "You would think you were a country girl. Is the King to be judged by ordinary standards? No? Then use your head. He watches me at the tables and winces inside but says nothing. I lose more. He nods his head and goes off to play billiards. I was down two hundred thousand livres and he commands the violins to play. And why is this? He has a guilty conscience. Take off these wretched diamonds. What good are they to me now?" She resumed weeping furiously.

"Madame," Claude soothed, "you perhaps exaggerate. Madame de Soubise is no more seen; Madame de Ludres is not so much as talked of. Your magnificence has dazzled all. This dress, Madame"—and Claude, who loved fine clothes beyond almost all else, held up the embroidered silk with pride—"it is the envy of the court. And with your new diamonds."

"You know him not. Where women are concerned, he is a man without refinement. It is La Fontanges! A country simpleton with pale hair and pretty breasts. What else does he care about? Get me a brandy."

"Yes, Madame," Claude said, hoping the Marquise would calm herself and stop worrying. Her mind was too subtle. A man who paid gaming debts of one hundred thousand livres was treasure enough and she would do better to turn a blind eye to any number of pretty young things with loose habits and ambitious parents. But Athénaïs continued to weep and stamp and denounce the King's faithlessness and La Fontanges's gall.

"We must do something," she declared.

"The powder was a great success, Madame. We can get more."

"I had not wished—ah, but even powders will do us little good if he takes to creeping into young Mademoiselle's apartments at night."

"He was with you this afternoon. He will come back."

"Ouch! You are pulling my hair. Take it all down. Ribbons, jewels. I shall never wear it up again. What is that?" Athénaïs interrupted the thread of the conversation to peer into the mirror. "The candle. Bring me the candle. The roots are showing dark. It must be dyed again."

"Tomorrow, if it pleases you, Madame, but you must be up early."

"Fairer, blonder." She banged her hand down on her dressing table, making the pots of paint and perfume dance. "I should let it go dark. Why should I change for him? When after everything, this is my humiliation: he prefers this girl and my children's governess!" Once again she burst into tears of fury and grief and wounded pride, which Claude stopped with the greatest difficulty.

"Something must be done," Athénaïs said finally. Claude waited to hear her commission, but Athénaïs got out her pen and began a letter which gave her a great deal of trouble and was not completed until full light. When she read it over after breakfast, she tore it up and decided to wait, scolded Claude and ordered more powders. It was early winter before she was again in complete despair. This time the letter was dispatched, and her sister's daughter, pretty, shy and pious Mademoiselle de Nevers, summoned to Clagny.

Athénaïs had resolved to try everything, but on the cold, clear afternoon when Mademoiselle de Nevers stood before her dressed for the court outing, she was attacked by doubt.

She stood up, tilted her head to examine the dress from all angles, had the girl turn around, walk across the room and sit down. Was it right? She was not quite sure about the blue and glanced at Claude and delicately lifted her eyebrows. "Well?"

"Mademoiselle is as pretty as a picture."

"Yes, yes," Madame said impatiently. That went without saying. Had Mademoiselle de Nevers been plain, she would never have been invited to Clagny. She was pretty—although it was unfortunate that her hair was light brown rather than blonde—her features were good, her figure and carriage handsome, her disposition, so far as anyone could tell, sweet and docile. But to put it plainly, the girl had no sparkle, no wit, no spirit. "The blue," she said, "is it right?"

"It brings out her eyes," Claude replied, but now her tone was doubtful.

Athénaïs stepped closer and peered into her niece's face as if the girl were a statue. "I would prefer green for her, I think."

"Then the jewels are a problem, Madame."

"Yes, and the hair, too. Will this style suit the green?"

"Is it not right yet, Madame?" Mademoiselle de Nevers asked plaintively. She had now been dressed and undressed, coiffed, groomed and criticized half a dozen times. "Shall we not be late?"

"When you go to court, all must be perfection," her aunt said sternly. "It is not some provincial ball."

Mademoiselle blushed and hung her head. "No, Madame."

"And do not sulk like a farm girl! The King does not like that. He likes wit and conversation."

"I am sorry, Madame, but I am so unused—"

"Yes, yes, you have been left shockingly ignorant. She must be changed," Athénaïs continued to Claude. "The green. And I think my emeralds would suit."

"Very well, Madame." Claude could not quite conceal the surprise and interest in her expression. So this was serious! Had Madame resigned herself? Or was this speechless fool just a stalking horse? Either way, it was unfortunate the girl wasn't blonde—or more forward. It was her impression that it was boldness and disregard of convention which had brought Mademoiselle de Fontanges into contention.

The other gown was brought in, but Mademoiselle de Nevers could not manage any interest. She stood blushing with her eyes on the ground as if she would burst into tears, the excitement of her prospects at court gradually turning to terror. She had not realized her aunt was quite this grand. It was one thing to hear at home of her bounties and triumphs; it was another to be at Clagny with its huge staff and extravagant decor, to see the constant stream of messengers between the chateau and the palace and to know that she was expected to impress the King.

"Oh, you were right, Madame," Claude said. "The green is perfect."

"More youthful," Athénaïs agreed, adding sourly, "which seems to be what's required."

"The emeralds, Madame?"

The Marquise inspected her niece again. The emeralds presented a difficult decision, for jewels were always a matter of precise calculation. Too many would make her ploy obvious, while too few would deny the girl the magnificence she required. It was necessary to introduce Mademoiselle as under her protection and patronage—and to suggest just how powerful and splendid that patronage was—and yet to leave the child innocent and beautiful. A certain simplicity was required. "The small emeralds will do, I should think. But no more than the necklace and the ear drops."

Claude nodded briskly. "Most suitable. And some simple rings will be needed as well, Madame."

Athénaïs sat down in her chair to play with one of her little spaniels, rubbing the dog's silky ears as she watched the final details of Mademoiselle's coiffure. The girl was very pretty. With such a figure, Athénaïs thought, I could conquer. I could sweep La Fontanges aside like a mayfly. She talked nonsense to the dog and considered whether she should pick a quarrel and send Mademoiselle de Nevers back home. Could she bear this—either way? To have the girl succeed would be intolerable; to have her fail, disastrous.

"We are ready, Madame."

The Marquise looked up, her brilliant eyes cold. It had to be done. This child was, at least, in the family. "Yes, she will do." The girl smiled uncertainly and bobbed her head.

"Remember," the Marquise said, "His Majesty expects to be entertained. He is easily bored. You must be clever and lively."

Mademoiselle de Nevers blushed more deeply and her aunt frowned. On the ride to the palace, she attempted a somewhat hasty and impatient social education which had the effect of so frightening Mademoiselle that she could barely open her mouth. The girl stood twisting her fingers together, waiting for His Majesty to arrive, and when that great figure appeared—looking, she thought, very red-faced, fat and serious—it was all she could do to curtsy without falling over.

This timidity proved unfortunate, for inevitably she showed poorly in comparison with her witty aunt, the sagacious Madame de Maintenon, the cheerful, gossipy Princess Palatine and her attendant lady-in-waiting, Mademoiselle de Fontanges, who, impetuous and ill-bred as ever, jumped out of the carriage with delight when they reached the frozen canal.

The younger courtiers were skating on the ice, the proficient astonishing the others with loops and flourishes. Footmen were panting up and down pushing the ladies along the ice, one party racing another with whoops and shouts, while their attendants split their satin jackets as they strained behind the sleds. Mademoiselle de Fontanges, very daring, ran onto the ice and slid, the hood of her cloak tumbling back, her long, blonde hair whipping loose from its ribbons. She shrieked with laughter, like a peasant girl at a festival, and if the other ladies tittered behind their muffs and exchanged snobbish whispers, there wasn't a courtier who did not feel his blood stir. As for His Majesty, he found himself anxious for a horse and hunting, and sniffed the cold, clear air and wondered if the ground was really too hard. Perhaps tomorrow they would try for a stag. He was tired of ceremony, tired of dignity. He thought of his newest chateau, small and private, and of how he would escape there when it was finished. Then he saw Mademoiselle de Fontanges cavorting on the ice, and in her grace, glimpsed another escape. She was as lovely as a young nymph, and when she turned and curtsied and waved, he felt he would like to race across the ice into her arms, so carefree and happy she seemed.

When they were well chilled, their faces red with the wind, their feet frozen, the court piled back into the carriages and rode off to the pretty Venetian village for hot wine, chocolate, coffee and cakes. The King chose to ride his horse, rather than go in the carriage with the ladies, and Athénaïs knew that was a bad sign. "You must be more gay, more lively," she said to her niece who was shivering and sniffling from cold and nerves.

"I know not what to say, Madame."

"You might begin by looking cheerful and forgetting your cold hands," her aunt scolded as they walked toward the buffet. "His Majesty never feels the cold or complains in any weather."

The girl nodded miserably, but it was hopeless. If Athénaïs did not already see this, it was brought home to her by her uncle de Ternes.

"Our niece is a picture," he remarked as he sipped a cup of hot chocolate.

"Truly," she said shortly, her eyes on the King, who, as usual, was strolling about, urging his guests to enjoy themselves with the delicacies of the tables.

"Though she lacks something in the way of charm, I admire

your resolution. You have the blood of the Mortemarts, true enough." He smiled and passed a tray of cakes. "Do have one."

"I am not hungry, uncle."

"You are not without hopes for yourself, then? Very wise. Between you and me, our Mademoiselle de Nevers will never capture His Majesty. A curious taste in a man, is it not, to prize intelligence in women so highly? As though it were a requirement of the sex."

"You are coarse, Uncle, and without much wit."

"I am desperate, niece, and without much money. The matter I spoke to you about—have you reconsidered?"

"Your poverty is your own fault, Sir, and the solution must be your own as well," Madame de Montespan said angrily, for the King had now slipped from her sight.

"You will deny me, then?"

"I neither can nor will help you, Uncle. It is impossible."

"You are not as wise as you seem. If you are in favor, he will grant anything. If you are out of favor, he will give you a parting present—and after the touching offer of the virtue of your niece, Mademoiselle de Nevers! Madame, you neglect your opportunities!"

"And you waste your breath to speak to me in such a way! I shall complain to His Majesty of you and he will send you from court as my parting gift!" Madame cried in a fury. She set down her cup and turned sharply away. De Ternes caught her arm.

"Is that your final word?"

"Uncle, I shall call the guards."

He stepped back. "You will be sorry! I have the means to make you regret this day." His voice was shaking with fury, but the Marquise was so angry herself that she took no notice. She was surrounded by fools and parasites! And where was the King?

With a jerk, she pulled her furred hood over her head and

walked quickly back to the shelter of her carriage. There she scolded her niece and sent the girl out to talk with the other guests.

The King, however, was already occupied with Mademoiselle de Fontanges. He had found her at the side of the tent that sheltered the buffet tables, nibbling the icing off a sweet cake. "It's delicious, Sire," she said. "Your cooks are marvels." Her pink tongue traced a swirl in the soft icing.

The King nodded, much taken with her azure eyes and the white curve of her throat. "Did you enjoy the ice?"

"Oh, yes, but I am waiting for the snow. Will there be lots of snow, do you think? Will we have sleds and ride in the park?"

"Indeed, Mademoiselle, if you wish it."

"If I might ride with you—"

"It would be my pleasure, Mademoiselle."

Her pink cheeks glistened. "But you always take such a crowd," she said, pouting delightfully.

This was obvious, but still the King's vanity stretched itself like a contented cat. She made him feel young. Foolish.

"Alas, I must have a care to disappoint no one," he remarked.

"Your regret, Sire, would almost content me."

He was touched by her simplicity, her directness. Oh, her mind was not quick, but even her hesitations and follies were perfection. He offered his arm to feel the touch of her lithe body. "A king has little time alone."

"But some, Your Majesty, there are some times, are there not?"

"Which I share, yes, with a special one."

Mademoiselle smiled and bit her lower lip, showing white, perfect teeth. "A privilege scarce to be dreamt of, Your Majesty," she said, but it was clear what her expectations were.

The King looked at her with all the pleasures of anticipation.

To his alert senses, the faint breath of woodsmoke and frost was better than the finest perfume. "Your wish, Mademoiselle, would be my pleasure."

Mademoiselle de Fontanges flushed crimson and curtsied very low, but when she raised her head, her bold eyes were bright with excitement.

"Shall we say this evening?"

"Your Majesty."

"The Captain of the Guards provides my escort. Have a servant inform him of the location of your chamber in the Palais Royale. Then, Mademoiselle, you may expect me around nine."

With this, His Majesty raised his hat. Mademoiselle, all of a flutter, made another deep curtsy, and the King strolled away without another glance to spend the rest of the party chatting with his sister-in-law, the Princess Palatine, who liked him enough to ignore his affairs with her pretty young ladies-in-waiting.

The carriages returned to Versailles when the sun was low. The ladies ran up the marble steps in their satin slippers to put their cold feet before their fires, while the gentlemen called their valets and demanded another brandy or more hot chocolate or both, and His Majesty had a quiet word with the captain of his Guards. But Athénaïs surprised the other courtiers by ordering her carriage to drive immediately on to Clagny. Without a word to anyone, not even to her frightened and disappointed niece, she went straight to her chapel and remained there a long time before going to her chamber. One of the footmen signalled to Claude, who went up and tapped on her mistress's door.

"Madame?"

There was no response. Claude pushed the door open softly and stuck her head inside. The Marquise was sitting at her dressing table. Although the darkness already looked in through the long windows, only one candle was lit, its flame reflected feebly in the mirror. The rest of the room, save for a few vagrant sparks flickering along the heavy gilt of the ceiling cornice and the gold leaf on the picture frames, was in deepest shadow. The nymphs and gods, clouds and horses, flowers and garlands on the ceiling, the masks and emblems and trophies ornamenting the walls were all invisible, but Claude sensed their presence: the shadows were full, the room itself pregnant with many uneasy shapes and feelings. She came in quietly and drew the long velvet curtains. Madame turned her head slightly but said nothing.

"You are expected at supper, Madame."

The only response was a wave of her hand.

"It would be unwise to miss."

"I think it does not matter."

Athénaïs looked into her glass. For several days, she had scarcely eaten, but the only result was the drawn look in her face. Had she the time, she would go back to the spa and diet, returning slim and youthful. At this thought, her face took on a sardonic expression: there was not time; there was not youth. "I will wager the chateau," she said, "my jewels, all this trash. Every sou. If I win, I will live like an empress. If I lose, I will become a Carmelite like Louise."

"Madame, this is nonsense. You are a great lady, with children, responsibilities. You must remember—"

"I must remember my soul," said the Marquise. "Is that not of more worth? I have gambled *that,* as you know."

"Madame, you take all too seriously. A few powders—why, even the Church cannot condemn such trifles."

"I was not thinking of that. You know there was more. All sacrilege is forbidden. It was for his sake," she exclaimed, suddenly angry, and with a sweep of her hand tumbled the bottles of perfume and pots of rouge from the dresser.

"That was a long time ago."

"The saints do not forget."

"And your good works, Madame? Donations to this order and that, prayers at abbeys and convents; gifts to the hospitals. Set your mind at ease, Madame. What was done was a foolishness, perhaps, but many prayers will wipe out error."

"That I believe."

Claude picked up the cosmetics and began straightening the dressing table. "Then Madame, let us light the candles and dress. You have no need for these dark moods."

"If I err again," Athénaïs said thoughtfully, 'I will surely peril my soul. That you cannot deny."

"Madame—"

"Is he worth it?" the Marquise continued in her false calm. "The price is high, and he is fickle."

"You might better pray, then, Madame." Claude said drily, "and leave the King to Providence."

Athénaïs caught her arm and dug the flesh with her sharp fingernails. "Do not mock me. It is on your hands as well. You have trafficked with that witch." The two angry faces stared at each other, then Athénaïs released her with a jerk. Claude stood rigid, her thin face cold and tight.

"Do not ask my advice," she said, "if you fear to take it."

The Marquise snatched the scissors from the dressing table and held their sharp points toward Claude's breast. "I fear nothing," she said. "There is nothing I would not do."

Her servant did not reply.

"I would shed blood. But his soul is too small." She turned back to the mirror and let the scissors drop onto the table. After a moment, she spoke again softly. "There is no answer. I have asked the saints and the Blessed Virgin, but there is no answer. Perhaps my soul is already lost. Perhaps it makes no difference. Had they but answered—"

Claude remained as she was.

"He spoke to her at the Venetian Village," Athénaïs said, "He talked to her as she ate a cake with white icing. She was too stupid to answer him, just nibbled on the cake and giggled and smiled. He took her arm, then released it. He lifted his hat to her and she blushed. Then he pretended to ignore her."

"His flirtations are transparent," Claude agreed, unbending a little.

"I was more than that! She is so mediocre! So dull! She has bewitched him."

"With her beauty," Claude said cruelly.

"Was all else then unnecessary?" Athénaïs asked in a low, dangerous tone.

"You have had a dozen years, Madame. No one else has managed so long. Or so cleverly. Was that not a marvel?"

"He grows older. Surely he will settle at last."

"This is a dangerous age. He will be difficult for a few years yet."

"But then he must settle. There will be one woman. He will grow bored at last with variety."

"I think that likely."

Then the court came to Athénaïs with a sudden rushing sound in her head: the chatter, the laughter, the click of the billiard balls, Lully's violins, the smell of the candles, the taste of intrigue and lemon ice, and her heart raced as if her life were on the edge. "I do not want to grow old in disgrace," she burst out. "To be sent away or ignored at court! I would rather die!" Her eyes were very dark in the glass and her pointed fingernails tapped on the silver blades of the scissors.

"There is a way," Claude said softly. "If you are resolved."

Madame bowed her head and appeared to study the arabesque of inlaid work in the dresser. "You have discussed this with La

Voisin?" she asked, half angry, half anxious. "I did not tell you to consult her."

"Madame, I always take thought for your interests."

Athénaïs hesitated for a moment. "What does she say?" she asked in a low voice.

"It is possible she can help."

"I would not need to be involved," Athénaïs said quickly.

This time, Claude hesitated. "Then she can guarantee nothing. The situation has changed. Things are more serious."

"I have not the time," the Marquise said with haughty impatience, but her expression was full of pain. "Is there no other way?"

"There might be. Madame Voisin says that next best is someone in your confidence. Someone of your household."

Athénaïs's voice was soft but intense. "Would you do this thing for me?"

A subtle change appeared in Claude's expression, a modulation of her cynicism, her hardness. She prized Athénaïs's surrender, as Athénaïs, the King's. "Yes," she said. "Yes, I would, Madame."

The streets of the quarter were icy and rutted. The overworked hackney horses hesitated and stumbled, causing the driver to go for his whip and the carriage to progress in a series of jolts and bumps. The Marquis de Ternes jounced uncomfortably on the hard seats, cursing the roads and the Abbé Lesage at whose insistence he was making this uncomfortable journey. But when through the curtains of the hired carriage he saw the moon appearing behind the tall, decayed tenements, he prayed to her to bless his revenge: his horoscope was favorable, and great things were at hand. De Ternes told himself that a life of pursuing favor, a life of delays, of the demi-poverty of minor courtiers, of dependence on his fickle, arrogant whore of a niece was soon to be—

what? Settled, avenged, changed in his favor? The Marquis thought, too, of the last few years which he had spent in cultivating the favor of the Dauphin. Now those afternoons, those dangerous hunts, those gifts of dogs, mares and curios for His Highness's collections would be repaid. He would wait no longer, for when the Dauphin was king, he would be a great man. And he would begin by sending Madame de Montespan from the court; that is, if she did not perish with the King or end on the scaffold. With this, de Ternes laughed, and he was still enjoying the prospects of his coming greatness when the carriage lurched to a halt before a miserable collection of hovels and tenements, all leaning hunched together like a group of drunken soldiers. A sign informed him that the low, evil-looking tavern in the center was The Bacchus. "You will wait," the Marquis said to the driver.

"The horses must have food," the man snapped, and the Marquis was forced to part with a coin, which most likely would go to inebriate the driver.

Blaming the villainy of hack proprietors and the deviousness of Lesage, de Ternes picked his way across the frozen ruts and filth of a track that was half street, half sewer, and entered the tavern.

The Bacchus was almost as cold within as without, the vine-leaved god on the sign being the only indication of jollity about the establishment. A few carters and demobbed soldiers dozed in a drunken stupor at the tables in the front, while at the back a pair of dark shapes sat before the small fire. As de Ternes approached, one looked up.

"At last," said the Abbé Lesage. "I'll finish your hand later," he told the farmer squatting on the hearth beside him, and, when the man had stumbled away, half stupid with drink, he gestured for de Ternes to sit on the narrow bench before the fire. A strong odor of wine came from the good Abbé, and de Ternes shook his head angrily.

"You have spent my money before you've earned it, Lesage."

"Abbé, if you please, Sir. I've given you value. Why, the identity of La Voisin's mysterious lady alone puts a great one in your hands. Do not deny it! You'll have a share in a privateer, at least, from the Marquise."

"Shut your mouth!" de Ternes said furiously. "We cannot talk here. What possessed you to choose this hovel? You told me you were well used to persons of quality."

"I'm a poor man," Lesage replied with an affected whine. "For a private room the landlord must be paid." He put out his hand and de Ternes was forced again to open his purse.

"Ah," said Lesage, "silver makes all possible. You'll like this place, Sir. Safe as a church." He disappeared none too steadily into the darkness, returning a moment later, followed by a thin blonde woman bearing a candle. She was barefoot on the freezing stones and, de Ternes saw to his disgust, nearly toothless.

"Best the house has to offer," Lesage said with a wink as the woman led them up a narrow and very dirty stair to the corridor above. She pushed open the third door, revealing a dark and dingy room furnished with a high, curtained bed and a plain wooden table with three straight chairs.

"And bring us some wine," de Ternes said, "and some wood for a fire."

He stalked over to the shuttered window and opened it, letting the cold night air into the fetid chamber.

"Shorten your life, that habit will," Lesage said cheerfully. "The pest rides the night air."

"This is a pesthole if there ever was one," de Ternes said.

"You were bred too nice," the Abbé replied. "For a man of my experience, this is a tidy hole, quiet, comfortable and discreet. I could cut your throat, Marquis, and there'd be not a word said."

This interesting topic was interrupted by the arrival of the woman with a handful of logs, and a bottle of wine. When the fire was crackling and the drink uncorked, the two men sat down on opposite sides of the table. Lesage took a long swig and reminded himself it were best to stay sober, while the Marquis touched the hilt of his sword and wondered if it would not be safer and almost as satisfying to run the Abbé through and depart for his own estates. In this congenial mood, they opened their meeting. When the bottle was about half empty, the Marquis spoke. "Would you be rich, Abbé?"

"As would any man of spirit, Marquis."

"The means are at hand," de Ternes said.

Lesage looked up, interested and curious.

"The lady who visits your associate, Madame Voisin, is the key to a fortune, Abbé. For men who are bold and knowledgeable."

Lesage grunted. "Tell me more, Marquis."

But de Ternes hesitated and took another drink. He did not trust the Abbé, and feared the old convict might be difficult to dispose of afterwards.

"Well?" asked the Abbé.

The Marquis decided. "You can get poison?"

Lesage shrugged.

"I know it is true," said the Marquis.

"Then you needn't have asked," replied the Abbé boldly.

"When next the lady des Oeillets visits La Voisin for those famous Galet aphrodisiacs, you must see she is given poison. Something very deadly and sure."

Lesage's face went pale. "Her mistress would give it to—"

"No names, fool. To even breathe it is treason."

There was a long silence.

"The price would have to be very high," Lesage said after a time.

The Marquis opened his purse and laid a handful of gold coins on the table. "In earnest," he said.

The Abbé's fingers trembled as he counted over the shining louis d'or. "Yet there are dangers."

"You drew my horoscope," the Marquis replied. "I am promised great things."

"A very favorable conjunction," Lesage admitted. The Marquis was the client of all time; the greatest pigeon ever. "There is no doubt you could be a great man."

"None whatsoever. And you, my friend," said the Marquis who could be subtle, too, "you could be free of that woman Voisin. A poisonous old trollop she is."

"The horoscope is very fair," Lesage admitted as he built the coins into three gleaming piles.

"It is an opportunity not to be missed," said de Ternes.

"Oh, it is possible," said Lesage, who was already thinking of the other gleaming coins he would extract from the Marquis. "But will she come again? Will we see the lady?"

De Ternes laughed. "She will need all her magic. She will come again."

"Then it can be done."

"But do not trust La Voisin."

"Think me a fool? There is another of these hags, a Marie Bosse, who deals in the deadly white powder. It is so simple, Sir, I can scarce believe it. The packets are switched and all are as you desire."

"Do it, and you will never want for anything again, Abbé."

"Yet the lady may perish with her lord. Have you considered that?"

"It is one of the attractions of the plan," the Marquis said, and Lesage gave a wicked smile.

"And that evil cow, La Voisin, will go to the scaffold for it!

Truly, Marquis, your horoscope was golden. It is a plan of genius."

"To our good fortune, Abbé," the Marquis said, raising his glass.

"To success."

Then, though the Marquis smiled, he drew out his sword, which he laid along the table, pointing toward the Abbé. "Fail me not," he said. "For if you betray me, Abbé, I'll cut your heart from your body."

"Mathilde! The candles, girl, and hurry. What are you dreaming about? You see the darkness coming on." Madame shivered at this and adjusted her shawl around her shoulder. "And my lace. Is it straight? No, don't touch it with your dirty hands, just point. Ah, yes, smooth now?" She waited for the servant girl's inspection.

"Yes, Madame."

"Very well." Madame's plump features assumed a maternal expression which Mathilde had long since learned to distrust. "You may go home tonight if you like. You should visit your mother."

The girl's face brightened, but a glance at the rapidly descending night showed her apprehension.

"Never mind the dark," Madame said briskly. "Take old Henri with you. For all it costs to feed that brute of a dog of his, he can walk you as far as the bridge."

"Yes, Madame, thank you."

"You may go at once." When the girl bobbed her head and ran out the door, Madame removed a key from the cord about her waist and unlocked her black wood cabinet. Quickly, she ran her fingers over the store of powders, assuring herself that all was in order, that everything possible had been done. Then she made a little face of disgust, as she remembered how La Lepère had really not been obliging. It would be wise to find someone else with her skill. Serve her right. And Madame began to swear under her breath at her colleague who had delivered the small bundle in a market basket just that morning, but who had felt this service entitled her to keep the usual commission! As if half her clientele wasn't due to me alone, La Voisin muttered, and when she counted over her packets, she decided to add a few ecus to the cost of each, which was only right, considering the very special service Abbé Guibourg intended. But was everything ready? She locked the cabinet again and ran through her preparations, nervous, yet pleased to be the organizer of great events. And Abbé Lesage? Yes, she had had his cassock brushed, his linen washed. He had been acting very strangely lately—ever since his mysterious new customers—getting above himself and unwilling to do anything but lounge in the kitchen and argue politics. She would have to ask him sometime if he had had a fever during his time on the oar, for he was full of fantastical plans. "Mathilde!" she called, forgetting that she had just allowed the girl to leave, then, remembering, Madame opened the door and shouted for Lesage.

The Abbé came nimbly downstairs, very clean and polished looking for once, with a smart new wig. "Have our guests arrived, Madame?" He was all control, all manners, all prosperity.

"Your turnout astonishes me, Abbé."

He gave a wolfish grin. "Better times, Madame, I have told you, and better yet if you would but take some timely advice."

"I have forbidden you to speak to me of such mischief. You will handle your end of the business, Abbé, and I will handle my own. That includes the powders and the locked cabinet." Madame Voisin nodded grimly and wondered if she might not be wise to feed the Abbé some of the black powders and be done with him.

"Ah, what spirit you show, Madame," Lesage exclaimed, and he began to tease and ingratiate himself. In the next few minutes there were many compliments and insinuations, a glass of brandy was drunk, and when the sound of the carriage came through the salon windows, Madame had to jump off the Abbé's lap in confusion.

"What nonsense is this! They will be here momentarily."

"Mathilde will see to them."

"Are you mad? I have let her go for the evening."

"Well, then, answer them yourself—they will be more impressed with our courtesy." Lesage laughed and, with the merest twitch of his long, strong fingers, the key to Madame Voisin's locked cabinet disappeared into the fold of his cuff.

"See you are not around. You should wait with Abbé Guibourg."

"Whew—he smells worse than a galley in August. I have a mind to wait here and meet the fine clients."

"Do as you are asked!" Madame exclaimed in aggravation, but as there were steps on the walk outside, she had to hurry through to the hallway. The moment the door closed, Lesage jumped up, palmed the key and unlocked the cabinet. There was a package folded up in a scrap of cloth and inside, wrapped in three—four!—layers were the packets. He opened one and sniffed the powder: white for love, black for death. From a fold in his cassock, he produced a handful of similar but deadly powders bought from Marie Bosse. He laid the new packets within the cloth and folded it up. So simple, so quick to kill—even a king—Lesage thought, and he was so touched with exultation that he lost his usual dexterity and had to wrap the little package again. By the time it seemed right there were voices in the hall, Madame's high pitched cooing, like a dove losing tail feathers, and the whispering of the clients. Lesage closed the cabinet and turned the key in the lock. The original packets vanished under his clothes; the key was left in the lock as if Madame had been careless in her haste. Abbé Lesage let himself out one of the floor-length windows as the door of the salon opened.

"Ah, Mademoiselle. Come in. Everything is in order."

Claude did not remove her mask as she usually did, but gave her thick traveling cloak to the masked woman accompanying her. This was Catau, an under ladies' maid, also familiar with the Voisin establishment.

"We have spared no expense, Mademoiselle des Oeillets. No efforts."

"And you have the new powders?"

"Of course, Mademoiselle," Madame Voisin said, bustling over to her cabinet. She felt a little spurt of anxiety when she saw the key. How careless of her to leave it there! Thank the saints that Lesage could not have noticed in so short a time. "They are perfectly fresh, and I will see that they are placed on the altar again tonight. Oh, yes, I must insist! The spiritual forces will be immense; it would be so foolish to neglect them. A case of spirit and matter, Mademoiselle, the conjunction of powerful forces cannot fail to do good. It cannot."

Claude adjusted the scarf that she still wore about her head. "Very well, Madame. I think we should begin. My absence may be noticed at the palace."

"Of course." Madame Voisin was smooth and eager, but she did not make a move until Claude produced a purse and placed it in her hand.

Madame felt its weight but did not stoop to count the coins. "This way, ladies, if you please." She crossed the hall, lifted the corner of a large tapestry, and pressed a recess in the paneling. The section swung inward with a soft creak, and La Voisin ushered her guests into her private chapel. This secret room, hung in black cloth, smothered with incense, and lighted only by the two black candles on the altar, was so dim that for a moment the visitors froze in the entrance, trying to orient themselves by the light from the hall. Then the door swung shut. Madame lit a candelabra, revealing a narrow, windowless room with a high ceiling, a crimson rug, several small wooden benches and, in place of a conventional altar, a curious raised pad or mattress. Aside from the carpet and the faint light of the candles, the only relief from the prevailing blackness was a large white cross embroidered on the draperies.

"Abbé Guibourg waits within," Madame said as she placed the powders beneath the cover of the altar. "When we ring, they will come immediately."

"They?" asked Claude, immediately wary.

"The Abbé Guibourg, who will perform the rite, and the Abbé Lesage. There must be an acolyte and the Abbé Lesage is most skilled. You will not be disappointed."

"It is an occasion for the greatest secrecy," Claude warned.

Madame Voisin gave a short laugh. "You ask your lady about the Abbé Lesage, Mademoiselle, though his name was Dubuisson then." Madame dropped her voice still further. "He and a priest named Mariette read the evangels over her head—for her success with the King. They knew her sister, too. A fine man, our Abbé Lesage, before his troubles."

"There will be no names," said Claude, unimpressed by this ancient history.

"No, no indeed, Mademoiselle! For an 'unknown lady' only. The abbés know their business, but, Mademoiselle, you must prepare yourself if we are to begin. As I have explained."

Claude appeared to hesitate at this, and it was perhaps fortunate that the mask concealed her flushed face and white, pinched nostrils.

"You may wear the mask," Madame Voisin added encouragingly and without a word, Claude began unfastening her bodice. When her skirts, underskirts and petticoats had joined it in a silky pile, Madame Voisin blew out all the candles except the tapers on either side of the black velvet dais that served as the altar. "Here, Mademoiselle," she said, "just make yourself comfortable. Yes, like so. And two candles, one in each hand." Claude's face was unreadable behind the mask, and Madame leaned closer to watch her eyes, sensing fear, disgust and other less definable emotions. "It will go well," Madame said. "I, myself, you know, have often—"

"I am ready," Claude said, her voice resonant and carrying as if she spoke from a stage.

La Voisin gestured for Catau to be seated. There was a rustle of silk. Then Madame rang a bell, once, twice, a clear ecclesiastical sound. The curtain moved at the back as, summoned from their little anteroom, Guibourg and Lesage entered, bearing a chalice and, on a cloth, a host stained red and black.

Guibourg walked to the center of the chapel, turned and faced the altar, which was the white naked body of Mademoiselle des Oeillets, and bowed. He stood contemplating her, his ugly furrowed face a broken mask of light and shade, as Lesage lit the tapers in her outstretched hands. Then he, too, bowed and Claude smelled the garlic and onions on his breath which mingled sickeningly with the smoky, perfumed air of the chapel and with the stench of unwashed clothes from Guibourg. She closed her eyes, but opened them immediately as the Abbé began to intone the prayers in his harsh voice, then shut them again, surrendering to the dizziness which engulfed her with the darkness. She could smell the Abbé, hear the congested snuffle of his breathing, feel, as he approached closer, the squalid, threatening warmth of his massive body. For you, Madame, Claude thought. She was freezing, and already her outstretched arms were beginning to ache.

How long? He was only on the Kyrie! Claude began to shiver: the very air seemed thick with ugliness, while the familiar perfume of the incense, now subtly changed in proximity to these renegade priests, seemed a cold, foul stench. It was possible that though angels failed to come, other spirits did not. Madame, this is for you. This is my devotion to all your interests. To your family, your wealth. To your powers over the King. And here Claude felt a surge of jealousy, of anger, of disgust. He discards us all, she thought, and the candles in her hands moved and flickered as she tightened her fists. The chanting began, filling her ears and making her head hurt, producing a dislocation in all expected things. The incense stank; the prayers conventionally begun turned corrupt, obscene; the chanting, once so soothing, grew shrill. From the corner of her eye, she saw Lesage staring at her feverishly and panting like an animal. There were sounds in the chapel—surely it is full, she thought in panic. The Abbé Guibourg took up a black napkin trimmed with lace which he laid over her breast. Lace, she thought, lace! This is for you, Madame. The chalice was silver, embossed with a dragon and as cold on her belly as a sword in winter. Trembling, she held herself rigid, stiff as a corpse, feigning death to survive. The hideous Abbé bowed close over her, his breath sickening, his filthy hands touching her breasts and thighs as he took up the chalice. He was babbling nonsense, a mixture of Latin and French, calling his fearful gods with strange, exotic words. For you, Madame, she wanted to scream, but she was too cold, too stiff, for it was blood she smelled, old blood, rank and rotten. The Abbé bowed again, kissing her body this time, so that Claude moaned with terror and revulsion. He raised the host, dripping blood in an unholy miracle, and the congregation howled as his enormous hand forced her legs apart to place a piece of the defiled host in her vagina. Madame, Madame! The cold, oily liquid from the chalice splashed her belly and dropped down her groin. The Abbé's voice dropped to a slobbering and unintelligible whisper as he bent over her, his body convulsed, his hands clutching frantically under his robes. Claude bit her lip and shivered, her rigid muscles aching, before a rush of disgust and exultation united in a cry, "Madame! For your sake!" and with a gasp, she let the candles fall and drew up her legs and threw her arms around her freezing body. There were sounds in the chapel, the wet whispers of bodies thrashing together with cries of pain, pleasure and anger. "Catau! Catau!"

Catau stumbled forward, past the Abbé, who was gasping and wheezing at the side of the altar, and Lesage, who was emptying the chalice, to wrap Claude in her cloak.

"The powders," Claude whispered. As she sat up, the room revolved and demons flew in the air.

"Let us go, please, let us go," Catau implored.

But Claude tore at the cover of the mattress. Touched, lost, found the packet and clutched it to her breast.

"Quickly, quickly," Catau said.

They reached the back of the chapel, unnoticed in the confusion of the celebrants—Claude was surprised to realize there were only three or four—and pushed at the panels to find the door.

"My skirts," she demanded. She would never be warm again.

Catau pounded on the wall for the door.

"The bodice, you fool."

Catau was weeping and slapping the wall. Then from the darkness Madame Voisin emerged, her dress and cap disheveled, her expression dreamy and malicious. She patted the wall with a plump hand and the panel opened. "This way."

Claude drew herself up stiffly, ignoring the sticky feel of the Abbé's disgusting potion and the rotten breath that clung to her clothes, her hair. She was not the child of actors for nothing. "Good evening, Madame."

"Mademoiselle." The old witch inclined her head, her usual effusive servility blocked by smugness.

"We must go," Catau said, impatient with ceremonial.

"Not without a brandy. It is so cold, ladies. So cold a night requires a brandy. But I must fetch it myself. Mathilde is not here." La Voisin winked. "I thought it unwise. A moment." She went into the salon.

"Let us leave now," Catau said, her voice quivering.

"We cannot," Claude said sternly, "Control yourself."

"Will you not come in, ladies?" Madame Voisin called from the other room.

"Alas, no, Madame. We are expected back."

She brought a tray and glasses. "To our success, ladies, and to the health of the King."

"Success and the King," Claude said, nudging Catau, whose "success" came as a faint echo. Claude swallowed the dark liquor in three burning gulps, while Madame Voisin watched her speculatively, her glass balanced against her lip. "A memorable evening, Mademoiselle."

"Yes," But Claude thought, I could watch this woman die with pleasure.

There was a sound behind the panel, and the guests immediately replaced their glasses. "Good night, Madame," Claude said. "We will delay no longer."

"A pity, a pity." La Voisin smiled as the two women wrapped their cloaks about them. She despised such nice-tempered ladies, and their fear and revulsion made her reckless. When the outer door had closed behind them, Madame laughed, drained the remnants of all the brandy glasses, and laughed again.

The panel moved behind her, and Lesage appeared. The service and his success had put him in a good humor, and he was willing to forget their quarrel. "Shut up, you old banshee," he said genially. "What? Not a drop for me?" He fetched the decanter and poured a hearty swig for himself. "Have they gone?"

"With the fear of the devil behind them."

"Good. They will think their money well spent." Lesage went to the door. From beyond the front garden he could hear the clatter of horses' hooves and he thought that if his plans matured even a coach of his own was not out of the question. The moonlight poured down like a stream of coins and all the omens were good. It was just a matter of time, of finesse. "A success, Madame," he remarked when he returned to the hallway. "There is no one like Guibourg for raising the spirits. True, he's a repulsive old hog, but he has the gift."

"Indeed. And where is he now?"

"Asleep in the back."

"Leave him," Madame said gaily, the brandy and her own power going to her head. There was no need to dismiss the Abbé just yet. He was a useful colleague, and if she decided to use the black powders, she would have to make sure there were no suspicions. "We will celebrate, Abbé."

"Another drink, Madame," Lesage said smoothly, refilling their glasses.

"A song!" And prompted by the brandy, Madame Voisin broke into a scurrilous ballad in her strong alto.

XII

Throughout the tedious ceremony of his lunch, the King had thought of nothing but Mademoiselle de Fontanges. With each change of course, with each new dish, cold like all the rest after its long journey from the palace kitchens, with each cry of the Gentleman of the Buttery, "Drink for the King," he thought of his escape. His pleasure in her was uncomplicated. When he was with her, he forgot everything—dignity, worries, time itself—and if his enjoyment was limited to her beautiful person, that happiness was sufficiently intense to be its own excuse. It is true that he seldom talked and joked with her, nor lingered in her chambers, nor kept her perpetually at his side as he once had Madame de Montespan. Nor was he so in love that he was blind to her weaknesses and flaws. For wit and amusement, Athénaïs was still supreme, while for serious conversation he visited Madame de Maintenon. Yet, Mademoiselle de Fontanges remained like a recurrent fever. He was well, cured, serious as any proper monarch, then sudden as a drug in his veins came desire, and he was as giddy as a schoolboy. Now, he was so distracted that he only touched the sweet to please the cook, and after a final sip of watered wine, jumped up from the table. He must see her.

Leaving the courtiers milling about the chamber, His Majesty slipped through the side door that led to Mademoiselle's suite. In his youth, he had run across the roofs at night to reach a certain lady's bed, but he'd never felt younger than now at Mademoiselle de Fontanges' threshold.

"Your Majesty." The cheeky red-haired servant curtsied deeply, but though he sometimes thought her very pretty, today the King had eyes only for her mistress, rising pink, blonde and lovely from her chair. Her low-cut dress was a wave of blue-gray satin, embroidered with flowers, and the little lap rug that slid to the floor was a soft white fur.

"Good day, Sire." When she curtsied, showing a slim white neck and masses of perfect curls, the King swept her into his arms and kissed her, making her saucy maid giggle. Mademoiselle was not disconcerted; she was always perfectly natural—another of her charms. Slipping from his arms, she summoned Arlette to loosen her corsets, then with a wave of her hand dismissed the girl and returned to him, her jeweled bodice half undone.

"You are the most beautiful woman in the world," he said and it was true: she was intoxicating, delight and oblivion in one. He lifted her skirts, making Mademoiselle squeal and laugh, and enjoyed her in the middle of her chamber. Then Mademoiselle pouted and scolded so prettily that the performance was repeated in the ornate satin bed, leaving His Majesty very red in the face and rather regretting her limited powers of conversation. She was not amusing, and no sooner had he satisfied himself with her than he was bored. It was unfortunate, but there it was. she was ignorant and stupid. In another day, he would be ready to give the jewels of his kingdom for an hour in her bed, but now he saw that there was snow in the air and he was anxious to be off. "Shall we walk in the gardens, Mademoiselle?"

Her expression lost some of its contentment. Although silly, she was not without sensitive feelings: the abrupt appearance and disappearance of His Majesty's ardor was wounding. "I think I had rather remain in the palace today, Sire," she said by way of a trial, for she had not, as a matter of fact, felt herself for several days.

"Why Mademoiselle, would you remain shut up in this stuffy chamber? A crime, Mademoiselle, to deny the winter its only sun." He pinched her playfully, making her giggle.

"You might remain with me," she teased.

"It were more compliant for you to come with me," he said, pulling on his satin breeches briskly, "but if you are tired, stay and rest for the ball." As the King's favorites were never allowed to be ill or out of sorts, this, in itself, represented a considerable concession, and Mademoiselle bowed her head.

His Majesty straightened his clothes, picked up his hat and stick and thinking that perhaps he would stop and visit his two clever ladies on the way, swaggered out.

As soon as he was gone, Arlette stuck her head around the other door and seeing the petticoats strewn about the rug, broke into a laugh. "Well, Mademoiselle, this is a fine thing."

Her mistress said nothing, but rubbed her eyes and sniffled.

"Oh, Mademoiselle, what is it? What has happened?"

"He wants to go walking. He's always like that. In a rush to go here or there as if he's ashamed of my company afterwards."

"His Majesty is very fond of the open air," the servant said carefully.

"He talks enough to that old shrew, Madame de Maintenon— or should I say the Widow Scarron, the little Duc du Maine's governess."

"Mind you do not say as much to His Majesty, Mademoiselle," advised her servant pertly, "for she is much in favor."

"Too much so, the old witch. It is not right and I don't feel like walking." Mademoiselle chewed her lip and tears came into her eyes, making her servant frown; it was not like her mistress to be tearful and ill-natured.

"See that he gives you something nice, Mademoiselle, if he is to be so rude. A pretty necklace, maybe, or a nice little chateau."

"You are wickedly greedy, Arlette," Mademoiselle de Fontanges said, but she wiped her eyes and considered. "A carriage, perhaps?"

"The very thing! With matched grays."

"Eight," her mistress added, warming to the idea.

"Not one less. He will not appreciate you if you set yourself too cheap. That is always a danger," Arlette replied and began putting Mademoiselle's hair in order.

"Must it all go up again? I think I'd like to go to bed."

"It is impossible, Mademoiselle. Tonight is the ball. His Majesty will expect you."

Mademoiselle stared into the mirror and rubbed her cheeks. "I am so white, Arlette."

"Just a little, Mademoiselle. Is it, perhaps, that time?"

"Yes, perhaps. A little past?" She bit her lips again and looked nervously at her servant.

"Oh, Mademoiselle, if it should be something, why it were good fortune for you! Think how he dotes on his children. You know it's said that the children are the foundation of his great regard for Madame de Maintenon."

"She is a mere governess."

"Their mother, Mademoiselle, erred in showing her children too little concern. They've been the basis of the governess's good fortune. So cheer up. Mademoiselle, a child would be worth a chateau."

"My mother died of me." Mademoiselle's soft face was serious and frightened.

"But you are a great, strong girl! In the very peak of health.

And wouldn't His Majesty have the best care of you? The best doctors, comforts, everything? Oh, Mademoiselle, you must be cheerful and think of the future."

Mademoiselle smiled and hugged her maid. "You are right, Arlette, you are right. But still—is my hair straight?"

"Just the ribbons, Mademoiselle, and then a little color for your face?"

"Am I really pale?" The anxiety returned to her voice.

"No, no, Mademoiselle. The dancing will bring a blush. You are right. It is best to leave paint—"

Mademoiselle giggled. "For such as Madame de Maintenon and her friend Madame de Montespan."

"For such as need them, Mademoiselle." Arlette made a final adjustment of the ribbons and held up a little hand mirror. "There. His Majesty will be enchanted," she declared.

Mademoiselle smiled at her image and nodded. "A face for diamonds, Arlette, don't you think?"

"For diamonds, chateaux, whatever you desire, Mademoiselle."

Her mistress paused a moment. "And if I desire but him, Arlette?"

"Why, Mademoiselle, he doesn't expect that," her servant said sagely. "One loves Kings for their station, which is proper and patriotic, as they love their servants for obedience."

"Well, I am warned, Arlette," Mademoiselle said with a touch of melancholy.

Arlette curtsied. "A lady of the court always thinks of her future, Mademoiselle."

Her mistress's smile was a trifle sad.

While young Mademoiselle de Fontanges and her servant were making their preparations for the evening, His Majesty's two clever ladies sat shivering in a pale, gilded salon on the ground floor of the palace. The room was so cold that the windows were slicked with ice and the ladies' breath hung in the air. Although Claude kept summoning the lazy, overdressed footmen, the logs they brought did not dispel the chill. Françoise de Maintenon had to keep stopping her needlepoint to chafe her frozen fingers, and even a third shawl over her shoulders did not block the drafts blowing in around the large, elegant casements. Outside, the gardens were white with snow. Apollo and his nymphs wore fluffy white wigs, and Le Nôtre's parterres were black and white like an etching, but Françoise was too miserable to see their beauty. White was cold; her feet ached with it, and soon His Majesty would arrive, hearty and in high spirits, to mock their fire and fling open the windows, demanding fresh air. Even her iron self-control could not suppress a shudder.

"Shivering already, Françoise?" Athénaïs asked. "Why, the windows are sealed tight. Our lord and master will claim to be suffocating." Her laugh was a throaty gurgle.

Well, she is fat, Françoise thought, and feels it less, but in truth one marquise was as uncomfortable as the other. For the last half hour, Athénaïs had scarcely touched her beautiful edition of La Fontaine, because her hands grew numb whenever they strayed from under her shawl. Now, however, she consulted the clock, saw that His Majesty ought to have arrived, and sat up straight, letting the shawl slip from her bare shoulders. Claude rose instantly.

"A moment, Madame." She began straightening curls, retying ribbons.

"He is late," Madame de Montespan said.

"He will come."

"Yes." Her drawling voice was touched with malice. "Else he will miss Françoise who must report on my children."

Françoise bent over her sewing, refusing to be drawn, and

Claude exchanged a glance with her mistress, but Athénaïs was in no mood for restraint.

"You are a fool, Françoise."

"Why is that, Madame?" When she was annoyed, Françoise de Maintenon took refuge in the most perfect formality, the most precise diction.

"Why, you sew when you might reap."

"I shall have my reward." She held up her embroidery.

"That you might buy of any needlewoman. I mean in other things. You might reap glory."

"But I seek it not," she replied, sensing the drift of the conversation.

"Yet you have returned to court. One might purchase sanctity in solitude and peace in a convent."

"I had not that vocation."

Athénaïs laughed. "There are few 'vocations' for women."

"That is too true."

"Having failed one—few others are open."

Françoise returned to her needlework.

"Why do you not sleep with him?" Athénaïs asked boldly. "Ah, how you blush! Your blood betrays you, Madame."

"If it did, you would have no need to urge such a vulgar course on me," the governess said tartly.

"You are too cool, Françoise. Yet think of the advantages. Who bears the greater reputation—a governess or the royal mistress?"

Françoise protested, but Athénaïs ignored her. "My perfume, Claude. And you are unkind. His heart has shifted. You would but complete the trio. I am mistress in name; that blonde strumpet, Fontanges, in fact, and you"—Athénaïs hesitated and narrowed her eyes—"in the heart. In the heart, Madame."

"Do not distress yourself; it will not be."

"No?" She took the perfume from Claude and applied the scent liberally to her shoulders, hair and wrists. The heavy smell of roses and musk mingled with the odor of burning logs. "Are there more cakes?" she asked.

"A few, Madame."

"I'll have some. Françoise, for you?"

"No thank you."

"How abstemious you are." She looked over the cakes decorated with pink and yellow icing, selecting two. "The tisane? Is it prepared for His Majesty?" She gave Claude a meaningful look.

"I will fix it, Madame."

"If he comes." She crumbled a cake to bits at the thought. Now Françoise glanced at the clock. He was late. Was it possible that La Fontanges might come seriously into favor—and what would that mean for her charges? Surely the Duc du Maine was safe! His father's devotion could scarcely be more obvious, and yet—she stuck her needle too vigorously through the canvas and pricked her finger, the blood welling up, round and bright as a tiny ruby. She would regret Mademoiselle de Fontanges's triumph for the girl disliked her, fearing clever women almost above all else; Athénaïs, despite faults and tempers, was bound to her permanently by the children.

"You are thoughtful, Françoise. Perhaps you will change your mind and betray me at the last," Athénaïs remarked, knowing as she spoke that this was uncalled for and melodramatic. Lately, she seemed less and less able to curb her tongue, but he was late; the salon was freezing; she was too fat, her perfume would be considered too strong. And Françoise was too moral, too self-righteous, and even Claude since the other night was too—too whatever. Athénaïs could feel the anger growing. She had begun to regard it as something separate from her personality. It was not her temper any longer, but an impersonal force, surprising in its virulence, that had chosen her for residence. She had had enough. He had asked too much. She had gone too far in attempting to satisfy him.

Françoise was protesting, her voice a controlled, well-modulated murmur, when someone scratched at the door. Claude answered, spoke to the valet outside, then went to Françoise. "A message from your household, Madame."

"Have him enter."

The man brought a letter which she read, then refolded. She turned to Athénaïs. "Please make my excuses and regrets to His Majesty. My confessor has arrived unexpectedly. He has made a long trip in this weather."

"Of course."

"I will return if possible."

"Please, do not trouble. I will send for you—if it is convenient." Athénaïs laughed to see Françoise blush, but after the governess was gone, she was bored and a little worried: lately His Majesty's visits had been better when Françoise was present. With a shiver, Athénaïs snuggled into her shawl, tipping her head to consider the nymphs, horses and cherubs cavorting through the clouds on the painted ceiling: not one of Le Brun's best designs. Perhaps she should ask His Majesty to order it redone in warmer colors. She was tired of these timid pastels, so cool, so polite. Then she stretched out her fingers, admiring the ring on her hand and turning it round and round reflectively. It was a sign when even Françoise was worried, and she was, despite that pious serenity. Better her than La Fontanges? She wasn't sure. He would leave a fool. Would he leave Françoise? No! It was all unthinkable. Surely this would work. She had risked her soul— was that not enough? The ring reflected darting red lights like the fires of Hell. She had paid; he would come. But despite this confidence, the Marquise now found herself genuinely regretting the failure of her niece, Mademoiselle de Nevers. Mademoiselle, at least, was in the family, the family for whom Athénaïs had labored, on whom she had poured such bounties as the Captain-Generalty of the Galleys, the Governorship of Champagne, the tobacco dues of the capital—though, in fact, her sister, Madame de Thianges, had earned those herself by little afternoons now and again with the King. Little afternoons—Athénaïs looked at the clock. An hour late! She had just decided he would not come when she heard the familiar steps in the hallway and the bustle of his attendants.

"Madame, it is the King."

Athénaïs threw off her shawl as she rose.

"Madame, good afternoon." The heavy velvet hat, drenched in plumes, made a sweeping arc.

"Sire."

The King's black eyes ran over the salon, seeking Françoise, then returned to her face. He smiled. "You are alone, Madame? In all this snow?"

"It is so cold, Sire," Athénaïs teased, "none dare even cross the corridor. I am as deserted as in the wastes of Tartary."

"I had thought your friend more loyal."

He did miss her, Athénaïs realized, and she felt her neck stiffen. "Madame de Maintenon was called away. Her confessor arrived, and she feared to have him waste his journey."

"A warm faith."

"Today, most suitable and necessary." Without the shawl, Athénaïs was freezing, but she could not waste her shoulders: they were the only place her extra weight was at all becoming.

His Majesty went to look out at his gardens, then he opened a window, bringing flakes of snow whirling into the room. He was pleased and restless. When he turned to look at her again, the Marquise saw that his eyes were secret and complacent. She felt a twinge of jealousy, but went and stood next to him, her arm entwined in his. "A magnificent vista," she remarked. Was there some unfamiliar scent? Could he possibly have visited La Fontanges?

His voice interrupted. "—most beautiful now."

"More beautiful than the summer, Sire?"

"I spoke of Le Nôtre," he said, reproaching her inattention. "But I understand his view. It is his specialty, after all. Now one sees the logic of the garden, the repetition and permutation of pattern. I had not thought until I met Le Nôtre that gardening might be susceptible to genius."

"Is there not a kind of genius in each art?"

The King was thoughtful. "I think, Madame, that may be true, but only in the most advanced civilizations. It is our wealth and refinement which permit Le Nôtre to exercise his art to the fullest."

"Then," said Athénaïs, "all depends on the wisdom of the sovereign, from whose presiding genius all else flows." But she looked so melancholy as she said this that the compliment was rather spoiled. The King drew away from the window and sat down.

"Did you walk in the park today, Sire?"

"No. The courtiers complained so of the cold, I had not the heart."

"I wondered—you are so late."

"I was delayed." He could sit like a statue, immobile. And he could hide his feelings, every one. Athénaïs folded her arms.

"Petitions?" she asked.

"A few."

A woman? she wanted to ask, but bit her tongue. "Will you have some tisane, Sire?"

"A little, thank you. My ministers make me thirsty."

Madame de Montespan signaled her maid. The powder was in the other room where Claude would infuse it in the hot water. She could imagine the white crystals separating, floating, dissolving. Claude said the priests had called up demons, but she had not let her tell more. Athénaïs sat still and watchful as though she held a powerful hand at cards. Everything depends on this, she thought. Everything. Her tongue was thick. I am growing as stupid as young Fontanges, she thought, and can make no conversation. But what to say? I have sold my soul for you? I despise your vulgar infidelities? Instead, she said, "I am tired of this ceiling."

The King looked up. "Le Brun thought it very suitable."

"One changes," Athénaïs said negligently. "What pleases once, grows boring on acquaintance."

"They are the horses of the sun," he said, putting them thus under protection.

"But so pale," Athénaïs protested. "That is a weak and sickly sun, a spring sun, young and immature. The sun in splendor requires stronger tints."

She hints that I grow older, the King thought. And this to cover her own age. He remembered the pale tints Mademoiselle de Fontanges affected, and her skin, almost silvery against the gray, suppressed radiance of the winter sky. "I shall see."

Claude brought the tisane, two cups and the pot. The King broke a bit off a biscuit, but indicated he was not ready to drink. Athénaïs smiled and leaned back in her chair. Pray God there was no taste. "I should like reds and deep purples," she said, looking up at the fresco. "And draperies the color of aubergines."

"Imperial colors."

Something in his tone. "If it pleases you not—" She shrugged and poured the tea.

"Le Brun is busy with the designs for Marly." This was his

new chateau. Already Versailles was beginning to weigh on him. He'd drawn all the nobles there and now he would, himself, escape.

"I have not seen the plans." Meaning: you have not bothered to share them with me.

"It will be charming."

"Perhaps we shall see it in the spring."

His Majesty picked up his cup, set it down. "We will take the carriages tomorrow if the snow stops," he said. "I will show you the site. An outing would be good. The courtiers are bored."

"You will take the court?"

"Madame, such jealousy if I were to ride out alone with you!"

"Better one to suffer such pangs than many?"

He had raised the cup to his lips, but this reproach made him set it down again untasted. "Madame," he said patiently, "one lives in public and for others."

The Marquise's smile was thin and bitter. "Once you laughed at them. Once they trembled to walk beneath our windows lest we be disturbed. A great king, Sire, can be indifferent."

"Madame, do not attempt to school me in my duties."

"Then, Sire, do not lie to me." Her eyes grew hot; she could feel anger as a tangible thing loose in her veins. Claude looked at her, trying to catch her eye, but it was too late. Something in his manner, the faint scent on his embroidered coat, the shadow of satisfaction in his eyes had told her too much.

"What do you mean, Madame?"

"You have come from her bed."

The King set down his cup carefully.

"I am sick of the humiliation of my position." Her voice was low and strained. "A great lady would be different—the pursuit of royalty is, after all, the sport of courtiers—but a mere girl . . ."

"Madame, you forget yourself."

"No, Sire, it is you who forget yourself—and me." The anger burst forth and she jumped up, rattling the pot as her skirts tipped the little tea table. "You forget our years together, and your years, too, to run after such a child. A girl more suitable for a son than a father."

"Madame!"

"Speak to me not in such a manner," Athénaïs cried. "I was more than that to you. Who knows you as I know you? Did you not beg me once to love you as a man, disregarding rank? I did so. Now do not assume so imperial a manner. I know it not. I have given you what you asked for and more. Our children are healthy and clever. My blood is good and I will bow to no man!" Athénaïs put her hand to her mouth and felt the tears running down her face.

"Calm yourself," the King said, rising and going to her side. "You make us both miserable with these scenes. You will kill the friendship that has lasted so long." He laid his hand on her shoulder, putting aside with an effort of will, how great she did not suspect, his grand and by now habitual manner. But a perfume lingered in the thick froth of lace at his sleeves, and Athénaïs would not be calmed.

"You have been with that little whore. And now you come to me." She whirled from the King and dashed the cups and the teapot to the floor, the fatal drink dripping down the furniture and staining the hem of her gown. "It is beyond bearing! I will not endure it!"

At the red edge of her anger, she heard the King's smooth and serious voice, commending her to Claude as though she were some madwoman, then felt her servant's thin, strong arms about her shoulders. Athénaïs tossed her head, jammed her elbows against Claude's breast and struggled to get up. The door of the salon opened and closed.

"Let me go! Let me go, you stupid cow!"

"So you can spoil things further? You are mad with self-will."

"Do you hear me? You will be gone from my service! Let me go!"

Claude's face was close to hers. She could see her maid's features pinched with anger, the whiteness around her mouth, the spatter of thin blood vessels in her eyes.

"You dare not defend him! His conduct is infamous. It is not princely—I carry the blood of Spanish kings as well as he. Let me go!"

"He has left others," Claude said as she loosened her grip.

Athénaïs sat back on her heels. "How dare you remind me? I could have cast that child of yours to the dogs, but I did not."

"Madame, you dared not."

Athénaïs struck her so hard that a little blood trickled from the corner of her mouth, but Claude did not move. "When you begged me to try to save you, Madame, I went. I went as a friend, for no mistress on earth could order such."

Athénaïs turned away, her proud face set, and Claude jumped to her feet and left the room. A moment later, she returned to kneel at the fire.

"What are you doing? What are you doing?" Athénaïs flew at her, but it was too late. The packets of Galet's powders, sanctified and demon-blessed, were already shriveling in the flames, their deadly white crystals sifting over the coals. The Marquise reached into the fire, cried out, reached again, before Claude grabbed her shoulders and thrust her away from the flames. For a moment, the two women lay in a confused heap on the floor, entangled in their skirts and petticoats, then Athénaïs gave a low cry and put her burned fingers to her mouth. Claude sat up without a sound and, after a moment, took her weeping mistress into her arms.

XIII

The chamber was full of ladies, their skirts and petticoats as bright and delicate as flowers unfolding. Around them squeezed maids and footmen and little pages bearing messages, cups of tea, plates of fancy cakes. Several small dogs quarreled under a table, while others sheltered in the folds of their mistresses' dresses or slept on unoccupied cushions, and the room smelled of dog, of perfume and lilies. But though the women spoke animatedly of dress and sermons, games of chance and love, the spring days, new jewels and current gossip, they did not know the very latest news. That information only the King knew along with the great ministers, Colbert and Louvois, Lieutenant Nicolas de La Reynie, chief of the Paris police, and a couple of alert valets and footmen, one of whom whispered it in the ear of Claude des Oeillets. Claude, fortunately, seldom lost her composure. When she entered the room where Madame de Montespan was chatting with her sister-in-law, Madame de Vivonne, she wore a mask of cool indifference. She curtsied to the gathering and sat down close to her mistress, whose teasing laugh rippled like a bird song. Undeterred by this interruption, Madame de Vivonne returned to her theme: her husband's toil with the galleys and his need for money.

"You must confess," Madame de Vivonne began, "that—"

"Madame, I do. I do confess. And despite my sins, I am allowed absolution."

"Do not joke," her sister-in-law exclaimed.

"But my dear, even the church allows me rest from its demands. I am absolved, forgiven. I cease to be harried, even by such energetic priests as the great Bossuet. But my brother, Madame, my brother is without pity. His rule is strict, his demands unceasing. I shall never be absolved by him!"

Madame de Vivonne's pretty features drooped into a frown. Athénaïs laughed. "You must become my angel instead of his. And plead for my rest before his pocket."

"You jest cruelly."

Madame smiled. She knew of Madame de Vivonne's ambitions to replace her with the King. "A weapon gentle enough, when one considers how I am beset for favors and"—she paused; watching her sister-in-law's eyes—"by rivals." Then she rose, having decided she would rather talk to Françoise, who, though a greater danger than the transparent Madame de Vivonne, was much more amusing.

At once Claude appeared at her side. "A ribbon undone, Madame." As she touched the thick curls, she whispered, "Something serious has happened."

Athénaïs took a deep breath and glanced around the room as if bored by her servant's ministrations, before asking, "What?"

"It is La Voisin, Madame. She has been arrested with her daughter, the Abbé and several other fortune-tellers."

For an instant there was silence in the room, so that the Marquise's first horrified reaction was that the whole crowd heard and knew her distress. Then the dull thunder of her heart reassured her: it was just the shock; the ladies talked on, a dog whined, the pages' hard shoes clattered over the marble floor. "We must leave at once," she said without thinking. But that was right. The room was unbearable; the women, unendurable. "This moment," she said to Claude. "I cannot remain here. Call the carriage at once."

"Of course, Madame."

The Marquise inclined her head to the others, who had heard the word "carriage" and were already wondering why and where and to what purpose. The instant Madame de Montespan left, the speculations would begin: she had gone to Clagny, to Paris, to a retreat, to the devil, and she was driven by those idle tongues as by the lash. Now, she fled the snickers behind the fans, the courtiers rising for another, the falling off in compliments, the indifference in the chambers as she passed through. Her pride was mortified. To have risked so much and to be discovered! They would laugh. Then they would sneer.

"Faster!" she screamed. "Faster, faster!"

"The carriage will overturn, Madame." Claude braced herself against the side of the swaying vehicle.

"I care not. They are cowards, all of them, and too tender of the horses."

Claude did not answer, but fixed her hard, appraising eyes on the Marquise. She was calculating whether her mistress could endure disaster. And what her own plan ought to be.

"You care nothing for me!" Athénaïs burst out. She hurled down her fan and lifted her bejeweled hands in despair.

"You tell me nothing." Claude was cold with resentment.

"I cannot stay at court. I cannot."

"Very well, you might have gone to Clagny."

"His Majesty would have sent after me." The Marquise wiped her eyes. "He did as much for Louise, did he not?"

"That was quite different," Claude said. "She had been replaced. You—"

"I! I have been replaced by two. Which at some point will give me satisfaction. When I am old." She gave a nervous, angry laugh.

"You surrender too soon," Claude said. She did not like this despairing mood. They would need all their wits and courage, and Madame, all her skill.

"Too soon? Too late! I had kept my soul if I had resigned myself earlier. And now——" She bit one of her jeweled knuckles and wiped the tears pouring down her cheeks.

"Then why are we going to Paris?" If Claude was to be blamed, she would at least be wicked.

"There are others. La Voison isn't the only one. Galet's powders are famous. We will see him ourselves. We will——but I cannot bear it!" she cried. "Have them go faster!" And she stamped on the floor and screamed out the window so that the driver cracked his whip and the fine matched bays leaped forward at a gallop, a pace they maintained until a muddy grade outside the city where, sunk in mud to their fetlocks, the weary animals slowed to a walk.

"We are near, Madame."

The lanterns were lit, and the flickering orange light in the carriage sank into the rich colors of Madame's cloak. The carriage halted, then lurched forward again as the footmen jumped down to lead the horses up the slope.

"You will see them all," Athénaïs ordered. "Every one. You will question them. Someone must sell those powders. They must!" Whenever she thought of the powders, the King or the future, her heart resumed its deafening thump, obliterating the sounds around her. This is what it is like to die, she thought. "What?" she asked. "What did you say?"

Claude spoke cautiously, knowing her mistress's deeper fears. "She will be discreet, Madame. They will get nothing from La Voisin."

Athénaïs twisted her rings. "Do not deceive yourself. She has sold everything else. She will sell us too. Unless we can be sure of the King, we are finished." She looked angrily out the window. "What are they doing? We should have reached Paris an hour ago!" The footmen in reply murmured about the mud. The Marquise flung herself back against the seats and tapped her foot restlessly. "Do you know the hour?"

"It was striking eight when we passed the Carmelites, Madame."

"The saints assist us! Nothing will be done until tomorrow. We are lost! His Majesty will notice my absence. We will need excuses, lies. How I loathe all this when I am so weary of his grandeur, his infidelities, his arrogance. To risk so much for such a man corrodes my soul." She wept the rest of the way into the city, but her eyes were dry by the time they reached her residence. There was nothing ready, neither dinner nor fires, because no one had alerted the servants, but Madame was indifferent. She withdrew to her chamber, ordered brandy, and left Claude to deal with the housekeeping.

In the morning, the Marquise's mood was changed entirely. She slept late, dawdled over her chocolate, had her hair changed a dozen times. Now she thought it unwise to contact any of La Voisin's associates. Claude was told, instead, to call in the tailor, Gautier, for Madame would have a new dress, something splendid. The morning was spent afloat on a gorgeous sea of deep blue-and-green satin flashed with white lace like sea foam, through which the tailor and his assistants waded with tapes and pins and matching ribbons. The embroidery promised was exquisite, a peacock's tail of silvers, golds and purples, the eyes of the feathers to be studded with jewels. There must be a fan to match, so the fan maker was sent for and the whole process begun again, with the tradesmen in ecstasies to catch the tide of her extravagance. Finally they left, orders and swatches of cloth catalogued, sample ribbons and laces and beads packed. A few stray feathers and scraps littered the floor of the chamber, and Claude was about to call in a servant to make it tidy when Madame stopped her.

"Order my carriage," she said in the peremptory voice of a woman who has just made up her mind and now fears hesitation.

"Very good, Madame." Claude waited to hear their destination.

"Well? Why are you hesitating?"

"Where are we to go?"

"I won't stay here," the Marquise exclaimed by way of explanation. "Order the carriage and help me change."

A footman was dispatched to the stable, and Athénaïs had Claude pull out her traveling clothes, but it proved more difficult than usual to satisfy her. She wanted nothing too bright, or too plain either, and one costume was rejected as too hot for the spring, another as too thin for the chill. The Marquise swore and stamped her feet and would have rent every thread of her wardrobe if her servant's cooler head had not prevailed. Then, when the clothes finally suited, when the horses were harnessed, the coach and coachmen waiting, her hair was pronounced horrible and had to be taken down and redone.

Claude remained in command of herself. "Are we to return to the palace, Madame?" she asked as she straightened the bunches of curls.

Athénaïs's bright eyes were defiant. "No."

Her servant shrugged, thinking it was childish of the Marquise to make such a mystery. This was to tease her, or to punish her, perhaps, for the failure of their dealings with La Voisin. Claude said no more, and the silence soon set Madame's long fingernails tap-tapping on the top of her dressing table. Now and again, the women's angry, nervous glances intersected in the mirror and Claude tied up the final ribbons more sharply than usual. "I must give orders to the coachman," she said.

The Marquise rose and waited for her dark velvet cloak. "North," she said as Claude arranged it over her shoulders. "We will go north. Let him take the rue Saint-Antoine."

Claude gave her a look.

"But I can trust no one here!" Madame exclaimed. "We must find Galet, himself, for the powders. Lieutenant Reynie may have arrested half Paris by this time. And to be compromised now— when La Voisin has been arrested—would be to be compromised forever! It must not be risked."

"You might remain, Madame, and avoid risk altogether," Claude suggested, but the Marquise would take no notice. She was restless, she must travel. Paris was unendurable. In the carriage, she wrapped herself in her cape and sat without a word until they were beyond the city walls. Then, as they approached the church of Saint-Antoine-in-the-Fields, she ordered the driver to stop. The brakes creaked, the horses blew their breath and shook their heads, the footmen jumped down into the road and stood by the doors. Claude rose from her seat, but the Marquise lifted her hand and shook her head. "Wait," she said and climbed out of the carriage to walk alone across the rutted ground to the small church.

With a sigh, Claude leaned her elbow on the window opening and looked out. At last the sun was breaking through the sodden clouds and the steaming, misty fields were touched with gold. She could hear water seeping into the ground and small larks and finches in the brush along the road. The coachman had gotten down to tend his horses, and the footmen now began stamping around, spotting their immaculate breeches and boots with country mud and telling lies about the female servants of their acquaintance. From the next field, a cottage chimney sent a faint smell of smoke and fat drifting into the carriage, and Claude thought of her childhood with the traveling players and of waking up in wagons just at dawn, surprised by new surroundings, new smells, new towns. Now that was a dream long past, just as the court, the service of a marquise, a child by the King, would have seemed insubstantial fantasies to the player's daughter who slept in the straw amongst the props and costumes.

But her marquise, what was she doing? The shadows lengthened; the tired footmen dozed on the back of the carriage, and Claude roused herself from near sleep to see her dark-clad mistress gliding back from the church. "Madame is coming," she called to the driver, and the attendants sprang to open the door.

Athénaïs resumed her seat without a word. The carriage rolled north again, and Claude began to consider practical matters: lodging for Madame, more clothes. The air cooled as evening approached, and the fields were saturated with a green that lay deeper than emerald against the dark earth and the pale lavender of the sky. The evening star came out and rooks and crows flew over the trees. "We must stop," Madame remarked.

"But there is no inn, Madame, nor any chateau where we can spend the night."

"I have slept out," the Marquise said easily. "Have I not gone to wars with my king?"

"The horses must have food, Madame—if we are to go north as far as Galet's village."

"I had intended that," she replied softly.

"And now, Madame?"

She did not answer.

"Did you seek advice, Madame, of the priest at Saint-Antoine-in-the-Fields?"

The Marquise sighed, thinking of the little low, damp church

with its thick walls and somber glass. The priest behind the
screen had been half deaf and unable to make much sense of her
confession. "What advice could he give me?" she asked. "He
knows not the court."

"Yet he speaks for the Church," Claude said cautiously, although privately she agreed with the Marquise.

"I had forgotten myself," Madame said. "Is it not His Majesty's
great genius that we forget our blood, our greatness, in the splendor of his court? I was faithful to him. I think there is no other
man I could have said that of. I have stained my hands for him."
She looked thoughtfully out at the twilight. "But to commit
crimes for one's sovereign may not be so very evil. The priests
have no reply to great warriors."

"No, Madame, lest they die in their churches," Claude said
cynically.

Athénaïs's tone continued reflective. "It is less crime than despair we must fear, the despair of losing our honor."

"That you will never do, Madame."

The Marquise nodded, then ordered the carriage halted. When
the women stepped out onto the verge, the sun was very low and
a little hill was enough to cast all the road in shadow. Athénaïs
walked into a field, and, after instructing the coachman to turn
the carriage around, Claude followed though the ground was low
and water stood in every rut and depression. Claude lifted her
trailing skirts and picked her way, but the Marquise strode on as
unconcerned as if she walked the paths at Versailles. When they
were out of earshot of the carriage, she stopped, her face severe.
"There is no hope," she said.

Claude wished to protest, to comfort, but a glance at the Marquise's face prevented her.

"Even with Galet," her mistress continued.

"Madame Voisin's arrest—"

"Exactly. There will be hints, insinuations, if not worse. We cannot withstand them as well as the interest in La Fontanges—and Françoise de Maintenon."

"That is not serious, Madame."

"It is over, though, for me. I had half thought to go to Galet's—I had also thought to go to some provincial convent. That would have caused a stir, would it not?"

"But then, Madame?"

"Yes, but then I could not have returned." Madame gave a dry laugh, short as a cough. "He has clipped all their wings—all the great lords' feathers. What are my kinsmen now but for my position, my bounty?"

"Then is this to be endured, Madame?"

The Marquise's eyes grew bright and hard as if she would lose her temper. "My brother wearies me with his demands. I will not regret his losses."

Claude knew there was no answer to this and remained silent.

"Remember," Madame said in a strange low voice, "I have had no direct contact with La Voisin—ever."

"But the Abbé, Madame? His name was once Dubuisson. He knew your sister."

The Marquise's eyes narrowed. "That was many years ago with the Comtesse at her chateau. My sister must take the blame for attempting to dislodge me."

"As you say, Madame."

"It is only you who have seen them," the Marquise said thoughtfully.

"Masked," Claude said, although the dampness of the early spring night now became a chill. There was a pause.

"If once you concede contacts with them, we are ruined. Both of us."

"I shall deny all, Madame, save for having my hand read. A small concession to conceal—"

"Yes, that is good. But can you maintain that? Else you must leave now. There would be plenty of money."

"I would prefer to stay, Madame. My presence of mind has not failed me yet."

The Marquise looked at her, then nodded and looked away. "You are protected by the child, in any case." She drew her cloak more tightly about her and shivered a little in the wind. "I plan to leave him." Her eyes were fixed on the flat, distant horizon.

"He will object."

"We will quarrel. I will leave. We will see what he thinks will bring me back to shield that little trollop, Fontanges. We will see." The Marquise stood straight, her face still and hard like one of her warrior ancestors, then she walked over to the waiting coach and horses.

Never did Athénaïs de Montespan dress with more care than she did the following afternoon at Clagny. Gautier and his assistants had worked round the clock for two nights straight to finish her new outfit and even that connoisseur, Claude, was ravished by the effect. "It is splendid! Splendid, Madame."

"Yes, we might pay Gautier this time and astonish him." She turned and checked the ruffling of the back in her mirror. "It is worth a dowry." Madame smoothed her skirts and adjusted her lace. Since her return, she had lost some of the tranquil stoicism she had found on the road north of Paris, and Claude could tell that she was nervous, perhaps even a little frightened.

"The effect is perfect. Such a gown has not been seen."

"He will appreciate it. But then, His Majesty expects his servants to die in splendor. It is right. I could not leave in any mean, defeated way."

"No, Madame."

The Marquise turned again, the dress shimmering like silver fire in the glass. She opened and closed her fan, touched her diamonds and nodded. Claude opened the door of the chamber and stood aside to let her pass down the stair to her carriage.

Of course, in their rooms at the palace, all had to be gone over again: every feather, every jewel, every ribbon. At last, the Marquise was seated in her salon with a cup of herb tea. "He will come," Claude said but it was a question.

"He will come," the Marquise repeated complacently. "No woman has left him in a dozen years. He will not be able to resist." She snapped open her fan and felt the anger inside her coil a little tighter.

Then the steps in the corridor, the self-important herald, the King's jeweled cane tapping the inlaid floors; there were greetings, ornate and allusive.

"The palace has been empty," His Majesty said, but his eyes were cool.

"As my heart, Sire." She smiled a tempting, wicked smile and flicked the painted fan that spread the warm breath of her perfume.

"There was no need for you to leave."

"On the contrary. Emptiness of heart drove me forth. A time to consider, Sire, is often invaluable."

The King watched her warily. He knew she was always challenging, always pushing to the thin edge of defiance. Once that had been exciting, proof her love was uncoerced, uncalculated. But as dignity had grown habitual, he had come to prefer more orderly companions—and women who inspired more manageable emotions. "People in our positions, Madame, must meditate among the crowd."

"Alas, Sire, few have your gravity or self-control." She did not smile. Perfect truth was a compliment needing no embellishment.

The King watched her shoulders paved with diamonds and wondered why he still found her attractive. It was no longer her person—that was quite shaded by the beauties of young Mademoiselle de Fontanges. Nor, Lord knew, was it her nature—which was bitter, unpredictable and satiric . . .

"Had I a vocation like my sister, I would withdraw from the world," she said.

He looked at her directly and sternly. "I would not approve."

The Marquise moved her fan. She was aware of flirting with both renunciation and danger and wondered if her predecessor, Louise, had felt this way, had flirted with the religious life as with an importunate, and perhaps sinister, suitor. "Is not my soul of moment, Sire? For years, my friend, Françoise de Maintenon, has sought to reawaken my religious duty. It seems her great passion," she interpolated drily. "Now if I take her advice, would I be wrong?"

His lips twitched. "Despite your friend's hopes, you have no calling, Madame, that would justify your withdrawal."

"No, that is true." Her eyes, half closed, gave her face a dreamy, sensual expression. "Yet ladies sometimes withdraw . . ." She paused, one white hand on her bodice. "My heart, Sire, has a defect," she said.

"Surely not, Madame! My physicians are at your command."

She laughed at his ready generosity. "This they cannot cure. Only one man can cure this heart."

His Majesty rose and began to pace slowly back and forth. "We quarrel too often for friends," he remarked. He was reflective, regretful.

Such tepid gifts were not for Athénaïs. "And know too much for lovers?"

This disconcerted him, though he concealed it well, as always, and the Marquise laughed and stood up, her peacock dress unfolding. She felt her old power to unsettle, the ability to break through the rituals of the court with the force of her personality. She was tempted by the thought of another chance, but she recognized this hope as her chief enemy. "Your Majesty, I tell you I would withdraw, for what made the court a pleasure to me has been withdrawn."

"You have duties, obligations. The children are here." In truth, now he did not want her to go. He sensed he would lose something with her gone, something, that is, beyond the aggravation of her temper and pride. When he had loved her, he had done mad things. He looked at her amazing dress—no doubt she'd had it made just for this meeting—and remembered his own extravagances: chateaux, jewels, fetes, orange trees in silver tubs for Clagny, a certain bank of moss beside the Porcelain Trianon . . . He had been man as well as king. Her next words gave him pain.

"The children have Françoise de Maintenon and their other attendants and need me not."

"It is not fitting." He lifted his head proudly, his eyes stern. The subject was closed, finished. When he set his face thus, the courtiers trembled and withdrew. It always surprised him a little that she was different.

"Well, Sire," Athénaïs said, "Louise de La Vallière wept, but I will not. She remained to shield me, but you must know I will never remain to draw scandal from my successor." Her fan swished back and forth like the tail of an angry cat.

"Madame, I will manage my court as I see fit." He was close to her, his stony face flushed, his fist tight on his cane.

Her smile was quick, malicious. To anger him was a kind of triumph in itself, stimulating, if dangerous. "When you loved me," she explained, "then I was frightened lest I lose your regard. Your indifference makes me brave, Sire."

"Rather, Madame, your own indifference makes you impertinent."

"Our seven children give me the right to speak plainly, Sire."

"You spoke plainly before you had any child of mine, Madame."

She laughed aloud. "That I concede. You see, I am not so changed."

There was, he thought, some truth in that, though her mirror should have told her much was different.

She touched his face lightly, her fingers warm, her jewels cool against his skin. I have ceased to want her, the King thought, and still I have regrets. Her eyes, close to his, seemed as dark as his own, and his head began to hurt, back behind his eyes, although his heart was racing. He recognized she was danger, disorder, extravagance, and as he bent to kiss her, he held her so fiercely that her jewels marked his hands and her white back. Yet he did not want her. His head ached. He could not have said why his eyes were sad when he raised his lips nor why the scorn in her face made him feel not anger but regret.

"You are afraid," she whispered. Or had she spoken at all?

"Madame, I am tired. I have no appetite for quarrels."

"Mademoiselle de Fontanges has exhausted you," the Marquise said. "I had not thought she had such passion in her."

"Do not speak in such a manner—or seventy children would not be enough to excuse your folly."

The Marquise did not flinch. Her light hand moved from where it rested on his shoulder to touch his cheek. For a moment he thought he would turn and stamp angrily from her room. The whisper came again. Yes, she had spoken; he could feel her breath soft against his lips. "I would say farewell in a better manner, Sire."

"You will remain."

Her smile was sensual but ambiguous. Had she spoken again, she could have told him that she had never wanted him with less calculation or with so scant an eye to the future. She had saved a rich gift for last, but it was a parting gift. He must take it on those terms.

"You will remain at court," he repeated. She must consent; he could not bear her rebellion. Yet his senses stirred as if nervous within the safety of his grandeur, his dignity.

"Yet you want me not."

"You will stay," he said, but his voice was soft. The Marquise drew closer; like a dancer's, her body was mistress of a thousand subtle messages, but when he took hold of her shoulders and kissed her, she made no answer, no assent, no promise. Over her shoulder, he saw Claude still working primly on her sewing. "Madame, we will retire," the King whispered.

Her lips grazed his cheek, his neck, before she turned toward her chamber.

"I fear, Sire, that I must call my servant," she said when the door was closed. In explanation, she touched the ornate bodice, tight as her skin and cunningly fastened with secret ties and laces.

The King traced the line of the heavy embroidery with a curious finger. "It is not necessary." He dropped his cane abruptly and seizing her around the waist, half lifted, half pushed her onto the blue satin covers of the bed. The Marquise laughed as he fell on top of her.

"This is magnificent. An extravagance worthy of you, Madame," he whispered.

"Yes, yes, it is fitting!" She felt suddenly that she might weep—but with rage, or sorrow or the poignancy of desire she could not tell.

The King took off some of his rings and began dropping them onto her breast. "I have given you fortunes, fortunes," he whispered. "I have made you splendid. Did you ever love me, when you have never obeyed me?" She had never seen him more ardent or troubled as now in the death throes of his great passion for her. "Did you?" he demanded. His hands rumpled her heavy skirts and marred the fine metallic embroidery of the bodice. "Have you loved me?"

"I have loved you as a man. Did you not always wish to be king?" It was anger she felt, rage at his demands, his selfishness. "Even here," she whispered, "you wish only to be king."

"And is this not kingly?" The fabric ripped under his eagerness with a thin, high sound, and Athénaïs groaned, for His Majesty's passion was always violent and short.

Then there was a little silence in which he heard his own breath and the Marquise's heart and the sound of horsemen in the court. Yes, it was spring at last and all the windows stood open. "You lead me into madness, Madame."

"I believe it not, Sire."

He lifted a torn fragment of her peacock embroidery and let it drop again as his answer.

"Yet you remain quite sane, Sire."

"And you, Madame? Are you quite sane and reasonable?"

"My madness, Sire, is of long standing."

He looked at her cautiously, sensing danger again. She was reckless and devious. "What is it you wish?"

"What I have asked."

"I have forbidden you. You must remain at court."

The Marquise sat up on her bed. "Then for my peace of mind, send away those who distress me."

"Madame—"

Her smile was wicked, yet resigned. "Mademoiselle de Fontanges is fit for a husband. Why not give her one? And Madame de Maintenon—likewise."

"You ask too much."

"And you ask too much of me—to stay."

The King rose and straightened his clothing, his face still. Now he was in the grip of his power as before of his senses. "I have ordered." He turned and walked sternly to the door.

"Yes, Your Majesty," The Marquise's voice was cold. "And you will see how I will obey." She jumped from the bed, sprang to the door and flung it open, then let him pass. "I have given you what you most wanted," she said in an undertone. "You will regret me when you are sated with the others."

He put on his hat and stood like a statue. "Madame, good day."

There were tears in her eyes, but as he started down the corridor she shouted to Claude, "Order my carriage!"

Beyond the door, the King stopped, touched the lace at his throat, then decided against risking his dignity. As he left the wing of the palace, he could hear Madame de Montespan's commands.

"Pack everything," she was crying. "Every single scrap. I shall leave! I shall leave the court forever."

XIV

"There really is no comparison," Madame Voisin said. Although her arrest had shaken her, she had not lost her society manners. As she spoke to Lieutenant Reynie, she sipped tisane from a fine china cup and emphasized her points with the wave of a lace handkerchief. Of course, the cell at the Chateau de Vincennes was not her usual setting. She spoke several times of her home, "her small retreat" as she phrased it, and complained of the difficulty of being away from it whenever there were questions she wished to evade.

The Lieutenant nodded. He had beautiful manners and, more important, patience. The cell high in the tower was dry and airy; if Madame knew other, less convenient accommodations existed, she gave no sign. A shrewd old bird, he thought as he examined her gray satin with its perfect white lace collar, her tasteful jewels, her furniture. There was even a mirror. He had not gone wrong; she would repay a good deal of time, whatever she might claim now.

"No, no," she continued. "Marie Bosse is the commonest sort of trafficker. Whatever you wanted, she'd try to supply, if you take my meaning, Monsieur."

"But your case, Madame Voisin—"

"My case!" She laid her hand over her heart. "Monsieur, you

take no thought of my sensibilities. My case! I would with more justice prosecute my enemies for slander. But my reputation stands. I take cover in my reputation and my friends." She paused before adding. "I have not inconsiderable friends who are in my debt."

Sly old witch, Reynie thought. "It might be good if some of these friends would speak for you."

"My ladies, Sir? Ladies of quality, remember. How could I call on my friends from this place? They trusted my discretion, Monsieur, as though I was their own mother."

Reynie ruffled his papers. "Had they reason to disown the connection, Madame?"

"No! I can deny that and deny again! I have explained. Since infancy—I was scarce out of my cradle, Monsieur, when my gifts were first known—I have had skill with the hand and all such arts. You will surely agree, Monsieur, that the art of discerning human character from the lines and the art of predicting the future from the hand are great gifts?"

"They seem much in demand in Paris."

"Yes, but there are so many charlatans about. You'd be a fool to trust your hand to the likes of Madame Bosse. That is my point. I gave my customers the benefit of genuine art and of my wisdom based on that art. A rare combination, I think you will agree, Sir."

"It is the rarity of the combination, Madame Voisin, that has brought you to the Chateau."

"I beg you, Sir, I beg to differ. It is the lies and libels and insinuations of a jealous, despicable enemy that have brought me here. I am persecuted by a most implacable fiend. In truth, Monsieur, seem I such a gypsy as might read your hand at the fair and pick your pocket afterwards?"

"Yet, Madame, your wealth of itself might raise certain little doubts."

Madame's plump face grew sharper. She really did have a very long, pointed nose, which, by its disharmony with the rest of her features, hinted at perhaps unpleasant complexities. "It is jealousy," she said, managing a sigh of resignation. "In all her days, Madame Bosse has had only one client of any distinction. She was a foreigner, of course, who could not be expected to recognize the levels of our Parisian society." La Voisin gave a little smile, as if out of pity.

"And who was this client?"

"A lady driven to dire extremity. I hesitate, Sir, to expose her sorrows."

"Madame," Reynie said sternly, "someone's sorrows will be exposed. That is how things stand. Yours or Madame Bosse's or this unknown lady's. It must be your choice."

"Do not upset yourself, my good Monsieur, you speak but the truth. We small people must be sacrificed for the mighty. Yes, it is our Christian duty, is it not?"

Reynie feared she might break into prayer, which was another of Madame Voisin's evasions and diversions. It had driven his deputy, Desgrez, quite beside himself. Reynie tapped the table softly with his pen and watched her eyes.

"Well, I'll tell you it was none other than a duchesse, Sir. The Duchesse de Bouillon, herself. A great lady, I am told. One of the nieces of Cardinal Mazarin."

Reynie stopped writing. "The Duchesse de Bouillon."

"As I live, Monsieur."

"And why does a duchesse seek out the likes of Madame Bosse?"

"Why, Sir, it is well known. It is only to such as Marie Bosse that one goes for evil things. A weapon picked up in the gutter,

Monsieur, is none the less deadly." She nodded sagely, sure of his attention, and allowed herself to be philosophic. "The arrangement of society, Monsieur, puts one and only one weapon at the disposal of dissatisfied wives. A great evil, most assuredly, but understandable. Would you not agree? In my work alone," she paused to sigh, "the tragedies I've heard. The advice of an angel could not solve some of the troubles, though, of course, I do my best to deserve my fee."

"Yes, yes," Reynie said impatiently, "but the Duchesse is a lady of the court and of the highest reputation. It passes belief that she would traffic with such as this Bosse woman. And"—his voice took on a sharper tone—"such tales do not bear far repeating without proof."

"Ah, Monsieur, forgive me. I thought you came seeking my knowledge. Of my own affairs, I have revealed everything of importance, but I believed you might like some insight into the nature of my accuser." Madame's face settled into a tight, hard expression and she added, "Ask La Bosse about the Duchesse and watch her well. You will see who is lying." Now her voice grew higher and shriller. "What are the charges against me? The word of such a woman. Well, I have given you the gossip about her. I see not how you can detain me longer, if it is but such a one against me."

"There is some truth in what you say. But, Madame Voisin, the Paris Police do not operate on gossip and innuendo. Your story will be checked—as Madame Bosse's was." He waited, and Madame Voisin moved uneasily in her chair and turned and refilled her cup. "We have also questioned the Abbé Lesage," he said.

Madame put down the cup and searched the Lieutenant's face to see if he was lying, then ran a weary hand across her forehead. "The poor Abbé," she said with only a faint rasp in her smooth and pious tone. "The poor Abbé. I was foolish with him. I think one can be as foolish for good reasons as for ill. Do you not agree? It was my piety," she muttered, hurrying on without waiting for the Lieutenant's opinion. "Yes, I took pity on him when he was lying in the galleys. Quite unjustly transported, I was assured, a case of mistaken identity. Well, I did what I could. When he was released, he came to me. What was I as a Christian to do? I took him in." She made a face to indicate her innocence and the extent to which she'd been deceived.

"He is not without certain skills, I believe."

"Skills? Schemes and tricks! But it was his sufferings, I do believe. May the saints forgive him, I believe it was his sufferings at the oar, Monsieur. We grow as we are treated. He has a vicious streak. None will deny it. It would have ended with him being put out of my house. But for pity, he'd have gone sooner. His head was affected, Monsieur, for he suffers from delusions. Many's the time he's believed himself back at his oar. Truly pitiful for any gentle mind to witness."

Reynie looked up from his notes. "I have seen the Abbé."

Madame Voisin shrugged. "Well then," she said without much conviction, "you know the manner of the man."

"So I do believe. In fact, Madame, his charges against you were so interesting that I have ordered him brought to your cell." At this, the Lieutenant rose and called to the jailor. A moment later Lesage, still in his clerical black but with his hands manacled, was brought into the cell. Despite his chains, he did not look much the worse for his misfortune, although he was missing his fine black wig. Without La Voisin's resources, the Abbé had been forced to pawn his possessions to secure the means to make prison life bearable, and now, when he saw Madame in a fine bright chamber, sitting on a red silk chair, he could scarcely conceal his fury. His thin, ill-shaven jaws clenched tight and he grew white about the nostrils.

"Abbé! My poor friend!" Madame Voisin exclaimed, rising all in a flutter. "We are ill met! I have just been speaking of you to the Lieutenant. Telling him of your tribulations and of your ill health since the galleys. The malice we have endured between us!"

"Shut up, you vicious cow! Don't listen to her! Not a word! She'll pour poison in your ears. Oh, she knows all the schemes! And to sit here, Madame! As you are, while I lie in filth below! Put her in chains and you'll hear a new story! A story of Madame Leferon perhaps, or Madame Dreux—both helped to profitable new estates by her aid. Yes, indeed. She hasn't told you that, has she?"

"Abbé!" Madame cried. "It is as I have told you, is it not, Lieutenant?" she asked in a plaintive voice, though she would rather have split Lesage's skull. "These meaningless furies, delusions, lies—all the fault of the galleys. Poor man, his sufferings—"

"This is a vile bitch," Lesage said, "who would kill before breakfast. Have you searched her house, particularly her—"

"Abbé, you do rant! A tisane, perhaps, to calm your nerves." Madame turned to the cups and pot, but the Abbé broke out into a stream of curses.

"I'd not touch a thing you prepared. Not a drop as I value my life!" He looked around the cell. "Why, you've the comforts of home here. Perhaps your little black chest, your private locked cabinet has come, too. Enough poison in it to kill this whole tower, there was."

"You know Madame's residence well, then?" Reynie asked mildly.

Lesage's jaws worked and his long, clever fingers touched his manacles. "I could tell you a thing or two about her. And the parliamentarians' wives. Dig in her garden, too. Oh, she had every device."

"The man is mad," Madame Voisin said, but she had grown very red. "I took him into my house, Monsieur, when he was in rags, crawling with ship lice. This is how I am repaid. By a man unfit to wear a priestly cassock, a man who even in the galleys managed all manner of schemes—even to counterfeiting. Ask if it is not true."

Lesage began to scream and rant like a madman, but almost at once he stopped and began counting on his fingers: "Madame Poulaillon, Madame Leferon, Madame Dreux, certain masked ladies—" Here even his recklessness failed him. He smiled at Madame Voisin and whispered maliciously, "Oh, I could tell much."

At the mention of the masked ladies, Madame Voisin had felt a pain around her heart. "Viper," she screamed, "whore's bastard! Can you believe this galley rat? He lies. May the saints witness. Now, I tell you, he is fit for the scaffold with his magic tricks." Lesage lunged forward at this, but Reynie and the jailor seized his chains.

"Yes," Madame fairly screamed. "Did you not kill pigeons and burn their hearts to secure my husband's death? The way he repaid my kindness, my hospitality, was to murder my husband. I had thought it was but nonsense. As a good Christian, Monsieur, I scorn all sorcery. I thought of it not! But now that I see his malice, I cannot doubt. He has murdered my husband, my poor Voisin, a harmless, gentle tailor—to secure power over a widow whom he could abuse."

This interpretation put Lesage beside himself with fury. "You whore, you lie. I never lived with her, nor killed her husband. More like she poisoned him herself, as she did so many others."

"You and Marie Bosse! You killed him between you. Oh, if you could see this low trash with a customer. You would believe, Lieutenant, you would have no doubts. And Madame Bosse—

how often have you wanted something 'special' and must go to her? How often? How often?"

Lesage began to swing his manacles wildly, and, as Madame seemed likely to take up weapons of her own, Reynie called for another jailor who cracked the priest on the head and hauled him off down the corridor. This was unpleasant, but the injury to the Lieutenant's dignity was soon repaid, for the ruin of the Abbé's hopes moved him to destroy La Voisin. He named names; she named others. There were charges and counter charges, and Reynie soon found himself in possession of the sordid conduit between the court and the gutter. La Voisin and her renegade priest were but two links in a chain that stretched from the most dismal and degraded to the glittering luminaries of the court. The latter soiled their hands with vice and crime in order to rise; the former, like the carrion beetle, carried away the rich corpse of honor to fatten off it in their secret places.

Reynie's reports grew long, for few of note had not dabbled in some folly—consultations over a horoscope, love potions, romantic advice or spells—and few lacked a spouse, rival or relative whose speedy passing would enhance the sum of human happiness. Spurred on by the lechery and idleness of the palace, the courtiers were frantic for more wealth, more freedom, more pleasure. Their moral decay made a dismal spectacle, but Reynie's superior, Louvois, was not squeamish—not, at least, until the names began to draw embarrassingly close to His Majesty. One morning, in the council chamber with the King and Colbert, he had to venture onto dangerous ground.

"You know, of course, Sire," Louvois said, clearing his throat softly, "that Lieutenant Reynie has pursued the matter of the poisons trade with the greatest diligence."

"You will commend Lieutenant Reynie. I am pleased. Have you the latest report?"

"Yes, Your Majesty, and I regret, I deeply regret, that a number of persons of the highest standing have been compromised. Reynie has questioned both the woman Voisin and the priest found at her house. As I have explained, their testimony has led to a number of other persons, so that evidence has been taken from several different sources." Louvois coughed again and the King's eyes strayed to the window. The sky was a clear, washed blue: this afternoon, he would hunt.

"The matter, as your Majesty realizes, has gone beyond the bourgeoisie, beyond such as Mesdames Leferon, Dreux—"

"They have been arrested, have they not?"

"Yes, Your Majesty. There were, of course, the usual complaints, protests—"

"To be sure. But we will have justice. No one is above the law. I have made that clear, Louvois."

"Your Majesty." Louvois bowed his head. "They will be dealt with. We cannot allow the members of Parliament or their kinsmen to flout the law. Your wisdom in setting up the special tribunal in the Arsenal will insure equality. But now, Sire, certain other names have arisen, and I thought it wise that you be informed before further arrests or interrogations." He extended Reynie's letter.

The King looked at his minister sharply, then ran his eyes down the letter. When he came to the names, he stopped and looked up. "He is sure?"

"I regret, Sire. The Comtesse de Soissons has been named by the priest Lesage as frequenting La Voisin. Her sister, the Duchesse de Bouillon, has most certainly dealt with poisoners. As for Madame de Vivonne—"

"Yes, yes." He sighed, put down the paper and looked out at the empty sky. Then he returned to the report and read the evidence carefully. "Madame de Vivonne," he said after a while, "has but been accused by this La Voisin, a most notorious woman."

"The evidence is still weak, Sire, but because she is related to Madame de Montespan and because of the affection you hold for Vivonne—"

"It was well to inform me. You will order Reynie to follow up this line of investigation immediately."

"Of course, Sire."

"The Duchesse de Bouillon and the Comtesse de Soissons are another matter."

"The evidence against the Comtesse is particularly strong, Your Majesty. The witnesses are unanimous and Reynie has, as you see, checked their evidence from other sources. It seems fairly certain that she made an attempt on her husband's life."

The King's hand tightened into a fist. "She is the niece of Mazarin. I owe the safety of my crown to that man and to the care of my mother."

Louvois bowed. The King's fidelity to the late cardinal was well known. It was also said there had been an affair between His Majesty and Olympe de Soissons. "It is a delicate matter, Your Majesty. Especially in view of the Comtesse's position as Superintendent of the Queen's Household."

The King's eyes again strayed to the window. Although he was used to difficult things and disagreeable decisions, he felt the weight of his responsibilities, of his power, even of his grandeur, in a way he had seldom felt since he was a young man. Since Cardinal Mazarin died and left him to rule by himself. "His niece," he repeated.

"Yes, Your Majesty."

The King's black eyes grew remote. Yes, they would hunt toward Marly, and he would spend some time afterwards with the plans for the new gardens there. He remembered that he had promised to show Madame de Montespan those plans before she left the court. That departure was very bad of her—especially when there was scandal and upset. It was important that she be there. He nodded his head decisively and looked at Colbert. "We will need some money," he said bluntly. "The Comtesse de Soissons must sell us her office as Superintendent. It is not proper that any person under such suspicions should serve the Queen."

"Yes, Your Majesty. I will make arrangements. But the Comtesse may be reluctant—"

"The Comtesse will not be reluctant. You will inform her of the charges against her. Say to her that I have broken my own rules to warn her because of her uncle—and our old friendship. She may stay to defend her honor or she may leave before the warrants are signed, but in either case she must sell her office." He folded his hands and stared back at his ministers. "You will purchase the office immediately. I have need of it."

"Yes, Your Majesty."

"I will be criticized for this," he said calmly. "I will be criticized justly."

"Your Majesty—" Louvois began to protest, but the King waved him silent.

"It is not proper. I have never wished to interfere with the workings of justice. It was to avoid the interference of lesser men that I ordered these cases before the Chamber at the Arsenal. I am setting a bad example." His lips tightened, but if he suffered, he suffered like a statue, by the merest change in a line or tightening of a contour. "She is of the family of Mazarin. For all that I owe the late Cardinal . . ." He looked again at the report, then spoke firmly. "You will see the Comtesse takes my warning," he said, "and that the money for her office is delivered immediately." He rose abruptly, forcing the ministers to scramble to their feet. "You will bring me word when it is done."

A light rain pattered against the glass, distorting the soft greens and yellows of the wood that began beyond Clagny's vast gardens. The Marquise was bored. She was feeling lazy and out of sorts, and as Claude worked on her hair, she kept pressing for news of the court, for the little tidbits of gossip and malice so good for cheering listless mornings. Some of these items Claude would rather have concealed, knowing how they must distress her, but at last she said, "There is some news of more matter, Madame."

Something in her tone caught Athénaïs's attention. "Well, what is it? Something about La Fontanges, I am sure. It is like you to save the news of her for last."

"No, Madame. It is said that certain ladies of the court have been compromised in the poison scandal."

The Marquise looked up quickly, her absorption in her toilette broken, her eyes meeting Claude's in the mirror. "What ladies of the court?"

"The Duchesse de Bouillon and the Comtesse de Soissons."

The Marquise laughed. "His Majesty will never touch them. Or rather, he touched them both in the past. They've been in his bed, and they are the nieces of Mazarin. This is but malicious tattle."

"Madame, the Comtesse de Soissons has left court."

Athénaïs's face grew still and cold. "God save us! Madame Voisin has spoken."

"No one says that, Madame."

"Why else would she leave? The Comtesse knew La Voisin for years." The Marquise tapped her fingers nervously on the dressing table. "Oh, leave it, leave it. Why will you fuss with my hair!" She took a deep breath and stared into the mirror. "We are finished. She will tell all, and I fear we cannot deny convincingly. Not if such as Olympe must flee the court."

"You are too hasty, Madame. Clearly, you have not been mentioned by anyone. Such a rumor would be about the court in an instant."

"But it is La Voisin, I am sure of it. Her arrest is at the bottom of everything."

"Perhaps La Voisin has given them the Comtesse to spare you, Madame."

"They will make her tell all. And why should she hesitate? I do not imagine such a one has any loyalty."

"Madame, La Voisin will go to the stake. But there are worse deaths. Very much worse. Any involvement with you touches high treason."

"For us all. You forget that—for us all." Athénaïs shook her head as if distracted. "I cannot bear this. There must be more news. Does no one read these police reports? Does no one attend these interrogations?"

"It is handled by the Chamber at the Arsenal, Madame. It is all secret, although Monsieur Colbert, of course—"

"You must see him! Yet not too obviously. I had not left court had I foreseen all this. We must proceed with the greatest care."

There was a soft knock on the door and the little under ladies' maid looked in and curtsied. "A visitor for Madame."

"Who is it?"

"Monsieur Colbert."

"Dear God, he has come to warn me!"

"Madame!" Claude exclaimed.

"Ask him to come up," the Marquise told the servant. When the door closed, she rose and stretched out her hand. "He comes to bring me my fate."

"You must have courage, Madame. If there is some accusation, your seeming serenity is your best protection."

"It is my only protection!"

"Not if such as Monsieur Colbert can be convinced."

"Bring my shawl. And is my hair right?" She touched her coiffure. "The ribbons! You had not finished with them. Quickly, quickly."

"Monsieur Colbert will not notice if you are in dishabille."

Athénaïs sat down at her dressing table and Claude took up her combs and brushes, so that when the servant knocked on the door and announced their visitor, they seemed entirely devoted to the gods of fashion and beauty.

"Ah, Monsieur Colbert, such a pleasure! Such a joy for an exile from the court."

"Madame, good day." Colbert bowed, his gallantry as stiff, bored and perfunctory as always, and in spite of her troubles, the Marquise smiled. She had seen Colbert on a thousand such errands—Oh, how many little services he had done her in the days of her glory!—and no man had ever seemed more ill at ease away from his desk. "I say 'Madame,' but I should, in truth, say 'Duchesse.'"

Athénaïs stopped breathing and even Claude froze, her hands still holding the brush and ribbons.

"Monsieur, what jest is this?"

"No jest but good news. The King, Madame, has honored you. As of this day you are made a duchesse with a pension of twenty thousand ecus and the right of tabouret. My congratulations, Duchesse. I take great pleasure in being the bearer of such splendid news." And he bowed deeply again.

Athénaïs released her breath. I am safe, she thought, and then she was annoyed. "Your pleasure, I suspect, is greater than the King's. I am made a duchesse in exile, a duchesse of Clagny, not of Versailles."

"You are in error, Madame. Your return is requested immediately, for you must assume new duties as Superintendent of the Queen's Household."

Claude put down the brush with a clatter and the Marquise rose.

"I have not the capital to purchase that office," she said.

Colbert produced some documents heavy with red seals and ribbons. "The transaction has been completed, Madame. Again, my most profound and sincere congratulations."

"Thank you, Marquis." Then she laughed, a low, throaty, triumphant laugh.

"What is it, Madame?"

Athénaïs stopped laughing and her eyes went cold. "I am paid off like Louise and in the same coin."

"His Majesty is most anxious for your return," Colbert said formally, adding in a softer voice, "especially now, Madame, with all the trouble and scandal. He feels it is important that you be beside him."

Madame de Montespan turned over the documents which gave her the highest position a woman might hold at court, then laid them down on her dressing table. "What of the Comtesse? Why has she sold her office now?"

Colbert sighed. "This is in confidence, Madame."

Athénaïs nodded.

"There was a woman arrested in the city, a sorceress by the name of La Voisin, along with a number of her associates. Much evidence has been uncovered by Lieutenant Reynie and his staff. More I cannot say, but the Comtesse was implicated in very serious charges. It was not fitting that she should continue to hold such an honorable post."

"I am shocked, Monsieur. But has she left the court?"

"She has left the country."

Athénaïs looked away, her heart pounding. "That is grave, indeed."

"The charges were of a most serious nature. Her choices were—limited, Madame."

"Are there others involved, Monsieur Colbert?"

Colbert was uneasy. "It is the King's intention to wipe out this scandal. Madame, I beg you, as your friend, do not hesitate to return to the palace. Friends and kinsmen have been involved, like the Comtesse and her sister, the Duchesse. Even Madame de Vivonne, your sister-in-law, has been mentioned. Yes, even she."

"I will believe no ill of Madame de Vivonne," the Marquise said, though her blood hammered in her ears and she was bursting to ask what the charge was.

Colbert hesitated for a moment, his blunt, square face blotched red. "You must return to court to protect your interests."

"Who uses all this information?" the Marquise asked. "Sit down and tell me, Monsieur Colbert. I am starved for news."

Colbert hesitated, then settled on one of the brocade chairs. "There is no doubt there is some evidence, some real scandal. Reynie has been investigating now for some months."

In spite of herself, Athénaïs put her hand over her heart: the risks, the awful risks she had run!

"It began with the cases of the three parliamentarians' wives. They were accused of murdering their husbands with the assistance of La Voisin and another witch, La Bosse."

"There has been little said about that matter."

"That is because of the new Chamber at the Arsenal, Madame. His Majesty feared that the usual courts would treat the ladies with excessive caution."

"Kinsmen were little use else," Athénaïs said. "This scrupulousness is Louvois's idea."

Colbert sighed. "He did encourage His Majesty. I could not block it; the King was determined that justice would be served."

"Is justice served by secret proceedings and closed chambers, Monsieur?"

Colbert shrugged eloquently.

"And this Reynie is part of it?"

"He has pursued the matter with the utmost diligence."

"That man had better been kept in your debt and under your control, Monsieur Colbert. Louvois should never have been allowed responsibility over the Parisian Police. The possibilities for mischief are endless."

"Since the wars, Madame, Louvois has made himself indispensable. I need my friends. Whatever your personal feelings," he added softly, "it is now vital that you return. The situation is delicate."

"I can scarce believe it. Some fool of a fortune teller, some charlatan, is arrested and"—she sighed and looked away—"the niece of Mazarin is sent fleeing for her life."

Colbert overcame his prudence. "It is said that she poisoned her husband."

"Poison?" Madame looked surprised for a moment before her features subtly relaxed. "And her sister, the Duchesse, whose husband still lives?"

"Attempted murder."

Athénaïs laughed cynically but there was relief in her voice. "They'll scarce prove that when he is on such good terms with her lover."

"Perhaps not. Yet, Madame, the King has taken this with the utmost seriousness. In such great ones, even the appearance of evil is a scandal. His Majesty will tolerate nothing that disturbs the grandeur of the court. Nothing, Madame, and no one."

"How many scandals did he give the world when he was young?" she asked, but her voice had lost its lightness.

"He is no longer young and now he would be serious," said Colbert. "In this your friend, Madame de Maintenon, encourages him. Duchesse, I must tell you they are often together."

"And Mademoiselle de Fontanges?"

Colbert looked uncomfortable.

"And Mademoiselle?"

"She is in very high favor."

"Openly?"

"She has a carriage and eight matched grays."

"I managed with six."

"So swift a rise must give us hope of as swift a fall."

"He has not waited for my return to shield her."

"No, Madame, yet he does desire your return most earnestly."

"Indeed, Monsieur Colbert, indeed he must, for he has loaded me with honors which must drag me back, however unwillingly. The Superintendent of the Queen's Household must perforce attend the court."

"When may I tell His Majesty you will return?" Colbert asked. Thank God, she was going to be sensible! He had experienced some of her rages: they took up an unconscionable amount of time.

"Tomorrow. Tell His Majesty I will arrive tomorrow. Tell him—" She paused, unable to continue. "Tell him my thanks, Monsieur Colbert," she said after a moment. "Your words will do that better than mine."

"He will rejoice, Madame."

The Duchesse smiled. Colbert rose and took his leave. The two women listened to his feet descending the wide marble steps, slowly and irregularly as though the weight of age and illness were unbalancing every step. How long they would have the great minister as an ally must be in doubt.

"Bring me some tisane," Athénaïs ordered. Through the open window, she could hear the minister's carriage.

"Did I not tell you, Madame?" Claude asked when she brought

the cup. "You are safe. The Comtesse and others may be ruined, but you have been honored."

"He gives me titles, offices, a seat in the presence of the Queen—what is this to past favor? Did I need a title to command the respect of the court? Did I need a great office to make the courtiers tremble? What are pensions, honors? I had but to whisper a request; I had but to open my hand."

"Madame, he cannot honor you more. This offers you safety."

"It was not safety for Olympe de Soissons." Athénaïs turned and slapped a jar from her dressing table. It bounced on the floor without breaking, then rolled in a curve beneath one of the chairs. Claude stood still. "Do you not see his selfishness? His subtle cruelty? He returns me to the court, to shames and humiliations, to the triumphs of—of my children's governess and that strumpet, Fontanges. And all the time, he loads me with honors, with gilded chains and empty titles."

"You might be in exile, Madame," Claude said coldly. "You might be in a convent or heading for the border. Think not on your rivals. Think of twenty thousand ecus, think of your new powers, think of your honors—or sure, Madame, some enemy will think to use scandal against you, it having worked so well against others."

The Duchesse raised her head proudly. "You will die peacefully in your bed, I can see, for you care for nothing but money and power."

"I believed you had some small concern with those things as well."

Athénaïs gave a slight smile. "But mine was subtler, more personal. When he loved me, then I had real power, genuine wealth. Now his heart is impoverished, he offers me substitutes and consolations."

"Love dies, Madame, but great houses survive on other things."

"I suppose I must defend Madame de Vivonne now," she said as she sat down and began examining her face and hair in the glass. "I suppose I must decry poison and accuse Reynie of over-zealousness."

"That would all be very wise, Madame."

"Then teach me to control my heart," the Duchesse said in a low, pained whisper, "for I was not born for such caution and calculation. Let the saints witness I am punished for my sins, for this return to court will mortify my soul."

XV

When he was annoyed, the Marquis de Louvois had a habit of pursing his full lips and tucking his round, shiny chin against his ruffled collar so that his plump, swarthy face took on a truculent air, befitting a man who faced the world on a permanent offensive. Normally, he conducted business with Lieutenant Reynie in a brusque and efficient fashion. Today, however, he delayed opening the matter at hand, and this, combined with his cross and sulky expression told Reynie something serious and potentially awkward was afoot.

Louvois took a turn around the room, glancing out the large, deep-set windows as he walked. The two men were in the new administrative wing at Vincennes, well away from the prying eyes of clerks, jailors and soldiers.

"His Majesty was much disturbed," Louvois said, clearing his throat hoarsely by way of emphasis. "Much disturbed."

"As was I," said Reynie. "Believe me, Marquis, only the seriousness of the affair convinced me to trouble His Majesty with the reports."

"It is fortunate, of course, that Madame de Montespan does not enjoy her former favor. Had she been still—"

"It would have been dangerous."

"Yes, yes, that is true," Louvois said sharply. "Well, is there nothing new? Nothing more? His Majesty responds that the evidence is inconclusive."

"Correctly so. The priest Lesage is not a wholly reliable witness. His charges against La Voisin are motivated by hatred and spite. Yet Madame Voisin, herself, admitted supplying Madame de Vivonne with poison and claimed that Madame de Montespan also consulted her some years ago."

Louvois stopped his pacing and sat down.

"'Consulted some years ago?'"

"That is correct."

"Alone that does not tell us much."

"What concerns me is the fact that Mademoiselle des Oeillets, Madame de Montespan's personal maid, has been mentioned and that among the others named as clients is Monsieur Le Roy of the Petite Ecurie."

"He has charge of the royal pages, but I do not see how——"

"His contacts with the sorcerers have been established beyond doubt, and the connection here is that his lodging is directly next to that of Mademoiselle des Oeillets at Versailles."

"Oh, that is bad business."

"I am further distressed by the length of this priest Lesage's career. As 'Adam Dubuisson' he was sent to the galleys for sorcery and for special and particular services. Madame de Thianges, Madame de Montespan's sister, was mentioned then as a client."

"When was this? You had not mentioned that in your reports."

"Just today I went through the records at the Bastille. That was in 1668. He was sent to the galleys, although the other priest indicted with him was spared—probably through influence."

"Who let this Lesage from the galleys is what I'd like to know! I'll have an answer to that, see if I don't," Louvois exclaimed angrily. "All this could have been avoided if that man had been kept in chains."

"Madame Voisin claims to have accomplished his release by the help of her 'prominent clients.'"

"Lending some substance to her boasts."

"I'm afraid it does. For that reason, I felt I could not delay—despite the unpleasantness for His Majesty."

"No, of course not. You were correct, Lieutenant Reynie, though I had rather it had not arisen. Still, it would be dereliction to neglect the evidence and folly to ignore the political ramifications." At this, Louvois half closed his eyes and settled himself more comfortably in the square wood-and-leather chair. It was interesting, he thought, how many of Monsieur Colbert's friends were involved. Of course, anything like a plot was out of the question, but if Colbert were to lose some of the courtiers who were his supporters over this matter—"You say you consider this Lesage's testimony unreliable?"

"I believe it must be weighed carefully," Reynie replied. "He obviously knows much and is quite willing to tell some in order to harm La Voisin and to buy favor. He is a man without moral scruple."

"But she, being under so heavy a charge, will lie out of fear, will she not? This La Voisin, I mean."

"If His Majesty will order her case to go forward, she will be examined officially."

"Her torture would be both ordinary and extraordinary."

"I'm sure that would be the decision."

"Yet some will stand firm, and then His Majesty is of two minds about the matter. He would know, but he would not know. And he would not expose Madame de Montespan to any distress." Louvois sighed. "This Abbé Lesage, as he calls himself, he speaks freely?"

Reynie nodded, and for a moment Louvois sat looking thoughtful and tapping softly on the arm of the chair. "It is the uncertainty of the thing which distresses His Majesty. And which, speaking for the ministers and the court, makes for indecision." He paused again, considering to himself whether he ought to back this new Mademoiselle de Fontanges more openly. Madame de Montespan was allied to Colbert and his faction, yet she had virtues: despite her extravagance, she lacked political ambition. "There are matters of state."

"As I am painfully aware, Marquis," Reynie said. "But as Lieutenant of Police, my chief concern must be the administration of justice—and the protection of the King's person."

"There was no sign of any threat?" Louvois's calm voice took on a note of alarm.

"No, there was not. Yet, if, as the Abbé claims, this Mademoiselle des Oeillets took aphrodisiacs to her mistress, the King's safety was compromised. Besides, there is the entire unseemliness of the situation."

"Precisely. His Majesty feels the latter most keenly."

Reynie nodded and sat watching the heavy and, at the moment, powerfully expressive features of his superior. Being a difficult, power-hungry man, Louvois demanded all the Lieutenant's tact. Reynie knew that the Marquis would be thinking how to make the most of the case and how to impress the King with his diligence—and, of course, his Lieutenant's as well.

"We must give His Majesty more facts. It is essential that the investigation be pressed with the utmost effort." He paused for a moment and straightened the lace at his cuffs. "I believe," he said, without looking at Reynie, "that I would like to see this Lesage."

"He can be brought to you at any time."

"He might repay—special consideration."

Reynie raised his eyebrows. "His one wish is to save his skin and to avoid the galleys. Were he offered certain guarantees—"

"Yes, that is a sound thought." Louvois nodded. "I will see this rogue. He may be useful."

"Remember, Marquis, the man lies without compunction."

"Lieutenant, I will find my way. He'll not deceive me or he will be back on his oar, and this time all the influence in the kingdom won't get him loose." Louvois rose abruptly and said "Summon the jailor. I will go to this Abbé's cell."

"Shall I accompany you, Marquis?"

Louvois gave a half smile. "I do not think that will be necessary, Lieutenant."

The hunt returned to Versailles with the dead stag borne in triumph, its fur matted with blood, its antlers rising above the packhorse's head like a crown of thorns. The afternoon light swam through the wood and the brown and yellow leaves dappled the paths of the park like gold and copper coins. When they broke out of the trees, the canal was shimmering before them, a sheet of silver under the whitish autumn sky, and the fountains shot up like strings of diamonds to bejewel the white chateau reclining along the top of the gardens. The King felt his return as a tangible weight. In the forest, he was free; only a few faint memories of young Amazons now gone disturbed the chase. At the palace, his troubles returned, and, with them, the miasma of uneasiness, the suspicion, which he would not have breathed even to his confessor, that the magnificence of his court, the splendor of Versailles, had somehow entailed an inexcusable taint. When they reached the Marble Court, he jumped down from his horse and, still unwilling to return to work, went upstairs to see Madame de Maintenon.

"I fear I disturb you, Madame." He was still in his hunting

dress and Françoise was surprised to see him at that hour, in that state.

"Never, Your Majesty." She laid down her needlework. "This is my constant companion, but being dumb, easily put aside."

"I wish that all my courtiers had such innocent recreations," said the King.

They exchanged a look. Their constant meetings had evolved a kind of shorthand. He did not need to say a great deal to convey what was on his mind. And by always being oblique and subtle, she had obtained considerable freedom to speak. "Has there been bad news, Sire?"

"There is no news but bad news in this matter, Madame, and still I can't decide how the situation stands." He went to push open a window. "They suggest terrible things." He paused, thoughtful, and Françoise surreptitiously pulled her shawl around her shoulders. "There is some thought that Madame de Montespan is involved. Her name has been mentioned."

Françoise gasped. Possibilities, fears, dangers lay in her lap, but before expediency could whisper, she said, "I cannot believe them."

"Nor I, Madame," he replied promptly. She could feel he was relieved at her loyalty and she knew she must be a friend. There was in Madame de Maintenon much goodness, yet goodness of a rather mechanical nature. No one was more dutiful, yet in none was duty so learned, so conscious. In this matter, however, her first gasp had been from the heart. "It is that woman Voisin," the King continued. "She speaks of knowing Madame de Montespan and some in her household. What more there is I do not know."

"I cannot believe there could be anything more than some foolishness, Your Majesty. Her devotion to you—and I will say, despite all our quarrels, to me—does not suggest evil-mindedness."

"That is what I think! Indeed, Madame, you ease my heart," he said, clapping his hands together and speaking with unusual animation. He sat down in a chair near the window then instantly rose again. "Lieutenant Reynie and the rest press me to bring this woman Voisin to trial, but I hesitate."

"For fear of injuring Madame de Montespan?"

"I would not distress her—especially not now." He had the grace to look awkward at that. "They tell me this, then they tell me that. There are no facts to support any decision, so I delay."

To give herself time to think, Madame de Maintenon worked at a flower in her pattern. "I believe, Sire, that suspense and uncertainty are the worst torture for a proud and sensitive spirit."

"Well, she is both of those."

"And she has no means of defense as things stand."

"I know, I know. I may wrong Athénaïs even to hesitate." He resumed pacing restlessly. "How did this happen? Why is there no order in my courtiers' lives? They run into the darkness when they might live in light and serenity." He leaned out the open window toward Le Nôtre's severe and elegant parterres. "Have I not provided a pattern of dignity and order, Madame?"

"Sire, you have and yet—"

The King turned, his stern and massive silhouette dark against the brilliant white light of the gardens. "And yet, Madame?"

She bent over her work for a moment. "And yet order is essential in all things, is it not? The court, the gardens, the palaces, the ceremonials, even your own great and regal command—these things are worldly."

"Admittedly, Madame. Yet we have provided for the Church as well."

"I spoke not of that, Sire."

His mouth tightened. Outside the gardeners were setting out

bulbs around the fountains and tidying the gravel. Their rakes made a rattling swish like waves on a stony shore, and the light breeze threw spray from the fountains over them like the vagrant foam of the sea. "You may speak freely, Madame."

"Your life, Sire, despite your great self-command, has also run beyond the moral bounds. How much more then your courtiers, weaker personalities, must be tempted to stray—in order to maintain themselves here?"

There was a long silence. A few voices from the gardens drifted into the room and out in the corridor the still afternoon was broken by the rattle of boots, the sound of passing workmen with their tools. Madame de Maintenon did not need to say more, for the King knew her theme quite well: his open adulteries had corrupted the standards of the court and shamed the Queen.

In the glare from the windows, his black eyes watched her unseen. She was the only woman to have refused him. That made her of some interest. And then, she was very subtle, idealistic and clever. She would have him return to his Queen. That meant he must give up Madame de Montespan, her great friend, and Mademoiselle de Fontanges—and certain other, less important ladies. Yet, of course, the Queen, despite her undeniable goodness, was a very dull woman. He had never, not even in the earliest days of their marriage, been able to tolerate a conversation of more than a few minutes with Her Majesty. It was certain, therefore, that he must have another companion of some sort. His lips twitched; Madame de Maintenon was perhaps the cleverest of all his ladies.

She continued to embroider the flowered garland, her thin white fingers making quick, dainty movements. "All things depend on you, Sire," she remarked after a time.

"God gives princes the strengths they need."

"But only God," she replied.

His Majesty turned to stare out at the gardens. He had an attraction for piety. Even in his wild youth, he had been punctilious about his religious observances; his mother had trained him well. Yet it had never struck him that piety might have a real, as opposed to a ceremonial, function, and this notion troubled him profoundly, with its suggestion that this unseemly scandal had some connection with his own flaws and lapses.

It could not be true, he thought, resuming his pacing. His care for the Church was exemplary—and he would defend it, even from Rome. Still, her words troubled him. He was sensitive to the example he must set, especially now when the Dauphin would soon be married. Not that the Dauphin had the spirit to get into great difficulties, but there were many temptations. Many. Kingship was a solemn business. And one that needed diversions, he added rebelliously. His face grew still, calm and implacable. He would not give up Mademoiselle de Fontanges. Not yet. Not when he was so harried and bored, not when there were troubles with Madame de Montespan, not with all this terrible business touching the court.

"Madame," he said, "we will speak of other things."

"Very good, Your Majesty, yet whatever we discuss, we speak of these matters, for your power touches all."

"You compliment me, Madame, in curious ways."

"For I flatter you not, Sire, but speak only the truth."

"In this matter, I believe that true." He sat down heavily and plucked aimlessly at one of her balls of wool, thoughtlessly unraveling it. "I must know, don't you see?" he asked suddenly in a loud, impatient voice. "I could dismiss all the charges, shut the whole thing down."

"But there is justice."

"There is justice and this: I must know what my court is about. I did love her much. More than was proper."

"And she loved you, Sire."

He looked at her sharply, then away. "I believed so."

Françoise hesitated, thinking over what she had to say, loyalty fighting with caution, before she pressed forward. "It appears—she took certain risks for your sake. Perhaps to secure your fidelity?"

"You would have it my fault," he said pettishly.

"No, Sire. I but mention her great anxiety as extenuation."

"I will not be blamed for everything. You know we have no choice in our marriages."

"I understand, Sire."

He read in her face thoughts of her own marriage, made out of direst poverty, and abruptly changed the subject to the children and their progress. They spoke no more of the matter closest to the King's heart until he took his leave.

"You believe this matter must give Madame de Montespan pain?"

"I do, indeed, Sire."

"It must be settled," he said. "One way or another we will settle it." But which way he would decide, he did not reveal, and his delays and hesitations were to allow Madame Voisin another six months of life.

The jailor rattled at the door, and Madame Voisin raised her head from the pillow.

"It's time."

Madame yawned, as if she had just waked up and had not been lying in her bed for hours, listening for the sound of his steps in the corridor of the fortress.

The man stepped into the dim chamber, shackles in his hands.

"Let me dress, for God's sake! To wake a lady at this time of the morning is bad enough without dragging her out in dishabille."

"The Lieutenant's there himself. You'll have to hurry."

"They can scarce begin without me," Madame said, sitting up and rubbing her eyes. She drew some coins from a pocket in her shift and set them on the quilt, then rose and pulled on her petticoats and skirts. With a glance over his shoulder, the jailor pocketed the coins, producing a small bottle of brandy from under his vest. Madame drank half with one swig.

"Hey, see you're not drunk. It would be worth my place."

"It'll not be half enough to get me through as it is." She wiped her lips, fastened her bodice, then wrapped her shawl around her shoulders. "Your brother will be on tonight?"

"Yes."

"See he brings me more. And I would send a message to the executioner."

"You'll see him this morning."

"Much chance I'll have to bargain in the Boot. See that I get a message to him and it will be worth your time."

"Putting it that way, it would be a pleasure," the jailor remarked as he fastened her shackles. "You have been a joy to do business with, Madame."

"We understand each other, Jailor, yet from your point of view, they have timed this near to perfection," Madame said sourly. "I'd have been broke had I been preserved much longer and left without the wherewithal to bribe the headsman. As it is, I will go to my grave with but my shift."

"Madame, such is the fate of all mankind," the jailor said philosophically. "We go to the grave naked and return to Mother Dust. But now, Madame, we must descend."

La Voisin grew quite white at this and touched the lace at her throat like a woman uncertain of her dress before an important party. "Another drink, I pray you, Jailor."

"You'll stagger not? Nor fall asleep? That," he added, "would be most impolite."

Madame grabbed the bottle and finished off its contents. "Is it very bad, Jailor?"

"To tell you the truth, that all depends. If you have a thick leg, why it will snap your ankles. Sometimes on the Ordinary. Then if, as in your case, Madame, you're due for the Extraordinary as well, you're in a very difficult situation."

Madame straightened her sleeves.

"'Tis a Spanish invention, you see. It was the Inquisition's device."

"Tell me no more. It will soon be apparent."

"Then come, Madame, for you are a person of importance," he said as they started along the corridor. "There's quite a crowd: the Lieutenant himself, and there are carriages here this morning, too." He smiled as he spoke, pleased with the bustle and with the change in his pocket from Madame Voisin. On days when they faced the Question, prisoners were always willing to pay for certain little helps and conveniences, and thus, so he put it to himself, the wicked paid their tolls to the just.

"Lieutenant, Sir, Catherine Deshayes, known as La Voisin," the jailor announced.

Reynie nodded, motioning the jailor and Madame Voisin into the chamber which was as tall and cramped as the bottom of a well. The room was lit by a high row of windows that cast long gray shafts into the brown and dusty murk, picking out the fortress staff, already frozen in their ritual positions. The magistrates sat on their upholstered chairs on the dais; the masked and hooded torturer stood with his assistant at one end of a stout wooden bench, while at the other the thin, stooped fortress doctor was stationed. Beside the magistrate's dais, a clerk sat at a small desk, ready to take down the interrogation, and in the center of the room, his eyes cast into fathomless shadow by the feeble and sinister lighting, Reynie stood ready to read the charge. Madame folded her hands together and shivered in the damp.

"Present the patient," Reynie said, for they were, from that moment, all doctors of her soul. She was accused of sorcery, of poisoning, of assisting in the procurement of abortions and in the concealment of dead babies. She would be questioned on these matters and on certain other concerns. Madame looked up at this and caught the Lieutenant's eye. What other concerns? She could feel his nervousness and knew there was something more. Oh, that she had ever mentioned Madame de Montespan! She would deny all. She would endure the Boot and go to the stake like a respectable woman, escaping the horrors of treason. Yet Lesage might have said anything in his mad hatred, and her face turned white and red with fear before the reading of the charges was over and another of the functionaries ordered the torture instrument presented.

The torturer and his assistant bowed, then lifted the Boot from its position on the floor and laid it on top of the bench.

"The patient will approach."

The torturer's face was partially concealed by his mask, but La Voisin could see his small, pursed mouth, and the gray and brown bristles on his fleshy, unshaven jaw. His assistant was barefaced, a thin, wiry youth with pale, crossed eyes. In her fear, their faces loomed like the repulsive phantoms of a dream, and giving them both an evil look, she forced her eyes toward the Boot. Consisting of four planks reinforced with iron bands and positioned to seize both the victim's legs, the Boot was operated by a heavy screw, which turned to produce a remorseless contraction of the device.

"We will ask you certain questions now, Madame Voisin," said Reynie, and once again she watched his eyes. What did he want? What could she safely give him?

"We will begin with the cases of Madame Dreux and Madame Leferon. Do you maintain that they secured poison from you to destroy their husbands?"

"Sir, I do." She twisted her hands.

"Have the ladies brought in," Reynie said.

Madame Voisin swallowed and closed her eyes. When she opened them, there were the ladies Dreux and Leferon, dressed very charmingly, although in quieter, more somber shades than usual. They sat down in chairs beside the magistrates' dais.

"Do you know these ladies, Madame Voisin?"

For a moment, she caught Madame Dreux's expression, like the nervous watchfulness of a beautiful bird, and felt regret that she should have to betray so genteel a client. But then Madame Dreux turned away, half frightened, half scornful, and La Voisin felt her heart harden under that contempt. "I do," she said.

"Repeat your charges."

She did. The ladies shook their heads, murmured denials. Then Madame Voisin was ordered to remove her overskirts and to lie down on the bench. For an instant, she thought she would cry, but she did not. Her legs, after all, were thin despite her weight. "Have mercy, Sir, for I am old enough."

The torturer did not answer, but fastened the straps of the bench across her shoulders and chest. Then he opened the Boot and, removing her shoes, positioned the boards between and outside her legs.

"The patient is prepared," he announced.

Near the dais, the ladies smoothed their dresses and cleared their throats and wondered if La Voisin might not considerately die of fright and leave their cases in suspension.

"Madame," said Reynie, "because of the gravity of your case, you have been ordered to submit to the Question both Ordinary and Extraordinary." Then he nodded and the torturer and his assistant turned the handles of the screws with a grating squeal. She felt the cold metal reinforcing bands against her calf and ankle. One turn. Three more for Ordinary, four again for Extraordinary.

"I will ask you now about Madame Dreux," Reynie said in his quiet and reasonable voice. Madame watched his eyes. Her fate lay there.

"She sought her husband's life and I sold her poison."

"And Madame Leferon?"

"The same."

Reynie nodded to the torturer and the screw turned again. This time Madame felt pressure on her ankles. Thank God, she had thin shanks. One of her friends, La Vigoureux, had died under the Question, but it had been water with her and doubtless she had drowned.

"The matter now of the abortionist, La Lepère," Reynie continued.

"She is guilty. It is true, I referred her customers." Was this the key matter? Some great lady of the court? Madame de Vivonne, perhaps, the wife of the King's good friend? She'd had some little trouble seven, no eight, years ago.

Reynie must have signaled in another way this time, for the horrid rasp of the screws in the Boot caught Madame by surprise and she gripped the sides of the bench against the pain, at once dull and piercing, like the crack of a heavy cudgel.

"How many?" Madame did not hear him, for the pain had swamped her senses, yet she knew the question.

"Hundreds, thousands. In my garden. That is true."

"I will ask you now again, Madame, about the ladies Leferon and Dreux. Is your answer still the same?"

"Yes, yes, the same." She screamed before the rasp of the screws, in fear and anticipation of the pain, and, for a moment, lost her concentration on Reynie's eyes, where she must read her salvation.

The Lieutenant walked over for a brief consultation with the other magistrates, and Madame lay rigid on the bench, opening and closing her eyes. She was trembling uncontrollably and it was a relief to her, when, Madame Dreux and Madame Leferon having been ordered away, the Lieutenant returned. In all the room only he was real, the pain reducing all others to mere phantoms.

"We will speak now of Monsieur Racine," Reynie said, "and Mademoiselle du Parc."

The Boot was tightened again, increasing the pain so that it raced the length of her body and bored into her brain like the agonies of childbirth. In spite of herself, La Voisin began to scream, and as the questions continued about this one and that, the town and the court, she could not focus her mind on the answers. Her brain was dissolving in pain and all sense of the questions—even of her own danger—was lost, the fabric of reason rent. Reynie ordered a halt for a moment, and, perhaps, had the torturer turn back the screws a little, for her ankles, that had seemed on the point of shattering, settled into a steady, sharp throbbing. The Lieutenant sat down beside her and spoke very quietly, his thin face stern yet pained. Although not immune to the opinions and prejudices of his class, the Lieutenant was a man with a humane and sceptical turn of mind. He had lighted Paris, regularized her administration, was paving her streets; these medieval proceedings gave him no pleasure.

"Now, Madame," he said, "the Question is endured to discover truth, to bring evildoers to justice, to clear the innocent and to ease the conscience of the condemned."

Blurred by her tears, the windows high on the wall merged into a flat, hazy bar of white light, against which the Lieutenant's dark wig and shadowed features appeared like an apparition.

"True, Lieutenant," she said, "though the great lovers of truth are seldom put to such pain."

"Much depends on your answers, Madame," the Lieutenant said, and Madame knew this was a warning.

"Then ask, Sir, for my heart is weak and this device may bring my death."

"Madame Voisin, you once mentioned a lady of the highest standing as being known to you. I speak of Madame de Montespan."

La Voisin drew in her breath and fought off the lethargy of pain and despair. "I did lie, Sir." Was there relief in his eyes? She could not be sure. "I knew her not, though I knew others in her circle."

"Did you know Mademoiselle des Oeillets, Madame de Montespan's personal maid, or Mademoiselle Catau?"

The torturer and his assistant threw their weight against the screws and La Voisin let out a shriek of agony. "Yes, yes," she cried.

"You knew one? You knew both?"

But Madame Voisin could not speak for the pain, and the Lieutenant had to wait while she bit her lip bloody and clawed the skin off her fingers against the wood of the bench. Then she shook her head.

"Which one did you know?"

"I knew Mademoiselle Catau, or rather, I knew well her aunt, Sir, for she has lived on the Quai des Grands Augustins these many years."

"Yet you originally testified you knew Mademoiselle Catau." Reynie persisted.

"Sir, indeed, I had met her. Perhaps I said a prayer for her employment. So many ladies, Sir, seek employment here and there. And knowing as I did her aunt—"

"You have not seen her since she took this employment with Madame de Montespan?"

"No, Sir, no. It was just vainglory. Oh, how I pay for that weakness," La Voisin groaned, but she had not read him wrong. This was their fear—that she had touched the circle of the King—and for a moment, madness tempted her. Then she remembered the terrible penalties: she would not be able to bribe the torturer on the scaffold.

"And Mademoiselle des Oeillets?"

"A lady I know not, Sir."

Reynie ordered the last turn, and there was a crack and another scream from Madame, who wept and vomited and whispered at the end, "I have never met Mademoiselle des Oeillets nor seen her mistress."

"Nor carried powders to either of those ladies?" Reynie asked despite his revulsion.

"No, Sir."

"Not to Versailles nor Saint-Germain?"

"Not to those ladies, for God's mercy, Sir. To others, but never to those ladies. As the fires of Hell may take me, Sir, I never did."

The Lieutenant rose at this, wiped his hands on his fine handkerchief and ordered the Boot removed. Madame lay with her eyes closed, feeling the terrible pressure released from her ankles and legs, feeling the stickiness of blood where the boards had cut into the flesh, feeling the nausea that flowed from the broken bone in her right ankle. The doctor came and felt her pulse with his cold, trembling fingers, then the sour, dirty odor of the jailor announced his presence. As they helped her to her feet, La Voisin opened her eyes and saw Reynie's sad and reflective expression.

"Should you wish to speak to me, Madame, I am prepared to listen at any time."

Dazed as she was, she made no response, but she was not surprised when his slight, solemn figure appeared in her cell the night before her execution. She and the jailor had been exchanging drinking songs through the bars, and she had just finished a parody of the Salve Regina that had set the corridor roaring with laughter when a sudden quiet fell, broken only by footsteps and the soft tap of an ornamental cane. Madame was sitting, swaying on her bed, holding a glass of brandy when the door rattled and opened.

Her visitor carried a lantern. She blinked and he moved his light so that she could distinguish his features.

"Ah, Lieutenant Reynie. Welcome to my humble salon."

"Good evening, Madame Voisin."

"Will you have a drink? I can offer you a glass."

"I must decline, Madame."

"Then you come on business. Yet you will not mind if I continue, Lieutenant?"

"In view of your situation, Madame—"

"Sir, you are a gentleman; alas that I am not more of a lady," Madame said, discarding her society manners. "They tell me I'm for the stake Thursday."

"Yes, Madame Voisin, though it was highly improper that you were so long forewarned."

She laughed at this. "Sir, we are cautioned to prepare for death always."

"That is true. And perhaps you would like even now to speak to a confessor?" He seemed hopeful and Madame Voisin's laugh grew dry and knowing: they wouldn't wheedle anything out of her that way.

"I mean, rather, Lieutenant, to go on as I've begun and to stay drunk and hilarious till they light the straw."

"Even brandy does not always ease the conscience," the Lieutenant remarked, rising from his chair and looking about at her possessions—the mirror, the folding altar, the silver brushes.

"I have confessed, Lieutenant; I have not been able to set weight on this ankle since the Question."

He turned with a sigh. "Not all speak truly or fully under the Question."

"And you fear that some have escaped through my discretion?" She gave a little nervous giggle, knowing she was on the edge, then wine and pain pushed her over. "Oh, it is true, it is true. Some ladies have escaped through my tact and some rogues as well."

His uneasiness was transparent.

"No one, Sir, will ever know the full extent of my clientele," Madame said, unable to resist a boast that was half a threat as well.

"Before death," the Lieutenant suggested, "many wish to speak to ease their hearts."

"There is some honor in all professions, Lieutenant Reynie. You may be sure my testimony will stand. As for easing the heart, song and wine ease mine." She began to hum and to rock back and forth, her face passing in and out of the faint glow of the lantern. She felt for an instant the true touch of prophecy, and the future might have been opened for Reynie if he had not taken his lantern and left the cell.

"Jailor, Jailor," she yelled when the Lieutenant's boots had descended the winding stair.

He came and leaned against the door. The recipient of some of Madame's drink, he was feeling lazy and obliging. "Well, Madame?"

La Voisin limped to the door and thrust her hand through the spy hole. "See this ring?"

The jailor lifted his candle. "You'll buy brandy with that. A ruby, isn't it?"

She pulled her fingers away before he could get his hands on it. "Tell the executioner it will be on my hand for him, if he kill me before the fire. If not, it can go with me to the angels."

"Well, Madame, I commend a prudent course, a prudent course. But remember your messenger, for you know it's not strictly proper to help a prisoner escape the full rigor of the law."

There was a little glimmer of light. "My last coin, Jailor, and if you take it now, there will be no more drink."

"Ah, give us another drink and we'll forget the bargaining."

There was a laugh, and Madame Voisin's dragging step. Then a bottle tapped the door and the jailor unlocked the cell and held out his glass.

"Sing, Jailor," Madame commanded, lifting the bottle. "Sing, sing!"

He took up a chorus which she joined, then halted, shaking her head. "To think I once had violins," she said.

XVI

By summer, the long-planned Gallery at Versailles was complete, a great hall of mirrors that reflected the company in all their expensive elegance and doubled the grandeur of the décor: the marble floors, the tables and candelabra of solid silver, the tender orange trees in scented flower. From the dark terrace, it was perfection, a fairy setting like the interior of a great sugar egg. Inside the impracticalities were more evident. The rooms were smoky with the thousands of tallow candles. In cold weather, the guests near the fires were roasted with the heat and crush and dizzied with perfumes, while those near the windows found the sweat had turned to ice on their bodies. In summer, the open windows brought in air off the stagnant canal, heavy with fever, and the mirrored walls redoubled the sun's glare.

Still, the courtiers were merry, their laughter as loud as ever—or perhaps louder. The voices still drawled compliments or whispered scandal. The gamblers in the Salon de Mars still swore when the cards went wrong and dashed their stakes down on the inlaid tables. The click of the billiard balls still echoed in the Salon de Diane and servants still filched rich cakes from the splendid buffet, and yet, like the perfection of the scene, this merriment was deceiving. For twenty years the court had done these things: twenty years of exclaiming "brilliant shot, Your

Majesty," of bowing to the lady of the moment, of the same iced wines and sweet cakes, of Lully's violins, of poisoned gossip. Twenty years of hopes, of dreams, of ceaseless maneuvering for place and favor. Though the courtiers would have died, cheerfully, in the defense of their niches at the palace, their boredom showed. Joy was a brittle shell over tedium; their high spirits had faded like their youth, their hopes. The young set were truant— off to costly ruin in the taverns, gambling dens and brothels of Paris. The old—the ex-Frondeurs, the last rebels—were dead or dying. Those of the King's generation were trapped at court, caught as surely as flies in honey, and now to their gilded prison came this new frustration, this new fear: the trials dragged on. Notables appeared—or disappeared. For the lower orders there was the Question, the stake, the galleys; for their betters, convents, jail or exile. Loving scandal as they did, the courtiers might have been revived by such tidbits, if secrecy had not thrown a pall over all with the closed chamber, secret indictments, ministerial silences. No one knew the whole story, but everyone knew that the Comtesse de Soissons had fled and her sister, the Duchesse, was exiled. The great Marshal Luxembourg was imprisoned and his protégé, the Marquis de Fellières, suspect; the Parliamentarians wives were away in Flemish convents, and the poet Racine lived in terror of an indictment. The charges were weird, indefinite, sinister. The investigation had entangled an ex-sheperd who collected toads in the Bois de Boulogne and a marquis who was a friend of the deposed Fouquet. There was a coven of witches and abortionists, plus herbalists, valets, unfrocked priests and political malcontents. As accusations bubbled up from the malice of the gutter and the rigor of the Question, uncertainty added an edge to court gossip, even in the languid heat of the evening *appartement* in the King's suite.

"They say she dies tomorrow."

Athénaïs de Montespan looked over her shoulder, suddenly alert. "Who, Monsieur?"

"Why that fortune teller, the witch La Voisin."

His friend, a much painted courtier, giggled. "She's to be burned on the Grève. I had it of a boy who knows the jailor."

Thank God, Athénaïs thought. Thank God! Might her secrets burn with her. After all this time! To conceal her agitation, she reached for another cake and signaled for another cup of tea, then found she could barely swallow the liquid. She had been martyred for over a year by soul-destroying anxiety, and now the witch was to be burned and her secrets with her.

"You'll go, of course," the courtier said to his companion.

"We'll take the carriage and get up a party."

"Oh, you'll see nothing—the mob will all be on the Grève."

"I've a friend who's invited us to her mansion—opposite the Hôtel de Ville. She's asked her whole salon."

"The best seats! You know half La Voisin's clientele will be there to see her off—"

"—and the other half waiting for their turn at the fire!" They laughed wickedly, then Mademoiselle de Fontanges, who had been watching them with her calf eyes, said, "I've never seen a woman burned."

A little break—as her stupidity registered.

"Not even in your wild Auvergne?" Athénaïs asked sharply.

"We had no witches. Though many died on the scaffold, it is true."

"Then you must accompany us, Mademoiselle," the Count said gallantly.

Madame de Maintenon spoke up. "It is a shame to make an outing of such things. Or to speak of them in the King's presence."

This made an awkwardness. True, Madame de Maintenon was

outranked by nearly all the court, but her forceful personality, her intimacy with the King, her recent appointment as lady to the new Dauphine, gave her a certain stature. The courtiers felt they had to watch their tongues around her and suspected, too, that she knew much they would like to discover. Young Mademoiselle, however, was too simple for prudence.

"She is a witch," she said, her voice high and a little too shrill. She was angry and humiliated to be called publicly to account by the old Widow Scarron. "His Majesty's justice is done. There can be no harm in witnessing it."

Madame de Maintenon looked at her gravely. "There can be no pleasure in such suffering—or in such wickedness and disgrace," she said.

Mademoiselle de Fontanges flushed and looked over her shoulder, but His Majesty, who must have been close enough to hear all, ignored her. As he so often did now! Her lip began to tremble, for she was not wicked at heart, only frightened and uncertain. They will say I've lost my chance, she thought, that he slept with her and gave her a jewel. Her pale cheeks produced two feverish red spots and tears came into her eyes. He should rescue her, comfort her, present her with some extraordinary mark of favor! But the King continued his conversation. He spoke of Pomme, his favorite hound, of some prodigy of tracking, while she was attacked, humiliated. Had she not lost the child, had she preserved her health—but at this thought the waiting tears spilled onto her cheeks and, with a gasp, she excused herself from the company, pushing her way through the rustling silks and stiff brocades, struggling for breath in the hot, flower-laden air. The King did not follow her.

"A shame," said the Princess Palatine, shaking her head.

"In the King's service," Athénaïs murmured to no one in particular, "one must expect to bear some wounds."

The courtiers nearby laughed, brittle and unfeeling, yet this displeased Athénaïs as well: their favors were poisoned, their regard as unreliable as the sands. Had she been disgraced, had she—dear God, she could scarcely think it—had she been taken to the secret chamber and condemned to die on the Grève, they would have gotten in their carriages as readily to make her agony a picnic. She had come so close: that witch La Voisin deserved to die a thousand times over to pay for her anxiety.

"You will go," she said to Claude when they reached her apartments. "And listen to what she says when she makes the *amende*. I would know."

"Yes, Madame," Claude said and thought—with pleasure.

"Go with the Count's party. For all the little favors he has asked of me, he can take you with him. I cannot go myself; I would not be seen to have interest." She picked up a book of poems, scanned the first one, then set the volume down. "Mademoiselle de Fontanges will go, but ignore her," she added.

"I think she will not go, Madame. There is some rumor that she plans to leave the court."

Athénaïs looked up.

"They say she is still losing blood."

"From the child?"

Claude nodded.

"That's what comes of doctors. What do men know? I would never let one of them touch me, no matter what His Majesty suggested."

"She does not look well," Claude continued, trying to give her lady hope, but Athénaïs shook her head impatiently.

"It will not help me and will only make more scandal."

"La Voisin dies tomorrow, Madame, and all dies with her. A day more. You must keep up your courage."

"We have had a year of this," Athénaïs exclaimed. "She has

been locked in the chateau for over a year. How many more must know something?"

"None, Madame, or you would have been questioned. Tomorrow is the end, and I will watch her die."

"You know she may speak even at the stake," Athénaïs said, cross and ready to quarrel. "Why did you tangle my soul with that woman?"

"Did you not beg me? Did you not say the King was worth any risk?" Claude's voice was scornful, and her mistress shouted, "Do not argue with me! Go to the city and don't come back until that witch is gone!"

Claude curtsied abruptly and left. The next afternoon, she arrived at the mansion on the Grève in a mood of grim anticipation. All Paris was there, carriages clogged the streets leading to the Hôtel de Ville, and every house overlooking the Grève had spectators hanging from the windows. The square itself sported a holiday air with musicians, beggars and street vendors, and, tiny from Claude's vantage point, a tumbler who clowned and pranced dangerously close to the soldiers and executioners who were busy about the straw and logs. The drone of a bagpipe issued from one corner, from another a drum punctuated the murmur and surge of the crowd with a restless staccato. In the rooms above the Grève, hostesses called servants to bring more chilled wine to cut the humid July heat, and ladies waved their fans and remembered Madame Voisin. Toward five, they heard a great shout from the island and while rumor ran about the eddying masses below, the gentry craned their necks to catch a glimpse of the tumbril bearing the condemned woman. From the top floors of the mansion, reports came that the procession was visible at Nôtre Dame, and shortly after, very flushed, dusty and out of breath, one of the courtiers puffed up the steps to report that La Voisin had refused to make the *amende*—the public confession—at the cathedral and was proceeding direct to the Grève. Claude breathed relief: Madame de Montespan's secrets were safe. Surely now La Voisin would die in her sinister faith and go to the stake in silence.

The rumble of the crowd was swept to a roar of excitement and Claude pushed her way to a window and looked out. The tumbril approached slowly, the heavy horses forcing their way through the mob that surged forward toward the wagon, shouting, laughing, cursing, encouraging. Their mood was volatile, and the soldiers thrust them back with their musket barrels, well aware of the mix of contempt, fear and excitement that could make the poor of Paris dangerous. This crowd might be content to frolic or it might decide to free the prisoner, or, conversely, to tear her to shreds and save the headsman the effort. Claude felt all this and nodded: she was part of the crowd still, not part of the gentry who stood, glasses in their hands, nervously teasing each other about the ecus Madame Voisin had cost them and the secrets she was about to carry to her pyre.

Then the tumbril reached the square before the Hôtel de Ville, and there was a great cheer, a rippling animal surge that rose from the cobbles to the balconies and up to the few daring watchers perched on the roofs. The driver halted his team and the soldiers jumped down and gestured for La Voisin to follow.

She stood erect in the cart, a small, stout, red faced woman with a large candle clasped in her hands. A soldier reached up to grab her, and she pulled away, cracking him with the candle so that the crowd, always eager for comic relief, laughed and jeered. La Voisin refused to leave the tumbril, and eventually two soldiers had to climb back up and lift her out, kicking and struggling, her white penitential shift revealing thin, veined legs and bare feet. They dragged her the final few steps to the stake and fastened her with lengths of chain. Claude gripped the window sill and thought how many times she had drunk cordials on cold nights with Madame Voisin and shared lemonade on hot and dusty afternoons like this one. The sun scalded the square, shining hot and white through the dust and haze, darkening the soldiers' backs with sweat as they arranged the straw and kindling. They laid their bundles around Madame's feet, but she kicked them away and dislodged the pile, rejecting her death as she rejected the crucifix the priest extended. To the hoots and jokes of the onlookers, the soldiers replaced the pile, but several times more La Voisin's desperate struggles disturbed their work until they had to load her with more chains. All the while, she shrieked at them, furious and profane, so that the crowd, hot now and impatient, roared, their unstable sympathies shifting back and forth between pity for the condemned and lust for spectacle. At last the straw was piled breast high, the logs arranged like spokes at the base. The executioner's assistants stepped back on either side, their long iron hooks ready to poke up the fire, to draw in the logs, to end the victim's suffering by tearing off her head. The troops took up their positions. The executioner lifted his torch dramatically to the crowd and there was a roar—of joy, of anticipation, perhaps, too, of rage. Then, slowly it seemed to Claude, the torch made a gentle descent, a bright rosy arc, to touch the straw. There was an instant, a pause, a silence, a time for the watchers to think on their sins, then the first white wisp of smoke rose, a soft sigh ran through the crowd. Madame Voisin struggled against her chains, turned her face from the crucifix that the priest with desperate persistence thrust before her. The top layers of straw shook with her efforts, but now it was too late: the pyre was burning red and black—as red and black as Madame's secret chapel, as the filthy host elevated by Abbé Guibourg—and its hot interior glowed orange. The logs were catching with a crackle, the smoke surging up, now gray and black, to choke the crowd on the windward side. They could hear for a time La Voisin's shrill, unintelligible screams, then the executioner nodded and his men stepped close to the smoke and flames and swung their grappling hooks at her head. One blow, two, three, another for good measure, for the executioner had been bribed by the good ruby ring, and then there were no more screams, only the whistle and stink of the fire, the crackle of the wood, the low moaning of the crowd. The figure on the stake slumped forward like a discarded puppet and Claude bent her head and took in her breath with a gasp. Madame Voisin was gone and all her evil secrets with her. They were safe. When the crowd began to cheer, she raised her head with joy, joining the unthinking roar that now celebrated His Majesty's justice.

The prisoners in Vincennes had heard the carriage rumble out before four, and the bells tolling the hour at five. Lesage got up, kicked Marguerite off the filthy pallet that was his bed and sniffed apprecatively. "Old bitch is in the air," he said. "Smell that?"

There was always smoke around the chateau and imagination easily added a burned smell. "Your mother's mortal remains, girl."

Marguerite had gone to huddle in the corner. Now she gave a string of curses, loud enough to stir Guibourg, who was slumped against the wall, his great bulk slack and useless, his filmy eye wandering up and down like a trapped animal. He crossed himself, and Lesage laughed. "Old hypocrite." The window bars were just out of reach, but on the second jump, Lesage managed to grasp them and haul himself up. The hazy summer sky was divided by a plume of white and black smoke. "That's it. That's her gone!" He dropped down, exhilarated in spite of the strain on his arms, and grabbed Marguerite. "Come on, again, for old times sake," he said, lifting her shift.

She resisted only lethargically. "With my mother dying?"

"Dead, dead. Can't you smell her?"

Marguerite began to laugh hysterically, then to wiggle suggestively in his arms. Hatred for her domineering mother was her mainspring; spite made the thin, dirty and sadistic Lesage possible.

"Filthy slut," he said, panting in the heat.

Guibourg began to giggle and shifted his bulk along the wall to see better. When they really got going, he would bang his food dish like a madman and slobber, for being too diseased himself to attempt much in the way of venery, these sessions between Lesage and Marguerite were his chief pleasure. Their rutting was a combination of lust and contempt which he found satisfying, especially when he could persuade Marguerite to come sit on his knee afterwards.

"For a drink," she said this time.

Lesage made a crude suggestion, but Guibourg hauled out his hidden bottle and Marguerite plopped down, her bare legs damp on his thigh. "A little rose," he said nostalgically. He stroked her coarse hair and thought with wistful pain of Didi.

"Shut up, you great hog. It'll take you longer to roast," said Lesage. "And the pain of it! It's a wonder you can accept that." He smiled and wiped his lips and crawled over to claim his share of the drink. This was a happy day; his revenge relaxed him, soothed the sharp corners of his soul, lifted the thick, angry clouds that had smothered his brain, kept him torpid, unable to plan. "They'll kill us off and let the gentry go unless we plan."

"What plan?" asked Marguerite.

Lesage gave a little grunt of contempt. She'd inherited none of her mother's abilities; that made her sweeter for some purposes, but only a feeble conspirator. And Guibourg now was a wreck, stinking of decay—physical and mental. It would all depend on Lesage himself, and that was an agreeable position, too, for the Abbé needed to have power somehow, over someone.

"Listen," he said, raising his head and pulling himself up to a sitting position. "The old bitch is dead—dead of sorcery, poisons, sacrilege. Are we less guilty?"

"She was my mother," Marguerite whined. "I'm not to blame."

"Stop that," Lesage said, slapping her. "They'll toast you in the straw if you're not clever. And you"—he poked Abbé Guibourg, who, sated, seemed ready to slip back into sleep—" "wouldn't you rather die of the pox?"

"The evidence against us will be strong," he said and began to moan.

Lesage swore and kicked them both and threatened to break the wine bottle. "Listen. La Voisin is dead. Guilty, finished. We're next—the Question, the stake, finished. Unless—" He stopped. It had seemed clear and right when he had rehearsed the idea in his head. Now, about to produce it in the fetid afternoon, he wasn't so sure. But what else to do? Nothing! "She didn't tell all," he said. "She held back. Fearing treason, fearing hot lead, flaying knives, the wheel. What did it get her?"

"A quicker death," Guibourg rumbled. "They can keep you alive for days you know. Kill you by inches like poor Ravaillac."

"Such delights are not for us," Lesage said. "I had this of the jailor: Madame was questioned about La Montespan. Very hard. She kept silent out of fear and they were relieved. Relieved! Think on that."

"La Montespan touches high treason. Think on that," Guibourg said, and Marguerite, who was a bit slow mentally, began to rock back and forth on his knee and whimper.

"Now, I have a gamble in mind, as I'm a gambling man," Lesage said. "I think Madame played the wrong cards. She played the innocent card, and she's in the air." He snuffled loudly like a hound on the scent. "I've a mind to play the guilty card, play it for all its worth, lay it on as thick as hog fat, and see what they do."

"They'll open your veins," Guibourg said, "and pour hot lead into them."

"Will they?" asked Lesage. "Or will they wet their pants with fear of the King and decide to forget the whole matter?"

The other two went silent.

"Do you follow me?"

They hesitated, and Lesage knew he would have to work to make them consent. "You would die!" he exclaimed. "You would die on the Grève when you might make yourselves untouchable. Listen, didn't the Marquis de Louvois come to visit me in person? Did he not sit in my cell with a wig as big as Guibourg's backside, stinking of perfume like a soldier's whore and carrying a staff that would keep us in drink for a month? He did. And what did he want? A few prayers, a quiet conference with a clergyman, a horoscope? No. He wanted names. Big names. The small fry he's willing to burn, but what gets him greedy are the marquises and counts, the big folk who are his enemies at the court, the army men who don't see eye to eye with his new reforms, and the old nobility down on their luck and ready to cause trouble. Isn't that so?"

They watched him uneasily, out of their depth.

"And who did I give him?" Lesage asked rhetorically. "I gave him Marshal Luxembourg. He was in my hand—for charms, for poison—and I opened my fingers." Lesage repeated the gesture, then snapped his fist shut under Guibourg's nose. "Where's the great Marshal now, eh? The door locks behind him as it does for us."

Guibourg and Marguerite nodded.

"So don't you think the Marquis de Louvois would be interested again if we were moved to talk? If I should hint to Lieutenant Reynie that I had information? If you, Marguerite, should be so overcome at your mother's death"—he spat on the stones, "that your tongue was loosened? If Abbé Guts here should back us up with the details he can so readily invent? Oh, we'll make them sweat like galley slaves."

"They'll put us in the Boot," Marguerite now protested. "Or the water. The water'll split your stomach or drown you as it did La Vigoureux."

"You know nothing. No Boot and no water if they don't bring you to trial! Trial first, Question after." Lesage laughed. "If it weren't for Reynie," and here he spat again, "I'd not risk it. Some jailors will take you down quiet and work on you on their own, but the Lieutenant's a civilized man. All by the book for him. And by God, I know the books," Lesage exclaimed passionately, jumping to his feet. Power was his goad and lording it over Guibourg and Marguerite had not been enough to quench an appetite sharpened by the barbarities of his time in transport and on the oar. But now he saw possibilities such as he had dreamed of: Louvois, Reynie! If he could put his lever to those wheels, he might yet touch the very workings of the crown. One opportunity gives way to another! There were great things before him still! Lesage was quite giddy with passion, with power, with fantasies, and before the last of the smoke from the Grève had vanished from the evening air, he had bullied Guibourg and Marguerite into agreeing to his scheme. Then he sat down and went over their stories with them, weaving a mesh of services and masses, of powders, poisonings and treasons. "But see you do not mention the lady too eagerly. Let her come out last and after a lot of work. Then they will hesitate. And while they hesitate, you, my friends, will live." Lesage laughed for sheer joy and cleverness, then snatched up the bottle. "To our lecherous King," he shouted. "His ladies will give us our lives!"

Soon after this rogues' council, Lieutenant Reynie started to send very disquieting reports to Louvois: Marguerite Monvoisin, daughter of the dead sorceress, had begun to speak of aphrodisiacs concocted for Madame de Montespan. Some of the material was so sensitive that Reynie was ordered to make extracts of the testimony for the palace alone, while the Chamber investigating the matter was left in the dark—and the court, too. Naturally, Athénaïs was told nothing, and she believed herself safe from the moment Claude returned from the Grève. She had jumped up from her chair and waited. Claude nodded without saying more and her mistress sat down slowly.

"She did not speak?"

"She resisted until the final moment and died without absolution."

Athénaïs crossed herself swiftly and touched her beads. "God save us from such a fate."

"She was brave," said Claude a trifle defiantly.

"And wicked—she deserved the stake." Athénaïs turned to the table beside her chair and idly picked through her books. She remembered the witch telling her fortune on the cold night at the Comtesse's and frightening her by describing the spotted hounds at Bellegarde. She remembered the corridors of the chateau at Avesnes where she had wandered seeking the King. Everything had led to this: to glory and the stake. Had Madame Voisin foreseen her own end or did fate surprise even a sorceress?

"Did it take very long?" she asked.

"Long enough, I suppose. They struck at her head with long iron poles."

"That's enough," said Athénaïs. "But we are safe."

"She preserved you, Madame."

But Athénaïs did not like to be reminded of obligations to such as Madame Voisin. "Bring me some brandy," she said. "And a glass for yourself. It will be the first swallow I've had without fearing I'd choke." Even as she spoke, she could feel her spirits rise. As she told Françoise de Maintenon shortly after, she was resigning herself to a new way of life; she intended to learn tranquility; she was going to consider her soul. "We can't change people," she said sagely. "We have to learn to live with their foibles."

Françoise nodded and Athénaïs poured more tisane for her. She thought the new marquise looked a trifle uncertain and gave a brilliant smile. So much had changed. Françoise had come very far, very fast, and neither of them had quite learned to accept her new role. But now that she was safe, Athénaïs felt some of her old spirit: nothing was impossible. The King still visited her daily. He would tire, perhaps, of pious chitchat with Françoise. "And the Dauphine?" she asked. "How do you like being her lady?"

Françoise smiled, touching the real gold lace that adorned her plain black dress. "It suits me, though the Dauphine would rather have had someone grander."

Athénaïs knew quite well that the appointment had stunned the court—especially the homely young Dauphine and her fellow German, Madame. "You know Germans," she said carelessly, "the petty marks of rank are important to them. When she has been at court long enough to see that all depends on His Majesty's favor, things will be different."

"His Majesty was kind enough to give me such a position," she said, dutiful always, "yet it will be hard to charm the Dauphine, no matter how long she is at court."

Athénaïs laughed maliciously and said what Françoise was too discreet to say: "And hard for the Dauphine to charm anyone. She is truly the ugliest woman ever seen."

Françoise allowed herself a smile. "But well-mannered and intelligent."

"Quite the ugliest woman since old—what was her name? The madwoman. Don't you remember, the one who talked to herself? The courtiers used to stick food in her pockets."

"That was before I came to court."

"A thousand years ago," Athénaïs admitted. "And now you sit very near the throne." Her eyes darkened, but she didn't seek a real quarrel. "They say La Fontanges is still seriously ill."

"That gives me no pleasure."

"Don't play the hypocrite with me," Athénaïs said good-naturedly, "she hated you, and, had she had children, would have sought to displace the Duc du Maine. You know that."

"His position must be made secure," Françoise said quickly. "I have talked and talked to His Majesty."

"There is a chance. Some property of his cousin's might change hands."

"La Grande Mademoiselle will never make Maine her heir!"

"No, but she still wants to marry Captain Lauzan. Still! It is thought," Athénaïs said carefully, "that a legacy—or a gift—to Maine might be the price."

"It would put him beyond danger," Françoise said eagerly. Though she was fond of some, Athénaïs's boy, the Duc du Maine, was still the only creature she loved.

"I am working on it," said Athénaïs.

"The sooner the better." Françoise's voice, which had been warm and concerned, dropped in temperature. "For now there is this new Mademoiselle Doré."

"I'm sure His Majesty is sleeping with her," Athénaïs said calmly, enjoying the flush that ran across her friend's features.

She had never taken the King's casual infidelities very seriously, and it amused her to see that Françoise was wounded by every deflection. "Come, come," she teased, "the Queen is no longer jealous. You have done yeoman work to persuade His Majesty to such fidelity as he now manages. That little trollop is nothing. And Fontanges is finished—even if she regains her health. That was an unlucky child for her," she added and thought of her own nine. "I hope your constitution is good, Françoise."

"Perfect, though so was La Fontanges's before she came to court."

"The court is said to be dangerous for young virgins."

"So it seems. You know, she now claims to have been poisoned."

"I had heard that," Athénaïs said, continuing boldly, "and feared it would be said even before she started demanding guards."

"The Germans agree—I mean, Madame and my Dauphine."

"They would. Madame's mad for gossip. She pays informants just to have something to put in those endless letters to her relatives. Truly! You needn't look so surprised. And what she doesn't know, she will invent."

Françoise was cautious. "I believe she already has."

Athénaïs remained calm. "And who do they think has endangered La Belle Fontanges?"

Françoise didn't answer, but raised her cup slowly and drank from it with deliberate ceremony.

Although she was not surprised, Athénaïs felt her back stiffen and her smile fade. "I see. Then you are brave to visit me, Françoise."

"I know you too well to have any fears. But that is the rumor. I am sorry. Her illness is laid to you. To some drink."

"And the death of her child, as well?"

Françoise was uncomfortable, but Athénaïs laughed. "You are too cautious. So their wickedness knows no bounds. That is jealousy. Learn from it, Françoise. All things have their price—even the favor of the King."

She flushed again, but said, "I will inform Mademoiselle Doré."

Athénaïs smiled and passed the cakes. When she wasn't mad with jealousy herself, she enjoyed watching Françoise operate. Such control, such coldness, such intellect. It was a pleasure to observe a lady who could plan. Particularly now, when her own anxieties had miraculously been lifted. Perhaps they should open a joint attack on Mademoiselle Doré. Then they would see who would corner His Majesty. Anything was possible.

XVII

This foolish happiness lasted until fall. Although Reynie had been questioning the sorcerers throughout the summer, it was not until another of their band, La Filastre, had gone to the stake in September, that the worst charges surfaced. La Filastre had implicated Madame de Montespan in the use of Galet's aphrodisiac powders, then denied all. As soon as she was dead, more serious accusations spilled from the rest of the coven. Marguerite was the first. She babbled about powders and poisons and first raised the idea that they had been trying to poison the King as well as Mademoiselle de Fontanges, a notion that turned Reynie as white as his paper. It seemed the sorcerers had poisoned a petition that Madame Voisin had tried to present to the King. They had also poisoned cloth to sell to La Fontanges via a valet named Romani, who had been Marguerite's lover. There had also been talk of compromising the powders Marguerite claimed were regularly delivered to Madame de Montespan. All this was her mother's doing, Marguerite maintained sulkily. She would interrupt the questioning to sniffle and blubber and curse her mother for leaving others to answer for her crimes. Or else, for she was childish at heart, she would go off into meaningless details of picnics they had had on the way back from delivering powders to Clagny or of a salmon and fried herring supper after an abortive trip with the poisoned petition to Saint-Germain. These curious details stuck in Reynie's mind and gave a certain substance to stories he felt were basically fantastic.

Nonetheless, even if the famed Galet's powders were never more than Spanish fly, the King's safety had been compromised. Full of fears, Reynie would go back to question the wary and unscrupulous Lesage or, the worst of the lot, the Abbé Guibourg. The girl was a simpleton; Lesage, a crook; Guibourg was something more sinister, and Reynie could always smell him before the jailor had even opened the door.

"The prisoner, Guibourg, Lieutenant."

"Bring him in."

The Abbé shuffled forward, blinking in the strong sunlight after his dim cell. Reynie nodded toward the stool in front of the desk and with a great clanking of his irons, the old man sat down, puffing and wheezing. His face was now thin; the baggy skin hung in folds from his cheekbones and jaw. His filmy eye rolled up and down; his good one, bloodshot and tinged with yellow, fixed on the Lieutenant despairingly. His large hands, once red, were now pale and spotted, and his great body, seemingly untouched by scant rations, spilled over the stool like a lumpy sack.

"You have told me various things about the business of the late Catherine Deshayes, known as La Voisin," Reynie began.

"Indeed, Sir," the Abbé wheezed. "A very vile woman."

"You have been implicated in black masses said at her house."

Guibourg's good eye now wandered from the Lieutenant's face. "It is true, Sir." He spoke with surprise as if he found such a thing hard to credit.

"For whom were these done?"

"For ladies of quality, Sir. Mostly ladies of quality."

"It has been said that one was performed for Madame de Montespan."

Guibourg looked vague and regretful and for a few seconds, Reynie had hope. "Yes, that's true," the Abbé said and cleared his throat, a disgusting mucousy rattle. "Cost me an ecu." His raddled face was distorted into a frown. "Cost me an ecu, the first one did."

Reynie looked up when he had finished the notation. "What for?"

Guibourg licked his lips and flapped his spotted hands on his knees. "For the service. The demons demand a sacrifice. 'Astaroth and Asmodu, I conjure you to accept the sacrifice that I present of this infant—'" His voice was hollow, resonant and disagreeable.

"These rites required the murder of a child?"

"A strong word," Guibourg said with another wheeze and snuffle. "See I had most of them of Lepère, the abortionist. Premature births they were." He snuffled and snickered and shifted unsteadily on his stool. "Some of the finest blood in the kingdom in those 'angels.' Cost me an ecu." He looked down, wiped his nose, and added, "Course, that did for two. Saved the heart and guts for a second mass and powders. Very sovereign for powders."

"What sort of powders?" Reynie asked with distaste.

"Powders for whatever you want, Lieutenant. For love, mostly. Now, the infant's blood powder is a good one, but better for inspiring passion, as it were, is another one Mademoiselle and I made up." He wheezed and winked.

"What Mademoiselle?"

"Why Mademoiselle des Oeillets—the masked lady. Oh, I'd recognize her again anywhere." He gave a little giggle and began to slobber. "A sovereign concoction, and entertaining in the making. It requires ground bat and sperm and menstrual blood. A bit of flour to bind it together—"

It was after this session that Reynie stopped questioning

Guibourg and the others and appealed to Louvois that something had to be done. "Think of the dangers," he said. "I fear the strain on Madame de Montespan—if she is involved. She could be driven to some recklessness by sheer anxiety."

Louvois stroked his chin and said it was a matter of state. His flushed face was tinged gray along the jowl and his small fat hands drummed on his desk. "His Majesty will not hear of distressing her. Besides, as you have pointed out, her accusers are trash of the lowest sort. That Lesage would tell any lie to save his skin."

"We may be able to avoid questioning the Duchesse directly. Her household has been compromised. That can be proved one way or another. This Mademoiselle des Oeillets is the key. We can say she has been implicated and give her a chance to clear her name. If that can be done, the connection between Madame de Montespan's household and this nest of witches and poisoners collapses."

Louvois fiddled unhappily with his thick lace cuffs, but at last he nodded. "You will prepare me a digest of the accusations and I will see her myself."

Louvois made this call toward the middle of November. Claude was quite at ease—ever since the elevation of her mistress, she, too, had been an important person at the court, someone to be pursued and flattered by those seeking access to the favorite. Even Monsieur Louvois was not a great surprise, although what he had to say upset her a good deal.

"A criminal investigation? Monsieur, I am horrified! My poor lady would be shocked. You know she would never tolerate such behavior from her servants."

"Indeed," said the War Minister, who tended to tread heavily in such matters, "the accusations are that you were merely her courier. That all was known to your lady."

"Yet you have not spoken to her of these things," Claude said shrewdly. "Your evidence cannot be very strong."

"In the case of His Majesty's safety, any suspicion must be investigated."

"Without doubt, without doubt, yet you haven't troubled my lady."

"There may be no need," Louvois said. "I'm sure you would prefer her to remain tranquil."

"Tranquil she is," Claude said, watching Louvois carefully. "She has no idea of these rumors and charges."

"Well, there you are," Louvois said. He was deeply suspicious, but Claude des Oeillets was so firm in her protestations of innocence, so upset for any smear on her lady's honor, so eager to assist his inquiries, that the War Minister began to feel easier. True, there was a kind of vagueness about her information: she "might" have had her hand read by La Voisin—many did such; she seemed to remember going to the witch's house once with friends for a party. She did not remember when; it was several years ago, and possibly that's how the sorcerers had gotten her name. She was indignant that the rogues would attempt to use an innocent frolic to damage her lady.

That might be true enough. "You know," Louvois said later to Reynie, "the valets and ladies' maids of Paris are all addicted to such recreations. It is not beyond belief that the Duchesse de Montespan knew nothing of her servant's contacts."

"It is not," Reynie agreed, "but still I would like to clear up the matter of whether des Oeillets did visit the witches."

"She says she might have met them once with friends."

"I would make a test," said the thorough Reynie. "I would take her to the chateau and see if the sorcerers recognize her."

Louvois frowned and raised objections. Having reaped considerable political advantage from the trials, he was keen to avoid losing his credit by bringing scandal near the throne. Finally, though, pressed by His Majesty's demands and Reynie's protests, he had to agree, and one freezing, sleety afternoon, Lieutenant Reynie and Claude des Oeillets visited Vincennes. As she stepped out under the open portico of the central block, Claude had to grit her teeth to keep from shivering with cold and nerves, and, not for the first time, she was glad for her good stage training. She had taken considerable pains over her makeup in preparation for the visit, lightening her hair a few shades, trimming her eyebrows, broadening her cheekbones with paint—a dozen little tricks. Thank God, Madame Voisin was dead! There would have been no hope with her. Even the Abbé Lesage presented a problem—he had probably seen her once or twice without her mask—and Marguerite? It was possible. She wiped her forehead, damp with sweat and rain and pushed her hood back from her hair. Beyond the doorway, the carriage horses stood steaming in the chill and the guardsmen clanked back and forth, their plumes and velvets sodden in the wet.

A jailor escorted them upstairs and over an open bridge a dozen feet above the courtyard to the tower of the old keep. The doors opened with a clang, and soldiers within presented arms. Then they climbed a narrow stair, smoky with the torches stuck in metal stanchions in the walls. Claude could smell the damp, the age, the musty mildew smell of cold stone, and, when they reached the landing, the acrid woodiness of open fires and the stale odor of dirty humanity. The jailor stopped and looked at Reynie for directions.

"Open the Abbé Lesage's cell."

Another clanking and scraping, then the thick, iron studded door opened. Lesage got up, wrapped in his blanket, and came to the opening. "Do you know this woman?" Reynie asked without ceremony.

The Abbé stepped closer. The jailor's fire flickered orange and gold and the smoke from the torch in the anteroom drifted across their faces. Lesage looked at her, then at Reynie. "It's Mademoiselle," he said, quite loudly. "Mademoiselle des Oeillets."

She could feel Reynie's glance, but kept her expression still. "You don't know me now," Lesage asked. "Or don't want to know me?" He reached out one scabbed and dirty hand, but the jailor pushed him back and Reynie nodded.

The next cell was Marguerite's, and whether she had overheard Lesage, which Claude thought very likely, or whether one careless night the girl had gotten a glimpse of her face, Marguerite did not hesitate for long. "That's the servant of Madame——"

"We will not mention that name," Reynie said quickly.

"Well, then, it's Mademoiselle des Oeillets. I've given powders to her many times."

"They heard Lesage," Claude said to Reynie when the hideous Guibourg had also identified her. "It is possible the first saw me when I had my hand read. The rest—impossible. It is collusion."

The Lieutenant sighed. "Yet the Abbé knew you instantly. If he had only seen you once, I doubt he'd have been so sure."

Claude felt the sweat running down between her shoulder blades. "Only once—if he ever saw me at all. I think it's uncertain. I believe he is mistaken. In this light, it is not hard to see how it could happen. There is a chambermaid of the Marquise de Castelman who much resembled me and—of course!" She stopped right on the stair and Reynie almost stumbled on her trailing cloak. "There is my niece. My brother's girl. They reappeared just a few years ago. She is enough like me to cause confusion."

Reynie watched her soberly. "A niece?"

"My only one. Raised around the army camps she would scarcely have feared witches, would she? Soldiers often go in for horoscopes and little charms, which seems only sensible in military gentlemen."

Reynie sighed and was dubious. And though by the time they left the tower, Claude had raised enough objections and qualifications and new suspects to leave at least a doubt, he still had to convey the bad news to Louvois that the sorcerers had all recognized her. As for Claude, she had to tell Madame de Montespan, but although annoyed, Athénaïs did not at first feel it could be too serious.

"La Voisin is dead! What are these but her hired priests, her small time confidence men? Were you not always masked?" Now her voice rose threateningly.

"I am almost sure, Madame."

"Almost!"

"They would perhaps have 'identified' me anyway, Madame," said Claude, who never lacked for some device. "Who else would be brought before them? If they were after you, they would seek to implicate me."

"That is true, I will mention that to Monsieur Colbert when he arrives." She looked at the clock, took a turn around the room and sat down. "The conduct of this whole business is shocking. If I could only speak to the King . . ." But this thought was painful. She could not speak to the King—not on such a matter. And in any case, he never gave her an opportunity. Though he visited her every day, he was careful never to be alone with her, fearing, perhaps, some confidence, some confession. As a distraction from his cowardice and her folly, Athénaïs called for a mirror, found fault with her ribbons and kept Claude running back and forth until a footman appeared with the news that visitors had arrived.

"Ah, Monsieur Colbert." She nodded to him and gave Claude a look that sent her into the anteroom.

"Madame de Montespan." The old minister, stiff, fat and leaden faced, bowed. "Duchesse, this is Monsieur Duplessis."

"Monsieur," said Athénaïs. The man who advanced and bowed was thin, solemn and grave. His face was furrowed, his eyes still. His linen, she noticed was clean but ancient.

"Monsieur Duplessis is a specialist in criminal law."

"Criminal law? I had not imagined I needed defense against accusations of any crime, Monsieur Colbert," she said archly and motioned for them to sit down.

The minister sighed and lowered himself unsteadily to the chair with the help of his cane. Duplessis laid a sheaf of papers on the table, then, without speaking, glanced at Colbert.

The old man wiped his face on his handkerchief, cleared his throat and said, "Madame, as you have heard, the Chamber at the Arsenal has been sitting on a number of serious cases all relating to this woman Voisin. Because of the extraordinary composition, secrecy and procedures of the Chamber, these cases have had an unfortunate tendency to take on political overtones." Here he stopped and Athénaïs had time to imagine all the worst before he continued.

"My concern with the way charges and accusations were being made led me to consult Monsieur Duplessis who has unusual expertise in weighing evidence. I have asked him, Madame, to look over the particulars which have—touched—on you."

So it was serious, Athénaïs thought. She was glad she had spent the last few months in marriage negotiations for Colbert's third daughter—and glad the match had come off successfully. "Am I to know what has been said against me?"

"The workings of the Chamber," Colbert replied, "are secret. However, so serious are the accusations and so elevated your position, that I was able to present to His Majesty that some specialist in the law should serve, as it were, as your defense."

"These are criminal charges?" Behind her, Athénaïs could hear the clock tick, the fire's whistle, the restless feet of her little dogs. Servants passed in the hall; the wind monotonously rattled the north windows.

"Monsieur Duplessis will explain," said Colbert. He leaned forward, his hands clasped on his staff, his heavy face damp.

Duplessis opened his papers. "You will realize, Madame," he said by way of excuse and introduction, "that your accusers are of the lowest criminal classes."

"It is a wonder they are given any credence."

Duplessis did not answer, just smoothed his papers and began reading in a dry voice. "Charges, with witness and date. The first, that Madame de Montespan did give love potions to His Majesty over a number of years—Marguerite Monvoisin, interrogations in July and August; also Galet, September, and La Filastre, September, later retracted."

"One, at least, was honest," Athénaïs said tartly, despite her horror and humiliation.

"Second, that sacrilegious black masses were said for the benefit of Madame de Montespan by the Abbé Guibourg, sacristan of St. Marcel's—La Filastre and Marguerite Monvoisin, interrogations in August and October; Abbé Guibourg, interrogations in September and October."

Athénaïs gripped the arm of the chair. "I have never even heard of these people," she protested.

"Third, that an attempt was made on behalf of Madame de Montespan to poison Mademoiselle de Fontanges by means of poisoned gloves and poisoned fabric stuffs carried by Romani, a valet, and a man named Bertrand—the same Marguerite Monvoisin in August; La Filastre, in September."

"This is the voice of my enemies," Athénaïs shouted. "As if I had taken La Fontanges so seriously." She would have said more and allowed herself a tantrum if Duplessis had not interrupted quietly.

"There is another charge—more serious than any of the others."

"You joke, Monsieur. More serious than murder? Than sacrilege? They make me a monster."

"It has been suggested by the Monvoisin girl that there was an attempt to poison the King—"

Athénaïs jumped up. "So this is what I am accused of! It is beyond belief and beyond bearing. I will confront those scoundrels; I will take the case before His Majesty. We will see if he will believe that the mother of seven of his children would connive at his death. What was I supposed to gain from this? What possibly could have been my benefit?" She swept the books from the table in fury and Monsieur Duplessis had to move quickly to save his legal brief.

"Madame," said Colbert. "You must be calm. No one here believes the charges, yet I am sure, admitting their gravity, you will agree that some defense must be made."

"My life at court, my children, my reputation, my years of intimacy with the royal family stand for nothing?"

"They have won you friends, Madame," Colbert said. "Yet in a court of law—"

"A court of law? A secret chamber with sealed indictments! This is not law, Monsieur, this is persecution," Athénaïs cried. Fear and anger had gone to her head like champagne. All the time when she had thought herself safe, had joked with His Majesty, had teased Françoise, these monstrous accusations, these charges, had been in the King's mind, and, bitterest of all, perhaps known to Françoise as well. She paced around the room in a fury of grief, humiliation and fear.

Quite coldly and methodically, Duplessis began to outline his work. Although Athénaïs was tempted to smash every vase, every picture, every ornament in the room and then to begin on the windows like her mad husband, the lawyer's gravity calmed her.

"When Monsieur Colbert asked me to consider these accusations, Madame, I decided to proceed on a number of fronts. I attempted to find other witnesses. None have turned up—not unexpected in such cases. Next, I examined the consistency of the accounts, the reliability of the accusers, and—a matter you yourself pointed out—the plausibility of the stories.

"All these," he continued, "I am able to attack. The characters of those speaking against you, Madame, are such that they would pass unchallenged in no court of law. Lesage, who, at various times, has corroborated most of the charges, is an ex-galley slave, a counterfeiter, an unfrocked priest, a confidence man."

Athénaïs sat down, closed her eyes for an instant and wondered how she had ever come to place her life in such hands.

"Guibourg is an apostate priest, the father of at least seven children, a pervert and, the police believe, responsible for the murder of a number of infants and young children; La Filastre, the witch who has already been burned, is accused of dealing in poisons and abortions. She contradicted herself a dozen times. In any ordinary court, her testimony would be thrown out as unreliable. Marguerite Monvoisin was her mother's assistant in all her dealings; she is reliably accused of aborting her own child by the valet, Romani. These, Madame, are your opponents."

"I am amazed that the words of such trash were even recorded," Athénaïs said haughtily, yet she was sick at heart because of the mention of the King.

"It was not only recorded," Colbert added gloomily, "but others are in jail or in exile because of it."

"There are many discrepancies," Duplessis continued in his methodical manner. "Madame Voisin, supposedly the ringleader, the person at whose home these schemes were purportedly hatched, mentioned nothing. She was questioned under torture and none of this came out."

"And the others? They have been put to the Question?" Athénaïs asked.

"Only La Filastre was brought to trial. She was put to the
Question but she retracted almost all of her confession afterwards. She claimed she lied under torture to end her suffering."

"The Question is not the final arbiter, it would seem."

Duplessis gave a little shrug. He was used to allowing for the
effects of pain and fear and accepted without demur the judicial
techniques he could so cleverly manipulate. "There are a variety
of inconsistencies within the Voisin girl's testimony; we can go
over them individually later. There are peculiar features to
Guibourg's testimony as well, especially in his account of your
supposed wishes, Madame. You will see"—Duplessis passed over
a sheet—"that he requests the demons grant the favor of the
Dauphin. The Dauphin was a child of"—he scrambled through
his notes—"of five, Madame, at that point."

"And my friend, anyway," she said. "The Dauphin's favor was
easily won by a little kindness."

"Finally, two more points," Duplessis said, his voice betraying
his satisfaction. The neat layout of a case, the precise demolition
of the opposing arguments were for him as exhilarating as a fresh
scent to a hound or a glimpse of the deer for a hunter. "Though
you are known to be generous, a fee of ten thousand livres for an
errand seems excessive, does it not?" He passed yet another sheet
from his rumpled pile and Athénaïs scanned it without taking in
the meaning of the characters. The situation was too fantastic:
she had to help this man unravel monstrous lies without letting
him touch the truth. She made herself smile. "It is absurd."

"And last," Duplessis said, "the plot against the King—"

Although she had been forewarned, Athénaïs felt her face
change, felt her blood chill.

"It was in two parts. The first concerned a petition. Reynie believes a poisoned petition is a technical possibility. Monsieur Colbert and myself—and, as a matter of fact, La Voisin's girl as well—doubt this. Nonetheless, the sorcerers produced one and La Voisin tried to give it to His Majesty at the palace. She failed to see him at Saint-Germain on at least one, possibly two, occasions. Had she known you, surely you would have eased her way, not knowing, of course, her murderous intentions?"

"It's not unlikely."

Duplessis smiled and nodded briskly. "That is what I told Monsieur Colbert. That is a very strong point in our favor, Madame."

"You have done excellent work, Monsieur Duplessis. Forgive me, if I have seemed insufficiently appreciative. You will understand this has been a severe shock."

"Surely, Madame," Duplessis said, inclining his head. "But I hope you see now that your defense is strong. In any court of law we could make a very strong attack on such lies."

Colbert cleared his throat hoarsely. "You are in good hands with Monsieur Duplessis, Duchesse," he said, pleased at the results of his intervention.

"So it seems. He will be able to show the world the absurdity of these charges. But," she added, unwilling to leave any possible doubt, "you mentioned two attempts against His Majesty. If the other was as foolish and bizarre as this petition business, I think I can rest easy." This time she found she could smile without effort. They had gone too far. In trying to entrap her more deeply, they had tripped and fallen.

"That they came up with the petition scheme at all, when they might more logically have proceeded differently, is a very strong proof that all is false," Duplessis said carefully, and this introduction allowed Athénaïs to compose her face and to be on her guard. "We must take it seriously only because of the mention of your uncle, the Marquis de Ternes."

"My uncle!" Athénaïs exclaimed with automatic indignation. "Monsieur Colbert, this is a terrible business. Why wasn't I informed immediately? I must speak to His Majesty."

"He was a client of the Abbé Lesage, Madame."

"I understand that many went to this Abbé for horoscopes," Athénaïs said, although the memory of her uncle's threats, his demands, made her heart race. She had run risk upon risk! "Can he have been accused for such trifles?"

"He is accused of seeking to procure poison," Colbert said. "He will almost certainly have to be arrested."

"I cannot believe it," Athénaïs said angrily, although she could believe it well. "Though we were not on good terms, he had bounties enough of me to have kept him loyal. I cannot take it seriously. Most like they think to get at me by mentioning him."

"Most like," agreed Duplessis, "for the initial scheme might easily have been employed had you really been La Voisin's customer. They spoke of switching the powders she supposedly sold you and of substituting arsenic for the aphrodisiacs."

Athénaïs gave a start of horror, and for a dreadful moment both she and her visitors thought she would collapse. The room darkened before her eyes and the red of the fire seeped across the pastels of the room. Then, as if it had materialized before her, she saw the pot with the tisane and the infused powders, saw it knocked over in her anger at His Majesty, saw the fluid drip down the leg of the table, saw Claude drop the packets into the fire. She had come so close; either the angels had saved her or the saints had chosen this extraordinary humiliation to point her danger. She pressed her fingers against her eyes and realized that in her shock and despair she had covered her face. She lowered her hands. Colbert and Duplessis were sitting on the edges of their seats, fearful of revelation. Athénaïs drew in her breath, touched her heart and said, "Excuse me, Gentlemen. The shock has been too much for me." She managed to smile, but she dared not call for tea or brandy. She could not trust herself to face her servant.

The two men nodded, embarrassed even to look at each other, and Athénaïs knew she had betrayed herself. "For the love I bear His Majesty," she said, then stopped, and wiped her eyes. "I fear I am ruined forever. The foulness of such accusations, though disproved a thousand times, must leave some taint."

"The character of your traducers, Madame, goes far in explanation," said Duplessis, recovering his suavity.

Athénaïs felt it would be unwise to say more. "Thank you, Monsieur. And you, Monsieur Colbert. I am grateful."

"We will let you recover yourself," the old minister said, rising with an effort. His eyes were sad, sceptical; his face, even more bloodless than before. They bowed and left. The sound of their feet descending the marble steps was unaccompanied by conversation. What was there for them to say, Athénaïs thought bitterly. What was there for her to say—or do. Only this. She reached out her hand and rang the bell. Claude opened the door.

"Madame? Have they given you some comfort?"

"Only one thing now will give me comfort," Athénaïs said. "That is never to see you or your brat again in this life."

XVIII

Sometimes in the *appartements,* seeing the same old faces, making the same brittle chat, Athénaïs wondered if Versailles was to be her purgatory as it had been Louise's. Beyond doubt she was trapped, trapped in splendor, true, yet caught as surely as the reflections that rippled from one end of the Hall of Mirrors to the other. Her shame was bitter; her wickedness had made her dependent on the King's mercy, and with beauty diminished, with favor lost, she could do nothing but await the inevitable verdict. The charges were so grave, her involvement so obvious, that he would surely send her from court, confine her to a convent, expose her to the snickers and malice of her enemies. When she thought this way, Athénaïs would lock herself in her cabinet, fall before her prie-dieu and attempt to reach the saints. Yet even her piety was marred, for though her heart cried out for confession and penance, for a spiritual director who would scorch her soul and burn away her pride, a certain caution remained essential. Some things could not be confessed. Athénaïs had to make do with fasting, with prayers, with a lavishness to her favorite charities, hospitals and convents that tempted their religious proprietors to greed. She prepared her soul for disaster, but disaster, flirtatious as always, now changed its mind.

The cold days stretched on; the ice thickened on the palace

windows; the courtiers' feet went numb on frozen marbles, and away from the huge, roasting fires, a lady's bare shoulders were chilled to gooseflesh. Still the King did nothing. Though sometimes Athénaïs thought she would faint or fall speechless from anxiety, by now charm, wit, even a semblance of gaiety, were almost automatic. She joked with the King, she impressed the ambassadors. She and Françoise, on decent terms, passed afternoons with the children. Helplessness brought out her courage; Athénaïs was as gallant now as any that served the King, but His Majesty saw only the tormenting appearance of innocence and thought he would never erase his doubts. He had bad dreams, awoke sweating in the night, but could not make up his mind. Though Lieutenant Reynie pressed each time he saw him for the completion of the trials, for a resumption of the Chamber, the King postponed everything. He ordered the sorcerers held, but the reports of their interrogations were locked away and an uneasy calm settled in through the winter.

Then one warm day months later, when the gardens were full of roses and their scent blew in the open windows, soft and insistent as a lover's perfume, the daily ministerial meeting was interrupted by a messenger.

His Majesty nodded and the courier advanced. He was young, the King noticed, as they all were lately, flushed with riding, smelling of expensive oils, leather and horse. The boy bowed and handed him a letter.

"From the Duc de Noailles."

The King knew. He waited until the messenger withdrew. Waited, until Colbert and Louvois found something to consult in their voluminous files, until the secretary's pen began to scratch, scratch, monotonous as a nibbling mouse. He broke the seal, scanned the pages.

"The Duchesse de Fontanges is dead."

While they read the letter, the King sat immobile. In his private cabinet, he had a miniature of her, painted during her brief glory. Had he been alone, he would have taken it out, and held it in his hand. When he had tired of her, when she had grown cross and weepy and swollen eyed, he had thrown it in the drawer, but it was there he was sure, still perfect while its original— His mouth tightened. A month or so before, they had been hunting near the convent where Mademoiselle lay ill. He remembered it had been wet underfoot, the horses and riders spattered with mud and water but warm in the early spring sun, the horses and hounds full of fire, full of eager, animal joy. The riders, too. When he recognized the area, he had pulled up his horse—with what ideas, what memories? He looked out at the sky, crossed by a swift flight of pigeons. He had thought of her as she had been the year before, a perfect rosy nymph, running happy and ill bred along the frozen canal or rising from her blue satin bed with her hair down and her pretty white throat bare. It had seemed possible that behind the gray convent walls she was as pretty and as perfect as ever; waiting for her lover to recall her, waiting for him to lift her across his saddle and race back through the woods with her to court. It seemed so obvious that he had laughed out loud at his dull moods, black dreams, old man's piety. Just to see her would be a tonic, so he shouted to his huntsmen and put the spurs to his horse and led the hunt racing pell mell across the fields and through the trees to the convent where they pulled up, dirty and gorgeous, horses tossing their heads and whinnying, the dogs barking, the young courtiers joking and laughing and flirting noisily.

At first, they thought they would all go in to see Mademoiselle, to cheer her up, but the mother superior, her sister, took him aside. "She is very weak, Your Majesty."

He had known then, instantly, that his hopes were fantasy, as insubstantial as a dream. He should have paid his respects, conveyed his good wishes, promised another contribution to the order and left. Instead, he went in, leaving the rest of the hunt roistering in the courtyard.

They walked down an ancient corridor, plain and bare with a low ceiling. Mademoiselle was in a little brick and masonry room at the left, and at first, though she raised her head and struggled to sit up, though she had the same yellow hair and blue eyes, he thought they had made a mistake. The rosy nymph was quite gray, her face puffy and swollen as rising bread, her shoulders shrunken, her splendid hair lank and unkempt; the Duchesse was dying, and she smelled of the grave.

The King took her hand, sat down beside her and wept: for her, for his sins, for the deaths of both their youths. In extremis, the poor child was clever; she said the one elegant phrase he had ever heard pass her lips.

"I can die happy," she whispered. "I have seen my King in tears because of me."

Colbert cleared his throat, and the King turned from the window, from his dying mistress, from his own failings. "What is to be done, Your Majesty?"

"She should be buried at the convent. Compose a letter expressing my deepest sympathy, request the usual masses, remind them of my continued friendship for the order."

There was a pause. "The body will have to be opened, Your Majesty," Louvois said.

The King frowned. Though an autopsy might answer many questions, he was inwardly furious. There was no need to know with such certainty. "Opened? Let us not butcher her. She had been sick for months."

Louvois repeated stubbornly, "Your Majesty, it must be done." He stopped, unwilling to rehearse the arguments the King must know as well as he: that the rumors, the charges from the sorcerers, La Fontanges's own insistence that she had been poisoned—all cried out for an autopsy. "It will be thought there is something to hide."

"There is no need. Send Reynie. He is to see that all her letters have been secured. Have him make a search; Noailles, after all, is not a policeman. See it is done," he repeated crossly.

"The family is sure to raise the matter of opening the body," Louvois persisted.

"Tell Reynie that is not my wish. Tell him I do not want it," the King said loudly and got to his feet.

The ministers rose and bowed, and the King left. But by the next afternoon, they had returned to the subject. Reynie reported that the mother superior was insistent; the rest of the family as well. The Lieutenant's thin, homely face was troubled. "I do not see how it can be avoided, Sire."

"There is no legal necessity. I do not wish her corpse disturbed—and for what?"

"There is no need in the law, Sire," Reynie said, "yet in policy there is every necessity."

Louvois and Colbert agreed and, at last, much against his wishes, the King gave his consent. A surreptitious buzz ran around the court. Madame, the Princess Palatine, told the Dauphine that poison would be obvious unless Madame de Montespan bribed the doctors. Madame de Maintenon contemplated the elimination of one rival—and possibly two—with less charity than was strictly Christian, and Madame de Montespan went into her closet, prayed for the soul of the departed and begged the saints that no one had fed the lady arsenic. At the convent, the doctors masked their faces and gutted the body of Angélique de Fontanges, sawed open her skull, weighed out her heart and lungs. The latter were quite decayed: the King's pretty lady had died of pneumonia.

"You sure of this?" the under jailor asked. He scratched his neck and rubbed at the lice in the neckband of his filthy shirt.

"By the saints," Lesage exclaimed, "give it back if you're hesitant. Why, I've had a marquis pay me gold for such a charm. But if the lady's virtue is not worth a few sous, give it back. I scorn to defend my wares, when I've had the cream of Paris at my feet begging for my skills."

"Don't be so hasty, Abbé. You say it is sure?"

"You brought me the bats yourself, didn't you? Now, bat's blood is a sovereign fluid, as is well known, they being creatures of the moon, so to speak."

"That is true."

"And the lock of her hair. You did not cheat me, now, did you? It wasn't cut from some tart in the common dungeon?"

"Abbé, I swear! On my mother's grave."

Lesage smiled. "Well then, it is as sure as certain to work. If you have not deceived me, it is a perfect charm."

The under jailor, simple fellow that he was, now denied up and down that he had tampered with the Abbé's ingredients, until Lesage could hardly keep from laughing. But he prudently contented himself with adding another few sous to the costs "on account of the quality of the ingredients" and after a little more haggling the turnkey went off with a potion to secure the favors of his landlady. This exchange left the Abbé in such fine humor that he was caught off guard by a commotion in the hallway: the thump of soldiers' feet, a rattle of cells, the bark of orders. He shifted his chains and squinted through the small opening in his door, which swung open so suddenly he was thrown back against the wall.

"Adam Lesage?" the military captain asked.

"Abbé Lesage," he answered, though his brain was racing like a cornered rat. What had happened? What would they do to him? They could not burn him without a trial!"

"This is the prisoner," the jailor said.

The captain handed over some papers and the jailor nodded. One of the soldiers stepped forward and seized the Abbé's manacles, another fastened a chain around his neck with an iron collar.

"What means this? Where are you taking me?"

Behind the captain's cape, he saw Guibourg and Galet, also in irons, and Romani. The other, noble inmates like de Ternes had been released a few weeks previously; now it seemed that all the rest were being turned out of their cells.

The captain gave a command and with a jerk on his neck chain, Lesage was propelled forward toward the stair. His legs ached before they got to the bottom and he was relieved to see a cart waiting, even if Guibourg began to whimper and whine that he was too old to burn. Lesage blinked in the strong light, so different from the few diffused rays that penetrated the keep, admired the exotic spectacle of trees and grass, and regretted the loss of certain useful stores abandoned in his cell. The under jailor's coins, however, were secreted among his rags. He thought they might buy him something—if he had any time for commerce.

The order was given. They climbed in the cart, Guibourg reluctantly and with such difficulty that at last the captain applied the flat of his sword to the old sacristan's sagging backside. Then they waited in the unfamiliar sun, silent, the horses shifting their feet, until the escort formed around them, muskets slung over their shoulders. They left by the east gate, and Lesage felt his hopes rise—though they could still turn, they could still be on the Grève in daylight. The cart rolled steadily east, however, and that evening when he slipped the youngest of the soldiers a coin, Lesage discovered that they were going all the way to the citadel of Besançon on the Swiss border. The Chamber investigating their cases had been shut down. He and Guibourg and the rest were to be confined in perpetuity in the border fortress. Lesage leaned back in the straw of the cart, watched the stars and laughed. Then he put his face in his hands and wept.

The heat let up a little in the afternoon, and the King decided that they would take out the gondolas that evening. The musicians were summoned and the barge that would carry them and their instruments prepared. The gondoliers bestirred themselves and checked their craft. The chefs and pastry cooks hastened to prepare the cakes and confections that would be required and pages raced up and down the length of the gardens bearing messages concerning the outing.

By evening, when the sun hung hot and pink near the horizon, all was ready. The ladies and gentlemen of the court trailed after the King, their fancy shoes crunching over the endless white gravel paths and slipping soundlessly along the lawns. Some of the younger courtiers lost themselves in the little groves or played tag like children amid the statuary. Walking decorously between Madame de Maintenon and Madame de Montespan, the King could hear their laughter, could hear the youthful sound of running feet amid the trees, as if his gardens were full of ghosts, echoing with fetes and loves long past.

There was some faded paint on the fountain of Apollo and the Nymphs, and the King stopped, disturbed by this hint of his bad dreams. It reminded him of the things he still had to decide: what to do about Athénaïs, where she should be sent and when. She stood beside him and now reached out to brush away some loose flakes of blue paint.

"It is the damp," she remarked. "We have had a similar problem at Clagny."

"I'm not sure now that I like the paint," the King said. "I may have it taken off and left plain in the Italian style."

"Perhaps just the gilt," said Athénaïs, who loved a little glitter.

"Like Madame de Maintenon," suggested the King, glancing at her plain black dress, trimmed opulently with masses of gold lace.

"She sets the new style," observed Athénaïs. Neither of them took her up on this, and she gave a smile at once bitter and triumphant.

"I will see," said the King. They moved down the long stretch of lawn between the groves of beeches. Ahead, Lully's violins began the serenade, a sign the Queen's carriage had arrived. In the flurry of excitement, Monsieur murmured something, and the King paused to talk, leaving the two women to walk on slowly, dark and fair against the silver of the canal, their parasols thin and delicate as the wings of evening moths. The King, used to being alone in the midst of his courtiers, listened with one ear to his brother's pleas for a chevalier who had fallen from favor, and gave the rest of his attention to his current problem: Athénaïs.

The Chamber at the Arsenal was closed now; he had shut it down as soon as he knew Mademoiselle de Fontanges had died naturally. That, for him, settled all the most serious charges; as for the others, he discovered he did not wish to know too much of Athénaïs's involvement. He was content that the obviously vicious should go to the stake, the galleys, or exile. The rest would be kept, neither innocent nor guilty, in close confinement; it was the best he could do. Athénaïs no longer needed his protection; her accusers were gone. Now was perhaps the time for her to depart, as Louvois and many of his other advisors wished. The children were all legitimized, living at court. He could do what he liked, though of course he would be generous: it would be a lenient, fashionable convent. She had spoken once of withdrawing; then he had forbidden it. He might simply announce that he had reconsidered her request. She would depart with her spells and charms and take with her his troubling dreams, his headaches, his moments of guilt and anguish.

"I will see, brother," he said aloud. "I will consider it."

Monsieur smiled and bowed, his plumes waving, his diamond earrings swinging against his perfumed wig. He makes himself ridiculous with paint and diamonds at his age, the King thought.

He smelled the night air, heard the swifts hawking overhead, adding their twitter to the violins. There was not a mark on the lawns, not a wave on the canal, not a weed in the flowers, not a flaw anywhere. Behind him, the chateau embodied his hopes, his good dreams. In spite of everything, he had succeeded. With Athénaïs gone, there would be nothing to remind him of the horrors of the last months, of the foulness of the trials, of—the thought came unbidden—his own sins and errors.

He walked forward toward the dock and the Venetian village. The courtiers bowed and the ladies curtsied, a ripple as natural as the trees swaying before the wind. Of them all, only Athénaïs met his eye. Her glance was ironic, appealing, defiant, voluptuous—he did not know. Yet he sensed her personality, her desires, her contrary self-will with vivid force. Once she had set him free; now he no longer sought freedom, but rather the dignity of rectitude. He would send her away, he thought, but even as his hand tightened on his cane in determination, he knew it was not possible. Around him the court was bowing, cajoling, flattering—worshiping even. They would make him an idol and leave him empty, lonely and inhuman: it was the price of his power, the bill for their impotence. She must stay. Without her, he would cease to be human, would dream of perfection, would fall into sin. She would stay and torment him with her demands, her resentments, her quarrels; she would stay and be humiliated for her folly. It was right.

At the dock, he nodded stiffly to her. "You must help me select the operas for the fall season," he said. "Decide what you would like to see."

Athénaïs caught her breath, knowing she was saved. Her face shone with relief, with joy; she had been cleared; he had believed none of it. The nightmare had lifted as quickly as a courtier's hopes. She gave a little curtsy and moved to take his arm, but the King now bowed, stiff and formal, and deliberately turned and offered his arm to Madame de Maintenon. Athénaïs saw the look between them, saw Françoise's black satin sharp as a shadow against the King's blue and gold, and saw her own future as clearly as if she looked through La Voisin's magic glass. She saw her life at court ending not in precipitate displeasure, but in a slow, polite neglect; she saw the courtiers gradually at ease in her presence, sitting when they ought to stand, speaking when they ought to be silent. She saw the King withdrawing, gradually but surely, from everything they once had shared, until her chambers, wherever they were, ceased to be the center of the court and became an obscure and distant anteroom. All this she saw in an instant: love and favor were lost, politely but irrevocably, and her heart died because she had loved power, had loved favor, had loved—in some way, at some times—the King.

The oarsmen steadied the boats, and as the court climbed on board, the violinists on the barge took up some sweet cheerful music. The boats cut cleanly through the flat water, leaving a flight of ripples, and the canal stretched behind them thin and neat. Athénaïs and Françoise sat uncomfortably, avoiding each other's eyes, but the King did not notice their discomfort, for he was looking back toward the shore.

A high, garishly painted vehicle with household goods piled on top and scenery flapping on the sides was crossing the garden. For a moment, he thought it was an apparition, unseen by the others, another residue of his bad dreams. Then the wagon halted.

"Wave," Claude told her daughter. "Wave good-bye to the King."

The child with the King's black hair, hooked nose and secret eyes lifted her hand—His Majesty saw the white blur against her dark dress—then her mother touched the horses with the whip. The wagon cut a track across the immaculate lawn and disappeared into the forest of Versailles and out onto the roads of France.